Harlem Girl Lost

A Novel by

Treasure E. Blue

Consultant: Stephen Williams

Cover design: Karen McInnis, kmcinnis@verizon.net

Photography: Felix Natal Jr. (201) 923-6800

Makeup: Sadé

First printing July 2004

Printed in the United States of America

10   9 8 7 6 5 4 3   1

ISBN: 0-9755974-0-X

This book is dedicated to my mother
Mrs. Ernestine Smalls Blue and Mrs. Debra Manson Wood

To Debra (Sunshine)

Debra, to this date I have yet to meet someone as loving and as giving
as you. You were the first person to recognize my talent, my gift that I
was too blind to see for myself. It was you who believed in me when
no one else had. I forever am in debt to you. Chalae and Shadae miss
you like crazy, but they will be o.k. cause I got them covered.

PS. If I get to heaven we gonna party like we use to
every New Years!

To my mother (Ernestine Blue)

As I write this dedication, tears are already falling from my eyes
because I miss you that much. In our brief lifetime together it seems
I've known two of you. The strongest, most loving, most beautiful
mother a child could ever have wanted. You were our protector, out
savior, our world.

Then there was the other one... the one none of us could ever
understand. The one we cried many nights for. Praying that no one
was hurting you too badly. The one, who use to come home bloodied,
robbed or raped.

No child should ever have to admit this, but I waited for you to die,
because I knew it was too hard for you livin.

It wasn't until I began writing this book did I truly understand. The
real reason you were so hard on me was because when you looked at
me you were looking back at yourself, because you
knew... I was next.
I love you Ma

Acknowledgements

First and foremost, I must thank God. Though I questioned your existence many times, it is clear and without doubt, your love and supreme compassion carried me fourth when I could not carry myself.

To my four beautiful children, Steven, Treasure, Trevor and Justice; I love you guys more than life it's self. Everything I do, everything I live for is for you. NEVER, and I repeat never, let anyone one tell you other wise. As long as you stay leaders and never the follower, as long as you say HELL NO to drugs, as long as you remember, never to use the worst word in the world, and you know what word that is, you will grow to become the fine individuals you are destine to be. Love Daddy.

To my father, Robert Smalls, over 30 years ago you used to tell people "Harlem is going to be a tourist attraction and brownstones are going to be worth over a million dollars" they all laughed at you. You are the most honest, giving man I have ever known. You would give a person the shirt off your back if they asked, I never understood that and hated that shit. But, in time I learn that "In order to receive, one must first give." You are truly a rich man, rich in love, rich in health and rich with family only because you gave unconditionally.

To my brother Rob, hold that shit down in the Feds nigga and I'll take care of the rest when you come home. To my sisters Rosalyn, Andrea, Karen and Gail; I hope I'm finally making y'all proud of me - it just took your Lil' brother some time to get his things together. My nephews and nieces, Tony, Michael, Lamont (Smalls), David (Nada is hot kid), Leon (My Twin), Adrian (A.O), Robert (My brothers boy), Cherice (My reesy neecy) Christina, Janaya and Ayanna, Uncle love y'all.

To my dear Aunt Geneva, words cannot express how much you mean to me. You always told me about my wrongs, and loved me so much you let me find out for myself, only if I had listened. You took me (and everyone else for that matter) into your home when we had no other place to go. Those were truly the best years of my life. I love you.

To Gentry, yo man, I don't know if you know this but, the only reason I'm still alive today is because of you. When we hustled on those streets of Harlem, you schooled me and never used me. I owe you kid. See you when you come home.

To Tyrone and Sandra (Dr. Love), thanks for holding me down through thick and thin. Whenever I got put out and needed a place to lay my head, a bite to eat, or simply just to chill, you were there for me. I spent many holidays with you and your family and I will never forget that. Ty Two Times, Tyrell (my Godson) and Crystal, Uncle love y'all. P.S, Crystal, you are going to be a star one day, believe that! To my godson Lil' Bill, stay up and watch out for the Beast.

To Stephen Williams, CEO, of Peaceful Storm Publishing, you are without doubt the greatest manager, agent, friend, motivator, counselor that a person could ever want. You are one of the biggest reasons I'm at this stage now, because you believed in me. There is not a person, an entity or a power on this earth, that would every come between us...I love you man! To Maxine. To Grandma Dot and Grandma Geneva and Stephen Williams Sr. and Aunt Normie, he love you all dearly, you all did a fine job.

To Glenn Krasner (G-6), I've used the word "Friend" many times in my life, but it wasn't until meeting you, and knowing you, do I know what the word truly means. You taught me true friendship, honesty and compassion. You saw my gifts over ten years ago and refuse to let me waste them...you didn't let me go! G-6, I will never be able to repay to you in what you have so freely gave to me, so I just want to let you know that "YOU ARE MY FRIEND" P.S, Thank you Mr. and Mrs. Krasner, he is a reflection upon you.

To Christopher and Joanna Barrett, it is so amazing how a simple meeting of chance could lead to a lifetime of friendship. I am now the Godfather to your son Christopher, and a surrogate uncle to your beautiful daughter Kylie, being there for both their births. Thanks for being there for me in my many encounters of hardship. I love y'all - to death!

To the Saunders family from Miller Ave in Brooklyn, thanks for accepting me in your family - R.I.P James Saunders, you are surely missed. Michael, Ty and Tori, y'all will always be my boys no matter what. Thanks for being there for me Junior and Kitten, when I needed you. Hey Blanche and Ms. Evelyn, love y'all. To Kia Ellis, Patrice, Tyrell, and Devante.

To my cousin James Riley, thanks for all the inspiration and being there for me with your almost prophesied words. Bill Riley, you use to be my homey now you act like you don't know me! We was closer than brothers at one time, we wore the same draws nigga. What happened? Call Me. To Rachael and Genine, you had my back when shit got funky and you said "that's my cousin, F*** all y'all" you think I forgot. Ron hold shit down on Washington Ave. To my man Cory Black, the realist nigga in the Bronx, Holla! Big Keith and Chris, I don't care what happened between me and yours, but I love y'all cats like brothers no matter what. Holla! To Keisha Greenidge, my home girl from John Jay, you are the real life Silver Jones, keep doing what you doing with your fine self.

To my publicist and business partner, Ms. Cheryl Corde, you are one of the most brightest and intelligent individuals I know. If not for you, I might not be here writing this now and you know what I'm talking about. You life story is amazing and you can help so many people with your words, your inspiration despite the odds that you were stacked with. Congratulations on the birth of your son. To Mary McGhee, God brought you to me, and I thank him for it. Thanks for teaching me and showing me love.

To the Men and Women of the Fire Department at 9 Metro Tech in Brooklyn; thanks for your years of support. To all my bosses, I know I was a piece of work and I put you through hell, but it is my hope that after reading my book you will understand. Sorry Lt. Johnson, sorry Chip, sorry Heath, sorry Macbeth, sorry Pierre, sorry Tuah, sorry Masood, sorry Sam, and sorry Nyron Grant. Damn, I got kicked out that many offices?

To Chief Laura Squassoni, there is no one in the Fire Department that I respect more than you. You never, ever judged me, only helped me with your kindness when everyone told you to fire me! I told you long ago, if you were a man, you would have been praised for your efforts, but unfortunate, society is filled up with a lot of assholes who felt threatened when a women didn't bow down to them. Your only crime was that you were smarter than them, you ran the most disciplined, the most professional unit in the Fire Department, and lastly, (which is a travesty) being a women.

To Daniel Macbeth, you knew how fucked up I was, but you still allowed me into your unit when everyone else said HELL NO! You gave me anything I asked for and to this very date you have yet to ask for anything back...and I'm a Yankee. LOL. Thanks Mac, I won't ever forget.

To Patrice Roper and Liza Horsley, you two mean so much to me that I'm having a hard time expressing it. Both of your life stories is nothing short of amazing. You two are perhaps the smartest individuals that I know. Both of you, after having minor setbacks in your lives, persevered despite your circumstances, and went on to graduate from college. Amazing! I'm waiting for both of you to pass the bar exam. Thanks for having my back. B.D (Turtle) whud up!

To all the District Offices, My boys, Dexter, Duane, Clinton(CPT), Carlo (The Italian), Hudson, where's your bowl, Darryl, Cecil, Lev, Alex G, Abraham, Abrams, John S, Buffy, Jackie, Emma, Awilda, Novelette, Vee, Richard, Cindy, Lal, Anthony Grant, Serge, French, To Chauncey McClary, Yo dude, you my dog for life, you always was down for me from day one, through all the drama I went through (My girl wants her bike back). To security to my man, FDNY Alan and Willie, and the rest. Naidu, Jimmy, Inez, Roseanne, Tonita, Tom, Bob, Benny, Randy, the Vitti's, Big Les and fam, Billy, to my man Lance, the greatest hustler in Brooklyn. To Pat, you held me down when they all talked shit, my home girl for life. Brenda, Sylvia, Elsa, Annette (Good girl), Vanessa, what's up. Jules, Murry, Linda, Sassy, Karen, Jannine. To my office D.O 6, my man Lloyd Ferguson, you don't know this, but I respect and envy you by the way you carry yourself as a man. Lilly, I love you babe, I'll be over this summer for the BBQ. Nyron, what can I say, you keep it real. I look up to you also; you are like a smooth panther, pretty motherfucka. Its o.k. cause I'm gonna be in micro-fibers and have a pretty girlfriend too.. Alicea Valentin, thanks for everything, you really looked out for me when I needed you, every time. To the richest gentleman in the Bronx, Mr. Elliot; write your book so I'll learn how to get rich too. Oscar, my man, Captain Save- a- you know. Leroy, you should have been doing comedy, you are the funniest dude I know. Mr. Tentler, you are down with the brothers, James, don't say a word just bring the Chicken, Doderick, you know more about music then anyone I know, One Love.

To all the Inspectors of the D.O, High Rise, Buried Tanks, Standpipe Sprinklers, Labs, FPCU and Rangehood Units, I want to go on record and say that you are the most dedicated, unrecognized, underpaid, thankless, bunch of men and women in the entire city. You guys prevented so many potential fires, which in part you saved so many lives, but never get credit for it. Not to mention the millions on millions that you create for this city, but nothing is ever given back to you.

To my buddy, Robert Francheschi, to this day I still miss your friendship; It's true when they say the good die young.

Too all the Newport niggas on 125th St, Green Eyes, what's up nigga.

To my people from Manhattan Avenue, Vito, Gerald, Jeffrey, and Face. To the gentlemen from 118th Street and 116th Street. To Fatima, Mercedes, Isiah, Verna, Dolly, Puz and the Gadsons, especially Pop from the Ice House.

To my peoples running the book vending business on the streets, Sidibe Ibrahima, (Sidi) and his brother Meitejean Ibrahima. You cats showed me love from day one, so that means I'm loyal. Lets make this money and bring this shit back to Harlem where it belongs!

To my author friends, Nikki Turner, author of A Hustlers Wife and Project Chick. I was just another nigga with a story and you took time out and showed a nigga what's what. You took me under your wing, and told me "don't worry, I got you." You gave me your number and told me to just call you up when I need advice. That's real. Forever Loyal Nikki. To Shannon Holmes, author of B-More Careful, Bad Girlz, my Bronx nigga, you came to John Jay, February 25th, 2003, February 26, I started writing Harlem Girl Lost. What can I say kid, you inspired me to start writing again. Thanks for the help along the way. To my home girl from Queens, Ebony Stroman, author of "The Hood", Yo for you to be only 23, you be gettin' it girl. See you on the takeover! To my nigga, a real live nigga from Harlem, author of Murder Inc. and Homo Thug, Asanti Kahari, yo thanks for keepin' it real, let's bring this shit back to Harlem kid! To my man, Mark Anthony, author of Paper Chasers and Dogism, thanks for keeping it real, and not trying to play high post like them other nigga's 'cause they got a book out. To my people from 142nd street Lenox and 7th where I really learned the streets, y'all raised a psycho. To my partner in crime Vincent Brown, me and you been through it all and we still standing and still got each others back, how many people can say that! To Joy Naylor, from Chicago; Yo we ain't forget you and we still love you for everything that you did for us, contact us, we miss you. Joyce Goodwin from Wagner, I still love you. To my Brother in laws, Herman, Adrian, and Tony, thanks for treating my sisters right.

To Tracey Sherrod, thanks for ever thing, I'm gonna make you proud of me. To my models, My Silver and Missy, Ms. Toni Hooks and Darmarie Bowen. Thanks for being the professionals that you are and tolerating that cold weather. Y'all both are dimes and I'll see you when we take this to film. To Felix Natal, the best photographer on the east coast, kid you blessed me. To Karen McInnis, you were an answer to my prayers. You hit me off with your book cover design. All I did was tell you what I wanted and you did the rest. You are the best! To my editor, Denise Clark, from Denise's Pieces, thanks for everything.

To my lawyer, Kenneth Russo, thanks for saving my life, and to Robert and Lenora from 205th St. Station, and Kim Rose from Echo Soul.

*A boy without his mother
is like a man without a country.
But a girl without her father
is like a woman without a universe.*

—*Steven B. Smalls*

Chapter 1

Dear Silver,

*What the hell is wrong with you? You are pissing your roommate off by waking her up with your nightmares and that shit has to stop. Gail's got every right to be pissed, because this is what...the fourth time this week? Plus finals are all week... shit, it's only so much the girl can take. She already bent over backwards for you when she took you to see the **school's** physician to help you out with your little problem. So it's only right to take her and the doctor's suggestion to seek 'other help.' I know you are scared but you simply got to get over it and face your fears and go see one, I hear they can really help, and... STOP! Who am I foolin', you know damn well black people don't get down like that! See a shrink... hell no, we're too afraid that we might find out we are really schizo!*

Beside, I already know I'm fucked up, so I don't need anybody trying to get in my head to tell me that. And if they do find out, that shit will follow me the rest of my life and ruin any chances of me becoming a doctor. I might be crazy, but I ain't stupid. Besides, I already know why I'm having these nightmares – I just don't know how to stop from having them. I know it's got a lot to do with what happened to me when I was little. Keeping all those secrets inside and trying to forget about it as if it didn't happen is my problem. But like all terrible secrets – they eventually catch up with you, and soon, after a while, they will drive you out your mind! I know I need help, but if I got any chance on making it into med. school I can't... strike that, it would not look good on my records.

*I asked the doctor if there were any alternatives other than seeing a psychiatrist. Seeing my reluctance, the doctor probably assumed that my problem was due to the stress and rigors of my studies, so she suggested that I try this shit, self- analysis, which is to put on paper anything that comes to mind. She said that in order to get to the root of my problem, I should unconsciously write and to let it just flow, and above all – **to be brutally honest**. She said that I would always be as sick as my secrets if I didn't expose them. I don't have no reason to be ashamed because nobody's gonna read this anyway, so I have nothing to lose. Besides, these dreams are fucking killing me!*

So the doc wants honesty…I'll give her mad honesty…here goes…I'll start out by writing about my mother, Jessica Jones. Mommy was the most loving and generous person you could have ever wanted to meet. She was the type of person that would give you the shirt off her back if she had to. She was gorgeous, perfect.

The thing I liked most about her was the love and honesty that she gave me. At times, it seemed like we were sisters because she didn't preach to me. She'd talk to me like you would talk to your younger sister, always schooling me. Mommy had to bust her ass real hard to provide me with shelter, nice clothes and to put food on the table. She worked the graveyard shift in downtown Manhattan, and she was good at what she did also – she was a professional whore and heroin addict.

As far as my Dad goes… I never knew him. Even though Mommy talked to me about everything under the sun, that was one subject she would rarely discuss. The only thing she said about him was that I got my hazel eyes from him and that she killed him with kindness. I'd be lying if I said I miss not having a father around, but like my mother always said, 'You can't miss something you never had'. Besides, I did have a father figure in my life … well sort of … I had my Auntie Birdie. He's a retired prostitute – a transvestite. He and my mom met while they were on the 'hoe stroll' over by the West Side highway in Manhattan. She was only seventeen, so young and inexperienced that Birdie (with the type of heart he has), felt sorry for her when a ruthless pimp started to beat the shit out of her because she didn't choose him. Everybody just stood there and watched this punk motherfucker beat my mother like she was a fuckin' man. She said just as she was about to lose consciousness, the pimp was lifted off of her by what he must have thought was a large woman. Now Birdie is 6' 6" and nearly 7 foot when he wears his stilettos, and when the pimp saw who it was, he pulled a switchblade and said he was gonna shove it up Birdie's ass – big mistake! Birdie not only took the switchblade from him, he gave the pimp such an ass whuppin' he had to spend six months in the hospital. Legend has it that Auntie Birdie was an amateur boxer in his younger days, so after that he took my mommy under his wing and we've been together since. He loved mother and me so much that we became all he had.

What I disliked most about my Mommy was her nasty heroin addiction. Remembering those days brings back so many bad memories that I become overwhelmed with emotional anguish. In other words – the shit fucked me up! It was so horrible. In fact, I used to watch her shoot-up right in her pussy because she couldn't shoot it in her arms. In her profession, a junkie whore with track marks on her arms was not too appealing or financially viable. I can't count the number of times Birdie or I had to revive her from a near overdose. I remember the first time I saw her O.D'ed, her skin was ashy white, her eyes rolled in the back of her head, and she had vomit all caked up on her mouth. It was fuckin' awful! I remembered all I could do was cry as I shook her and begged her to wake up. I thought she was dead. I was so scared that she had died that all I could think of was that there would be no one to take care of me. In fact, to this very day, I still have a fear of being alone.

After the overdose incident, Mommy taught me how to bring her back to life in case it happened again. She told me that I should get a bunch of ice and put them inside her panties and to place some under her armpits. She said if that didn't work, I was to shove a couple of cubes up inside her twat – I was six years old! But needless to say, after a while, it became as normal as shampooing my hair. I became her personal resuscitator. But that wasn't the worst part. Did you ever see someone you love dope sick? Oh my God…there's nothing worse. Its like… how can I explain… it's like watching your child get their fingers crushed in a door, and their pain is so excruciating, but nothing you do can take the pain away. I wanted to take Mommy's pain away so badly, but I was fuckin' helpless. I would ask her, 'Mommy what's wrong? Can I help?' With a forced smile she would always say, "I'm okay baby… Mommy's just a little sick. I ran out of candy (or medicine as she put it), but not to worry because the 'doctor' was on his way." Now you know who the 'doctor' was – he was the friendly neighborhood dope man. Even though I despised him for pushing the dope on my mother, I remembered being so relieved when I heard him knock on the door. Mommy would rush to door and rip it open and then pass him something real quick and run to the bathroom. I would smile because I knew when she came out; she would instantly be cured of her sickness.

Mommy peddled her goods on the famous Times Square, Forty Du – Wop, The Deuce, or whatever you want to call it. She made no bones about what she did and most importantly she made damn sure I wasn't lame to nothing that she did.

When it came to her profession, she had her own philosophical way of putting things. She would say, 'Show me a women with a pussy and I'll show you one rich bitch' or 'selling pussy is the oldest and the most respected profession in the world and that behind every great dick was a greater pussy. It has broken some of the strongest and most powerful men in the world, from Kings of Africa to Kingpins of Harlem – pussy has brought them all to their knees – it's called 'Pussy whipping!' That shit used to crack me up. If you look at it she was right, cause look what happened to Bill Clinton, the president of the United Fucking States, mind you. Women are real Dons …or shall I say Diva's.'

But to hear a lot of girls tell it, you'd think that they are doing something different from my mother. They sell their ass and do drugs like their shit don't stink. They're only delusional, fooling themselves. They run around saying, "I don't do drugs, I only smoke weed and drink a lil' bit of thug passion." Duh… what do you think weed and alcohol is? It's a fuckin' drug! "But weed is innocent, it ain't like crack, weed is from the earth." From the earth…dumb bitch, where the hell do you think coca leaves come from… Mars? Do me a favor and ask any crackhead, any heroin user or any addict for that matter, what drug did they start out using first, and I'll bet your ass a thousand dollars to one, that they'll either say, 'Innocent Weed or Innocent Alcohol'.

How many girls you think actually aspired to become a fiend and degrade themselves by sucking and fucking niggers to get that next hit? What I'm saying is that you just never know, so why take the chance? To this very day, I don't even know how alcohol tastes, cause Moms told me 'once you had a taste of any of that shit you're gone'! I'm not going to be fooled by the illusion that one drug is worse than another, 'cause that shit leads down the same road of destruction! See, that's how Moms got caught out there, which is why she schooled me to the fact that a drug is a drug is a drug! She knew better and did everything in her power to make sure I knew the truth!

And how about those girls that are spreading their legs to every Tom, Dick or Rapper just because they have a record deal or a fat ride and fatter pockets? Most of these dudes are just lookin' for a quick chick to pick up so you can suck their dick till you fuckin' hiccup. 'But he said he love me'. Hoe pa   leaseeez! If I could get a dollar for every time these same Cats called you a chickenhead (extra crispy at that) after they twisted you out, I'd be one rich sumptin' – sumptin. They don't respect or care about you once they got the draws. If you don't believe me ask to meet their mommas and see how many excuses you'll get.

At least my Moms kept it real. She didn't care what them other heifers said about her, cause her motto was, "I'd rather be a rich talked-about bitch than just a talked- about bitch any day!" She told me if any bitch ever tells you she never tricked a little, she's a lying bitch, 'cause every girl does. Once a girl figures out that she is a walking ATM, them same cats can call her a chickenhead all they want, because she'll be one Filet Mignon steak eatin', Dolce & Gabbanna wearing, shine glistenin' chicken from then on.

She broke it down like this… how many times have they dated a man who took them out to dinner, bought them an outfit, or gave them some jewelry or some money? I don't care if he's a boyfriend, husband, lover or lovette (for those who lick…I mean 'like' the female persuasion). Any chick that answers yes to one or more of those above… Welcome to the Good-Pussy Society! Your pussy, his loot! Pre-paid pussy plan.

Realistically, I had to think like that to keep things in perspective to help rid me of the shame and humiliation I had coming up. I didn't feel normal – I felt nasty. No matter where I went or how much I achieved, I still felt dirty and less than other people did. I would constantly imagine, 'what if these people knew that my mother was a whore, or that my auntie was a transvestite, how I lived, the things that happened to me?'

But in spite of it all, I managed to keep my head up, because I reasoned that my mother had to do what she had to do to survive, and what she did has no reflection upon me. It took me a long time to learn to think like that. What's done is done! Even if I didn't understand it, I just had to respect it and move the fuck on. For people like me, who saw the truth – I cry a river for them, because I, like them, saw a glimpse of how fucked up this world can truly be. I know how it feels to suffer, suffer only because we were born, born into a hellish world that no child need not see, nor have to bear. But here we are.

If they were anything like me, I blamed everything on somebody else. My motto was a simple, 'If there's no one else to blame, say fuck it and blame it on my Mama.' But blaming somebody else was so easy, moving on was the hard part. So that left me with two choices. Should I feel sorry for myself and live a lonely miserable life, or should I shake that shit off and live out my life till the motherfucking wheels fall off?

*You're damn right, I chose the latter. See, little did I know Mommy knew she was caught up in the grips of that madness, so she sacrificed her own life while preparing me for combat, 'cause she knew that it would be harder for a sister to make it. So she groomed and inspired me with the only thing she could possibly offer me – pure and unadulterated truth – even if it hurts. She knew that the **real truth** (when confronted with it) is very scary – but it's how you handle the truth that's going to make the difference in one's life.*

If I had one wish, I would tell all the children or all the people who were children who suffered because their parents were addicts or alcoholics and saw all the horror that came with it, I would tell them that it's 'not your fault'! Because it's not! It's not your fault if you were molested – like I was; beaten like I was; or homeless and abandoned – like I was! And it's definitely not your fault if you developed some dreadful disease or addiction. Whether it's an addiction to drugs or alcohol, sex or crime, it really doesn't matter, because it's not wholly your fault - and believe that!

She taught me that everything that glitters isn't gold and everything that looks sweet damn sure isn't sugar. Because the things in this world that look enticing are really a ploy to get you hooked. Whether it's money, fame, fast cars, beautiful houses, or sex and drugs, it's all a set-up to deceive us into thinking that these are the most important things that we need in our lives. Mommy made damn sure I didn't fall for that fake cellophane okie doke shit those cats be talkin' in Harlem. She told me that if I don't stand for something I'd fall for anything, and standing up for myself was something I definitely did.

Chapter 2

Junior High School 196 - Harlem

The girl named Silver Jones sat quietly at first, but her patience was running thin. The longer she watched the jump-off go down, the more she began to get heated. She knew it wasn't her beef, but being the person she was she couldn't just sit there and let her two classmates get victimized by those two punks.

Catching a first glance at Silver, one would naturally assume that the eleven-year old honor student was nothing more than a skinny, stuck-up little Daddy's girl because of her flowery amberish hair, striking hazel eyes, and flawless fair skin. But as many students found out, you should never judge a book by its cover, because in addition to her fragile soft looks and almost Erkel-like demeanor, she was also one of the most fierce fighters in the entire school. She was definitely a freak of nature, almost chameleon-like, because she could change from a mild mannered angel to a fucking Tasmanian Devil in an instant if you rubbed her the wrong way. Silver wasn't the type to start a fight – she only ended them.

Silver's mother, Jesse, was determined not to let her only daughter be anyone's fool, so she taught Silver about life, straight with no chaser. She saw fit neither to talk to nor treat her like a child. Jesse felt that life was too hard to sugarcoat things, especially to a poor black girl from Harlem. Jesse saw far too many girls, including herself, fall victim to the streets because they were naïve and ignorant, and Jesse preferred Silver heard the ugly truth from her rather than hear a beautiful lie from anyone else. Although many of the lectures Jesse told Silver were chilling and explicit, she felt it was far better that her daughter knew about them and not need them, then to need them and not know them. Jesse programmed principles so deep into Silver's mind that it was as if she had wisdom beyond her eleven years.

One of the many things Jesse taught Silver was to always do what her gut told her to do if she felt she was in the right. So Silver did what came naturally. She stood up at her desk and yelled, "Why don't you leave them alone, Problem!"

Problem and Tyrell, the school bullies, had Beastly and Diego, Silver's two classmates, hemmed up in the back of the class as they rustled through their pockets.

The other students turned to watch as Silver stared at them with her arms folded, waiting for them to jump bad and say something slick, especially Problem, because she couldn't stand his ass anyway. Problem, whose real name was Doyle, was blue-black and sloppily fat. He stared at Silver with his dark, sullen eyes. It was silent enough at that moment you could hear a pin drop as the students watched and awaited his response.

Problem glanced at Tyrell, his partner in crime, for insurance. Everyone knew that Problem would have to say something or he was gonna look like a punk, but by the same token, he knew that he didn't want to say anything that would piss Silver off. He knew very well about her and also knew she could fight like a boy, so he harbored no quick desire to get in a battle he knew he couldn't win. The two boys he was robbing, Beastly and Diego said nothing.

Beastly was the smallest boy in the class. He had recently arrived in the United States from Kingston, Jamaica. His real name was Beasley, but his classmates called him Beastly because of his huge Rastafarian dreadlocks, which made him look like a lion. Diego, on the other hand was a pudgy Spanish kid who was just as big if not bigger then they were, but he was a punk and got robbed every day because of it.

Tyrell, rail thin, with missing front teeth, urged Problem to handle his business, he assured him that she was only a girl and that he was the fucking man.

"Yo" said Tyrell, "you gonna let that skinny bitch front on you, dog?" Sucking his teeth he added, "nigga, you know I got your back!"

Problem tossed Diego aside and sneered at Silver. "And if I don't, what the fuck you gonna do about it?"

Problem's defiance quickly deflated when he heard 'Click...clink!'

Missy, Silver's best friend, clicked open an orange box cutter. Missy Anderson was a tall girl for twelve, with pretty dark skin and hair that hung down over her shoulders. She often lost her temper if she didn't get her way and would fight anyone for any reason, especially boys. She was third generation project and simply didn't give a fuck. She grew up in a family of all women, no males, so they had to hold it down. She grew up watching her mother, grandmother and aunts, fight and maim their boyfriends or other women around the projects.

Their weaponry varied from straight razors, butcher knives or N.B.C sticks (Nigger Be Cool Sticks), which were bats with rusty nails sticking out of them. But their favorite weapon of choice was a special concoction that consists of Red Devil lye, ammonia, and urine, a secret family recipe that was handed down for generations. If they felt other women wanted their man, a bitch looked at them funny or some typical 'he said she said' shit, these infractions were dealt with swiftly. Everyone knew that if you fought one Anderson broad, you had to fight them all. That's how they got down and this kept the entire Anderson clan fighting year round in the projects.

As a matter of fact, that was how Silver and Missy met, fighting each other. When they first met in the fifth grade, they hated each other's guts and fought like Royal Gladiators every day, neither girl backing down an inch. It got to the point that they simply kept their faces greased with Vaseline and their hair braided at all times because they never knew when the other would stage a sneak attack.

Then one day after school while both girls were serving detention for fighting, of course, a third person was needed to play double-dutch and Silver was the only one around. So Missy approached Silver, who stood immediately ready to throw down, when Missy nonchalantly asked "Yo, bitch you want to play rope?"

Silver looked her in the eyes, then at the rope and spoke with attitude. "Yeah, hoe, I like to play… but I'm jumping first!"

From that day on, with a simple rope and a common love for double-dutch, they became the best of friends, having each other's back through hell and high water. They had no choice, because they found it easier and a lot less bloody to be friends than enemies.

Both boys eyed Missy as she towered over them. Problem turned toward Silver.

"Yo, I ain't messing with you, so why you gots to be all up in my bidness?" he asked, his tone less confident.

Silver stepped closer, both hands on her hips. "I'm making it my business."

Problem was shook, especially when Tyrell backed away and bounced from the classroom, leaving him alone to handle his business by his lonesome.

Missy stood behind him and whispered chillingly in his ear as she placed the box-cutter to his blubbery neck. "Talk that shit now, bitch?"

Problem stood speechless and ready to shit on himself. Silver stared at him with disgust. "Yo, why you only pick on people you know won't fight back?" Before he could answer, she rolled her eyes and swayed her head from side to side. "Because they'll kick your fat funky ass," and mushed him in the forehead for good measure. The entire class busted out in laughter, taunting and hissing him. Silver waited for Problem to make a move, but amazingly, all he did was smile.

It suddenly occurred to her that the entire class had gone silent and sat properly in their chairs. With a sense of dread, Silver slowly turned and saw her teacher, Mister Bonds, standing in the doorway, wearing a stern look.

"Miss Jones, I want you to go straight to the principal's office and tell him about that filthy and disgusting mouth of yours."

"But Mister Bonds," Silver pleaded, "Problem's not even in this class and he was—"

Problem quickly interrupted. "Ms. Horsley asked me to find some chalk...and that's when she," he said, pointing at Silver, "started messin' with me for no reason."

"You's a goddamn liar," Silver snapped. "I'm not going on detention because of your lying ass!"

"Mister Bond's eyes widened. "Curse one more time, Miss Jones, and I assure you that detention will be the last of your worries!" Silver realized her mistake. "I'm sorry Mister Bonds, but he's lying...I mean you can ask Beasley and Diego, they were—" Hearing none of it, he simply pointed toward the door. "Now, Miss Jones!" Silver looked toward Diego and Beasley to back her up, but they remained silent because Problem was eye screwing them. Missy stepped forward. "Mister Bonds, she's right. Problem was—..."

"Did anyone ask you Ms. Anderson?" Mister Bonds coldly cut her off. "And why are you out of your seat in the first place? Now sit your contemptuous self down before you go with her!" Missy looked like she wanted to curse him out something awful, but Silver gestured for her to remain silent. The entire school knew Mister Bonds was soft on little boys and harder on the girls, so it made no sense for both of them to get detention.

"Leave now, Miss Pretty," he mocked. Collecting the books off her desk, Silver turned to glare at smart-ass Problem, who was smiling and waving bye-bye.

Principal Hudson's Office

As Silver sat in the main office awaiting the principal, she smelled a musty odor that smelled like a dead rat. She frowned and held her nose, hoping that the principal would hurry up. It sounded like the principal was already in a conference with Ms. Horsley, who taught the dumber students downstairs. She heard every word of their discussion in the office. Apparently Ms. Horsley was talking about one of her students, who wasn't participating in her class.

"Come on, Andrea," the principal said. "You are a teacher for Christ's sake! Do your job and work a little harder with the boy."

Silver turned and noticed a scruffy looking boy sitting silently at the other end of the room, staring impassively at the walls. She knew immediately they were referring to him. His clothes were tattered, and his hair so nappy it was turning into beaded dreads from lack of combing. Ms. Horsley spoke her voice heavy with frustration.

"Listen Bill...I'm a teacher, not a miracle worker. The boy needs to be in a Special Ed program or something...he can't read, he can't even write. I have other students I have to focus on instead of trying to teach the boy his A B C's! No," she said shaking her head "there's nothing I can possibly do for him and to be quite honest with you, I personally think the boy is retarded or something."

"Anything else?" the principal asked defeated.

"A bath from time to time wouldn't hurt him either, he smells like raw sewage!"

Silver looked at the sad-looking boy, but he showed no emotion or reaction to the cruel words the teacher said about him.

* * *

It was sixth period at Junior High School 196, lunchtime for all the seventh graders. Silver had just gotten off the canteen line after purchasing some butter crunch cookies and chocolate milk. No seventh grader in their right mind would be caught dead eating a school lunch. Silver, still fuming over receiving two days detention, spotted the boy she had seen in the principal's office earlier that day. He sat alone in the corner of the cafeteria eating a tray of hot dogs and pork and beans. Silver watched him for a moment, ignoring Missy and the rest of their crew as they waved for her to come and sit with them. Acquiring the same compassion for the less fortunate as her mother, Silver decided to go and sit with the lonely little boy.

As Silver approached him, the students in the cafeteria looked on in silence as she placed her cookies and milk on the table in front of him. When she sat down, the boy stopped chewing and stiffened. Silver didn't have any classes with him because she was in the Advanced and Gifted Student class.

The boy had seen Silver before, jumping rope during recess. He thought she was the prettiest girl he ever saw especially her eyes. He had many encounters with white people with colorful eyes, but never a black person with eyes like hers before, and now here she was sitting right in front of him. He had but one burning desire at that moment, and that was to have the power to become invisible. He looked out the corner of his eyes and just as he suspected, all eyes were on them.

As he sat shaking nervously, he waited for someone to pull some cruel joke on him as they had done to him all his life, or worse yet, for her to do something cruel to him. He didn't mind other students treating him badly, he was used to it, but to have this 'Angel of a girl' hurt him would surely humiliate him beyond what he was used to. He held his breath and waited tensely for the grand finale at his expense.

Silver watched the timid little boy shiver like a wet puppy and began to feel even sorrier for him. She decided to break the ice. "So how long you been coming to this school?"

"Not long," he mumbled, mouth full of food

Silver could not understand him. "Excuse me?"

Embarrassed, he quickly gulped down the remaining food. "Not real long," he repeated. "So, what's your name?"

Face still averted, he answered. "Chance."

Silver frowned. "Chance… what kind of name is that?"

His eyes remained on his food. "Well, my real name is Chancellor…Chancellor Haze, but I don't like it, so I just tell people to call me Chance for short."

"I think Chancellor is a beautiful name," Silver said. "But if you prefer to be called Chance, I'll respect that." She smiled. "My name is Silver."

As if he was talking to his food, he shrugged. "Silver," he said. "And you talkin' 'bout my name?"

Silver chuckled. "You're right…I should be the last person to talk about names."

"How'd you get a name like that?" he asked, still looking at his food.

As if she had answered the question a million times already, Silver opened up her milk. "Well when I was born, the nurse was cradling me in her arms when I opened my eyes. She said to my mother, 'Oh what beautiful eyes she has… they look almost silver. What is her name?' She handed me to my mother, who took one look at me and said, 'That's her name…Silver…Silver Jones'." Silver picked up her napkin and wiped her hands and extended them for him to shake. Not noticing her hand, she waved it to get his attention. He quickly shook it and pulled back. Silver smiled widely and said. "Now it's official, that makes us friends right?"

Chance shrugged and said, "I guess."

"And since we are friends now…" Silver bent lower to get his attention, "I ask but one favor."

"What?" Chance looked up suspiciously and then lowered his eyes again.

Silver answered seriously. "When we talk, I would appreciate it if you looked at me when you do…okay?" Slowly, Chance raised his head and looked into her smiling face.

Chapter 3

Uptown Harlem

The train station on 116th and Lenox was noticeably empty as a tall and exceptionally beautiful woman wearing a blond wig emerged up the stairs. Jessica Jones, whom everyone called Jesse, returned home from a long evening shift of carnal exchange. Jesse has a statuesque, almost regal look about her. She took long, confident strides in white knee high boots and seemed oblivious to the freezing temperature. She wore only a short buck leather skirt and matching jacket. Jesse had grown accustomed to the cold – she was used to it. As she turned the corner, a powerful gust of wind greeted her head on, breaking her stride and causing her to readjust her frazzling wig. Everyone in the neighborhood came alive when they saw Jesse round the corner, from local merchants opening their sturdy black gates to downtrodden winos that slumbered about waiting for the liquor store or check-cashing place to open.

"Whassup, Miz Jesse?" Stickbroom Johnny, an old toothless man who delivered newspapers around the neighborhood from door to door greeted her.

"Hey Stickbroom, what was Brooklyn last night?" Even though no one was within twenty feet of them, Stickbroom Johnny cautiously peeked around with his bugged-eyes.

"Seven Twenty Eight," he whispered.

Though Stickbroom was older than dirt, he had the mentality of a ten-year-old; everyone from the neighborhood loved and took care of him because of his contagious sense of humor. He was particularly famous for knowing any and everything that was going on in the neighborhood. If anybody wanted to know who was fucking who and who was getting fat, you need only ask Stickbroom. "I dun put ya paper at yo doow, Miz Jesse."

"Thanks Johnny," Jesse said, handing him a dollar. "I'll throw you something extra on my way back down, okay?"

"I sho appreciate Miz Jesse," he said with a gummy smile.

One by one, people on the street greeted her or asked for some spare change, which she happily gave them. This was her neighborhood and she was happy to help them out.

Turning the corner on 117th and 8th, Jesse slowed when she saw Mitts, the neighborhood's most notorious dope fiend. Mitts was one of those grotesque dope fiends that had repulsively swollen arms and legs that made him look like Popeye the Sailor Man due to years of heroin abuse. Everybody called him 'Mitts' because he had hands that were the size of catcher mitts. No one could bear the sight of him because the legion of crust-filled, pus-induced sores that covered his hands and body. Because of poor eyesight and cataracts, he wore thick dark glasses to prevent sun exposure. Seeing Jesse, he nervously rocked back and forth, because he knew the kind-hearted Jesse was a sure score. As she approached, he extended his freakishly huge hands towards her. Jesse stared at him in remorse as he squirmed like he had to pee real bad. Because of his addiction, butterflies in his stomach gave him the urge to defecate. Feeling sorry for him, she reached inside her purse and handed him ten dollars. Taking the bill, he strained to see the denomination as he held it close to his dark glasses. Once again he began to rock back and forth, for ten dollars wasn't nearly enough to get past his morning sickness. Seeing his reluctance, Jesse reached inside her bra, peeled off a twenty and handed it to him. He snatched the bill quickly and raced off down the block. She turned and watched him hobble off to the nearest shooting gallery for his wake-up, or as they say in the streets, their 'breakfast.' Jesse knew first hand how it felt to have 'The Beast' on her back.

King Heroin – The Ultimate Slave Master! In Harlem and throughout the free world, it is known by many pseudonyms: "Smack," "H," "P-Funk," "Boy," "Horse" "Snow," "Diesel" "Dope or D," but no matter what you call it, it'll eventually be called one thing – Death…a slow and miserable one! To many that used it, it was the closest you'll ever get to heaven on earth. But to all that are hooked, it was a guarantee of suffering hell on earth! Jesse had been off the poison for six months now, after vowing never to use the cunning, baffling and insidious drug ever again, not only for herself and her sake, but for the hell she put her daughter through.

Jesse put the entire episode out of her mind and continued about her business. She heard a loud commotion coming from the alley and stopped in mid-stride. Normally Jesse would abide by the every ghetto's golden rule of 'hear no evil, see no evil', but she faintly recognized the voice and took a chance.

Stepping over a jungle of dirty hypodermic needles, broken wine bottles and trash, she happened upon a man brutally beating another man with the butt of his guns. Edging closer, she stepped on a bottle, crushing it and alerting the man to her presence. In one swift move, he turned his weapons toward the unwanted intruder. Jesse instantly lost her breath as she stared down the barrel of two large weapons. Frightened, she quickly threw her hands up. "Chubby!" Jesse said quickly "It's... it's me... Jesse!" The generously proportioned man squinted to see who was disturbing his business. After recognizing her, he lowered his weapons, smiled widely and began rocking back and forth like Stevie Wonder. He took a Tootsie Roll pop out of his mouth and said, "Oh shit... Jesse, that you? Fuck you doing back here?"

Jesse dropped her hands in relief and stepped closer. Staring down at the beaten and bloodied man beneath him, she recognized Dupree, a neighborhood kid who used to hustle coke for Chubbs.

Chubbs lived on 116th St. between Manhattan and Morningside Ave. He was big, black and the meanest motherfucker on the black side of Harlem. A diagnosed manic-depressive with horrible mood swings, he stayed on medication to keep him out the mood of premeditation – murder, as per the New York State Mental Board and stipulations in his parole. But it was apparent – they weren't working. Chubbs had four older brothers, all felons who've been doing dirt since they came out of Pampers. Vonda, Chubbs' older sister, was Jesse's best friend since grade school. Their family took Jesse in when her mother kicked her out when she got pregnant with Silver at fifteen, and lived with them for nearly two years. Even though Chubbs owned many legitimate businesses such as bars, a barbershop and some Laundromats, he remained street. Money to Chubbs didn't mean a thing, he could care less – it just came along with being a gangster. He and his four brothers grew up with artistic backgrounds because they perfected the art of stick-ups; the art of kidnapping and the art of extortion and they made use of those skills on drug dealers.

The only thing sweet about Chubbs was the Tootsie Rolls he had a habit of sucking.

Though Chubbs had many faults, the neighborhood loved him - especially the older folks. His minor transgressions were overlooked as inconsequential because he kept the neighborhood safe from petty thieves and stick-up kids who preyed on women and the elderly. Chubbs hated them ever since one of them had robbed his mother years ago. Legend had it that one crackhead made the unfortunate mistake of robbing a seventy-three year old neighborhood lady of her social security check as she exited the check-cashing place on 116th and 8th. That same day, Chubbs and his brothers found the man, threw him inside the trunk of their car and drove off. The next morning the police found the man completely naked, beaten to a bloodied pulp and an inch away from death. He was tied and gagged to the very gate of the check-cashing place that he robbed the old lady from with a bloody note pinned through his flesh that read ' I will not rob my neighbors ever again,' written one hundred times. After that, needless to say, niggas' took their chances robbing white folks downtown before fucking around in the hood.

Still rather nervous, Jesse stared at the bloodied boy beneath Chubbs. "I'm all right Chubby... but what's going on with you?" Out of habit, whenever Chubbs had to explain himself, he nervously swayed his head and rocked his body to the side while looking away from you. He had had this habit since he was a child and turned into a perpetual liar because he got into so much trouble. Stuffing one weapon in his belt, he held a tight grip on the man's Afro, as if he didn't have a single care in the world.

"Ain't shit... you know my style, work hard, live long and taken care of bidness."

Jesse walked a little closer. "I hear you Chubby, but umm... shit don't look too good back here though." He frowned and surveyed the garbage in the alley, took a slight whiff and nodded "Yeah you right, shit is nasty back here... and it stinks too."

"Chubbs man!" Jesse said in exasperation. "I ain't talking about the garbage... I'm talking about Dupree... he's bleeding pretty bad." Brows lifted in surprise, Chubbs pointed to Dupree.

"Who...you talkin' bout this nigg?" He grabbed Dupree even tighter. "Oh, you ain't got to worry about this lil' nig, dis nigga aight. I got this!"

Suddenly, Chubbs unleashed a vicious slap across the boy's face with the butt of the weapon, cracking his facial bones. "Chubby...what tha fuck!" Jesse yelled, cringing.

Barely eighteen, Dupree was an undercover crackhead who owed Chubb's some money, which was a no-no in Harlem. A drug dealer didn't give a fuck how much a nigga owed – ten dollars or ten thousand dollars – shit didn't matter. All that mattered to these cats was the fact that you tried to fuck them, and they would surely kill you.

This was the perfect opportunity for Dupree to make a plea for his life.

"Yo Chubbs man," he pleaded, "... I was gonna pay you but—"

Whap! Whap! Chubbs slapped the boy senseless across his head with the butt of his forty-four long, cracking that open too. Chubbs looked at him with his fierce, black eyes.

"Nigg...I'll fuck you up if you interrupt us grown folks again'!"

Cringing again, Jesse asked in disbelief. "Chubby damn... what the hell did he do to you to make you beat him like that?" Chubbs paused as he tries to recall.

"Oh yeah..." he remembered. "This punk tried ta duck a nigg and taking advantage of nigg kindness...talkin' shit in the streets sayin' he ain't gonna pay Chubbs his money ... ain't that right, Dupree?" Chubbs lifted him by his collar and stuck the cannon deep inside his mouth. "Talk that shit now, lil' fucka...talk it now!"

Dupree's bowels bubbled loudly, as the foul odor from his shit filled the alleyway. Chubbs frowned and immediately tossed him to the ground like discardable garbage as he stared at Dupree with disgust.

"Look at that shit, Jesse... its niggas' like that," he said, pointing the weapon at Dupree, "that be given Harlem niggas' a bad name. They be walkin' around talkin' mad shit like they some muthafuckin' mobsters...now look at 'im." Chubbs spat on him. "He shits his muthafuckin' pants when he run into a muthafuckin' monster!"

Growing angrier, Chubbs pulled out his second pistol and cocked the triggers. "Yo Jess," he said as he stared down at Dupree "you better step now, you don't want to be part of this shit." A little confused, Jesse wasn't sure what he meant. "Chubbs…you not gonna…" She looked around in disbelief. "Damn, Chubby you gonna kill him?" Chubbs rocked nervously and could not answer, but Jesse knew the deal. "Shit, Chubby, how much he fuckin' owe you?"

Chubbs looked down at Dupree and asked "How much you jerk me for, lil' fucka?" Dupree looked up at Chubbs and answered softly. "Five dollars."

Jesse looked at Chubbs in disbelief as he started rocking faster. "Shit, Chubby," she said, "Here's fuckin' twenty dollars if that's the case." He shook his head.

"Naw girl… you know it ain't about the money…it's the fuckin' principle yo."

Jesse threw him a sarcastic, knowing look. Shifting his weight from one leg to the other, he avoided eye contact with her until, after a few uncomfortable seconds, he relented.

"Alright, Jesse, damn! I ain't got no principles, I just like doing this shit!"

She grabbed his black army jacket and black hoody. "Then do this favor for me Chubby… just this one time, let him go." She extended the money toward him but he waved her off.

"Naw, Jesse, fuck dat… you keep yo dough, you know I'll do anything for you. Shit… you my maafuckin' peeps." Relieved, Jesse let out a big sigh.

"But…" said Chubbs, grabbing his crotch, "It is something you can do for me!"

Frowning, Jesse gave him a wary look and put her hand on her hips. "What is it, Chubby?" He gave her a knowing look "You know goddamn well what I want? I want a big ass pot of lima beans, that's what the hell I want, just like you use to do it back in the day."

Jesse smiled. "Deal!"

"With pigtails and smoked- neck bone too" he added quickly.

"Okay, you got it," Jesse assured him.

Chubbs grimaced at Dupree and barked. "Get the fuck outta here, lil' fucka…"

Dupree blazed the fuck out the alley without looking back while Chubbs yelled at his retreating back.

"And don't let me see ya bitch ass on the humble, nig!"

Jesse hugged Chubbs by the waist as they walked out of the alleyway. "Silver asks about you all the time."

He smiled and folded his arms. "You don't say? How's my god-daughter doing academically this year in school?"

"Actually, she's doing extremely well. She got skipped to the seventh- grade and is still at the top of her class... she said she's gonna be a doctor."

Chubbs shook his head as his smile broadened. "My goddaughter, a doctor...whoa!"

Jesse gave him a big hug and a kiss. "Thanks, Chubby... make sure you tell Vonda I said hi."

"You make sure you give my goddaughter a kiss for me," Chubbs said, opening the door to his black Pathfinder.

As an afterthought, Jesse turned around. "Yo Chubby, were you really gonna kill that boy for five dollars?" With the same devilish smile he had since he was a kid, Chubbs looked away and started rocking back and forth. Jesse smiled. "Forget I asked," she said, knowing oh so well what the answer was anyway, she should have known better.

Chapter 4

Auntie Birdie

As Jesse climbed the three flights of stairs of the decrepit, dimly lit tenement that she called home, Birdie, her roommate and Silver's 'Auntie' greeted her at the door. Birdie was like a mother hen when it came to Jesse and Silver. He was always overly protective, and detested Jesse giving people in the neighborhood money all the time.

He stood waiting by the door filing his nails, wearing a satin green robe with huge pink curlers in his hair. "How much of your money you gave away today?"

Jesse only smiled as Birdie read her face

"I fuckin' knew it!" Birdie said knowingly. "Why you always giving these no good niggas your cash, Jesse?"

Jesse entered the apartment. "Because they're my people, and they need it." She plopped down on the couch. Birdie slammed the door shut and folded his bulky arms over his broad chest.

"Yeah well, I wouldn't give them niggas' shit! If anything..." Birdie paused and then said defiantly, "I would've made they're asses "earn" those dollars, if you know what I'm saying, child?"

Jesse gasped in shock. "Stop it girl, are you serious?" She knew very well that Birdie wasn't joking.

"I'm nasty" Birdie said snapping his fingers for emphasis, "but times are too hard to be just giving away ya hard earned cash, cause a buck is a buck and a fuck is a fuck child, and I ain't getting too much of either these days."

Looking toward the bedroom door, Jesse hushed him. "Shhh girl, Silver might hear you."

Birdie waved her off. "Oh child, please...she's sound asleep." He walked to the kitchen. "Do you want any coffee?"

Jesse kicked off her boots with a weary sigh. "No thanks, girl, I gonna walk Silver to school so we can catch up and come back and take a hot bath and get some sleep."

"Rough night?" Birdie inquired.

Jesse shrugged. "You know, same old same old, damn tricks wanting something for nothing." She sat upright as if she had an epiphany. "Oh yeah, I almost forgot, it was this one trick last night …and girl you won't believe this shit!" She drew Birdie's full attention as he rushed over with his coffee and sat down beside her.

"Now spare me all the details…what happened girl?" he asked, nearly breathless with excitement.

Since Birdie retired from hooking, his life consisted of *General Hospital, As the World Turns* and babysitting Silver while Jesse worked at night. So when Jesse came home with tidbits of 'Hoe Stroll', he savored it and lived it through Jesse's eyes.

Birdie's real name was Benjamin Alton. When he was sixteen, thirty years ago, he ran away from Alabama to New York after he no longer could take the repeated rapes by his stepfather. Soon after he arrived in New York, he fell on hard times and began sleeping on trains at night and spending his days at Times Square's bus terminal. One day, cold and hungry, an old white man offered Birdie twenty dollars for a blow job – he accepted it, and he'd been on the hustle ever since.

"Well," Jesse continued, "I'm working Times Square last night…out there by the water…when this big, black, shiny limousine with tinted windows and everything is cruising around peeping out us hoes. Everybody knew this nigga is hunting for some pussy cause he done circled the block three times. I'm thinking he's just trying to make up his mind which one of us he wanted to get with." She paused to catch her breath. "And you should have seen all them bitches posing and profiling and shit… breakin' their damn necks to get his attention cause you know that trick was good for at least a hundred dollars".

"I know that's right child," Birdie agreed.

"…Anyway, all of a sudden he starts slowing down and the motherfucker stops right in front of me."

"Then what?" Birdie asked, brows lifted in anticipation. "Then the passenger side window starts to roll down and I walk over and look inside and this black dude was driving. He was wearing one of them black chauffeur outfits, and he says, *'My boss in the back would like to know if you're interested in a date?'* …I said, 'Why can't your boss tell me himself?' Cause you know I ain't getting in no ride if I don't see how a motherfucker looks."

Birdie nodded in agreement. "You got that right girl, 'cause they still ain't catch that motherfucker that been killing all them girls… you got to be careful! I just heard on the news that he struck again and cut this girl up so bad her head was damn near off her body."

For nearly a year, dozens of women in the metropolitan area had been killed – primarily women of the night. The deranged killer's 'Modus Operandi' (mode of operation) was horrid. After he butchered them, he drained the blood from their bodies and thoroughly bathed them. Then, he dressed them in a wedding gown and made love to them. The newspapers dubbed him 'The Butcher of Broadway' and 'The Groom of Frankenstein'.

Waving her hand, Jesse dismissed his comment. "Please girl, he ain't doing nothing but killing up them white girls. He ain't interested in no dark meat".

"Still Jesse, that Frankenstein motherfucker is a sick bastard, so you just be careful. Now go head and finish telling me what happened."

"So anyway," Jesse continued, "I tell him why can't his boss tell me himself…that's when the back window started rolling down and I looked inside and I said to myself, *I be damned'!"*

Birdie grew impatient with anticipation. "Come on girl…what was it? A celebrity… Ooh, a celebrity with big ass dick?"

Jesse frowned. "You are fuckin' nasty; all you worry about is dicks, hoe!"

Birdie paid the comment no mind. "Yeah, I'm a hoe but don't forget my evil twin and her name is Moe! Now tell me what you saw."

Shaking her head at the outrageous comment, Jesse continued. "I looked inside once again to see if I was seeing thangs, but goddamn it, there it was again…" She enjoyed keeping Birdie in suspense, and purposely paused again to build him up till he burst.

On edge, Birdie shouted. "What bitch … what was it?"

Moving closer, Jesse looked him straight in the eyes. "A midget!"

Birdie frowned in disappointment. "A midget?"

"Yes girl, a midget… I looked back at the driver and he had this 'What could I do looks' on his face. I turned and looked back at this lil' white Gary Coleman, and he had on this big ass Kool-Aid smile on his big-ass face."

"Then what you do?"

"I said fuck it, a trick is a trick, right? So long as he got money, and trust me, this little motherfucker ain't gonna be out here in no limousine without no paper. I tell him yeah but its gonna cost ya two hundred. He said, 'Get in!' I got in and looked around, trying to act like it ain't no thang right, but it was hard 'cause this bitch was laid the fuck out! Plush chairs, T.V.'s, champagne and any kind of liquor you want. Then he peels off two crisp one hundred-dollar bills. I take it and put it inside my bra, then I tell him to tell the driver the directions to the motel, and the lil' motherfucker said he wanted to take care of business right there in the limo while we rode around."

"No he didn't," Birdie said astonished.

"Hell yeah girl, so I give him this leery ass look and he begins to peel off another two hundred and holds it up in front of me."

"What did you do?" Birdie asked.

"Bitch what you think… I took that mutherfucker!"

"No you didn't girl," Birdie giggled.

"Yes I did…shit, for four hundred dollars I would have fucked his lil' ass in Macy's window during rush hour!"

"And you call me nasty," Birdie said. They both laughed "Then what?"

"Girl, that little motherfucker went straight to eatin' the coochie!"

"Stop!" Birdie said, edging closer as the story got meatier.

Jesse nodded proudly. "Yep, like Pac-Man. And the lil' motherfucker was fierce too! Girl, he licked me from my asshole to my elbow and from the rooter to the tooter." Birdie placed both hands on his chest. "Stop!"

"Hell, yes girl! I ain't never got my pussy ate like that before! Shit, that big-headed motherfucker was so good that I came about sixteen times."

Hands over his mouth, Birdie's eyes widened. "Sixteen… Stop!"

"No shit! Sixteen…had my toes curling and everything. Hell, I should have paid his ass." Birdie couldn't believe her good fortune.

"So what about the fuck? Did he fuck you? How big was his little ass dick?" Birdie shouted, unable to contain himself any longer. "Come on girl, tell me!"

Before she could finish the rest of the story, Silver walked into the living room.

"Good morning baby!" Jesse said.

Silver smiled and ran into her arms. "Mommy!"

"Did you sleep well baby?"

"No, I had another bad dream, Mommy, it was about you again," Silver said, hugging her mother tighter.

"Aw...everything's okay, baby. You don't have to worry about Mommy," Jesse said softly rubbing her back. She looked up at Birdie. "Anyway, girl, I'm going to change and get Silver ready for school so me and my baby can catch up on things." She reached inside her bra, pulled out a thick wad of cash, peeled off a hundred-dollar bill and handed it to Birdie. Birdie stared at the large wad of cash.

"Damn child," Birdie whispered, "I might have to come out of retirement and show y'all bitches what a real lady can do! And none of you hoe's would make any money".

"What happened to waiting for your tall, dark and handsome"? Jesse teased.

Birdie chuckled. "I'll settle for short, white and bigheaded... Ooh, by the way, did you happen to get Gary Coleman's number?"

Chapter 5

The Rules

Jesse chose to walk uptown to Silver's school rather than take the bus because she was giving Silver the first portion of her daily education – the streets. The core of central Harlem had many decaying yet beautiful structured brownstones that were now abandoned and served as transient flophouses, occupied by horror-flickish addicts seeking temporary refuge to get off a quick hit or nod. As they turned the corner on Lenox Avenue, they watched the slew of addict's looming about enthralled in futile conversation while waiting for their daily methadone dose from their program. Many of these addicts were there for business purposes also. When they got their orally ingested medicine, they sometimes refrained from swallowing it, so they could sell it on the street in what they called 'spit-back'.

With each corner they turned, or each block they walked down, there was always something that she could teach or show her daughter. As they walked to school, it seemed everyone stopped to greet Silver and Jesse. They ran into Stickbroom Johnny and Jesse handed him some money. Stickbroom stuck out his wrinkled, midnight-black hands

"I sho tank ya, Miz Jesse," and give her one of his famous 'Good Negro' shuck and jives. "No problem, Stickbroom."

Stickbroom looked at Silver. "So how ya doing, Miz Silva?" he asked, displaying a wide, gummy smile. "I'm fine, Stickbroom," she answered. As they continued on, she asked, "Mommy, why did you give Stickbroom all that money when the newspaper only cost a quarter?"

"Because some people are not as fortunate as others. So as human beings, we have to help those people out because you never know when they will help you. Do you remember when I taught you about the 'The Law's of the Universe'? Silver shook her head. "Well, it is quite clear and never fails. In order for you to receive, you must first give." Silver pondered her words.

"Is that the reason why you give that man Mitts money all the time? 'cause he need it?"

"Well, yes."

"But he uses the money for drugs and you said drugs are bad."

She looked at Silver, searching for the right words. " Yeah, but people like Mitts been using drugs for so long that they can't help themselves. I'm sure they would stop if they could, but if they did and don't get their drugs, they can die."

Silver stared up at her. "But you didn't die, you stopped it."

"Yes that's true, but some people are different. Some people are so far gone that they give up rather than stopping."

"That's bad, but if the Laws of the Universe is true you will receive something from him, right?"

Jesse smiled. "Yeah, that's true but you don't necessarily expect something in return. A blessing can come from anywhere, that's why I have you."

Arriving at the school, Jesse, as usual, drilled Silver with precious and necessary information she felt her daughter needed to know and remember. Every single day, Jesse asked Silver the same questions over and over again, until she could say it backwards if needed. She had been doing this since Silver could talk. Jesse did this for several reasons, knowledge, self-esteem and wisdom being the most important. Jesse knew just how hard this world could be for blacks, especially a black girl. So Jesse groomed Silver with information to offset any and all misconceptions that might hinder her. She programmed her to look at things through a totally different spectrum, and the notion of possibilities instead of complacency and unreasonabilities were taught to her all her life. This was all Silver had known. Jesse was so adamant about it, she etched these principles so deeply in Silver's mind that she would be forced automatically to do the right thing, because that's all she knew.

Standing at the gate of the schoolyard, they began their morning ritual. Arms folded Jesse spoke. "Okay Silver, who's the smartest person in your class?"

"Me, Mommy," Silver said with all the confidence in the world.

"What kind of degree do you have?"

"I have a PhD in Common Sense."

"Who's the prettiest girl in your class?"

"I am."

"Why are you in school?"

"To prepare me to become anything I want to be!"

"And what is it you want to become?"

"A doctor," Silver said with enthusiasm.

Jesse grew stern. " Is it going to be easy?"

"No, it's going to be extremely hard and challenging."

"Why do you expect it to be hard?"

"Because if I expect things to be hard, everything will eventually become easy."

"What can you expect out of life?"

"The only thing to expect out of life is the unexpected!"

"Do you follow or do you lead?"

"I lead," Silver said.

"But?" Jesse asked with a frown.

"But is word used by procrastinators."

Smiling now, Jesse bent down. "Now lastly, what is the absolutely worst word in the world?"

"The worst word in the world is "Can't.""

"Good!" Jesse said, her smile growing. "Now give Mommy a kiss and go play with your friends." They hugged and kissed and then Jesse stood and watched Silver run over to her friends who were jumping double-dutch. Jesse smiled a moment, and then turned to go home for a well-deserved rest and a hot bath.

On her way home, Jesse spotted her mother, Thelma Jones, walking down Lenox Avenue toward her. Jesse wanted to turn and run the other way, but it was too late, her mother had already spotted her. Their relationship had been strained since she had gotten pregnant twelve years earlier. As Jesse got closer to her mother, she felt as if the air was being sucked out of her. She so badly wished she had taken another route home. She thanked herself for at least changing her clothes before she left the house. As they met, Jesse took a deep breath and forced a smile. "Hi Momma, how you doing? I haven't seen you in a good while…so how's it been?"

With a smug look, her mother looked her up and down. Uncomfortable, Jesse tried to change the subject. "Your granddaughter asks for you all the time. She says, 'When I'm gonna see my grandma…and she said she wants to be a doctor some—"

With a disgusted glare, her mother cut her off. "Are you still selling your body for money Jessica?"

Caught off guard, Jesse grew speechless as she cast her eyes toward the ground in shame and embarrassment. Mrs. Jones continued with her sour disposition and wickedness.

"You should be ashamed of yourself!"

Jesse raised her head, sad but defiant. "Momma, why do you always have to put me down?"

"Why not?" she said quickly. "You degrade yourself by prostituting your body and shoving that…that poison in your veins. It's just disgusting I tell you!"

Jesse had heard this many times before. "Momma… I'm sorry I didn't turn out the way you wanted me too, but I've changed." In earnest desperation for forgiveness she pleaded. "I haven't messed with those drugs in six months." Hoping this new development held weight, she continued. "I also plan to go back to school and start going to church."

"Church!" her mother said with astonishment, "God don't want any two bit junkie whore in his house!"

Crushed and defeated, Jesse fought back tears, realizing that nothing she said could ever change her mother's mind about her. Deep down though, Jesse wanted so badly for her forgiveness, but her mother was relentless, content it seemed, on making her suffer for the rest of her life.

Seeing her humiliation, Mrs. Jones continued. "What? Are you ashamed? Are you ashamed like you shamed your father and me?"

Just hearing about her father made Jesse feel lower than she already did.

"God bless his soul," she continued. "You killed him! That's what you did, you broke his heart when you got pregnant and left!"

Angry and in tears, Jesse protested. "But you put me out!"

Without hesitation Mrs. Jones barked. "You damn right I put you out! No no-good pregnant whore was gonna lay up in my house! You shouldn't have been out there spreading your legs to every nigger you met. Now look at you …you live in some beat up building with some faggot and your bastard child!"

Jesse could not believe her ears. The cold venom of her mother's words had pierced her very soul, to call her child – her granddaughter – a bastard was too much for her to bear and Jesse could only stare at her with anger as she walked off, crushed beyond words.

* * *

Jesse walked aimlessly through Harlem, stinging from her mother's wickedness. As she turned up 115th Street on St. Nicholas, she happened upon a familiar voice.

"Jessica?"

A tall man stood in front of the Japs restaurant. "What's happening, baby?"

Jesse looked up and saw Fast Eddie, one of her old dealers, who eyed her from above his sunglasses. Out of habit, she smiled said hello and kept moving. Ever since Jesse got clean, she had learned to disassociate herself from the 'old crowd'. Lifting his sunglasses, he stared heartily at her ass and hollered.

"Girl, you looking good! Go ahead with yo bad self!"

Jesse had walked five feet before she was suddenly hit with a familiar and overwhelming feeling – she wanted to get high. Feelings of pain, guilt and compulsion were a combination that awakened the old monster within her that had been sleeping for six months. The sudden need for just 'one' fix took over. She cursed herself for this notion and tried to walk off, but she was stuck. Doubt convinced her she couldn't win, so she reasoned, *'Hell…I deserve it, I'll do just one and that's it, I can handle it, just one!'* She turned on her heel and spoke to the dealer. "Yo Eddie, are you straight?" Her stomach was already starting to flip with anticipation for the drugs. It was said that your body releases epinephrine adrenaline when you're about to cop some drugs, causing you to get high before you even use the stuff. But his smile turned into a frown.

Eddie looked down over his sunshades. "Naw Jessica, you done beat that monkey down baby, long time ago, you doing so good!"

"Look man I ain't got no time for no preaching," Jesse snapped impatiently. "Either ya holding or ya not, 'cause if you ain't gonna sell to me it's plenty nigga's out here that will take my cash." In a stand off, he shook his head in pity. But business is business, and with an attitude and all business now, he snapped back.

"How much?"

She reached inside her purse. "Give me two." He looked around to make sure everything was everything and reached into his shirt pocket and pulled out two small glassine bags. He attempts to make one final plea to her, but she impatiently extended the money and stared him down. Reluctantly, he snatched the money out of her hand and shoved the bags in her hand. She stared at him for a second, and then headed home.

Chapter 6

Just An Illusion

Saturday was 'Girls Night', and no matter what, Jesse made sure nothing came between them and having a good time. Jesse, Silver and Birdie would just stay home and get dressed up, pretending to be some rich royalty types. They would do each other's hair and nails and bug-out singing and dancing all night. '...*Come on boy see about me....* *Come see about me...*' Jesse loved the Supremes, especially Diana Ross.

"Everybody thinks she's a bitch," Jesse said. "She probably is, but she fought for what she wanted and she is paid! But now, she can go anywhere she wants, buy anything she wants, and be who ever she wants. See Silver, like Diana Ross, she was poor and from the projects but she refused to accept the fact that she had to stay that way. She had a dream, and that's all you need to start with to get what you want."

Jesse turned to Silver. "Tell Auntie Birdie what your gonna be when you grow up."

"Oh, let me guess," Birdie said. "A Ballerina?"

"Nope," Silver laughed. Like a big kid, Birdie tried again. "Ooh wait...wait, let me guess again... a nurse?"

"Close," Jesse said.

"Tell Auntie what you gonna be."

"I'm going to become a doctor." Silver answered proudly.

Even prouder now, Jesse spoke up. "That's right, my baby gonna be a doctor so she can help all the people when they get sick."

"That's beautiful, baby," Birdie said. "And you can do that, all you have to do is believe in yourself and work real hard and you can become anything you want. Yeah, I can see them now ... 'Paging Doctor Jones.... paging Doctor Jones, please come to the emergency room...paging Doctor Jones!' "

"But you can't get side tracked," Jesse said. "That's why you got to be strong no matter what, 'cause the only person you can rely on in this world is you and don't ever forget that. You remember the rules?"

"Yes, Mommy."

"What's the worst word in the world?"

"Can't."

"Why?"

"Because, if I don't use the word in my vocabulary," Silver answered, "I can do anything."

"And what about boundaries?"

"If I don't place boundaries in my life, I'll never know when I'm out of bounds."

"Love?" Jesse asked.

"Don't expect to find love in others if you don't have love yourself first."

"And lastly?" Jesse inquired. "Always do what you say and say what you mean, because if you lie to a friend, you may only lose a friend, but if you lie to yourself, you may lose your soul."

"My baby!" Birdie said.

Jesse jumped to her feet. "Bonus question," she asked enthusiastically. "What is the secret girl rule?"

Silver jumped up smiled. "God gave man strength to conquer the world."

At the same time the three of them loudly said, "But God gave women a nana to conquer man!"

They all laughed and started dancing once again to the Supremes.

After partying all night Jesse put Silver to bed.

"Mommy," Silver asked, "Why do you always make me recite the rules?"

"Because I want to prepare you for life so you can be ready for anything this world have in store for you, because life is an illusion."

"How is life like an illusion?" Silver asked.

"Well, sometimes in life you are given choices, and the choice that you choose you may sometimes have to live with," Jesse replied. "The tricky thing is everything that looks good or feels good is not really good for you, it's only an illusion. Sometimes people spend their whole lives chasing something that's not really there, and after a while they come to their senses and stop chasing it only to find that they wasted a lot of time and effort."

"Mommy, did you ever chase an illusion?"

Jesse turned her head, stared up into space and reminisced back to her teenage years.

Chapter 7

12 Years Ago

Summertime in Harlem ... ain't nothing like it in the world. It seemed everywhere you went there was a party bumping. It was party fucking central and music was everywhere, so people partied at the drop of a hat. Hip-hop was just starting to take over, but Disco was still king. Go to any block, any parks on any given weekend, and nine times out of ten they were throwing down! From 111th Street to Sugar Hill, from Spanish Harlem on the eastside to the Bronx, which was right over 145th Street Bridge, it didn't matter; 'cause niggas was up in there. And it didn't matter if you knew who was throwing it either, cause bottom line was, the more the merrier.

There was just some unwritten laws to go by: Don't step on nobodies fresh kicks, carry a blade or box-cutter; roll thick with your crew and most importantly B.Y.O.B.B., (bring your own brown bag). A dollar was all you and your crew needed to stay toasted and blessed all night because that would get you a bottle of Cisco or Swiss-Up. If you were lucky, you had enough for a trey bag of smoke and some Big Bamboo.

The main crew was Vonda, Jesse, Lynn and Tiny. They went to an all-Girl Catholic School together. Vonda and Tiny lived in the same block on 138th and Lenox and 7th. Lynn lived only a couple of blocks away in the Drew Hamilton projects. Jessica's parents however, owned a building in Harlem's affluent 'Strivers Row'. The bugged thing about Strivers Row was that when you walked through it, it was like stepping in the Twilight Zone, because one minute you're surrounded by abandoned buildings, junkies and trash, and the next, you walk through these well-maintained tree-lined blocks and you wouldn't see any trash, or anyone hanging out on his or her stoop, you barely saw anybody, period. They had the most beautiful and expensive brownstone homes, owned by black doctors, lawyers, and actors.

When Vonda met Jesse, they clicked and been down for each other ever since. They had to be, because they were the targets of public school girls who hated them. It wasn't uncommon to see dozens of public school girls beat the shit out of a couple of Catholic schoolgirls. They thought all Catholic girls were stuck up and thought they were better than they were because they attended private schools. But to Jesse and her crew, they were better, so it just built their egos up even more and over the years they grew tighter.

At first glance, you would have thought a party going on, but Jesse and the girls were inside Vonda's room preparing for a big party that night. Torn out pictures from Right On magazines and posters of Parliament and the Funkadelics, The Jackson Five and The Sylvers covered the walls. Talking mad shit, the girls were bugging out, getting fucked up as they passed around some Panama Red. As they danced, a disco strobe light caused the room to have a psychedelic effect, enhancing the ambience. Vonda, the shot caller of the crew had smooth dark skin, sharp piecing eyes and was tall like Jesse. She was more tuned to the streets with hipness and fashion. She was the only girl in her family of five brothers- all street niggas. Nobody on the block was stupid enough to fuck with her on the strength of who her brothers were.

Lynn and Jesse were practicing a new hustle move they saw some Puerto Ricans do on the eastside, killing it as they finally perfected intricate moves in succession. Standing on the sideline, Vonda watch the two spin and turn with flair to the beat.

"Oh that shit was fly, do that shit again," Vonda said, passing a joint to Tiny.

Tiny however, was totally disinterested and sat lazily in an armchair inhaling the reefer. Tiny eyed the group and took a final pull before she got up to pass it to Lynn. Arms folded, she stood in front of them and blew smoke in Jesse's face. "Wack! Wack! Wack! That bullshit y'all doing is straight wack!"

The mood was broken and the girls turned to look at Tiny.

"Bitch, you can't do it!" Lynn said.

Tiny wiped ashes off of her clothes. "Don't even try it, y'all bitches ain't doing nothing but bitin! But me..." she patted herself on the chest to emphasize the point. "I'm gonna be original with mines!"

Jesse sucked her teeth. "Aw Tiny, you just mad cause you can't dance."

"What?" Tiny said defiantly. "You shouldn't even talk, bitch – I don't even know why you dancing 'cause you mama ain't gonna let you go to the party anyway!"

Everyone stared at Jesse, who grew silent.

Vonda shut off the disco lights and switched on the regular lights. "Jesse, ya mom's gonna let you hang tonight"?

Deflated, Jesse walked away. "I don't know I ain't asked her yet."

"Bitch," Vonda said. "I don't know what you waiting on, 'cause this shit is gonna be the joint. My brother told me D.J. Herk is gonna be spinning there at Stevo's house party, so you know all the playboys gonna be up in that piece."

Tiny was the smallest of the crew, but she talked the most shit. Tiny had a serious Napoleon complex, and swore she could kick anybody's ass. Tiny held a constant undercurrent of contempt and envy towards Jesse because Vonda, who she knew longer because they had grown up on the same block, took a liking to Jesse as they got older. Tiny resented it, and hated Jesse's guts for this intrusion, but she got used to it only because they still hung tough. Still, she harbored deep, deep resentments toward Jesse and tried to show her up all the time.

"Her mommy ain't gonna let her go, just like last time," Tiny said spitefully.

Jesse looked at Tiny with contempt. "Fuck you Tiny," she snapped. "You don't know what the fuck you're talkin' about... I ain't wanna go to that hot box party Shay-Shay had any ole way."

"I don't know why cause that shit was the serious joint, everybody was up in there," Lynn added.

Vonda looked at Lynn as if she were stupid. "Get the fuck outta here, ain't nobody but them bummy ass project hoes was up in there."

Lynn, the only one from the projects, turned toward Vonda. "What the fuck you mean 'project hoes? Ain't everybody from the project is a hoe or bummy!"

Lynn had developed a complex because of the stigma of living in the projects and thought everyone looked at her as if she was poorer than the rest of them.

"Don't be so fucking sensitive," Vonda said.

Lynn rolled her eyes. "Then don't be calling me no project hoe."

Vonda laughed it off. "You know you got problems, we weren't even talkin' about you. The minute somebody mentions the word 'Project' you swear they are talking about you. You ain't the only person that live in the project."

Being the shit starter she was, Tiny put her two cents in. "Jesse be thinking because her parents own a house, she better than the rest of us and shit."

Jesse hissed, "Bitch, I ain't said a fuckin' word about where she live, so better keep me out your mouth before I close that shit." Tiny said frankly with a dry, bitter laugh.

"Yeah bitch, picture that…at least my Momma don't give me a 7: 00 o'clock curfew!"

Jesse knew from experience not to let Tiny know what anger button to push because she fed off it and used it against you. The only way you get back at Tiny was to check her hard. "You just mad nobody want you with your no-titty ass."

Tiny's face flushed. She hated it when anyone talked about her physical attributes. Tiny had no curves at all; she was built more like a boy – chestless. Enraged, she jumped in Jesse face with blind anger.

"Then kick this no-titty bitch ass, you fucking hoe!"

Vonda quickly stepped between them and separated the two before any blows were exchanged. "Y'all ain't gonna be fighting in my Mama's house." In bitter silence, Vonda glared at Tiny. "I'm so sick of hearing your bullshit, Tiny!"

Tiny pointed at Jesse. "Why the fuck you yelling at me and not her?" she yelled.

Vonda spoke sharply, staring at Tiny. "'Cause you are the one always starting some shit." Before Tiny could reply, Vonda continued, her voice icy. "And don't be raising your motherfuckin' voice in my house!"

Tiny paid no mind and simply turned around and dismissed the whole thing like it didn't happen.

Lynn, the chubbiest and peacemaker of the crew, sensed the tension and changed the subject. "Anyway," she said, "I heard Kenny's gorgeous ass gonna be there, so you know I'm gonna freak his ass!"

"You gonna be waiting all night too, cause bitches be waiting in lines just to dance with that nigga," Vonda said.

Lynn rolled her eyes. "Shit… all I got to do is throw this chunky ass on his fine ass until he can't take it no more and he'll be begging for some of this pussy. He ain't gonna want nobody but me."

Lynn started to imitate grinding her ass against his penis. Everybody cracked up laughing.

Vonda's younger brother Chubbs was listening by the door. He boldly walked into the room. "Yo Lynn, fuck dat nigga Kenny, and throw dat chunky maafuckin' ass on a real playa."

They all looked at the pudgy boy simulating a sexual act and busted out laughing.

"Lil' nigga," Lynn seductively said, "If I throw ya lil' ass some of this," she turned around, showing him her ass to emphasize the point, "Yo lil' fat ass is liable to pass out!"

"You crazy, I'll bust you out big time!" the pudgy boy said in defiance.

Tiny jumped in with her two cents. "With what, lil' nigger? You're little dinga-ling?" She stuck out her pinky finger and wiggled it in front of them. As they all begin to laugh at little Chubbs, he grew angrier.

"Tiny, you shouldn't talk with yo bony tooth-pick ass, you can't handle it!"

As if it was comical, Tiny frowned. "Handle what nigga? You ain't got no dick, that shit is all up in your big stomach."

Sucking his teeth, Chubbs retaliated. "Bitch, please..." He unzipped his Lee jeans and pulled out his penis. All the girls could do was stare wide-eyed in disbelief at the size of the pudgy, foul-mouthed boy's abnormally large genitalia. Smiling from ear to ear, he spoke proudly. "My weight ain't the only reason they call me chubby... I got's me a chubby ass dick too!"

"Shut your mouth and put that shit away and get out of my room before I tell Mama," Vonda yelled.

Chubby zipped up his pants. "Yeah and I'll tell her y'all smoking reefers."

Vonda gave her conniving brother a mean stare, but relented because she knew Chubby would rat her out if he didn't get his way. "Just get out my room," she said.

"But I'm hungry, and you got to fix me something to eat."

Frowning, Vonda shrugged. "Nigga, you better wait till Mama get home, 'cause I ain't fixin' you shit."

Chubbs quickly responded. "Mama ain't getting home till late. She's working late and she left a note for you to feed me." He held up a note to prove it.

Paying the note no mind, Vonda shook her head. "You better fix yourself some cereal or something."

"Ain't no milk!"

"Then make some peanut butter and jelly."

"Ain't no bread!"

"Then lick that shit off a spoon, just leave me alone," Vonda said, at her wits' end. "I'll call Mama at work if you don't."

"You do and I'll kick your fat ass."

"Watch me," the defiant boy said, attempting to leave.

Vonda caught him and put him in a headlock. Lynn and Tiny joined in by lifting his tee shirt up slapping his fat Jell-O-like stomach. The fat boy pleaded, calling out to Jesse for help.

"Leave my little man alone," Jesse said. Vonda tossed her brother to the floor and threatened him. "You better not call Mama, 'cause if you do you won't eat shit till she comes home at midnight."

He yelled, wiping tears from his eyes. "But I'm hungry!"

"Ooh...look at the big cry-baby," the girls taunted.

"Leave him alone," Jesse said. She hugged him like he was a baby. "Don't worry Chubby, I'll make you something to eat, I don't mind cooking."

"Why you still treat him like a baby?" Vonda asked. "That nigga done changed a long time ago. He's bad just like them other niggas now!"

"That's okay. He'll always be my little Cubby Bear."

While Chubbs hugged Jesse, he stuck out his tongue at the three of them.

"You're lucky you little fucka," Vonda said, "'cause I wasn't gonna fix you shit! You would have been sucking on those tootsie roll pops till Mama got home."

Walking out of the room, Chubby spoke to Jesse. "Can you fix me some lima beans like you did last time? We got smoked-neck bones, pigtails and everything."

"Sure, Chubby," Jesse said. Chubby smiled as he ditty bopped out the room toward the kitchen. Chubbs suddenly stuck his head back in the room and smiled wickedly. "Yo Lynn, I'll settle for a half of those big titties and make a big ass titty sam'mitch!"

"Get out!" Vonda and Lynn yelled.

Chapter 8

Silver's Father

Kenny Duboise was tall, slim and drop dead gorgeous with the most radiant hazel eyes that you'd ever seen. He represented 142nd between Lenox and 7th even though he didn't live on the block. All the girls from the neighborhood, as well as most the guys were on his shit.

Nobody... and I mean nobody, could fuck with Kenny in looks or dancing. The kid had it all. He only shopped at A.J Lester's on 125th Street or Delancey Street in lower Manhattan to buy his Mock-Necks, Ice-cubes and A.J.'s, not to mention his Gators. The nigga defintely stayed dipped keeping his Lee's razor sharp, and was the only nigger to switch up gear twice a day. He had every colored British Walkers, Pumas or Pro- Keds and was the first nigga to sport a Sheepskin Quarterfield. It was rumored that his father was Ron O'Neal, that nigga from the movie 'Super Fly' because they looked just alike, only Kenny had a curly Afro and no mustache. Though nobody really knew much about him, he hung out with the older players from the block, who let the seventeen-year-old pussy magnate hang with them partly because he always bought wine and weed.

Unknown to everyone in the crew, Jesse too, had a big crush on Kenny but never had the heart to reveal such an outrageous idea. Kenny could have any girl he wanted. Even the older, more sophisticated girls would try to get with him. Jesse knew she didn't have a chance in hell, but at least she could watch his fine ass dance, she thought.

Later that evening, Jesse was home talking to Vonda on the phone. Jesse didn't want to miss this party for the world but wasn't sure if she'd make it. "So what time is the party?" Jesse asked.

"Your Moms said you can go?" Vonda asked excitedly.

Frustrated, Jesse stuck her lip out like a small child. "I didn't ask her yet." Jesse's mother was real strict when it came to her going out, especially to a party. Jesse could never understand the reason behind it, because she was doing well in school and rarely ever went out in the first place. The biggest thing, she thought, was that she was still a virgin compared to most of the girls she knew.

"Bitch," Vonda shouted, "You better do something 'cause you ain't got that much time left, it starts at ten o'clock and it's already five."

Looking at her watch, Jesse bit down on her bottom lip. "I know, but Moms don't come home from work 'til six thirty."

Vonda paused. "Where is your Pops?"

Jesse shrugged, knowing what she was leading up to. "He's here, but you know damn well my Moms runs shit."

"Bitch, that's it!" Vonda shouted. "All you have to do is tell your Pops we are going to the movies and after the movie you might stay over my house 'cause you won't have anybody to walk you home."

Jesse pondered this notion for a few seconds. "But what if they call your house checking to see if I'm there?" Vonda was used to getting over on her own mother and had this lying shit down to a science.

"Bitch, my Moms ain't gonna know where we going... even if your Moms calls my house and talk to my mother she just gonna tell her we ain't back from the movies yet." Vonda paused to let the plot sink in. "After midnight, you go to a pay phone to call your house and say that you're back and that we are going to sleep."

Now this really made sense to Jesse, but she was just unsure of just one thing. "But what if she calls the house for me after midnight?"

As if it was the stupidest question in the world, Vonda chided her. "What parent you know is gonna call another parent's house that late to see how their child is doing...think about it."

Jesse did and confessed. "You are one smart lying ass bitch, you know that?"

"You know it!" Vonda said. Satisfied, Jesse was now in a rush to get ready. "I'll call you when I'm on my way, okay?"

"Okay," Vonda said, and then hung up.

Jesse knew that Vonda was truly happy her home girl was going because it just wouldn't have been the same without her Ace - Cool - Boom! Even though she would have had Lynn and Tiny with her, she wouldn't have been as comfortable because both their conversations were one tracked and limited. Lynn was always unsure of herself and complained all the time, and Tiny who was too sure of herself, but constantly plotting and scheming on someone when she didn't get her way. Besides, she and Jesse were the same height, both of them stood almost six feet, and Jesse made her feel more comfortable, opposed to Lynn who was squat fat, and Tiny...well Tiny was just like her name, she stood five feet nothing. Vonda hated being the only one asked to dance by the guys. This made her feel guilty for the other two girls. She and Jesse were the dimes of the bunch, which made it a lot easier on Vonda.

They all met up at Vonda's house about nine-ish to change, and by the time Jesse got to Vonda's, everybody was already their taking showers and changing into their Sassoon or Jordache jeans.

"Oh shit ... it's on now!" Vonda said with a grin. They gave each other high fives. "Your Moms and Pops went for it huh, bitch?"

Jesse put her overnight bag, filled with clothes, on the bed. "Yep, my Moms started talking shit at first, but my Pops smoothed her out. All she said was that I had just better call when we come back from the movies." She reached in her pocket and pulled out a bill and opened it, smiling. "They even gave me ten dollars for some popcorn."

Vonda's eyes lit up. "Yeah girl, we could buy a lot of popcorn now!"

"I thought you said we was going to Stevo's party," Tiny whined in disappointment. "Y'all ain't said nothing about no movie's."

They looked at Tiny as if she was a dunce while Vonda shook her head. "You know... you are one simple bitch!" They burst out in laugher, as Tiny stood dumbfounded.

Fixing her hair, Lynn turned to Tiny. "That's where Jesse told her parents she was going to get out of the house... duh!"

This made them all laugh even harder. Humiliated, Tiny silently fumed as she stared evilly at Jesse. "All right bitch..." she muttered under her breath, "Let's see who will be laughing tonight!"

* * *

The house party was in full swing when they arrived. Everybody was doing the Hustle, the Bus Stop, the Spank or the Freak. It seemed everybody who was anybody was up in that piece, including Kenny and his crew. Even though it was a House Party, niggas were acting like they were up in the Fever. Jesse and her girls were the Queens of the dance floor, and she silently thanked those Puerto Rican's for the routine they stole.

The guy Jesse was dancing with couldn't keep up with her, so Lynn jumped in to show him how it was done. The shit they were doing was so fly everybody just stopped dancing to watch them get down. Jesse was sure all eyes were on her, including Kenny's, but she purposely edged closer to him so he would definitely see her. Being the case, she accentuated every toss and every step with extra snap and flair. Suddenly, the D.J mixed to a new song.

"Trans-Europe-Express!"

This was the song everybody was waiting for. It was said that if you danced to the hottest song with the hottest nigga, which was Kenny of course, you would become a sort of ghetto princess, talked about and envied for months to come. All the girls rushed towards Kenny for a chance at the title. Jesse, Lynn and Vonda knew they didn't have a prayer, so they went to the punch bowl for a drink.

"Look at all them desperate bitches," Lynn said, shaking her head. "They ain't got no class."

"I'm telling you," Vonda added, "I am not gonna play myself for nobody." She nodded agreement with Lynn, and then glanced away. "Oh shit! Look at Tiny's little ass pulling at him."

As they watched Tiny go for hers, Kenny was paying her no mind. He seemed to be looking for someone else.

"Yo, you got to give Tiny credit though, she stepping to her business," Jesse said.

"Get the fuck out of here," Vonda said. "That bitch is straight up embarrassing herself... look at her... he's pushing her lil' ass aside like she ain't even there."

They watched Kenny push Tiny aside as if she was a bothersome gnat or something. Suddenly Kenny started walking their way.

"Ooh shit," Lynn said. "He's coming over here." Lynn frantically checked her clothing and patted her doo.

They all stood still as he approached. When he reached them, he stood directly in front of Lynn and stared at her with his piercing hazel eyes, causing her to nearly pass out. Kenny smiled softly. "Can I get some?" Speechless, Lynn could only stare at him in disbelief. "Can I get some?" he said again, and then pointed to the punch bowl behind her. She turned to see where he was pointing and a goofy laugh escaped her throat. "Oh... oh, yes I'm sorry," she stammered. Blushing, she moved out of his way.

He took the silver ladle from out of the large bowl and poured some into a plastic cup. He raised the cup to his mouth but stopped to sniff it first. He frowned. "Yo, this ain't spiked, is it?"

" I don't think so, Kenny" Lynn nervously answered. "It didn't taste like it when I had some."

He looked at her. "Good... 'cause I don't like no alcohol." As he drank his punch he looked over at Jesse. "Yo Jessica, you was fly out there on the floor. I didn't know you could get down like that. You wanna dance?"

Shocked, Jesse couldn't believe what she was hearing. *Was he talking to her? How did he know my name, she thought. Am I dreaming? There must be a mistake. But he is looking right at me with those divine eyes.'*

"Yo girl," Kenny said. "You don't hear me? I asked you did you want to dance."

'Oh shit! He is asking me to dance. Say something, nod, smile, do anything. But I can't... I can't move... I can't...' An elbow jab from Vonda did the trick and Jesse elegantly cracked a broad smile. "Sure," she said, regaining her composure. Kenny took her by his baby soft hands and led her to the middle of the floor. As they walked by Tiny, she narrowly eyed them. As they started dancing, she quickly exited the party, searching her pockets.

Kenny and Jesse were perfect together. They flawlessly fed off each other's rhythm, not missing a beat or a step. An outsider would have thought that they had been partners for years. The other girls stood on the sidelines watching with covetous envy as they laughed and talked about everything from Jesse's shoes to her outfit. Jesse knew they were hatin', but it didn't matter. She knew she was on and she smiled in their faces as Kenny turned and tossed her to the pulsating groove. After three songs, Jesse and Kenny were still throwing down when the music stopped.

"Okay y'all," the D.J. suddenly announced. "It's that time. Fellows get ya girl and girls get your guys, 'cause it's time to grind to some Al Green."

Sweating profusely, Jesse shyly thanked Kenny for the dance and was about to leave when he gently pulled her hand.

"Hold up...we ain't finished." He pulled her into his arms. "You sure can get down girl, what club you go to?"

Jesse blushed and thanked him. "I don't go to no club, me and my girls just be inventing shit."

"So you're a natural," he smiled. "Is that what you sayin?"

Jesse felt heat flame her face. "Thanks Kenny, I wouldn't say that, I just like to dance."

"So what block are you from?" he asked.

"138th Street," Jesse replied.

"What... Lenox and 7th?"

He spoke the words as if they were a curse. "No," Jesse whispered. "No, 7th and 8th." He smiled knowingly and shook his head. "You from the Row?"

"Yeah... why do you ask?"

Kenny spoke frankly. "Cause, you got to be a rich motherfucker to live over there." Having heard this all her life, she downplayed it. "I ain't rich."

"Yeah, but your parents must be."

Not wanting to appear like most of the kids from her block – stuck up, Jesse wanted to appear normal as possible.

"My father works for the Post Office and my mother is a schoolteacher. That's not exactly the best jobs in the world you know."

"Chill down, baby," Kenny smiled. "You should be proud that you live in a nice neighborhood, and don't let nobody tell you different." She looked in Kenny's eyes. "Can I ask you something, Kenny?"

"Sure baby, your fine self can ask me anything."

Jesse felt heat flame in her face again. "Is it true you father is Ron O'Neal?"

Kenny laughed. "Naw, baby girl...that's just a rumor."

Jesse smiled. "But you look him just like...only better, and you dress in all those nice expensive clothes." Kenny downplayed what she said. "Well, I can't change the way I look, and the reason I dress well is because I got my own lil' business, if you know what I mean." It took Jesse a moment to get the hint, and when she did she put her head down because she didn't know he was a scrambler – a dealer. She looked up when he shrugged.

"Nigga got to do what a nigga got to do to survive."

Just as Jesse was about to ask another question, he stopped her.

"Listen can we talk about that another time, I just want to enjoy this moment with you."

Jesse looked up at him and saw that he was dead serious. She placed her head on his chest and closed her eyes and let the music captivate her soul. Never before in her young life has she experienced such feelings...she was in love!

Inside a phone booth, Tiny dialed Jesse's number. A woman answered. "Hello... Missus Jones, can I speak to Jessica?" she asked in the most innocent voice she could conjure. "Who is this?

"Oh I'm sorry, this is Tiny... I mean Claresse... Jessica's friend from school."

"Oh yes, how are you Claresse? Jessica's not here if that's what you're calling about." Tiny spoke with false disappointment. "Oh darn it!"

"What's the matter, dear?"

"Oh nothing..." Tiny said. "They must already be at the party, 'cause they're not at Vonda's house either." Tiny had to force herself not to laugh as she placed her hand over her mouth. "Party... what party? They're supposed to be at the movies tonight!"

Tiny said nothing. "Claresse, is there something you're not telling me?"

Tiny faked a plea. "Miss Jones, please don't be mad with me, but I'm not sure I'm suppose to be telling you about the house party they are having at 1132 St. Nicholas Avenue, Apartment 3B..." She hung up.

On the dance floor, Jesse felt Kenny's manhood rise as he thrust his hips from side to side to the rhythm as his hands explored her entire body. She felt an overwhelming guilt as she began to get moist, unable to control herself. After the third slow song ended, Jesse was too wet to continue and stepped away from him. "Thanks for the dance, Kenny."

Kenny held her hand and stared down at her. "Here girl, I want you to take my number and call me some time."

He wrote it down and gave it to her. She noticed that his friends were waving their arms trying to get his attention. He looked up and acknowledged them with a wink and a nod. She grew puzzled when she saw a couple of them waving money around, but paid it no more mind as he turned to talk to her.

"Listen Jesse, is it all right if I talk to you in the back room about something?"

Kenny led Jesse into a back room. Jesse looked around nervously. "You think it's okay to be back here, Kenny?"

"Yeah," Kenny said, "This is my man's pad. His parents are gone for a week... it's cool."

Not wanting to act uncool in front of Kenny, she decided to stop asking stupid questions.

"The reason I ask you to come back here is because..." He paused. "You opened up some things in me I ain't talked about in years...you talking about your parents and all made me think of my parents."

"What, your parents don't live together?" she asked softly.

"Parent's ... girl please, I never knew my Daddy and my Mom's died five years ago in a car accident. I only wish I had a family like you."

"Oh that's so sad, I'm sorry that I asked."

"No it's alright; I'm okay with it now."

She felt sorry for him. "But how did you take care of yourself?"

"Well," he shrugged. "You know, since all my mother's family was from all over the south, they couldn't contact nobody, and even if they did they was so poor they couldn't feed another mouth anyway. So they put me in a group home, and if you know anything about group homes, you know that ain't no place you want to be. So I ran away, and been surviving on the streets ever since."

"Oh baby I'm sorry... I didn't know," Jesse said, full of concern.

"No... it's okay, but you know what? You're the only person I ever told that story too, and now I'm thinking why was it so easy to tell you out of all the girls I know about my deepest secrets?"

He had her full attention, and Jesse silently listened to every word he said. He suddenly rose to his feet and walked over to the dresser.

"See, all my life, I've managed to hold onto my feeling's 'cause too many people has let me down, so I decided not to trust anyone. That's when you came along. That stuff you said about family made me think how much I miss having a family of my own. Now I know we just really met, but I feel something real deep inside of me for you. Tell me you feel it too." She looked at him and nodded.

"See, I knew you felt it too! See, all my life I had to make choices. Some was choices I was right about and some choices I was wrong about. That's why I know I'm making the right choice now." He turned around, walked over to her and got down on one knee. "Jesse, can I trust you?"

"Of course you can trust me," she said.

"Now I'm gonna ask you a question I ain't ever asked anybody." He grabbed her hand. "Will you be my lady?"

Jesse could hardly believe it as she searched his face. "For real, Kenny?"

He smiled widely. "For real."

As if she were dreaming, she answered him. "Yes, yes of course, Kenny!"

Kenny dug into his shirt pocket and pulled out a wrapped up ten-dollar bill and showed it to her. She watched curiously as he unfolded it.

"Do you know what this is?" he asked.

She looked down at the white powder inside the bill. "No, not really."

Kenny put the bill on the table and looked deep into her eyes. "That there is what keeps me looking good." Standing up, he opened up his arms and turned around slowly like he was modeling. "I look good to you right?" Jesse blushed. "Yes Kenny, of course."

He got down on his knees again. "Well, I think you are fly too." He picked up the bill. "And this stuff here… will tell if you are down with me."

Jesse didn't know what he meant by the comment and was afraid to ask. She cursed herself for being so unhip and lame. If only Vonda were in the room with her she would know what to do. In the meanwhile, she thought, she'd play everything by ear. She watched Kenny take out a matchbook, tear off the cover and crease it at the pointy sides, making it into a scooper. Slowly, he put the match cover into the bill, scooped up a small amount of the white powder and put it up to his nose. Jesse watched him closely as he ferociously sniffed the white powder up his nose. He smiled at Jesse, and then fed his other nostril.

"Yeah…that's what I'm talking about, smooth as ice, baby, ain't nothing to it. Now you try it."

Reluctant, Jesse shook her head. "I don't know, Kenny… I don't be digging on no heavy drugs." Kenny looked offended. "Heavy drugs…this ain't no heavy drug, baby," he said with great assurance. "This here is a feel good drug. Shit…everybody takes a toot every now and then …well at least everybody I hang with does!"

She didn't move.

"Let me ask you a question," he said. "Did you ever take an aspirin for a headache?" She nodded. "Yes."

"Well, what you think this is? It's the same as an aspirin only this is in powder form."

Jesse still felt leery. "But it's still a drug."

"Well what you think aspirin is? It's a drug! When you eat dinner what do you put on your food for taste? "

"Salt?"

"Now what do you think salt is?"

"A drug?" Jesse said, still unsure. Reacting as if she won the million-dollar question, he slapped his hands together. "Bingo baby! It's the same thing. I tell you what… just take two hits. If you don't like it, you don't have to do no more, okay?"

Looking in his innocent face and eyes, she submitted. "Okay. If I don't like it I'm stopping." He smiled again. "Cool." Not giving her a chance to change her mind, he dug into the powder, pulled up one big scoop and raised it up to her nose. "Now sniff this real hard to make sure it goes all the way up."

Jesse looked into his eyes one final time. He nodded to her, and in an instant she took a deep sniff of the powder up her nostril. She sneezed, but Kenny already had another mound of the powder in front of her.

"Good girl, now one more."

To get it over with, Jesse quickly snorted it again. She sneezed again as the strong powder burned the inside of her nose. The powerful drug immediately started taking effect, and she suddenly felt dizzy and queasy. Kenny quickly raised a paper bag to her mouth as she started throwing up. After she finished, Kenny gave her a tissue to clean her mouth and sat her on the bed.

"Good girl. Now don't you feel better?"

Unable to respond, she felt like she was in a calm, soothing dream. Kenny began to rub her breasts and undid her blouse. Stuck, all Jesse could do was gaze back at the most gorgeous boy she ever laid eyes on. Slowly, he began kissing and admiring her fresh youthful breasts as he expertly pulled down her already saturated panties. His fingers began to explore her virgin vagina, sending millions of tingling sensations throughout her naked body, causing her to have yet another orgasm. Kenny took his time as he turned her on her stomach and kissed her with his steaming hot tongue from the top of her neck down to the small of her back with all the gentleness of a lamb. Never in a million years would Jesse have believed that such feelings were possible. In her blissful sexual journey, Jesse had exploded multiple times as her organic juices saturated the bed and sheets. He turned her over and then, without warning, Kenny put his huge, throbbing dick inside of her dripping wet pussy, ripping her hymen to shreds as he plunged deeper and deeper inside of her. The pain became unbearable, but she could do nothing – the drugs were much too powerful. As she received him, she entrenched her fingernails deep into his back. But soon, with every powerful thrust, the pain was replaced with euphoric pleasures. Jesse had yet another orgasm as her brain registered unbelievable sensations. Kenny spread her legs wider and pounded faster and faster as he put every inch of his manhood inside of her. Suddenly, his short strokes turned into long strokes as he began sexing her like a madman. With an animal-like howl, Kenny released a massive explosion deep inside of her guts, causing her to have yet another orgasm before he collapsed, exhausted into her arms.

The heroin still worked its magic as she lay helplessly on the bed. She watched, as Kenny looked down at her, seemingly ashamed now as he lay upon her. He fumbled around the room looking for her panties. He cursed when he couldn't locate them and simply slipped on her jeans without them. After several minutes of struggling with her, he grew tired and frustrated and simply gave up, leaving her lying half-naked on the bed.

* * *

Vonda and Lynn noticed a crowd milling around in one of the back rooms and became curious at what everybody was gawking at.

"Yo, what's going on back there?" Lynn asked.

"I don't know," Vonda said. "I can't see." She stood on her tiptoes to get a better view. "Probably some niggas fighting, as usual."

Lynn smiled. "C'mon, let's be nosey."

As they walked toward the crowd, Vonda noticed people staring at them. As they got closer, they saw a female body hanging half-naked on the bed.

"Get the fuck out the way!" Vonda yelled, pushing her way through the crowd at the door. When she reached the room and realized it was Jesse, she nearly cried. She and Lynn quickly covered Jesse and asked her if she was all right. Jesse could only babble incoherently. Lynn turned around and noticed the crowd in the hallway still looking and laughing.

"What the fuck are y'all looking at?" She demanded. She ran to the door and slammed it shut.

"That motherfucker must've given her some type of drugs," Vonda said, tears in her eyes. "We got to get her to the bathroom."

They made sure she wasn't exposed as they carried her limp body to the bathroom.

Inside the bathroom, they put Jesse's head under cold running water. After about twenty minutes of running cold water and puking her guts out, Jesse began to respond to their questions. Vonda asked Jesse what had happened. Still slurring slightly, Jesse told them that she and Kenny were talking, and the next thing she remembered he offered her some kind of white powder.

"That snake nigger must've gave you some dope," Vonda said angrily.

"I didn't know what it was," Jesse said. "He said it was like aspirin."

Vonda stood up. "That wasn't no fucking aspirin that dirty bastard gave you. It was heroin and he fucking raped you." She gritted her teeth and spoke to Lynn. "Stay here with her. I'm not gonna let that bastard get away with this shit!" Moments later, the bathroom door slammed shut behind her.

When Vonda spotted Kenny she moved coldly in his direction with the stealth of a panther and leaped on him without warning. Vonda hooked off with blind and ferocious rage as she punched and tore into his face until she was on top of him. She moved so fast that Kenny hadn't known what hit him as he cowered from the barrage of blows that rained upon him, until finally, his boys pulled her off of him. Vonda kicked and fought mercilessly to be released, but they held on firmly.

In a daze, Kenny adjusted his eyes and it was then had he realized that his molester was a girl. Angry, Kenny sets to retaliate, but his boys held him back also. Tears falling from her eyes as her jaw twitched wildly, Vonda screams, "You dirty motherfucker...you gave my homegirl some dope and then fucking raped her? Nigger I'm gonna fuck you up" and went on the attack again. Vonda grabbed his Afro with one hand and began punching and clawing him with the other. It took his entire crew to rip Vonda off of him as she yelled like a mad woman, "Get y'all fuckin' hands off of me!" Not quite finished getting her shit off she struggled fiercely to be released, but they held tight. Not able to get to him, Vonda threatens, "Motherfucker this ain't over... I'm gonna get your bitch ass for this shit... you best to believe that!" Realizing she drew blood, Kenny said "Bitch! You scratched my face...are you fucking crazy?" With a deranged and cynical glare, Vonda sneered, "Bitch? We gonna see who the bitch is when I tell all my brothers what you're punk ass called me." Vonda continued "And when they do... they gonna bury your punk ass you can best believe that you raping bastard!"

Kenny and his boys put their heads down because they knew this wasn't an idle threat, but a promise. They knew all of Vonda's brothers and they equally knew that they murdered nigga's for much less. Seeing the fear in Kenny eyes calmed Vonda down. Smiling now, Vonda said, "Yeah, I thought so... you fucking chump!" And walked back to the bathroom.

A half an hour past before Jesse began to feel reasonably better, only now she was embarrassed and ashamed. Vonda was tired of waiting around.

"Fuck them people out there, you ain't got nothing to be ashamed of, it wasn't your fault. Now we going out there with our heads up, so lets get the fuck out of here and go home okay?"

Jesse managed a slight smile as Vonda and Lynn helped her to her feet and checked her appearance one last time before they opened the door. The first thing she noticed was that the lights were on and the music was off. The second thing she saw stopped her heart cold. Jesse's mother - Mrs. Jones. When Mrs. Jones spotted her daughter, she walked directly up to her, her face stiff with anger.

"You lying bitch!" her mother snapped and slapped her senseless.

Partygoers squirmed as they witnessed the vicious and brutal smack. Embarrassed beyond belief, all Jesse could do was run toward the door with her mother still beating her from behind. The entire place erupted in hysterical laughter as her mother beat her all the way out the door. She heard their laughter three floors down as she exited the building.

Chapter 9

Three months later

Jesse was on her knees in the bathroom, violently throwing up. Her worst fear was becoming real – she might be pregnant. Her mother kept her in the house the entire summer as punishment, but since school was approaching in a week her mother loosened up a little and allowed her to run simple errands and go shoe shopping. This gave her just enough time for her to go to the free clinic to get a pregnancy test. Vonda went with her, and as suspected, the test came back positive – she was three months pregnant. They both cried all the way home. Jesse had begged Vonda for months not to tell her brothers about the incident, and Vonda had reluctantly agreed.

Jesse decided it was time to call Kenny and tell him the news. She called the number he gave her for over two weeks now but never seemed able to catch him at home. Maybe this time, she would be successful.

"Hello…can I speak to Kenny?"

"Kenny's not here," a woman answered.

Disappointed once again, Jesse sighed. "Okay, can you tell him Jessica called?"

There was a slight pause over the receiver. "Are you the same young lady that's been calling all week?"

A little ashamed, Jesse put her head down. "Yes ma'am, it is."

The woman spoke gently. "Listen, Jessica…I'm only telling this because you sound like a really nice young lady… Kenny has a lot of young girls like you calling for him. Do yourself a favor and find yourself a good young man. Kenny is just like his father and believe me, I should know."

Jesse grew curious. "Ma'am if you don't mind me asking, but who are you to Kenny?"

"Why I'm Kenny's mother, dear!"

She slowly hung up the phone and began to cry. Kenny had lied to her, played her for a fool. And a fool she was, for she had believed his every word.

As time passed, Jesse's stomach and breasts began to stretch and swell rapidly. She had to make a decision soon, because she could no longer keep ducking her parents. It was time to confront Kenny with the news. Deep down, Jesse prayed Kenny hadn't used her. She naively thought that if she hadn't been so fucked up on the drug, things wouldn't have gotten out of hand. Besides she reasoned, she was now pregnant with his child and she had to give this Harlem cat the benefit of the doubt.

The history of Harlemites is legendary. Some of the greatest masters of *'Game-o-logy'* were from Harlem – second to none – unlike any other place in the entire world. Never the imitators or duplicators, they are trend setters and invigorators. The men and women of Harlem simply have a different persona about themselves – a different grandeur. They talked different and they walked different. If you saw a person wearing an outfit that you never saw before – they were from Harlem. If you heard somebody talking some slick shit you haven't heard before – they were from Harlem. Since the 30's, blacks have been settling in Harlem from all over the country. They came to New York penniless... broke... nothing! The one thing that they did bring with them was 'game'. Game from the South, game from the West, game from the Midwest – all over. Times were so hard back then that you had to survive off your wits or bounce back on the train, bus or boat that you rode in on. Beg, borrow, steal or kill – whatever...whatever, you had to do what you had to do to survive. Now just imagine all that game rolled into one like a mosaic melting pot, and what you get is thousands of the most trend setting and ruthless motherfuckers walking the planet earth. Over the years, it was more lil' nigglets getting educated on the street than in the entire Board of Education system. And then in the seventies came those Blaxsploitation films like 'Super Fly' and 'The Mack' and Oh – My – God, damn nigger's really lost their goddamn minds. Those movies' single handily set young black boys back fifty years. It created false images and made all those black boys play roles of wanna be playas, drug-dealers or pimps. It was all just an illusion and they fell for it. Over the years every single wannabe would eventually pay for it with their lives. They would eventually get murdered, go to jail, or become junkies. But one underworld pedigree of Harlem's finest remained unscathed, and that was the 'Gangster' – the true gangster that is.

Gangsters make the world go round, but you would never know who they were because they remained invisible…they were silent!

As Jesse walked down 142nd Street in her Catholic school uniform, she spotted Kenny on the corner, surrounded by his boys. She had not seen or heard from him since the night of the party. Jesse stared at them for a moment, trying to get the nerve and the words together. She had decided that under no circumstances would she have an abortion, so she knew where she stood. At least, if she knew where Kenny stood, she would have a better sense on how to handle things before she told her mother. If things worked out, maybe, just maybe, Kenny would do the right thing and get an apartment for them together before the baby came. Besides, telling Kenny wasn't the hard part, it was breaking the news to her mother that would be doomsday. As Jesse approached, the group of men all fell to a whisper.

"Kenny," Jesse said, "I'd like to talk to you." As if she was interrupting a major conference, he threw her a bored look.

"Fuck you want to talk to me about?"

Caught off guard by his venomous sarcasm, she shrugged it off and continued. "I'd like to speak to you… in private."

He looked at his boys and smirked. "Bitch, anything you want to say, say it right here."

All the guys Kenny hung out with was much older than he was, and they were so call 'bringing him along' cause he had potential and was building his rep as a player. A niggas' rep was like precious gold and nigga did anything for it – anything! His boys added fuel to the fire by calling him soft. So Kenny set to prove to the older heads that he can be 'Dat Nigger'

Jesse could tell he felt compelled to put up this tough front to impress his friends, but surely, after he heard her news, he would soften up. She took a deep breath, and tried not to let the coldness of his words affect her, she decided to take off the gloves and blow up his spot.

"All right then. Kenny, I'm pregnant!" she said, pointblank.

"Aah …Sukey sukey now…Poppa Muthafucken Doc," his boys began to mock.

Kenny appeared to be unfazed by the revelation and spoke almost casually.

"So fuck you telling me for?"

Taken aback by his attitude, she felt momentarily stunned. "'Cause you're the father!"

Kenny barked. "Bitch, I don't know what the fuck you talkin' 'bout, so you better take your freak ass up outta here and find the real daddy."

"Ooh Shit, that nigga on the come up!" one of the boys shouted, giving each other daps. Unable to comprehend his denial, Jesse spoke in hurt surprise. "What are you talking about Kenny? I ain't never been with nobody but you."

Sucking his teeth, he waved her off. "Yeah right!" He turned to his boys and pointed his thumb back at her. "All you Catholic School girls are undercover freaks"

"Sure you right, nigger!" the boys howled.

Hands on her hips, Jesse grew angry. "Why you acting like you don't know what happened at the party, Kenny?"

"Look here, bitch…" Kenny said quickly. "I remember two things that happened at the party that night. One…you sucking my big black dick and two…ya momma beating ya ass while you ran out the door!"

His boys let out an eruption of laugher as they gave him high fives and yelled.

"You the Goddamn Man Nigger!"

"Pimp fuckin' Daddy!"

Jesse sadly realized a side of Kenny she had not known and shook her head. "You're wrong, Kenny… this is your baby and you want to deny it!"

Enjoying every moment, his crew told young Kenny to pimp harder and pushed him closer toward her. Stepping in her face now, Kenny had the decency to look chagrined as she continued to stare at him in disbelief. He was unable to look her directly in her eyes. Jesse sensed his dilemma and took him by the hand, pleading softly.

"Kenny please, baby, don't treat me like this, this is your child… yours! And together we can make this work." Kenny remained silent. "Kenny," she said, glancing at the men behind him. "Let's go somewhere alone where we can talk." His face softened and he opened his mouth.

"Oh don't tell me this lil' nigger is getting soft!" one of the boys demanded.

"Hell, yeah," another man said. "Like a sho' 'nuff bitch!"

"Lil' nigger ain't ready for the game, he's in love!"

In an instant, Kenny jumped back into character and smacked her hand away from him. His voice and eyes turned cold once again.

"Bitch," he said. "I done told you once to get ya raggedy ass off my block before I get mad now. My name ain't *Herbie* so I ain't *Handing* out no *Cock!* This dick is closed, and it don't come for free like last time!" He turned around to his boys. "Even though I did win some money off your tired ass in a bet that I could fuck your skank ass in less than hour, and guess what bitch… I won!"

His boys ran in circles as they let out an eruption of laughter.

"Pimp hard, nigga'!"

Standing alone and humiliated, tears streamed down her face as she made one last plea. "What am I suppose to do now, Kenny"?

Kenny stared coldly at her, reached inside his pocket and pulled out a thick wad of cash. One of his boys laughed.

"Oh no…what this nigger gonna do? I know he ain't gonna go out like a sucker and pay for an abortion!"

Kenny calmly peeled off a single dollar bill, balled it up and threw it squarely in her face and said,

"Buy a hanger, bitch!"

"King pimp *supreme!*"

"That's right, nigger, money, clothes, and hoes!"

"I said he gave the bitch too much!"

Back to Reality

Jesse had her coat on as she headed out the door. Birdie stepped out of his room and startled her.

"Where are you going this time of night, girl?" Birdie asked.

"Oh…um…my period just came down and I'm out of pads. I gotta pick some up from the store, I'll be right back." She slammed the door behind her.

"Bring me back some vanilla ice cream on your way back" Birdie yelled.

An hour later, Jesse was in the bathroom on her knees, sweating profusely as she frantically prepared her fix. She held two burning matches under a silver spoon, eyeing the steaming liquid until it bubbled. She quickly dropped a small piece of white cotton inside the spoon to absorb the liquid, quickly tore open a newly purchased hypodermic needle and slowly drew the heroin up through the cotton and into the syringe. Working with the expertise of a seasoned nurse, she tightly wrapped a rubber hose around her arm to halt the circulation of blood. Holding one end of the hose in her mouth, she frantically tapped her arm with her fingers until a greenish, squiggly vein protruded. Anxiously, she grabbed the drug-laced needle from the sink and carefully plunged the prickly, dripping barb into her arm.

In an instant, her eyes began to flutter and her lips quivered as the powerful drug raced though her bloodstream. At that moment, life and all its problems no longer existed, for Jesse was in a utopia – a blissful womb with total disregard for time, life or worry.

After an hour or so of peaceful nodding, a long slime of spit hung amazingly suspended from the side of her mouth. It was then that the bathroom door suddenly swung open – it was Birdie. Seeing Jesse on the toilet, Birdie turned away.

"Oh… I'm sorry Jesse," he stammered. "I didn't know you were in here."

Jesse glanced up to see Birdie staring wide-eyed at her, more in remorse than shock. He shook his head, speechless as he stared at the needle protruding from her arm. Drops of dried blood had spewed on her arm and porcelain floor and walls.

"Oh Jesse," he said teary-eyed.

* * *

Over the next few weeks, Jesse's drug addiction spiraled downward. In addition to her heroin addiction, she was introduced to heroin's deadly sister, 'Crack.' Needless to say, it started affecting her family dramatically and worse than before. Saturday's Girls' night out became a thing of the past, nor did Jesse have time to walk Silver to school. Jesse no longer tricked in Times Square, opting for the seedy eastside of Harlem's Park Avenue instead, right under the elevated train on 125th. This area was reserved for the sleaziest of whores and transsexuals, most of them with a drug habit themselves. They favored this area because of the easy and accessible availability of their drug of choice. Drug-dealers stood by, waiting for the whores to finish a trick and cop soon after.

Jesse's appearance fell off rapidly as she sank deeper and deeper into the grips of addiction. A cycle so vicious it caused mothers to sell their own kids, or a man get on his knees and suck another man's penis. And just when you think you hit rock bottom, you find out that those bottoms have trap doors and then you sink lower and lower into squalor, degradation and humiliation. The vast majority of these unfortunates have few options to get away from these monstrous and abominable cyclones, and they are death, jails or mental institutions. The ones who survive must live with the trauma and damage that they've done to themselves and others for the rest of their lives.

No longer could you see the regal beauty Jesse beheld only weeks earlier. After endless talks to stop the madness, Jesse became tired of Birdie's constant preaching and soul saving efforts. She wanted to be left alone to enjoy her high, so she began spending weeks, then months in the drug spots, hotels or shooting galleries.

A shooting gallery is a typical abandoned building converted into a one-stop drug haven. Inside you could cop any and every kind of drugs you needed. The in-house dealers sold everything from China white heroin to dirty beige Peruvian scale cocaine. You can cook-up to smoke it or powder for speedball. Pushers even sold the syringes and glass pipes so you had no reason to want to leave, so they could get every dime of your money. In some cases, the dealers would even buy you food to eat, not because they were kind-hearted – no, never that – but because they knew that you stayed higher for a longer period of time on an empty stomach, and that would take profits and residuals out of their pockets.

You could get high peacefully without worrying if someone tried to roll your pockets while you nodding or geeking out because the dealers wouldn't have it. White boys were treated no different from Blacks or Puerto Ricans, because in the dismal world of addiction, it was a mosaic brotherhood among dope fiends – color didn't matter. The only color that matters in their world was Dead President Green.

Addicts could spend days, even weeks inside these houses shooting and smoking themselves into oblivion without once seeing the light of day. Walking inside these hellholes was like entering the accommodations of the Devil's Den – they reeked macabre and morbid death. Spewed and decomposed blood cast upon the floors and walls, causing the filthy candle-lit apartments to reek a mixture of rotting flesh and constant vomit. Dirty pee-stained mattresses were scattered sparingly throughout the rooms, as scores of dope fiends greedily stab themselves into any viable vein in their body – arms, legs, necks, or groins – anywhere! Many, in order to save a buck or two, systematically used the same dirty and dull needles over and over again, only cleaning it when blood clogged up their works, causing horrible, black and insidious abscesses all over their bodies. Opened wounds oozed yellowish pus. Some men, who got a dope dick – if you can imagine – openly received sexual service from men or women alike in the midst of these abominable and repugnant conditions. In a matter of time, Jesse was reduced to one such person, and it became common for her to turn tricks for two dollars, if that, the way she now looked.

Chapter 10

Chance's story

Before the crack of dawn, Chance ran out of the tenement, looking behind him all the while, when a older man yelled out the fifth floor window

"I see you, you little fucker. I ain't stupid! When ya lil' ass come from school you better come straight home. I'm giving you a bath...you hear me?"

A frightened Chance could only nod as he continued to run away.

"And don't think I didn't see you go in that 'fridgerator and take that food out!" the old man hollered after him.

Breathing easier, Chance walked about two blocks and looked over his shoulder before he entered an alley. About halfway down, he removed some boxes and kicked rats out of the way. Under the boxes shivered a frightened little street boy named Hollis, wrapped in heavy layers of blankets. He held a knife for protection but smiled when he saw it was Chance, handing him some food wrapped in aluminum foil and a half a loaf of Wonder bread. Chance sadly watched the pitiful homeless boy dig heartily into the food, as if he hadn't eaten in weeks. He reached in his pocket and pulled out a bag of bones, signaling to the little boy. Hollis reached under one of the thick blankets and pulled out a little mixed breed puppy.

* * *

As time passed without her mother, Silver and Chance grew even closer. She found sincerity in Chance that she had never known in any other person other than her mother. Even though she and Missy were close, Missy's answer to everything was to kick ass and ask questions later. Chance didn't act or talk like anyone her age. He was more serious and focused, as if he was a grown man at times. Even though Chance was only twelve, his deepness enthralled her. When Silver asked him about his parents, he turned unresponsive. She had learned from her mother never to pry into anyone's business and made a mental note never to bring the subject up again.

As they grew closer, she began to tell him all her darkest secrets. He never even batted an eye. That's what she loved about him, he listened and didn't judge – which was the ultimate way to a person's heart.

One day, while walking home from school, Silver looked over her shoulder and gestured. "Chance...I don't know if you been noticing, but that dude has been following us since we left the school."

Chance turned around and saw the straggly looking boy walking some distance behind them.

"Oh, don't worry about him, he's a friend of mine. His name is Hollis...he lives on the streets, so I be helping him out from time to time. Don't worry about him though, he's harmless." Silver remained silent as she stared at the crazed looking boy.

During the next few weeks, Silver and Chance often stopped in the park, where she taught Chance how to read and write. She borrowed a second-grade book from the school to teach him the most basic of English, 'The How-Now-Brown-Cow Book.' As she read, she pronounced each word for him to repeat. "How," she said, emphasis resounding on each word.

"How what?" Chance asked.

"Say the word."

"The word!" Chance answered.

"Not word... How!"

Chance frowned in confusion. "Who's notwordhow'?"

He gave her a sly smile and she gave Chance a love tap when she realized he was joking with her. "No, Chance, stop playing...we've a lot of work to do it's gonna get dark soon. Now, say 'how.'"

In a deep voice, Chance lifted his hand like an Indian Chief. "Sayhow... Me Tonto." Silver couldn't help but laugh.

Chance stared at Silver for several moments and said, *"As I gaze into your eyes, so full, so enchanted,*

> *I close my eyes, for they're still unhampered,*
> *As they dance in blissful darkness as I sleep,*
> *I pondered your trust, your heart, so deep,*
> *I long conquered wonders of sincerity,*
> *because I open my eyes,*
> *for your eyes are still near me!"*

For a moment they just stared at each other, Silver more perplexed than surprised. "Wha…where did you learn that from?" she asked.

Chance smiled. "I just made it up for you… you like it?"

"Liked it… Chance, I loved it. It was beautiful. How did you –"

He interrupted her. "Silver, I haven't been totally honest with you."

Silver frowned in confusion. "Honest about what, Chance?"

"Well I think it's best I show you."

Chance stood up and walked to the other end of the park to the trash bins and began looking though each of them. She watched curiously as Chance pulled out a newspaper and walked back to the bench where she sat. Still silent, he sat down beside her and began scanning through the pages until he found what he was looking for and proceeded to read the editorial section. Chance read every word with perfect enunciation and diction. He even read words she didn't even know how to pronounce and didn't stop reading until he completed the entire editorial. After he finished, he looked up at her. She was speechless.

Taking her by the hand, he paused to gather his thoughts. "Silver, right now, you are the only friend I have on this planet. You are my only true friend, and for that I will be forever loyal to you." Looking into her eyes, he continued. "You asked me some time ago about my parents, and I thinks its time I tell you … I have none. I'm what they call a 'ward of the state', which basically means the State of New York owns my black ass until I'm eighteen. Over the past three years, I've been bounced around from one foster home to another for being too much trouble." Chance stood up in front of the bench. "Which actually means I fought back when I didn't let them touch me or put my mouth down where they wanted me to."

He paused to see how she would react. A knot developed in Silver's stomach, but she remained silent.

"They sent me from one place to another and each one would be worse than before. So I got to the point where I was tired of fighting and just gave up and let them have their way with me." Putting his head down in shame, Chance continued. "I learned it was easier to get it over with and maybe they would leave me alone for a few days or if I was lucky, a few weeks." Seeing Silver's pained expression, he reassured her. "But it's okay these days because the family I'm with now has only one horny old fart and he can't even get it up. He just likes to watch me bathe myself, so I guess that's why I smell so bad." Chance tried to laugh. "Anyway, I just stop trusting or responding to people anymore, especially adults because I don't trust them. So I just play dumb. That way, they don't want much from me, and that includes teachers. Since nobody seems to give a shit about me, I started not giving a shit either. I just stopped giving a fuck!" His voice grew strained. "Why should I care what they thought of me, if my own mother didn't?"

It was the first time Silver detected anger in his voice since she met him.

"Mother made me, mother fucked me... that's how I look at it." He turned toward Silver, as if making a confession. "My mother was what they called an alcoholic... I can still remember, as though it was yesterday, my mother staggering up the block with all the kids following behind her, imitating her drunken walk." He shook his head. "That shit was so embarrassing. The kids on the block teased me every day. But nothing was worse than coming home from school and seeing a gang of guys from the neighborhood with their dicks out, running a train on your mother, some of them no older than I was." He threw up his hands as his voice began to crack. "Everything happened so fast. One minute my mom and dad lived together and we were a happy family. Then one day they started arguing all the time, which was strange because they never used to argue. I would hear my mother pleading with my father that she was sorry. I found out my mother had cheated on him with his best friend." He began pacing back and forth. "As she got bigger, he tried to act normal and dealt with it because he loved my mother that much, but I knew he was crushed." Chance seemed to be in a daze as he somberly reflected. "My dad was like my hero. To hear your hero cry, that did something to me, yo." He gritted his teeth. "And I hated my mother for doing that to him."

Silver wanted to just take away his pain but knew he had to get everything out. "After my sister was born he stopped coming home altogether. I guess he couldn't look at her without catching feelings." As if it didn't matter anymore, he shrugged. "And to make a long story short, he started smoking crack and lost his city job and eventually..."

He stared at the sky. "He lost his life by owing some drug dealer some money and he got himself murdered. After my father got killed, my mother musta felt guilty and started drinking a lot and soon she began to have boyfriend after boyfriend... none of them staying with her very long." He let out a big sigh.

"After a couple of years of moving around 'cause she couldn't pay the rent, we started living in shelter after shelter until welfare put us in public housing." He shrugged again. "Then one day the bottom just fell out and she cared about nothing but her bottle. She would leave my sister and me home by ourselves while she was out drinking somewhere. My sister, Karen, was about four or five years old, I was about nine.

"My sister never talked because the doctor said she was a little slow due to my mother drinking while she was pregnant with her. Anyway, when my mother didn't show up for days, we ate the ice from the refrigerator freezer because we were so hungry. When she finally stumbled in, she would be broke anyway. Even though we were on welfare and my Moms got food stamps, she would exchange them at the store and get seven dollars cash for every ten-dollar food stamp at the bodega. Between her cashing in the food stamps and those no-good men robbing her, my sister and I were left with no food or no nothing." He shook his head and sighed. "But I wasn't about to let my baby sister starve, so I got to the point of not relying on my mother to come through for us. I decided to take to the streets to hustle for some change. I would go out and beg people for some money and as soon as I had enough for a loaf of bread, we would go home and make some mayonnaise sandwiches.

"After a while, I started packing bags at supermarkets and I had enough to buy us any kind of cereal that we wanted, Captain Crunch, Frosted Flakes, Cocoa- Puffs and Fruity Pebbles. You name it, and we had it!"

As if he won a slight victory, Chance smiled. "And we ain't never starved after that. We ate cereal for breakfast, lunch and dinner, but it was cool because I didn't know how to cook anyhow. I did everything for my sister, I fed her, I bathed her, brushed her teeth and did her hair, or at least I tried to do it." He laughed as he reminisced. "And she couldn't go to sleep unless I read to her, so I would read to her old newspapers, history books, science books, cereal boxes, hair care products, ingredients and all – anything."

He looked at Silver. "Did you know that a bar of Irish Spring has Pentasodium Penetate, Tetrabutyl Pentaery – Thrityl Hydroxyhdrocinnamate with a tad of Titanium Dioxide? So I guess that's how I got to read so well. I loved my little sister more than I love myself – I was all she had – I had to protect her. No matter what I did or where I went- I took her with me. I would place her in my shopping cart and simply pull her everywhere with me. Leaving her home with my mother was too dangerous, because the men she brought home were unpredictable when they were drunk."

He turned and explained. "I remember this one time… I woke up in the middle of the night and this man was just standing there zipping up his pants. I looked at my lil' sister who was still sleeping when I noticed what I thought was white glue all over her face and pajama's." Chance gritted his teeth in anger. "That fuckin' bastard had just jerked off on my little sister! After that, I got into the habit of setting up a makeshift bed in the closet for my sister to sleep in at night. I would place these old clothes over the top of her so they wouldn't see her. I wasn't about to let them dirty bastards touch my sister."

Chance took a deep breath in an effort to control his anger. "After a while, my mother stopped coming home altogether. By then it didn't matter none, 'cause I hated seeing her … she wasn't giving us nothing but grief anyway. Shit… welfare paid the rent and light and gas was free in the projects so what we need her for?"

Silver knew he didn't mean it, it was written all over his face.

"The only problem we had though was B.C.W…you know… those child welfare people? They kept coming around trying to get all up in our business. Our nosey neighbors musta ratted us out or somethin', but I didn't answer the door for anybody anyway. It got to the point that they would begin to stake out the front of the building every day. But I would dick them and sneak out the back exit. After while they got hip and started coming in pairs to post out both exits." He smiled at his own cleverness. "No problem, I just go up to the roof and cross over to the next building."

He sat down beside her and spoke with serious intensity. "See, I knew that if they catch us they would try to break us up and I just couldn't live with that." He closed his eyes as if in pain as he remembered. "Then one day out of the blue, me and Karen came home from packing bags and my mother was home. We hadn't seen her for five months and I quickly noticed how different she looked. My Moms was always skinny, but she was skinnier, almost half of what she was. Her bright white eyes and fair complexion was now yellowish. For the next two days she stayed in bed – she was very sick. For some reason, she kept asking me to get her some cold water because she said her insides were burning.

"The next day, I woke to my mother crying in intense pain. She told me to go call an ambulance, so I went downstairs to the payphone and called 911. When the ambulance men came, they lifted my mother off the bed and into one of those chairs, and I saw the reason why they had acted so crazy. The sheets were saturated with thick blobs of blood. She was bleeding from her anus." Chance put his head down as Silver rubbed his hands "At the hospital, they kept my mother in intensive care because they said she lost her liver. The next day, my sister and I spent the entire day with my mother right by he side." Looking into space, Chance smiled. "That's when it dawned on me... this was the first time since I could remember that my mother wasn't drunk – she was sober. She spoke to me clearly without that slurring sound and I didn't smell that horrible rotting odor from her mouth. Then suddenly it occurred to me." He smiled brightly.

"Everything was finally gonna be all right, she was in the right place getting cured, and besides, she had a white doctor. At that moment all the pressure and burden was lifted off my shoulders and just like that, I felt normal again. My sister and I went home, to return the next day to enjoy another day with our mother. When we got to the hospital I told the reception desk lady I was there to see my mother in room 416. The lady looked through the chart and made a phone call and whispered into the phone and hung up and told us to have a seat for a moment. After twenty minutes of waiting, I saw my mother's doctor get off the elevator and walk towards us. With him was a woman that I knew I had seen somewhere before. She was black, with a large purse over her shoulder, and behind her was a man in a uniform. They all had these fake smiles on their faces, except the man in the uniform who didn't smile at all. Bending down, the doctor spoke first.

"Hi, I'm Doctor Epstein, Clara Haze's doctor. Are you her children?"

All I could do was nod. That's when it hit me... I remembered where I saw the lady from − she was one of those Child Welfare people that used to stake out my house. *They were there to get us!* They must have followed us, I thought. I immediately wanted to jet out of there with my sister, but I knew I wouldn't make it. The lady bent down and introduced herself.

"I'm Mrs. Cherice Mayo, with the Bureau of Child Welfare," she said in a sad, sincere voice. "I'm sorry I have to tell you this, but your mother expired at 2:17 this morning."

As if Chance was right back at the moment, he shook his head in dismay. "For some reason it didn't register. I was unable to comprehend those words. All I could do was stare at them. I went numb and began to think, *'How could this be? My mother was getting better... she wasn't drunk... she was getting help... there must be some mistake... I just saw her yesterday... this was the best condition I had seen her in years- this just cannot be!* ' But the two faces in front of me told me a different story. It wasn't until I looked over at the receptionist wiping tears from her eyes that it hit me... my mother was really gone. All the while the social worker's mouth was moving, but I couldn't hear a single word. Time had suddenly ceased to exist and began moving very slowly. It wasn't until I heard the cries of my little sister that I came back to reality. Not only were they there to tell us our mother was dead... they was there to take us apart."

Chance shook his head in anger. "So I went after my sister, who was crying and reaching out for me, but the guard held onto me. I broke loose anyway and ran to her. We held on to each other for dear life as we both sobbed, but they finally pried us loose. All I could do was call out for her over and over. The next thing I remember was waking up in a hospital bed and I was handcuffed to the railing. After that I went from one group home to another, and I never saw my baby sister since."

Silver's eyes swam with tears. She had no idea how much suffering he had been through. All at once things began to make sense to her. "Oh Chance... I'm so, so sorry, I didn't know. Why didn't you tell me?"

"Silver," he said. "I never told you this because I was afraid that you would look down on me like everyone else. But..." he quickly added, "It's not like that with you... you're so different from anyone

I've ever met". He stared into her eyes for a moment. "That day, in the cafeteria, when we first met... you remember?

Silver nodded.

"And you asked me to look at you when we are talking?"

She nodded again.

"Well... when I did, oh my God." He smiled at the memory. "I looked up and saw the most beautiful thing I've ever laid my eyes on. I thought to myself, 'My God... could there be anything more beautiful on this earth?' Well... the more time I spent with you, the more I realize how wrong I was... because there is something more beautiful than you..." He paused. "And that is...your heart, Silver."

Silver melted from the depth of his sincerity as she explored every feature in his amazing face.

"Never... would I ever have imagined that something as lovely as you would come into my life and bring a glimmer of happiness into the world of a smelly broken bum like me and make me feel so complete." Tears welled up in his eyes. "I never believed that after all I've been through that I would ever trust or feel for anyone again... but you changed that, Silver. You did all that by simply being a friend to me... and for that, I just want to say... I will forever love you."

Overwhelmed, the air seemed to have been removed from her entire body as she gasped. "Oh, Chance...I love you too!" Caught in the grip of emotions and tears, they hugged each other dearly. As they pulled apart, they gazed into each other's eyes, and it seemed as if nothing in the world existed or mattered anymore. Slowly, they edged closer to one another to kiss for the first time.

As they pulled apart, a mysterious and overwhelming calm embraced her young soul, for at that very moment, she had found unequivocal love. The kind of love that some people searched their whole lives for but were never able to find. Silver knew that she would forever be a part of Chance's life, as he would forever be part of hers, for their two worlds had aligned at precisely the right second... the right minute... the right hour. From that moment on...they truly will... and forever will be... one!

Chapter 11

A minute to pray, a second to die

Birdie tried his very best to keep Silver's spirit's up. He even walked with her to school on occasion. Today, Birdie was dressed as a man so he would spare Silver any embarrassment in front of her friends. Birdie knew just how cruel other kids could be. They spotted the ever-familiar Mitts, the dope fiend, nodding as he begged people passing by for change. The most amazing thing about heroin addicts was that no matter how low they descend toward the ground while nodding out, they never fell or faltered. When Birdie and Silver approached, he straightened and grimly stared at them. As Birdie and Silver passed, she turned around and noticed that he was still watching.

"Auntie, why didn't you give him some money like mother does?" Silver asked.

"Because that nigga ain't shit!," Birdie snapped. "The more you give those types some money, the more you help them kill themselves and that nigger back there done killed himself long time ago."

"So, is that how my mother is going to end up?"

Birdie stopped in his tracks. "Baby, your momma is far from what he is," he tried to assure her. "That won't ever happen to your mother because she is too strong." He nodded, as if trying to convince himself. "You know as well as I that your mother been through this before and she always pulled herself together. Just you wait and see."

Silver was not convinced. "But why doesn't she come home anymore? I miss her, Birdie."

"I know you miss her baby," Birdie said. "I miss her too, but all we can do is wait for her to be willing to stop on her own. As bad as it may sound, that's the only way for her to see."

Silver looked up at Birdie. "What do you mean by only way to see?"

Pondering the question, Birdie bit down on his lip. "Well…it's sort of like when a mother eagle teaches their baby eagles how to fly to survive. See, when they are born the mother eagle fly out all day getting them food. As they get older the mother eagle know that they will die from starvation if they don't learn how to fly and learn to feed themselves. The problem is they got so comfortable having their mother hunt for them they don't want to leave their nest. So the mother eagle takes them out one by one, high in the air, and drop them."

Silver gasped in shock. "That's cold."

Birdie nodded in agreement. "Yes it is, but guess what happened after she dropped them?"

"They learn to fly?"

"Exactly," Birdie said.

Silver frowned in confusion. "So you saying we should drop Mommy off a cliff?"

Birdie laughed softly. "No, it means just like the baby eagles, they are the only one's to decide to either fly or fall." He paused and looked Silver in the eyes. "Your mama has to make that same decision; no one can spread her wings but her."

"What if she doesn't spread her wings and falls?" Silver asked sadly. "What is going to happen to me?"

Ever since Silver was a little girl, she had developed a deep phobia of abandonment. She became stigmatized as a result of her mother's erratic drug use and near death experiences. Most children of alcoholics or drug abusers will eventually develop issues due to their dysfunctional upbringing in some shape form or fashion – all of them – and Silver was no different. She had many nightmares that something bad would happen to her mother and she would never come home.

Birdie bent down and looked her in the eyes. "Silver, look at me... no matter what happens; I will always be there for you. I will never ever... let anything happen to you...I promise!"

With that he wiped the remaining tears from her eyes and hugged her tightly before they continued on their way to school. As they neared the school, they unexpectedly ran into Silver's grandmother Missus Jones. Both parties slowed as they neared each other. Birdie gripped Silver's hand tighter and took a deep breath as they proceeded. Birdie had met her once before with Jesse and he immediately got bad vibes from this woman.

Birdie particularly didn't like it when she called him a freak behind his back. Normally, Birdie would have quickly told someone off for such offense, but since she was Jesse's mother, he acted as if he didn't hear it, but like Birdie always said, a person only got away with that shit one time, no matter who they were. As they stopped, Silver spoke first.

"Hi, Grandma."

"Hello, child." After a moment, the older woman spoke again. "So child, I haven't been seeing your mother around these days, is she missing in action... again?" She then turned toward Birdie and covered her mouth with one hand. "So... is she still on those D-R-U-G-S?"

Birdie scowled at her, but spoke to Silver. "Silver, baby, why don't you go ahead on to school now. Auntie Birdie would like to speak to your Grandma alone."

Silver looked up at Birdie, knowing exactly what was going to happen next. "Okay Auntie," she said. She said her goodbye to her grandmother.

"Goodbye child," the elder woman replied.

They watched Silver walk off to school until the older woman spoke again, her tone heavy with sarcasm.

"Auntie would like to speak to her grandmother huh... where is she?"

Birdie took off the gloves. Hands on his hips, he moved his head from side to side, trying his best to control his temper. "I don't know who you think you are, but don't you ever talk that way in front Silver about her mother again. You think she can't spell? And it is none of your damn business where she is and what she does anyway."

"Why, I have every right to acquire the whereabouts of my daughter," she smirked.

"Your daughter?" Birdie's voice rose in disbelief. "Since when have you been concerned about your daughter? You ain't never did anything for Jesse or Silver and you have the audacity to want to know her whereabouts? You don't have that right; you gave that up long time ago."

"How would you know what I ever did for Jessica?" she snapped. "Her father and I gave Jessica everything she ever wanted... and what did she do the minute she got a chance? She spread her legs to anybody who came along, got pregnant and embarrassed her father and me."

Birdie stepped closer. "For your information, Jesse was a virgin and that was her first time…it was a mistake, but you wouldn't know nothing about that because you put her out the first chance you got!"

Dismissing Birdie's account totally, she shook her head. "It doesn't matter, I gave her a choice, and she could have stayed."

"Choice," Birdie said, astonished. "What choice? Have an abortion or get out?" He let his words sink in. "If it weren't for Jesse being strong enough to make her own decisions, that precious little girl would not be here today." In a sincere effort to reason with her, Birdie continued. "Do you see how beautiful your granddaughter is? Do you know how intelligent she is? She's in the top of her class in every subject and is planning to become a doctor when she gets older." The old woman looked away from Birdie and he thought he had struck a cord. Sadly, he continued. "Jesse made a mistake…a bad mistake, but she was only fifteen years old."

After a long pause, the older woman spoke again, her tone laced with contempt. "Well, she's certainly paying for it now."

Birdie stared at her in dismay. "What type of person are you? It's almost like you get off by seeing Jesse suffer! If you can't find compassion in your heart for Jesse, you could at least have some sympathy for your own granddaughter. Does she have to suffer for the rest of her life too? You should be ashamed of yourself! And you call yourself a Christian…huh… I've seen dogs get treated better than the way you treat Jesse!"

"Suffer?" she cried in exasperation. "I'm not the one who has that poor little child around … you…you… freaks and living in that inhumane and deplorable building." She rolled her eyes. "And you would know how it feels to be a filthy dog."

Vexed and at his wits end, Birdie grew tired of being nice and decided to let her have it. He pointed his finger in her face. "Let's get one thing straight you old bitch, I ain't Jesse and I'm damn sure not a child. So I suggest you watch what comes out of your mouth, 'cause I'm the right one to be fucking with. You talk slick to me one more time and I gonna forget I'm a lady and proceed to putting these size 14's up your ass!" The woman's mouth dropped open in shock, but Birdie wasn't finished. "You are nothing but an old miserable woman who is incapable of loving anyone else because you really hate yourself. I'd rather be a filthy dog and happy than being a snooty miserable bitch any day." Birdie then turned and walked away, but felt compelled to add one more thing. "And your granddaughter... her name ain't Child...it Silver! That's S-I-L-V-E-R and my name ain't freak, its *Miz* Freak to you... and you can K-I-S-S my entire black A-S-S!" With that, Birdie proudly swaggered away.

* * *

Since it was the end of the month, the shooting gallery was especially busy with an abundance of customers spending their welfare or disability checks. A drug dealer's favorite numbers are 1st and 15th. They would keep more than an ample supply of product on hand to be sure they didn't run out. Dealers knew that once a crackhead beamed up, it was over and they would spend every dime before the night was through. It was always just a matter of who they spent it with, and they would find every way to keep them inside the house and not let them out of the spot until all their paper was gone. Dealers lied to the fiends, claiming five-o was staking out the spot and grabbing niggas' as they came out, so it was best if they relaxed until the coast was clear. Believe me, fiends, already paranoid and geeking, weren't in any condition to chance it. So the fiends sat and smoked for hours, sometime days until they were on their knees searching for little pieces of anything that looked white and once that happened, guess what...you got to go. That's the Harlem way!

Jesse no longer craved the more expensive heroin. She now preferred the instant rush of the pipe. The house tolerated Jesse because she could suck the shit out of a dick – straight deep throat – without complaint. Though Jesse couldn't sell pussy any longer because of the way she looked, it didn't stop niggers from getting quality head. One thing about men is they joke and say they wouldn't let one of them crackhead bitches suck their dicks, but let another nigga say that one of them could suck a dick like Michael Jordan played ball, and trust me – that nigga is gonna want a shot! Jesse became the official in- house hoe, only this time she didn't get paid cash, it was strictly for a blast.

At the moment, Jesse was making good on a promise to one of the dealers to deep throat him and to swallow all his cum. Jesse was on her knees in one of the backrooms serving homeboy something lovely. Caught up in the moment, he had both hands on her head while thrusting her head in and out with rapid successions. "Yeah bitch… right fuckin' there…oh shit… oh shit…don't stop that shit, bitch…don't stop…! He was in blissful pleasure when suddenly a loud crash from out front stopped them both cold. He quickly tucked his limp dick back in his pants and pulled out his silver forty-five automatic.

Eyes wide, Jesse cried out nervously. "Oh shit, it must be the police! I can't go to jail." Homeboy eased toward the door and slowly turned the knob, but a volley of gunshots followed by loud screeches and cries stopped him short. Jesse watched in alarm as he paced the room, obviously looking for a way out. He glanced at the windows, but curse when he saw they were bolted with Master locks. All the rooms were heavily bolted to keep out thieves and desperate dope fiends looking to break in and find their stashes, regularly hidden in walls and floorboards. She heard more gunshots and screamed.

"Shut the fuck up," Homeboy hissed, glaring at her. Easing toward the door again, he placed his ear against it.

A cop's voice, crackling of radios, something… anything to signal him to what he's dealing with. The unknown, he thought, was just as worst as the situation. Jesse suddenly heard footsteps and watched as Homeboy braced himself against the wall. As the footsteps grew louder, he gripped the weapon tighter and closed his eyes. He decided at that moment that if he was to go out he wasn't going out like a chump, and he damn sure wasn't going back upstate. Hell no, he reasoned, he couldn't take another bid, so he was down for whatever-whatever! He looked toward the ceiling, mumbled a quick prayer and cocked the trigger. Fear rushed through Jesse as she read his eyes when he looked at her one final time. She knew what would happen next. Frantic, she searched the room for cover until her eyes fell upon a pee-stained mattress. She ran toward it and quickly slid under it.

Under the shelter of the mattress, Jesse had a limited view of the door at floor level before Homeboy suddenly jerked open the door and started blasting. The noise was deafening as rapid flashes of gunfire lit up the hallway. Then, just like that, it was all over. Jesse heard a loud thud, and when she opened her eyes, she saw Homeboy laid out like a rug. She closed her eyes and prayed that this was some kind of demented dream, but what happened next confirmed her greatest fear— a green pair of puma's appeared. It was then that she realized how much trouble she was in. Jesse never saw a cop wear those kinds of sneakers. Police wore those track running shoes – all of them! No…these weren't cops… they were killers! 'Lord … please save me,' she silently prayed. 'Please help me!' But all hope diminished when she heard a man give an order to kill everyone. It seemed like the gunshots lasted an eternity. She silently cried, sure that she would also meet her maker. When the gunfire stopped, the eerie silence gave way to the pungent smell of blood, death and gunpowder. Terror overcame her when she heard the familiar '*Voice of Death*' order the back rooms to be searched for 'the rest of the shit.' She thought of just getting up and begging for mercy, but she was physically incapable … she couldn't move. Holding her breath her heart dropped when she saw someone enter the room and step toward the closet. She heard the rickety closet door open and close. She watched the sneakers turned and pause and inch slowly toward her hide out and bit down on her lip until it bled. She felt something poke the mattress.

In one swift toss, the mattress was lifted off her, and just like that, her cover was blown. Blinded by the sudden exposure to light Jesse scurried like a cornered rat. Gasping for breath, she looked up and saw a masked man take aim at her head with a sawed-off shotgun. She knew it was over then and there, and didn't try to plead, but instead accepted her fate. Ready to die, she closed her eyes and awaited eternal darkness. Seconds passed, but nothing happened. She wondered whether she was already dead and just didn't know it, so she slowly opened her eyes and saw the masked killer staring at her the way a curious K-9 police dog would. The killer lowered his weapon and continued to stare at her until the voice of death yelled.

"Yo nigga, you find anything?"

The gunman quickly picked up the mattress and threw it back over Jesse. Once again, she was covered by the darkness of the mattress, and confused, did not know what was going on, but she thanked God anyway.

"Oh shit nigger, it's fuckin' payday!"

An unseen man entered the room and showed his partner stacks and stacks of cash and large bags filled with hundreds of colorful caps of bottled crack. "Look my nigger… we fuckin' rich! Let's be out this bitch!" The man with the cash and drugs turned and ran out of the room.

Suddenly, the masked man turned his attention back to the mattress and spoke softly. "Get your shit together, this shit ain't for you."

"Yo Dupree, let's bounce out this bitch!" a man yelled.

Jesse realized that the masked killer was none other than Dupree, the kid that she saved from being murdered by Chubbs in the alley. Slowly, Dupree turned to walk out of the room. He stopped and turned.

"Now we're even."

Chapter 12

Payback

Silver was doing her thing as she skipped and twirled through the rope when she suddenly stopped. "Look," she said. The girls turned to where she pointed and saw Problem and the rest of his crew pushing Diego to the back of the schoolyard. Missy shook her head. "Yo, Silver, I know what your thinking, but why the fuck you want to help Diego after he punked out on you in class?"

Silver knew she was right and remained silent.

Missy continued. "I'm saying, yo… I don't mine throwing some joints and all but yo, you can't keep fighting his battles for him. Diego got to learn to start standing up for himself."

"I hear you," Silver answered. "But he was just afraid Problem would get him later. Besides, this ain't helping Diego. I want some payback for him getting me on detention." Silver pondered the situation and smiled. "Yo, I just thought of something …just follow my lead." She stepped from between the ropes as Missy and the rest of the girls followed closely behind. Seeing Silver and her crew coming, Tyrell tapped Problem on the shoulder and gave him the heads up. Looking around at the girls, Problem tried to act tough.

"Fuck do y'all want?"

Silver only smiled and remained silent. Her mother had always told Silver that if a person was doing wrong or done wrong, remain silent and let them tell on themselves. Problem attempted to carry on to his business of robbing Diego, but was uneasy now with all the eyes on him. He continued to look over his shoulders until he yelled in frustration.

"Fuck is y'all all over my dick for sweatin' me and shit?"

The other girls caught on, and simply folded their arms like Silver and began to smile also. It was a silent standoff until Problem's cohorts began to walk away not wanting any part of it. Seeing his boys desert him, Problem quickly attempted to run away, but Silver and the girls blocked him. "You ain't so bad without your friends around are you?" Silver said. Looking around at their faces, Problem remained silent.

"What's the matter?" Missy asked. "Cat got your fat tongue? Why you ain't saying something now...are you afraid?" Problem sneered. "I ain't afraid of nothing."

That was exactly what Silver thought he would say. "Well, if you're not afraid, you'd give Diego a fair one?" Diego's jaw dropped. Problem looked at Silver as if she was insane.

"Diego said that if you ain't had your punk ass friends with you all the time, he would kick your ass a long time ago."

By now, other students started to crowd around, smelling a fight.

Problem looked at a terrified Diego. "A'ight punk... lets do this." Problem got even bolder when he saw Tyrell had come with some backup. Confident, he began to boast. "And when I finish waxing this punk," he said loud enough for everybody to hear, "I'm gonna end that other shit you talkin' and bust your skinny ass for always being in my bidness. "

Silver smiled. "Yeah right nigger, you better just worry about getting past Diego."

"We'll see!" Problem said, pounding his fist.

Silver and Missy surrounded Diego as he nervously began to plead.

"Silver, I...I don't know about this, I don't know how to fight."

Missy jumped in and did her best Ali impression. "It ain't nothing to it Diego, just bob and weave, nigger!"

"What?" Diego asked.

"Stick and fuckin' move!" Missy said.

What?" Diego asked, still blank.

"Just kick his ass!" Missy yelled in frustration.

Shaking his head Diego started making excuses not to fight. "But I never had a fight! I don't know how! I'm afraid!"

Terror filled his eyes as he lowered his head in shame. Silver lifted his head up and looked him square in the eyes. "Listen Diego, you ain't got no time to be scared! Turning away from her, the scared boy watched Problem loosen up for the fight. Silver turned his face back to her. "Look at me Diego...you got to stand up to Problem or he's gonna rob you every day. Is that what you want?" He shook his head and she pointed to Problem. "Now look at him, Diego... that's the nigger who robbed your mama!"

"What?" Diego asked, confused.

Silver winked at Missy. "Yeah, you remember that time you told us that somebody snatched your mother's purse?"

"Yeah," Diego said.

"Well… it was Problem, but I ain't want to tell you, since I ain't no snitch or nothing, but I'm telling now." She pointed directly at him. "That fat fucker right there was the one that stole from your mama…" She paused to let it sink in. "Look at him, Diego… he laughing at you."

"Laughing at you and yo mama!" Missy added.

"Picture it in your mind, Diego" Silver said. "Your mama minding her business when he …that nigga right there… runs by and snatch your sweet old mama's purse!"

"And knocked her down, scraped her knees and everything!" Missy again added.

"Can you see it?" Silver continued. "She is crying and asking for help, *'Help Me Poppy! Poppy Help Me!'* How do you say help in Spanish?" Diego began getting angrier and angrier as his nose began to flare.

"You gonna let that thief get away with that shit, big boy?" Missy said.

"Hell no!" Diego said angrily in Spanish.

Missy carressed his face and spoke seductivly in his ear. "As a matter of fact… you kick his ass and I'll let you get some of this ass."

Not believing his ears, Diego looked at Missy to see if she was serious. Looking in her eyes, he turned and looked at Problem, then back to Missy. Out of nowhwere, Diego let out a hostile yell and charged Problem. Problem tried to intimidate him with 'The Rikers Island C- 76' shit called the 52, by swinging his hands and slapping them while bobbing and weaving. Silver and Missy instructed Diego how to fight like real trainers would in professional bouts.

"That's right Diego, left hook, Diego!" Whap! Amazingly, Diego caught him with a left. "Now with a right hook, Diego…" Whap!

"That's right, Diego, fuck him up… Yeah, yeah… you got him down, Diego…Now stomp him!… Stomp his fat ass!"

Problem was on the ground curled up in a fetal position, protecting his head, as Diego stomped him, letting out years of frusration. Problem tried to get up and run away but falls and scrambled to his feet several times before finally gaining balance to get away. The entire school laughed at the school bully break his neck as he struggled to get away, and moments later, everybody surrounded Diego, cheering him on as they patted him on his back, congratulating him. Missy stepped through the crowd and gave him a seductive kiss on the mouth. Astonished, Diego looked at her and then passed out.

* * *

A knock on Birdie's door startled him. "I done told y'all niggas to stay away from my door!" He looked through the peephole. ""Who the hell is it?"

"It's me, Birdie ... Jesse!"

Recognizing the voice, he looked through the peephole again. "Jesse?" he said, and quickly unlatched the door, but when the door opened, his hands flew to his heart. "Dear Lord!" Shock and disbelief shot through his body as he stood before Jesse. Even though it had been only five months since he last saw her, he could not fathom the trauma and destruction that she had done to herself. Jesse was a mere shell of her former self, barely recognizable. What stood before him now was a filthy, wretched eighty-five pound woman in tattered, stained rags. Though Jesse was only twenty-seven, she now looked closer to sixty-seven. The damage she had done to herself was so extensive, Birdie could only cry, not believing his eyes as he stared into her sad, tear-filled ones. Arms outstretched, Jesse was in desperate need of a hug.

"I want to come home," she pleaded. "I want to come home."

Birdie felt overwhelmed. "Oh, Jesse…of course you can come home!" He pulled her into his arms and tightly hugged her. "Don't cry, baby… it's okay. You're home now, you're home now." Cradling Birdie for dear life, Jesse cried like a lost child.

"I'm ready to kick this shit, I can't take it no more!"

"Alright, alright Jesse, I'm with you," Birdie said, taking her inside. "Do you want me to take you to the hospital?"

"No…please, Birdie, I …I can kick it if you help me, like…like we did last time, you can tie me down real good, you remember?"

Birdie did remember, and it was like hell fighting the drug cold turkey. "Okay, Jesse, I'm here for you."

"I want to get cleaned up before Silver gets home. I don't want her to see me like this." Jesse babbled incoherently about her hair and her clothes, while all the while, Birdie gently patronized her. Suddenly, the front door swung open and Silver ran inside.

"Auntie Birdie…Auntie Birdie, you should have seen the fight at school today, this bully named Problem—" She stopped short when she realized Birdie had a rare guest in the house. The three of them stared at each other for several moments before Jesse smiled, revealing her yellowish teeth.

"Silver, baby…it's me … Mommy!"

Silver looked at her, then to Birdie, then back at Jesse and ran to her room and slammed the door.

Birdie showered and cleaned Jesse up the best that he could, but she still looked like hell. Her clothes were now four sizes too big and fell off of her. Jesse was so upset that Silver was hurt at the sight of her that she asked Birdie if she should talk to her, but Birdie said that he would talk to her first.

Birdie softly knocked on Silver's door and walked in. Silver sat on her bed doing her homework as if nothing had happened. "Silver… are you okay?" he asked cautiously. Silver continued silently working on her homework. Moving closer, Birdie bent down and smiled. "Didn't I tell you your mother would come home?" Still silent, Silver continued to write in her notebook. Birdie put his hand on Silver's, stopping her from writing. "Silver, aren't you happy that you mother is finally back home?"

"That's not my mother," Silver snapped. "Now get out of my room!"

Birdie nodded in understanding and quietly left.

Later that night, Jesse began to experience the tremendous pain of heroin and crack withdrawal. Birdie had to tie her legs and arms to the bedpost. Jesse became drenched in sweat as she became delusional and began to hallucinate.

"Birdie, please…I…I'm only gonna get just one hit…just one hit and I come right back, I swear. Please, Birdie…let me go you bitch! Please let me go."

Crying, Birdie felt her pain, but this was the only way. He wept, not only for Jesse, but also for Silver, who could surely hear the shrieks of madness coming from her mother's bedroom.

"Do you hear her? She is coming to get my baby!"

"Who?" Birdie asked.

"Shh! You don't hear that?"

Jesse was spooked. Her eyes bulged out as she listened earnestly for the sound.

" I don't hear anything," Birdie said. "What is it?"

"She coming to get her...my mother... don't let her in, don't let her in...she's coming to get my baby... Birdie, don't let her get my baby!"

"I won't," Birdie assured her. "It's okay."

"Birdie, promise me!" Jesse snapped. "Promise me that if something should ever happen to me you won't let her get my baby, don't let that women do to her what she did to me... promise me!"

"I promise, Jesse, I promise," Birdie soothed her, trying to calm her down.

Hours, then days passed, and Jesse survived the critical moments. The drugs oozed out of her pores and through her nose and mouth. At one point, Silver walked timidly into her mother's room to have a look at 'this woman who claimed to be her mother.' Still looking like death, Jesse nevertheless managed a slight smile even though she felt as if she was dying. This was the best opportunity, she thought, to educate her daughter on the dangers and effects of drugs. It was better for her to suffer through seeing her this way than to suffer from the same thing herself some day. "Silver," Jesse grunted as she fought through the pain. "I want you to listen...they got this new shit out...it's called 'crack'." She shook her head and explained. "Smoking that shit...that glass fuckin' dick... is like sucking the Devil's dick himself... that shit makes heroin seems like an Excedrin!" Her bloodshot eyes stared at Silver as if her whole life depended on her words and she began to cry. "That stuff messed me up bad, baby, it will take your soul from you...bring you to your knees." Tears began to fall from Silver's eyes. Jesse fought sleep and glanced around the room, looking for her daughter. "Silver! Silver!" she cried.

"She's right here, Jesse," Birdie said.

Jesse continued. "I saw a whole lot of people die just for being in the wrong place at the wrong time...I'm supposed to be dead right now, but I guess God got different plans for me." Turning her head to see if Silver was paying attention, she lashed out. "Silver, don't let no motherfuckers ever tell you no different, don't let none of them fool you about these drugs! Don't you smoke a joint, don't you pop no pill and don't let them fool you in thinking alcohol is okay 'cause it's not! That shit is all the same." She grew desperate. "Do you hear me, Silver?"

"Yes, Mommy... I won't," Silver cried.

"Birdie!" Jessie called out.

"I'm here, Jesse, I'm here."

"Take these fuckin' sheets off of me!"

Fretting the thought, Birdie looked over at an already shaken Silver and shook his head. "I...I don't think that's a good idea Jesse."

"Bitch! I don't give a damn what you think," Jesse said, incensed. "She's going to see everything! Now take these damn sheets off of me!"

Full of apprehension, Birdie looked from Silver to Jesse and reluctantly complied with her orders and slowly pulled the sheets off of her. Silver's eyes widened as she observed the protruding bones and sallow skin that was now her mother's rail-thin body. Her body was covered with hideous black and blue sores that blotched her entire body – she looked like death. Silver shuddered.

"Look at me, Silver," Jessie implored. "Look at it...and don't you ever forget this shit as long as you live. Do you hear me?"

"Yes, Mommy!"

She gasped for breath. "Always remember, it's not going to be some big bad man who gonna offer you to do drugs for the first time... it's either going to be so-called friends or your own fucking family, believe that shit... You hear me, Silver? A family member or friends!" Teary eyed, she continued. "Silver, promise me, baby ... promise me that you will have nothing to do with drugs...nothing! Don't use it because you will end up like this." Jesse rolled her eyes across her body. "Don't ever have nothing to do with drugs because this what that poison does to a human being. Do you understand?"

Wiping her eyes, Silver answered. "Yes Mommy...I understand."

"Come here," Jesse said softly.

Silver walked slowly over to her mother and gave her a hug.

Chapter 13

The Birthday Surprise

Over the next few months, Jesse remained true to her word and recovered magnificently. She gained most of her weight back as Birdie and Silver waited on her hand and foot. Slowly and surely, her appearance was coming back as well, and she used lightening cream to get rid of the darkened sores. And a month after that, Jesse felt well enough to go back to work in Times Square. Silver cried when Jesse went out alone that first night. Jesse assured her not to worry and that she was through with drugs forever. Jesse even told her that she had a surprise for her very soon.

It was Silver's birthday, September 18, and Jesse had promised that this would be a birthday that she wouldn't forget. She promised to be home early to celebrate. When she told Silver she could have any gift that she wanted, she simply asked for a Black Barbie doll and a new jump rope.

Jesse punched her time card, finished with her shift at Macys on 34th Street. This was the big surprise that she wanted to tell Silver and Birdie. Jesse had searched all week for a job and Macys had interviewed her for a sales position. They hired her on the spot after her friend, Lynn, who she went to school with, put a word in for her. Jesse smiled from ear to ear as she envisioned giving Silver her Barbie doll and jump rope that she just purchased, and giving them the news that she was through with prostitution and had found a regular job at none other than Macy's Department Store. She decided to walk over to the motel that she formerly rented on 47th Street and 11th Avenue, to get her three hundred-dollar deposit, since she had retired from hooking.

While walking to the motel, a car pulled up beside her, driven by a goofy looking white boy wearing glasses. The wiry white man bumbled over his words and smiled. "Excuse me ma'am, but I would like to know... I mean I was wondering... if... you know... well, if you might be interested?"

Jesse knew exactly what he wanted and decided to help him out a little. "You would like to know if I was interested in a date."

Relieved, the shy looking man looked down and confessed. "Yes ma'am!"

"I'm sorry honey, but I'm retired." Disappointed, the man seemed let down but apologized for asking.

"I'm sorry for intruding, I didn't mean you no harm, I never did this before."

Jesse told him he had nothing to be sorry about and he bashfully offered her a ride. Jesse looked around to see if any buses were coming and saw none. She looked back at the goofy looking man and agreed to let him drop her off at the motel, which was still a good distance away, and jumped in. He told her his name was Stanley, and they shook hands. He explained that he got tired of doing it to the nudie magazines in the bathroom all the time, and after two weeks of thinking about it, had finally got the nerve to do it.

Jesse smiled. "Stanley, are you a virgin?" Embarrassed, he let out a goofy laugh and looked down. "Stanley," she said. "If you don't keep your eyes on the road, you will never get a chance to get any."

He straightened out the wheel. "How did you know I was a virgin?"

Jesse smiled. "Just a lucky guess." She looked at the bashful, blushing man and started to think. Since she was already going to the motel, there wasn't no sense in turning down a perfectly good trick. She looked at her watch. "Stanley, I tell you what. If I was to do this, it would have to be quick and worth my while."

"How does a hundred dollars sound? He quickly said. "Talk about quick... shoot, no sooner do I touch myself, I splatter holy hell all over the place."

Jesse smiled. "I believe you, Stanley." Pointing, she continued. "Okay, take this turn on Forty-seventh Street and go over to Eleventh Avenue." Stanley smiled like a kid who was just promised a brand new bicycle while Jesse thought to herself, *'One more time for the road never killed anybody.'*

Inside the motel room, Jesse undressed down to her bra and panties while Stanley stepped into the bathroom. "Come on baby, I done told you I ain't got much time," Jesse called. The bathroom opened, and Stanley nervously walked toward her with a white towel wrapped around his rail thin body. Jesse looked at him. "Everything gonna be alright, mama is gonna take care of you." Positioning herself at the side of the bed, she rubbed his hand to calm him down. Slowly, she unwrapped the towel from his waist and told him to relax. She began to give him a blowjob. He seemed more relaxed and began to find a rhythm. He began to move, and at the same time, to mumble. After a few moments, the mumbling grew louder and she heard what sounded like biblical chants as he started thrusting faster. She glanced up. His facial structure had changed, hardened into a scowl as spit started to form at the sides of his mouth. She grew alarmed, but figured this was just his way. She felt his entire body tense, and glanced up toward his face once more. His eyes blazed open, revealing bloodshot eyes as he spoke down to her while removing a large, jagged knife that was taped to his lower back.

"So God said, 'He will set forth his disciples to rid the earth from all sins and abominations'. Redemption will be mines for the sake of purity, for I am the purveyor of his goodness, his answer to his resurrection."

Jesse never saw it coming. She felt a harsh blow, and the last thing she saw was the uplifted knife, its shiny surface dulled with her blood as it spattered over his face and body.

A circle of candles flickered in the darkened room. He carried Jesse's body from the bathroom where he had thoroughly bathed and cleaned her. After dressing her in an all white wedding gown, he slowly placed Jesse on the bed and laid her down ever so gently. Her body had been drained of blood and her skin appeared ghastly white. Stanley stared at her and smiled proudly. "You look beautiful, mother. Wasn't it a lot of people at the wedding? Gosh, I didn't expect such an outcome. Did you see everyone's faces when we gave our vows? Oh it was just beautiful. I bet Dad was really surprised. " He snickered, and then looked down at her pale body. " Mother, you are now granted full clemency, cleansed of all your sins and granted full redemption, and thus now worthy as my concubine and worthy for my entry." He unrobed and proceeded to mount her dead corpse to consummate the incestuous marriage.

Chapter 14

Bad Luck Does Come in Threes

Nearly a week passed since Silver or Birdie had heard anything from Jesse. Their mood was somber and silent because they both knew it would be only a matter of time before Jesse came home, beaten down from the streets again. After all the broken promises, they weren't sure exactly how they could trust her any more. They still loved Jesse, but all the worrying she put them through was very hard on the both of them and this particularly had an effect on Silver, who became more and more withdrawn in her classes. Guilt and shame became constant companions in her life. If it wasn't for the trust and confidence she had in Chance, she wasn't sure how she would have handled such burdens. Though she was tight with Missy, she knew that she could not offer any advice to her. She and Chance became inseparable; he comforted his girl with all the compassion it took to get her through the bad times. Silver must have cried on his shoulder a thousand times, but he was there for her whenever she needed him, no matter what. He even snuck out of his foster parent's home and once spent the entire night with Silver at her house, hugging her tightly as they slept. He promised Silver that no matter what happened, he would be there for her when she needed him the most. When Silver was with Chance it was the only times she really felt safe. It was as if they truly became a part of each other, feeling each other's pain, as if they were intertwined.

Silver waited for Chance after school so they could walk home together. Since she got out of school twenty minutes before he did, she simply waited in front of the school for him. As she waited, Problem, Tyrell and an older boy ditty bopped toward her. As they surrounded her, Problem spoke to the older boy.

"Yeah, that's that bitch... she's one of them that jumped me."

The older brother, who was about sixteen, fresh out of Spofford, a juvenile lock up in the Bronx.

"Yo, I heard you and your crew held my little brother down while some nigger punched him in the face?"

Silver defiantly looked at Problem. "I don't know what he's talking about. I didn't need to hold him down, he got his ass kicked fair and square."

Problem quickly defended himself. "She's lying... she's lying... I was winning the fight when she and her friends grabbed both my arms and that's when the dude started punching me in my face... right, Tyrell?"

Tyrell nodded. "Yep, that's exactly what happened."

"Yo, you got to pay for fucking with my brother," the older boy said. He shrugged his shoulders. "But since you're a girl, I'm gonna give you a chance to make it up to him. I want you to say sorry and bend down and kiss his Jordan's".

Problem and Tyrell laughed while Silver looked at them. "I ain't saying sorry and I'm damn sure ain't gonna kiss his funky sneakers!" She dropped her bookbag. "Me and him can throw down right here and right now before I do that shit!"

"Hold up," Problem's brother said. "You ain't got no fucking choice! Either do like the fuck I said or you gonna have to deal with me."

He edged closer. Silver looked over the boy's face and knew he was serious.

"Now what the fuck you gonna do?"

She did the only thing she knew to do. She put her hands on her hips and looked him square in the eyes. "Do what you have to do, nigger." The older boy seemed amused.

"Oh, this lil' bitch think I'm playing." He ordered the two boys to grab her arms.

Problem and Tyrell grabbed Silver's arms. She struggled to escape, but they were too strong. The older boy squared himself in front of her.

"Now, lil' cunt, I'm gonna give yo ass one more chance to apologize, only this time you haft to bend down and kiss my Jordan's too."

"I ain't kissing shit," Silver said angrily, and spat in his face.

Enraged, the older boy slapped Silver across the face, causing her lip to split open and bleed. Without warning, Silver administrated a hard, swift kick to the boy's groin, causing him to wrench over in pain. Angry, the boy struggled to his feet. "Bitch, you done fucked up now!

" He punched her in the face, causing her to drop instantly. Out of nowhere, Missy appeared and jumped on the bigger boy's back and began whuppin' him from behind as she tried to gouge out his eyes. The bigger boy screamed in pain. In the background, Diego and Beastly watched the fight with the other students, but they were both too afraid to help Silver or Missy.

"Bitch!" the older boy, yelled. He grabbed hold of Missy's hair and tossed her to the ground. Angry, Missy rose immediately and went on the attack again but he punched her, causing her to fly backwards.

This struck a nerve in Diego and he suddenly burst through the crowd and tackled the older boy to the ground, punching him and cursing ferociously. " Te voy al mata...Te voy al mata! ... "I'll kill you... "he swore as he pummeled the boy. Problem and Tyrell jumped in, grabbed Diego off of their friend and began stomping him out. Watching, Beastley gritted his teeth, let out an eerie yell and sprang in to attack as well.

"Bumbo cloth meki me kill tha pussycloth boy im na know who im a bumbocloth a fuck wid!" Little Beastley snapped, swinging wildly as he began whupping both Problem and Tyrell senseless. He served one and then served the other before they could get to their feet. Finally gaining their balance, they both ran as if their lives depended on it.

"A bwoy nu cum back round ya tis teach you not tu not tief me no more!" Beastly yelled, chasing both boys out of the schoolyard.

The older boy and Diego were on their feet now, Diego with his hands up in a fighting position, and though it was evident that Diego wasn't a boxer. The bigger boy looked at Diego as if he was a bad joke, and then punched the pudgy Diego with a hard left, then a brutal right that knocked him out cold. Tired, Problem's brother then stepped over to Silver, still on the ground. "One more time, bitch, you gonna kiss my sneakers or what?" On her knees, bruised and battered Silver grimaced. "Why don't you try kissing your mammy's ass first, motherfucker?"

Pissed off, he pulled back his arm and landed a crushing blow to her face. Silver went down instantly. "Hell no, bitch, you ain't getting off that easy... get your smart ass up! I ain't finished!" He hit her again.

Behind him, Missy grimaced as she reached into her pocket and pulled out her ever-ready box cutter. Staggering to her feet, she went on the attack. Without warning, Missy came up behind him, raised the razor high in the air and buck fiftied the older boy across the face, splitting his right cheek open like a parting red sea.

Enraged, he held the side of his face as blood gushed between his fingers. In fervor, he dumb-rushed Missy and quickly disarmed the much smaller girl and punched her so viciously in the face that her eye swelled the size of a small grapefruit before she hit the ground. Teeth gritted, he stared at the blood on his hand and then at Missy.

"You little fuckin' bitch!" He taunted "I'm gonna cut yo fucking ass to pieces!" He went on the attack, but before he could give Missy a taste of what she gave him, Silver jumped on his back in a futile attempt to stop him from deforming her best friend. A brutal elbow to Silver's throat knocked her off his back and she sprawled unconscious on the pavement. The bigger boy stood over both girls as if debating which one he would cut first – then stepped toward Silver.

He bent down. "Yeah bitch, this is gonna be a little something to remember a nigger by." He grabbed Silver by her collar and pulled back his shoulders to ox her a permanent Frankenstein smile across her pretty but battered face.

Like a streak of lighting, Chance appeared and hit the bigger boy across the side of his face with a brick, knocking him down instantly. Chance pounced upon the bigger boy with blind fury, relentlessly hitting him from all directions. Out of control, Chance dropped the bloodied brick and brutally beat the boy until his face turned into a bloody pulp. Seeing this boy, this nigga – strike his beloved Silver – his woman – his wife – his life – was just too much for him to bear. His mouth foamed with built up spit as tears and the boy's blood fell from Chance's face. Diego was the first to reach him, but to no avail. Chance beat the boy unconscious but wouldn't be satisfied until the bully was dead. Finally, five other boys joined in to help Diego pull Chance off him, but in a psychotic frenzy, it took four more boys to subdue Chance. Chance struggled violently to be released as the boys begged him to calm down. It took several minutes for Chance to return to normal and the fight left him when he spotted his Silver. "Silver?" He rubbed his eye. "Silver!"

The boys released him and he walked slowly over to his battered girl. Unable to believe his eyes, he cried when he saw her bloodied and swollen face. He bent down and lifted her head into his arms. "Everything is all right baby… don't worry, I got you now, I got you," he moaned. He softly kissed her wounds and helped her to her feet when Diego yelled. "Chance… watch out!"

Chance and Silver turned around to find the bloodied boy on his feet, reaching into his back pocket. He pulled out and flicked opened a switchblade. Chance and Silver stared at the boy in horror when Mister Bonds, Silver's homeroom teacher, pushed his way through the crowd.

"What the hell is going on here?" he yelled. He looked at the bloodied boy. "Young man, what in God's name happened here…what is your name?" He grabbed him by his shoulders. "Who did this to you?" he asked, looking around.

A sense of relief came over Silver when she saw Mister Bonds, but it was short lived as she watched the older boy raise his blade and slice Mister Bond's throat.

The students watched in horror as blood spurted from the teacher's neck like a water pump. Mister Bond's face turned colorless as he stumbled uneasily and held his severed neck before collapsing. The student's fled in all directions as the knife-wielding killer approached his next victim, but Chance pushed Silver out of harms way.

"Get out of here, Silver, run!"

The older boy circled Chance and smiled mockingly as he tossed the knife from one hand to another. Without warning, the older boy swiped at his hand, slicing it. He winced in pain and quickly backed away, feverishly searching for an equalizer, but there wasn't a bottle or stick to be found anywhere. In one swift and brazen move, the older boy charged in for the kill and lunged directly at Chance's heart. With lightning quick maneuvers, Chance sidestepped, shoved him off balance and ran toward a group of trashcans and out of the schoolyard in a desperate search for a weapon. He tossed the trashcans behind him but the older boy simply swatted them aside and gave chase.

After running two blocks, older boy on his heals, Chance turned into a dead-end alleyway. Trapped with nowhere to run, his mind raced a hundred miles an hour. The older boy stood at the entrance of the alley, smiled and walked slowly to savor the moment.

"You done fucked up!" the older boy said as he showed Chance his knife. "In a minute you gonna feel this cold blade in yo motherfuckin' stomach and as I twist this motherfucka around, I'm gonna be watchin' yo motherfuckin' eyes as you die slow, motherfucka!"

Chance grabbed the nearest thing to him – a garbage can top, and began to back away, swinging the lid to ward him off. The boy kicked the lid away and Chance fell, stunned. The older boy stood over Chance, gritting his teeth.

"You's a dead motherfucka!"

Moments later, a police car pulled up in front of the alley in time to see the bloodied, older boy walk out with the knife still in hand. Silver, Missy and Diego jumped out the squad car in a panic.

"Oh my God, where's Chance?" Silver cried.

The police immediately pulled out their guns. "Freeze! Drop the weapon!" one of them yelled.

The older boy turned to see two officers pointing their weapons at him while four more squad cars screeched to a halt. With a tired, zombie-like look, he continued walking as if they weren't even there. The group of police officers jumped out of their squad cars and yelled once again.

"Drop the weapon! Now!"

Suddenly, the older boy paused, dropped the knife and fell to his knees. They ordered him to lay on his stomach and spread his arms. He complied. As the officers cautiously approached him, they noticed a stream of blood flowing from under his still body, forming a dark puddle on the pavement.

Suddenly, one of the officers turned. "Freeze!" he yelled.

Everyone turned to watch Chance slowly walk out of the alley holding a huge, bloodied knife. "Oh my God!" Silver gasped.

All weapons were now pointed at Chance as he dropped the knife and followed their orders, dropping to his knees with his hands behind his head.

Moments later, the police pulled a white sheet over the victim and were handcuffing Chance. As they handcuffed him, Silver, being treated by paramedics, frantically ran toward the police.

"What are y'all doing? He didn't do anything, why y'all taking him away?"

The detective spoke nonchalantly. "Young lady, this is police business. Step to the curb."

Following the detectives, Silver nervously jumped in front of them. "Why y'all taking him away? He didn't do nothing but defend himself."

Missy and Diego tried to calm her down, but it was fruitless.

"I'm not going to ask you again, young lady, "the detective said. "Move to the curb! This is police business!"

In a raging fit, Silver lashed out. "Fuck you, you stupid motherfucker! He ain't do shit!"

The white detective turned to Missy and Diego "If you don't get that little black bitch out of here right now, I'm gonna take her smart ass downtown too!"

The comment made Silver even angrier. "You're mother's a bitch, you white bastard!"

Beet red, the detective pulled out his Billy club to hit Silver, when a black officer stepped in front of him and shook his head.

"Not while I'm around. I suggest you just calm down!"

Eyes aflame, the white detective looked around at all the eyes cast upon him, and knocked the black officer's hands off his suit and spat on the ground as he tossed Chance into the back seat of the car. He looked around at the mass crowd that had formed and gave Silver and the black officer an evil look before hopping in the passenger seat as the squad car drove off.

Silver cried as she saw Chance somberly watching her from the back of the squad car. "Chance!" she yelled. She broke free from Missy and Diego and began running alongside the squad car. Chance placed his face against the glass as she touched the window. "Chance, don't leave me baby...don't leave me, I need you." As the car picked up speed, Silver lost her balance and stumbled to the ground. "Channnnce!" Silver yelled, pounding the pavement and weeping uncontrollably in the middle of the street.

Battered, bloodied and bruised, Missy and Diego walked and comforted Silver all the way home. When they finally got to her building, they noticed two white detectives standing in front of Silver's building, talking with Birdie.

"Goddamn Silver," Missy said surprised, "that detective musta really been pissed at you. They already found out where you live."

Birdie moaned when he spotted Silver with her friends.

"Silver," Birdie yelled, his voice breaking. "I got to talk to you right now."

Her mouth swollen, Missy tapped Silver on the shoulder. "Yo, Silver, you know I got your back if you want me to testify."

Birdie grabbed Silver by the hand. He appeared not to have even noticed her battered face as he led her into the building with the two detectives closely behind them.

"Baby..." Birdie said sadly. "I got ...well ... I got some bad, bad news to tell you." Looking down, he slowly continued. "Your mama ...well your mama has gone bye-bye, and she won't ever be coming home again." Birdie broke down and hugged Silver tightly as he sobbed. "I'm sorry baby! I'm so, so sorry!"

Silver grew numb and her mind went blank – she was speechless as she stared into Birdie's wet face.

Two weeks had passed since the funeral. Silver remained sullen and silent. Losing her mother to a violent death and Chance, now placed in Spofford, a juvenile detention hall in the Bronx, was too much for her to handle. Birdie, who believed in superstition, knew that death and bad luck came in threes. He simply hoped for Silver's sake that he was wrong. Silver has seen more hell in her short life than most adults had in an entire lifetime. Birdie allowed Silver to stay home from school for the two weeks, understanding how she wanted and needed a break, but then felt it was time for her to start going back to school.

On her first day back to school since the occurrence, Birdie chose to walk with Silver. They happened upon Mitts, the dope fiend. As they approached, Mitts reached inside his tattered and stained coat, pulled out a single stemmed red rose and held it toward her. Silver looked at him for a brief moment and then slowly walked over and accepted it. She looked up at him and spoke softly. "Thank you." It was the first time she had spoken since learning of her mother's death.

When they reached the school, Birdie slowed when he saw Silver's grandmother standing in front of the school with two police officers. With them stood a woman wearing a tweed jacket and carrying a briefcase. As Birdie approached, he got the uneasy feeling that his premonition was right, tragedy did come in threes. The lady with the briefcase spoke first.

"Mister Alton?" the lady inquired.

"What is this about?" Birdie asked suspiciously.

"My name is Sandra Corde, I'm a social worker from the Bureau of Child Welfare, and I'm here to serve you notice negating your custody of one Silver Jones to the custody of Thelma Jones, her maternal grandmother."

Birdie shook his head while looking at the papers. "Oh no, there must be some sort of mistake. Jesse did not want her to have Silver, she told me…"

"Mister Alton, the State of New York makes the decision over who a child is awarded to after an untimely demise of her guardian," Miss Corde coldly informed them. "Since there are no records of

Silver's biological father, she automatically goes to the next of kin…which is her grandmother, Mrs. Jones."

Birdie pulled Silver behind him. "No, this ain't right, I can't allow you to take Silver away from me."

"Mister Alton," Miss Corde said sternly, "You have no say in this, this is a matter of the courts."

Pulling Silver closer to him, Birdie exploded. "Bitch, fuck you and fuck the courts, I'm not gonna let you take my baby from me!"

One of the police officer's got on his radio and called for back up.

"Mister Alton," the social worker said. "It is not necessary to display such rage in front of the child; she's already been through enough."

Growing agitated, Birdie snapped. "Bitch, if you try putting your hands on this child, I'm show you real rage!"

The police officer attempted to calm Birdie down, but made the fatal mistake of getting too close. "Take it easy buddy, or we'll have to—"

Birdie hauled off and punched him in the face with a crushing blow. The other officer immediately pulled out his Billy club and swung at Birdie's head, but Birdie was much quicker than the overweight cop. He blocked the blow with his arm, disarmed him and began beating them both with it. Within moments, four police cruisers screeched to a halt. A handful of uniforms jumped Birdie from behind. Birdie put up a valiant fight but yielded to the ten Billy clubs raining down on him.

"Silver, Silver…" Birdie managed to gurgle. "I'm sorry…I'm sorry, Silver! I'm sorry… I'm sorry…I'm—"

Birdie's skull split open, but the police refused to let up as they beat him senseless until he slipped into unconsciousness.

* * *

Inside her new home, the same home her mother grew up in, Silver's grandmother set the rules of the house. She ensured Silver that it would not be a vacation if she were to live there and that if it weren't for the State checks she was getting for her, she would have let them put her in a foster home. Her grandmother vigorously controlled every waking moment. Silver assumed the bulk of the household chores, including scrubbing the floors, doing the laundry and taking out the trash. Silver wasn't even allowed to watch television or go outside to play with her friends because her entire day was filled with homework or chores, a move carefully calculated by her domineering grandmother.

After dinner, Silver usually went straight to bed, partly due to boredom and partly due to exhaustion. At those times, Silver thought about her mother, Birdie and Chance- she missed them all. These were also the times that she cried herself to sleep without a single person to comfort her or tell it wasn't her fault and everything would all right.

Over the years, her grandmother began to detest her as she had Jesse. If things weren't absolutely perfect to her grandmother, she would beat her. If Silver came home a minute late, she would beat her. Her grandmother's weapon of choice was a six-foot brown extension cord. She would whup Silver so viciously that the beatings left hideous and permanent scars on her back. It seemed at times as if Silver could not do anything that satisfied her grandmother. Her grandmother would strip her buck-naked after a beating, run hot bath water over her and then pour a bottle of Witch-Hazel over her. Then she was forced to sleep in the tub to cleanse her of what she called 'the Devil in her'. She regularly made cruel comments comparing her to her mother. *"You ain't shit just like your damn momma! You gonna wind up just like her... a dirty whore, you watch! But I be damned if you kill me like that bitch kill her father!"*

Chapter 15

Five Years Later

After enduring five years of virtual hell, Silver had grown into a beautiful young lady. Her grandmother despised her for it even more, so much so that she forced her to wear old women's clothing to disguise her sex appeal. Over the years, the insults, beatings and slave-like duties did not let up – they grew worse, and so did her grandmother. After her grandmother retired from teaching, she began to drink more and more wine, and the more she drank the more miserable she became.

With time, Silver developed a habit of walking with her head down, shamed by the way she looked, but since the tenth grade, Missy, who still attended the same school and classes with Silver, convinced her to begin changing into sexier clothing. Every morning, Silver made a beeline to Missy's house in the St. Nicholas projects and changed into clothes loaned by Missy before going to school.

Now in her final year of High School, Silver was one of the top students in the city and she anticipated receiving a full scholarship to any college that was as far away as possible from her grandmother. She had dreamed about this moment for years and in a matter of four short months, she would be free forever, never to return. At night, Silver thought about her mother, but eventually, she seemed like a distant memory. And then there was Chance. There wasn't a single day that she didn't think about him, but since that fateful day five years ago, she hadn't seen nor heard from him.

For the past two weeks, Silver and Missy had been discussing their prom, but under no circumstances would Silver's grandmother allow her to attend. She told Silver that all she would do was open up her legs to any nappy head nigger and get pregnant. Silver knew that when her grandmother said no, it meant no. In fact, the entire five years Silver had lived with her, she hadn't been allowed to go to the movies or anyplace else for that matter by herself. But Silver didn't care at this point. She knew that if she stayed home, she would regret this one crowning moment of a lifetime. Besides, she felt it was her right to attend the prom – she earned it and she was determined to go…somehow?

She changed clothes at Missy's house. Missy was smoking a fat blunt and grooved to some L.L Cool J. Missy had also grown into a beautiful and sexy young lady, and was even more appealing and irresistible because she stayed dipped with all the latest fashions, compliments of her many hustling boyfriends.

"Yo … you see how diesel that nigger, L.L is getting lately? And the way he always licking his fucking lips? Now you know that nigger can suck a mean pussy!"

"Yeah, but you will never find out 'cause I hear he's happily married," Silver said.

"That don't mean shit! All them rapping niggers are fucking like it's Fuck Fest 2000."

Silver frowned. "That's why I would never mess with no entertainer, that includes ball players or drug dealers, 'cause they have too many girls sweating and hawking them. You would always have to wonder if they out screwing…naw… not me."

"Bitch, you crazy! I would get with one of them rich motherfuckers in a second, 'cause niggers gonna cheat anyway. I rather be with a rich cheating motherfucker, shopping and spending his loot while he's out boning some hoe, than being at home with a broke motherfucker who ain't got pot to piss in or a window to throw it out!"

"You're a fucking hoe."

Missy started dancing freaky style. "Yeah, but I be a paid hoe, believe that shit!"

"One day, you gonna wake up with ten kids by ten different baby daddies running behind them for some milk and pamper money."

Missy paid Silver no mind and continued dancing. "You know I don't get down like that, ain't no semen touching my insides. I make them nigga's wrap up."

Silver frowned. "But why you got to mess with so many dudes at one time? Don't you get tired of that shit?"

Missy popped her coochie to the beat. "You want to know why?"

Silver nodded. A new song came on with a heavy beat and Missy began rapping.

"Cause I love to fuck nigga's, all I do is fuck nigga's, but when I fuck nigga's, I'm like...fuck Nigga's!"

Silver shook her head and laughed. Already dressed, she waited for Missy to finish dressing. The process seemed to take hours as she smoked and talked mad shit. Silver loved these moments because their worlds were like night and day. She stay hip and lived her teenage years through Missy's eyes. Missy was a Hip-Hop head and had every hip-hop publication such as *The Source, XXL, Don Diva* and *F.E.D.* magazines.

Silver continued to scan through one of the magazines. "Uhh, look at these girls in here, they ain't wearing nothing but strings up their asses." Missy took a look and saw where Silver pointed to a girl with a very large buttock posing with some rappers.

"Chickens," Missy said bluntly. "Only reason them bitches are in the magazine in the first place is because they get those birth control shots to make their asses fatter!"

Silver grew perplexed. "Get the hell out of here...you serious?"

"Hell yeah, girl, remember Rasheeda from 114th Street and how she had a white girl ass?"

Silver nodded.

"Well how you think she blew up like that? The bitch been getting shots since the 9th grade and now she got a dooky ass."

Silver was surprised. "So is that why your ass is so fat?"

Missy threw her a strained look as she took a pull from her blunt. "Bitch please." She blew out the smoke. "I got my butt the old fashions way...I let a nigga fuck me in the ass."

Silver frowned. "Uhh...you are so fuckin' nasty."

Missy smiled. "Yo, that shit works yo, it hurts like a motherfucka, but it's worth it." This was vintage Missy, and you would never know if she was joking or for real, but Silver knew Missy wasn't the kind to talk about it, but be about it. Missy took another pull from the blunt and passed it to her. She frowned, "Bitch, don't even try to play me."

"What?" Missy smirked.

"You know goddamn well I don't fuck with that shit," Silver said. "You need to stop fucking with that shit too before you graduate to some other shit you can't come off of."

"You could kill that shit... the only thing I'm ever gonna fuck with is weed or some fucking Yac."

Silver frowned as she watched her smoke the blunt. "Why you smoke so much anyway?" Missy plopped into an armchair and spoke matter of factly. "'Cause it takes away stress and shit... you need that shit to function around this house. All these motherfuckers in this house are starting to get on my nerves. It's already crowded enough, and my Moms fuckin' moves her boyfriend up in this small bitch. And the nigger ain't shit either. He just came home from up north after being locked down for three years and don't do shit but lay up all day and argue with my Moms. If he ain't doing that, he's tryin' ta look up my ass...my Moms is real stupid. So I smoke to tune all these motherfuckers out. Shit, you talking about me, this is what your stiff ass need. Stop being so stuck up all the time."

"Friends and relatives," Silver said, remembering what her mother had told her years ago. Missy had heard this from Silver her whole life, but it never stopped her from testing her.

"Yeah, yeah, yeah... friends and relatives," Missy said. "I know what your mother said, but this is only weed. It's from the earth, put here for us to relax, so chill the fuck out, you almost grown now."

Silver put down the magazine she was reading and grabbed her book bag. "Naw, that's all right...I'm like Nancy Reagan, I just say..." She walked behind Missy, bent down and screamed in her ear. *"Hell, no!"* She ran out of her room smiling.

Missy, holding her ears, shouted back. "Oh no you didn't, bitch!" She grabbed her school bags and ran after her.

On their way to school, boys, men and even women tried to rap to them. They simply stood out, like two runway models, the streets being their stage. Their natural beauty shined easily, but wearing their Lil' Kim-esque gear, they epitomized 'Ghetto Super Stardom', and they acted the part by not giving anybody the time of day. Students in their High School had nicknamed them Salt and Pepper, Silver being the salt and Missy, of course, being the pepper.

"Yo guess what"? Silver said slyly.

"What?" Missy asked.

"I made up my mind... I'm going to the prom!"

Surprised, Missy stopped in her tracks. "Stop playing...your grandmother said you could go?"

Silver smiled. "Nope, but I'm going anyway."

Missy gave her a pound. "That's right girl, go for yours! You deserve it! I mean... how the hell your grandmother gonna stop you from going to your own prom anyway? You bust your ass for four years... four hard fuckin' years at that! Shoot... plus you the Valedictorian and she thank you by saying you can't go to your own prom. Fuck that shit... you doing right, girl." Missy shook her head and continued. "I'm glad my grandmother ain't like yours."

Silver laughed. "Nobody's grandmother is like yours."

Curious, Missy frowned. "How's that?"

"Missy, what grandmother you know smoke trees with their daughter and granddaughter?"

Missy was not impressed. "So...what grandparent doesn't? My nanna is no different from anybody else's in the projects."

Silver was surprised by Missy's nonchalant outlook and laughed. "Oh my God! How 'bout the time you caught your grandmother fucking your boyfriend?"

Still not impressed, Missy shrugged. "At least she kept that shit in the family!"

Silver was amazed at Missy's cavalier attitude and degree of bluntness. "That's fucked up!"

Missy enjoyed grossing Silver out and shrugged again. "That ain't shit. I heard she fuck my daddy too back in the day. Shit, she's only forty-four and she still look good, so what you expect?"

Silver's mouth opened in shock. "You lying?"

"Nope, I heard she had that nigger fiending too!"

Silver waved her off. "Stop! I don't want to hear anymore." Missy loved it.

"Anyway," Missy said, moving on to another subject. "How you gonna get out to go to the prom?"

"I'm gonna wait until she get nice and drunk, and then I'm gonna sneak out when she falls asleep."

"Sounds like a motherfuckin' plan to me... but what if she wakes up?"

"The prom is on Friday, right?"

"Right."

"Well... Friday's is her main night that she get blitzed and she'll get so fucked up that she will sleep through the entire night."

"I hear that shit, it's on now... my girl is coming...ooh, we gonna walk up in there like what! Them niggers ain't gonna understand it! But what are you gonna wear?"

"I made a dress, and the shit is the bomb too. I took one of her old dresses, shorted it and redid it to fit me... and 'Voila'! All those years of sewing her clothes finally paid off."

"Damn... you been scheming on this shit for a while, huh?"

"Hell yeah... I deserve this shit."

"You damn skippy you deserve it."

"But there's only one problem."

Missy stopped in her tracks, disappointed. "What now?"

"I don't have a date."

"Bitch, you can have any nigger you want to take you to the prom!"

"Yeah, but the prom is tomorrow and everybody is already locked up with a date."

Missy thought about the dilemma for a moment. "We just go together!"

Silver stared at her. "But, what's up with Justice?"

Missy shrugged. "What about him? Yo, I like Justice, but you are my motherfuckin' girl, yo! That's what's up!"

Silver again realized just how much of a true friend Missy really was. "You sure Missy, cause I can go by myself."

"Look, that Spigger is just gonna have to handle that shit."

"What the fuck is a Spigger?"

"Oh, Justice is half Black and half Spanish...so that makes him a cross between a Spic and a Nigger... Spigger... get it?"

They both laughed at her pun.

"Besides," Missy continued. "He's gonna get some pussy after the prom anyway, that's all them niggers are worrying about anyway. The Spigg will pick us up in a limousine from my house and we gonna do our thing from there on...besides, that nigger is gonna get mad props stepping out the limousine with both our gorgeous asses."

Missy paused and extended her fist. "You down, bitch."

Silver smiled and tapped her fist. "I'm down, hoe!"

"We finally graduating," Missy said. Yo, I can't believe that shit, I ain't never gonna sit in nobody's classroom ever again. I'm just gonna find some rich ass, Rico Suave nigger and let him take care of me for the rest of my life."

"Why you always fucking with them Spanish guys?"

"'Cause they ain't afraid to eat no pussy!"

Silver laughed as Missy continued.

"You think I'm lying? Them Spanish niggers ain't afraid to go scuba diving on you, shit... you don't even have to ask them either. They like..." Missy held her nose and simulated someone going underwater.

Silver laughed even harder. "So what you saying...you just stop fucking black niggers all together?"

"Hell no, bitch..." Missy snapped. "I love myself some Shaka Zulu dick just as much as the next bitch, but it's just sometimes I feel like a lick, and sometimes I feel like a stick. These niggers out here act like they too good to give a bitch mouth to mouth resuscitation on the pussaaaay!" Silver died laughing as Missy continued. "For real though...my rule is 'No Licky, No Sticky'."

"You are one crazy hoe."

"Yeah, I'll be crazy hoe, but a least I'm getting some, unlike some people I know."

Silver smiled again. "I'm saving myself."

"I don't know why, give me one good reason why?"

"I'll give you three...one, I don't want to get pregnant. Two, there are too many diseases out here. Three, I'm waiting until I get married."

"Married? To who, bitch...Chance?"

Silver grew silent, and when she didn't respond, Missy turned toward her and stared.

"Oh shit...don't tell me you still stuck on that nigger? Yo, I'm sorry to bust your bubble, but that nigger is probably still locked up doing life or something!"

Silver remained silent.

"Besides, you ain't seen or heard from that nigger in what... five...six years? For all you know that nigger could be—"

"Just forget about it," Silver snapped.

Missy frowned. "Damn, Silver, I'm sorry, I didn't know you still had feelings like that for him." Eager to cover up her mistake, she changed the subject. "Yo, you know I got an audition downtown next week."

"You didn't tell me about no audition."

"Yes I did, I told you they had open call for dancers for this new off-Broadway play."

Silver smiled, genuinely happy for her friend. "Go girl! I'm happy for you, I wish you luck"

"Fuck that, I ain't gonna need no luck, it's all skill baby... 'cause you know none of them bitches can work it like me." Missy did a little dance combination to prove her point. "You know that's right girl," she said, giving her a pound.

"Besides, if I get this gig, I'll have enough money to move the fuck out my mom's house and get my own apartment."

"Yeah...I know exactly what you mean, 'cause I'll be so glad when they send me my scholarship so I can get the hell out of here!" She didn't notice Missy's smile disappeared. "I'll go to Timbuktu if I have to, just get me far away from here." She frowned at Missy's sudden silence. "What up, Missy, why you going silent squirrel on me all of a sudden?"

"'Cause"

"'Cause what?"

"You don't know?" Silver grabbed Missy by the arm.

"No, I don't know...what is it?"

Missy looked away for a moment and just came out with it. "'Cause I'm gonna fuckin' miss you!"

Silver felt surprised and sad at the same time. All the years that she had known her, Missy had been far from the emotional type and held her feeling inside. This was the first time she had ever showed any outward sensitivity. Silver didn't know what to say, so she just gave her a big hug.

"Oh, Missy... you know you're my girl, and no matter what, me and you will always be down for each other. We have been down for each other this long through thick and thin and good and bad. I know for a fact that you definitely been there for me when I had no one else, you remember?" Missy stood with her arms folded as tears began to well in her eyes. She simply nodded as Silver continued. "Through all the shit you and me been through, you remained by my side like a motherfuckin' trooper. When I had beef, you had beef; if you had a dollar, I knew I had fifty cents." Silver caressed her smooth, dark skin. "True friends like you... are few and far between. That's one thing you can't ever get new... and that's old friends, and it's nothing in this world I wouldn't do for you." Silver lifted her chin and looked her square in the eyes.

"I will fucking die for you, hoe!"

Tears streamed from Missy's eyes as she stared at her only true friend and hugged her tightly.

"I'll die for you too, bitch!" she whispered.

Silver wiped away her tears. "We're always gonna be girls, and no matter where I go, all you got to do is call and I'll be there for you, no matter what."

"For real?"

Silver smiled reassuringly. "You didn't know? For real!"

Chapter 16

Queen To Be

The next day, Silver stared impatiently at the clock. It was 8:30 p.m. She looked at the clock once again and then walked to her grandmother's room to ensure that she was still sound asleep. Silently scanning the room, she observed the empty wine bottle that lay at the side of bed, satisfied that the older woman was still fast asleep. Cautiously, she closed the door and called Missy, telling her that she would be there in fifteen-minutes. She hurried into her room to get her pre-packed bag and slipped out the front door.

At the prom, Silver and Missy had the time of their lives. Missy wore a tight fitting red dress that highlighted her slender, long legs, making her look like a Paris runway model. Silver wore an elegant white satin dress that fit her body like a glove. Missy designed Silver's face with lipstick and make-up that made her look flawless. Up to that point, Silver had never really used makeup before and she was more surprised than anyone else at how beautiful she looked. Everyone knew Silver was a cutie, even when she wore drab clothing, but on this night she looked absolutely radiant and drop-dead gorgeous. It was the best time Silver had had in a long time. As a matter of fact, this was the first and only school party that she had attended in her entire life, and she loved it.

At Silver's house, a gust of wind from an open window caused a vase to fall to the floor. Startled and groggy, Ms. Jones called out. "Silver!" she yelled several times, to no response. "I know that damn girl hears me," she muttered angrily as she searched for her slippers. Putting on her robe, she opened her bedroom door and noticed the living room window was wide open; curtains fluttering over the broken vase lay on the floor. She yelled for Silver once again and headed toward her room. "Girl, I know you heard me calling you…" She realized that Silver was not in her bed or room and walked into the bathroom. She paused to clear her head and then stepped to the telephone and pressed redial. After few rings, a female voice answered.

"Hello?" Mrs. Jones said. "Who is this?"

"Bitch, you calling my goddamn house, who the hell is this?"

"I'm Mrs. Jones, Silver's grandmother."

"Oh… Mrs. Jones, I'm sorry, this is Mrs. Anderson… Missy's mother… I thought you was one of them scandalous ass bitches calling my house for my man."

In the background, Mrs. Jones heard a male voice.

"Bitch, why the fuck would I give a hoe my number to call me here?"

Missy's mother angrily retorted. "Motherfucker, that ain't stop them bitches before, I know it's them bitches that be hanging up when they hear my voice!" The voice paused. "Miss Jones, sorry, what can I do you for?"

"Well, I was wondering if you knew my granddaughter's whereabouts?"

" Girl, stop playing, you know they at their prom. They left here over two hours ago, and girl, them girls looked good, too."

The man's voice came over the line again.

"Yeah, especially that red one!"

Angry, Missy's mother yelled. "Get the fuck out my house, motherfucker … get your nasty ass out of here!"

Miss Jones heard the receiver drop.

"Hello? Hello?" said Mrs. Jones.

Missy's mother still shouted. "You getting your ass out of here tonight, you dirty motherfucker!"

"Hello?"

"What?" Missy's mother demanded.

"Can you tell me where the prom is?" she asked.

"Yeah, they over there at that fancy place in Central Park, you know, that tavern place… listen, Mrs. Jones, I got to go! You dirty motherfucker…"

She hung up.

"That slick little whore…we'll see who is the slickest one!" She dialed for cab service. "I need a cab at 1545 west 138th Street. Yes, I going to Tavern on the Green in Central Park…okay, fifteen minutes, fine." She hung up and went to her room to get dressed.

At the prom, the Master of Ceremonies announced that it was time to present the award and dance to this year's prom King and Queen.

"And this year's Prom King and Queen of the graduating class of Nineteen-hundred Ninety-nine is presented to Mister Trevor Smalls and Ms. Silver Jones."

The crowd gave a round of applause as the two held hands and walked up the stairs to the waiting Principle and Dean, who held a tiara crown and bouquet of flowers. Trevor shook hands with the Principle and Dean as they hand him a plaque and then turned to wave to well wishers in the crowd. Silver stepped forward and was crowned with the tiara and given the bouquet of roses. She smiled and the crowd grew wild. It was the single greatest day in Silver's entire life.

Trevor stepped to the podium first. "Thank you, thank you... I like to thank God for blessing me and allowing me to be here today. Secondly, I like to thank my mom and dad for supporting me in all my endeavors, and lastly I like to thank my date for making me look better ...and most of all...you, my fellow students and the staff for nominating me as this year's Prom King. I won't let you down. Thank you."

The Master of Ceremonies stepped forward. "I can see that God must be missing an Angel, 'cause we got one right here on this stage! And I present to you not only this year's Prom Queen, but also this year Valedictorian... Ms. Silver Jones!"

Shyly, Silver walked over to the podium and surveyed the crowd. She grew serious and the crowd became silent. "I would like to thank God, the staff, and my fellow students for having me as Valedictorian." She put her head down toward the podium and paused, but looked up moments later. She took a deep breath. "About five year's ago, my mother was murdered in a Times Square motel room by a deranged killer – my mother was a prostitute." Some staff and students gasped. The Principle and Dean exchanged nervous glances, but Silver waited for everyone settled down before continuing.

"What I remember most about my mother was when she used to walk me to school every morning after she finished work. She would make me repeat these little affirmations and sayings, hundreds of them! I would ask her if I didn't need this for school, then what were they good for? Well, she never really explained that part to me. She just would say that in time, I'd understand. Well that time has come…I now understand. One of the things that I remember her asking me was, *'What was the worst word in the world?'* And I would say 'can't'. She would then ask me, 'Why?' I would answer, 'Because if you exclude that word out of your vocabulary you 'can' do anything you want!'" Silver paused, looked up toward the ceiling and shook her head.

"When she died … when she died, I thought to myself, I can't go on… because there was nothing in life I had to looked forward to. I felt that if I couldn't have my mother, what's the point? Well, over the years without her, there were plenty of days when I honestly didn't know if I could make it through another day. I could have given myself a reason to just give up and quit, take the easy way out like so many people that I've known. Doubt tried to convince me to give in, but I couldn't and I honestly never knew why. It wasn't until this very moment, this very second, that I realized why I never gave up and quit." The room was silent enough to hear a pin drop, everyone captivated, hanging onto every word.

"It was because I didn't know how. That was something she never taught me how to do. You see… I realized that all those years when she was alive, what she was doing was preparing me for rough times, knowing that they will surely come. She told me how she got tricked into using heroin and became an addict, she told me how she was given a choice at the age of fifteen when she got pregnant with me to either have an abortion or move out. Since she was unfortunate to have made those life changing choices, she made sure I didn't fall for the same illusions and misconceptions that had ruined her own life. So I guess that's why she started instilling in me something more valuable than gold and something more precious than the largest of all diamonds – and that something is the truth!" She smiled. "It's funny, but my mother told me that this was going to happen, and I'm not just talking about graduating from high school. She said that I was going to graduate at the top of my class and become the Valedictorian. She would describe almost to the letter how I would stand before my peers and graciously accept my awards. That was almost seven years ago. How did she know that it would become reality? Tonight is not just an illusion, but it is reality of her life long vision that shines through her and through me. The truth is that she really didn't leave me… she's very much alive within me, because she is inside my heart, my soul, and in my mind."

Tears began to flow as she emotionally continued. "In parting, I would like to thank four people, especially my best friend, Missy Anderson. If it weren't for you simply being a friend, I wouldn't have had any. I'll die for you, girl."

Missy, overwhelmed with tears, called back." I'd die for you too!"

"And to my Auntie Birdie and Chancellor Haze, wherever they are, I will never will forget you. Lastly, I want to thank and dedicate this award to my mother, Ms. Jessica Jones." Silver looked upward. "Thank you mother… I will always love you."

Many in the student body and several teachers were in tears. Stifled sniffles gave way to slow clapping that turned into a thunder of applause. There wasn't a dry eye in the entire audience as Silver smiled back at them. This was her greatest moment of achievement—her smile faded when she noticed the distinct and grim face of her grandmother, staring imposingly back at her from the crowd. Not missing a beat, Missy looked toward where Silver was staring and her jaw dropped. Silver grew weak-kneed and put her head down as she slowly began walking off the stage. Hands patted her on the back and some hugged her as she made her way toward the exit door. By the time Silver reached her grandmother, Missy was already there, taking responsibility for everything. Her grandmother wasn't hearing any of it.

At home, her grandmother screamed. "So you want to be a fast bitch, huh? I'm gonna show you what I do to fast bitches like you! You know what to do, get out of that funky dress, wipe that shit off of your face and come back with the extension cord, 'cause I'm gonna whip your fast ass!"

Silver reluctantly complied. She went to her room and changed out of her dress. All the while she heard her grandmother calling her everything but a child of God. Silver stared at herself in the mirror and washed off the makeup. She imagined her mother standing behind her and visualized her gently placing her hands on her shoulders and smiling at her. The image disappeared when she heard her grandmother yelling for her to come out and bring the extension cord with her. Silver slowly walked to the kitchen and came out with the extension cord, which she handed to her grandmother.

"Since you want to be cute, I'm gonna teach your ass not to disobey me. Now lift up your shirt."

Silver reluctantly lifted up her shirt and turned around for yet another beating. Ugly scars from past whippings were exposed. She bit down on her bottom lip and closed her eyes to brace herself.

"You want to be grown huh? I'll teach you to stay in a child's place. You are just like your no-good mother, but I'll beat the black out of your ass before you disrespect me!" Suddenly, Silver opened her eyes and turned around. "No more!"

"What did you say?" her grandmother snapped.

"I said no more!" Silver said in defiance. It was the first time Silver had ever remotely talked back to her.

"Bitch, have you lost your motherfucking mind?" her grandmother shrieked.

She raised her arm to hit Silver with the extension cord, but Silver grabbed it and wrestled the cord out of her hands and threw it down. "I'm tired of you beating me for no good reason," Silver said calmly.

"Bitch, have you lost your goddamn mind?"

"Have you?" Silver replied. "All I wanted to do was go to my prom! My prom… and I'm wrong?" Silver stared at her. "I don't ever go anywhere, I put up with everything you tell me to do, I get straight A's in school and nothing I do seems to ever satisfy you! What did I ever do to you to make you hate me so much?"

The older woman sneered. "You want to know why? Because you are a lying, filthy slut just like your mother… and you gonna be just like her…a dirty junkie whore!"

Silver sadly shook her head. "You know what? All these years, I used to think that my mother died on my birthday in that motel room, but you know what? I was wrong. She died long, long before that." Shaking her head in pity, Silver continued. "I feel sorry for you because you ain't nothing but a miserable old woman who doesn't have an ounce of happiness inside you."

"Since you want to be grown up, you can get the hell out of my house."

Silver smiled. "That ain't a problem, I was gonna leave out of this prison anyway." She went to her room to pack her clothes, her grandmother close behind her.

"Oh no, you don't, bitch. You ain't taking none of them clothes I brought you. Since you're ass is so grown you go sell your pussy like your mama and buy your own."

Silver laughed. "You call those clothes? You can keep them. I can get better clothes at the Salvation Army." She walked out the front door, her grandmother on her heels as she headed out the door.

"And don't come back!" she yelled. "Don't come calling me when you get into trouble, 'cause you gonna turn into a whore and drug addict just like your simple-ass fucking mother!"

That was it. Silver stopped in her tracks. The words had cut through her like a razor and all the years of pent-up anger finally made Silver snap. She turned around quickly and stormed back toward her grandmother, who watched her until she closed her eyes, preparing herself for the worst. Suddenly and unexpectedly, Silver placed a soft, gentle kiss on her cheek. Her grandmother opened her eyes to Silver's smiling face.

"My mother use to say, 'For your worst enemy, you don't ever have to do or wish them any harm that they aren't already putting on themselves. She told me that instead of hating your enemy, love them, and that would kill them quicker than a bullet ever would. You have so much hate inside of you, you're not even able to love yourself. So here's what I'm going to do. Since you're incapable of loving yourself, I'm going to love you until you learn to love yourself, so until then grandma, goodbye. My mother and I still love you." Silver smiled and walked away, leaving her grandmother standing speechless.

Chapter 17

Welcome Back Birdie

Knock! Knock! Knock! Silver had not been in this building in over five years. She wasn't even sure if Birdie still lived there or was even alive for that matter. She would have stayed at Missy's house for the night, but knew that she would not have anywhere to sleep because Missy's apartment was so crowded. Silver could only pray that Birdie still lived here. She heard the bedroom door inside the apartment squeak open.

"Nigger, why you waking me out my sleep... where the hell is your key?"

Silver smiled when she heard the familiar voice as apartment door 3 F swung open. Smiling from ear to ear, Silver looked up at her favorite Aunt, who she hadn't seen in years. Birdie, much older now, bore multiple scars across his face and an ugly webbed eye from the beating years earlier. He did not recognize her.

"Can I help you, young lady?"

Silver couldn't contain her excitement. "It's me, Auntie Birdie...Silver."

As if a bolt of lightning hit him, Birdie's jaw dropped. "Silver? Oh my lord ...is that you?"

She nodded. "Yes... it's me."

Finally recognizing her, Birdie embraced her with a big hug and began crying as he looked toward the ceiling. "Lord, I knew you would bring her back to me. Come in, child." He ushered her in from the hallway. "Ohh child, I miss you so much, I got so many questions to ask you... what brings you here this time of night?"

Silver looked down, embarrassed.

Birdie nodded knowingly. "Your grandmother, right?"

Silver nodded again.

"It's okay, baby... you don't have to explain," Birdie said. "I already know. We'll talk about that later. For now tell me everything that's been going on in your life... ooh, I miss you so much!"

Birdie and Silver sat up and talked for hours before Tommy, Birdie's boyfriend, entered the apartment. Tommy was a tall, wiry man with yellow beady eyes and bad skin. "Oh Tommy," Birdie said, "I want you to meet my niece, Silver... she's gonna be staying with us a little while until she goes off to college."

Silver tried to smile but Tommy gave her the creeps, the way he stared her up and down with his cadaverous like face. He nodded to her and then turned to Birdie.

"Fix me some breakfast, I'm hungry."

With that, he walked into the room and closed the door.

"Don't mind him," Birdie said. "He's just crazy like that. It just takes some time to get to know him, but he's harmless."

Silver nodded in acknowledgment, but that didn't ease the bad vibes she felt from the man.

"By the way, where is your clothes?"

"What you see is what I own," Silver said, patting the clothes she wore.

"Girl, don't you worry, 'cause your Auntie Birdie is taking you shopping for a new wardrobe first thing tomorrow."

"Auntie Birdie, you don't have to do that. You doing me a big favor by just letting me stay here with you."

"Child, look at me, we are family... I'm not doing you any kind of favors by letting you stay here, or by buying you some outfits. I changed your diapers with these hands right here. Me and your mother, God bless her soul, was everything to each other, and before she died, she made me promise her that I would protect you." Birdie swallowed hard. "They took you away from me once and I refuse to let that happen again, so what I do for you, Silver, never look at it as a favor. I'm doing because we are family, understand?"

Silver hugged Birdie. "I understand."

After spending the entire day shopping on 34th Street, Birdie and Silver had acquired tons of Macy's and pink Conway shopping bags. They had so much fun together that day that time seemed to fly by. Silver in particular found a newfound freedom that she had never known or experienced. In her seventeen years, she had never shopped or been allowed to pick and choose what she wanted to wear. To top things off, Birdie took Silver to the Dominican's hair salon to get her hair done, and to the Korean's to get her fingernails silk-wrapped and a full pedicure. This was such a new and refreshing experience that, at times, Silver couldn't help but feel guilty.

Exiting the train station back in Harlem, Silver and Birdie wearily headed home, arms filled with bags.

"Oh child," Birdie suddenly said. "I got to go to the number hole and play my numbers. You go ahead to the building and wait for me."

Silver nodded and continued toward the building. Stopping at the light, she suddenly saw a man fall out of the rear of a black sedan. The car screeched to an abrupt halt and she watched another man emerge from the rear in quick pursuit as the fallen, disheveled man tried desperately to regain his balance. The dark-skinned man quickly grabbed him from behind, ending his brief chance at freedom. As the pursuer pulled the bearded man back toward the car, he fell limply to the ground and pleaded for his life.

"Aw come on, man," he pleaded. "I ain't talk to nobody...it wasn't me, I swear!"

The dark-skinned man remained silent but continued pulling the man by his collar.

"Aw man," the first cried, pounding his fist on the ground. "This is fucked up, this is fucked up...why y'all doing this, man? I ain't talk to nobody... I ain't tell nobody shit, please man!" Unable to get the man to hear his pleas, the fallen man lay limply by the curb. "Man, we can work this shit out... just let me talk to them niggers...you got the wrong man, I swear!"

The driver of the car yelled out. "Yo, Hollis, this shit is getting hot...handle that shit!"

Hollis wasn't a tall man, but he was built like a Sherman tank. Though he seemed young, to Silver, he had deeply defined eyes that reminded her of a shark. If it weren't for the hideous long scar that he had on the side of his face and neck, he could have been considered handsome.

Hollis pulled out a high caliber weapon. "One time nigger... die on your feet like a man or die in the gutter like the filthy dog that you are... snitch!"

The frustrated, terrified man continued to pound the pavement. "Man, I done told you, I ain't—"

Before he finished his sentence, Hollis fired a single bullet through the man's cranium. Brain and skull fragments splattered the pavement in a starburst pattern. Silver jumped as she watched the man's head burst like a dropped melon.

Hollis coolly watched the man's body shake violently. "Bow-wow, bitch," he said, and then casually walked back to the sedan, closed rear the door and hopped in the passenger seat. As the men screeched off, they saw her. The car slammed to a halt as the driver's gaze locked on Silver, as if straining to get a good look at her. Silver stared back in horror as she watched a long, black gun extend out the window, pointed directly at her. Suddenly, the car took off, burning rubber down the street, and instants later, Birdie snatched Silver off of her feet and out of harm's way. Inside their building, Birdie rushed up the stairs, shopping bags floundering everywhere. At the door, he nervously fumbled through his purse for his keys.

"It's getting worse and worse around here," he cried. "One day I'm gonna get the hell out of this place."

Silver stood in a daze. "They were going to kill me, I…I saw it."

Birdie stopped fishing for his keys. "What did you say?"

Silver looked up at Birdie. "I saw the whole thing…he blew that man's head off right in front of me, Birdie."

Birdie finally got the door open and pulled her inside the apartment. Dropping the bags, he grabbed Silver by both shoulders. "Listen child… you ain't seen nothing, you ain't hear nothing… you understand me, Silver?"

Birdie shook her. "Yes, Auntie Birdie, I understand, I understand!" Birdie obviously felt some remorse for handling her so roughly and gave her a hug.

"I just can't afford to see nothing happen to you baby, it would surly drive me crazy if I let something happen to you, Silver… you understand, baby?"

Silver gave him a wan smile. "I understand, Auntie Birdie." They hugged and then Birdie pulled away.

"Now let's try on our clothes like we used to do."

Silver agreed, but knew that it would be a long while before she get the incident out of her head, especially the driver's eyes as he drove past her. Silver felt a strange impulse – something had been very familiar about them—just then, Tommy rushed through the door.

"Did you hear about the shootin'? They done blew that nigger; Five-dollar Freddie's head clean the fuck off. That nigger won't be talkin' to no cops no mo'... he fucked over the wrong niggers this time! I heard that nigger, Heartless himself, pulled the trigger."

Birdie gasped. "Oh, my God ...Hollis was the one who killed that man?"

"Yep, Stickbroom Johnny said he saw it too, and you know that nigger know everything."

Birdie clutched his chest and fell to the couch. Tommy frowned. "What the fuck is wrong?"

"Tommy, Silver saw the whole thing too."

Tommy threw his hat down in anger. "Goddamn it, Birdie, you know goddamn well if them niggers find out she is staying here, they gonna send a motherfuckin' hit squad back here to kill all our asses up in this bitch." He turned to glare at Silver. He shook his head and continued. "I knew when I first saw her she was gonna be nothing but goddamn trouble!"

"Maybe they didn't see her," Birdie said. "Maybe they didn't notice her."

Tommy pointed to Silver. "How the fuck they gone miss her high yellow ass?" Shaking his head, he stormed out of the room.

Driving uptown, the two men pulled up in front of their spot on 144th and 8th Avenues. Hollis signaled a kid over, who swiftly scooped up the bag of hot guns and bounced.

"Yo, nigger," Hollis yelled to the driver, emerging from the vehicle. "Yo...why the fuck you drive off before I could clap that bitch?"

Chancellor Haze had grown considerably from the slight, frail thirteen-year old he had been five years prior. He now stood 6 foot 2, with a slender muscular build and a sharp, keen handsomeness that was hard to miss in a crowd.

Hollis chuckled. "Yo, nigger...you getting soft, that's a sign that a nigger getting' too much money."

Chance ignored him.

"See me, I'm gonna remain a soldier, 'cause I'm true to this and I don't give a fuck!"

Chance grew tied of listening to him. "Yo, shut the fuck up! You run your fucking mouth too much, man, that shit is gonna be the death of your ass."

Hollis paid him no mind. "Yeah, whatever nigger... but yo, I'm gonna go to Willies and get me some burgers or sumptin, I be right back."

Chance looked at Hollis as if he was sick "Yo, what the fuck is you on? This whip is hot as a motherfucker and you thinking about eating?" He shook his head and looked around for police. "Naw, fuck that...we gonna handle this shit now and then burn this shit!"

Hollis walked off. "No doubt nigger, let a nigger cop a couple of burgers first an' then we out."

Annoyed, Chance pointed at the ground to emphasize his point. "Nigger, you ain't hearing me. I did you a favor on this job here. My prints is in this bitch... we doing this shit right now!"

Hollis turned around. "Damn, dukes...calm ya motherfucking ass down... damn!" He lifted his arms as he scanned the area. "Po-Po ain't that muthafuckin' good."

Chance closed the car door. "See, that's what I'm talking about; that's exactly how stupid ass niggers get knocked... over some dumb shit! You ain't gonna get me trapped the fuck off because you want a fuckin' burger!"

"Nigger... fuck you stressing for? We ain't dirty... we ain't got no weapons on us!"

Chance waited for a couple to amble past, not wanting them to overhear their conversation, watching Hollis with a hawk-like stare the entire time. Hollis finally threw his hands up in frustration.

"What?"

Teeth gritted, Chance spoke in a low, angry tone. "Come the fuck here!"

Hollis reluctantly walked up to Chance, who whispered in his ear emphasizing his point as he spoke. Hollis finally glanced up into Chance's eyes, and then reluctantly conceded.

"Alright man. Damn!" He strode to the rear seats and began to clean out any type of evidence before they dumped and burned the rental he had been driving for the past week on a stolen credit card.

Looking over his shoulder, Chance glanced at him. "Yo, where the rags at? I'm gonna wipe down the front."

Hollis was in the process of tossing old McDonald's bags and soda bottles from the back of the car. "I think I got some towels in the trunk."

Chance opened the front door, pulled the keys out of the ignition and took them to the trunk. He opened it and stared for several moments. Then he glanced up. "Hollis."

Busy cleaning the car, Hollis didn't hear him. Chance looked around the block and called him once again, only louder. "Hollis!"

Hollis stopped cleaning and stuck his head out of the car. "What now, nigger?"

Chance motioned. "Come here." He lowered the trunk. Annoyed, Hollis stepped out of the rear of the car.

"What?"

Angry, Chance gritted his teeth. "Come the fuck over here!"

Hollis dropped what he was doing and hastily stepped to the back of trunk where Chance stood. Chance looked around before he lifted the trunk again. "What the fuck is that?" Looking inside the trunk, Hollis displayed a surprised expression and spoke almost casually.

"It's a body."

"Motherfucker, I know it's a body…what the fuck is it doing inside the trunk?"

Lost for words, Hollis shrugged. "Man, I don't know. I musta forgot about him."

"Nigger…how the fuck you forget a—"He caught himself and lowered his voice. "How the fuck you gonna forget a dead body in your motherfucking trunk?" He grew even more vexed when he remembered the hit they had just completed. "Nigger, you had me driving this bitch while we did a—"Unable to control his anger, he slammed the trunk hard. "You motherfucker…" Pissed off beyond control, Chance knew that if anything had gone wrong – like it did – or worse yet, the fucking cops caught him, he would have been doing double life for both bodies over some stupid petty shit. Beyond angry, Chance decided to leave before he did something he might regret, like put a bullet in him, something he wouldn't hesitate a second to do to *anyone*.

Chance first met Hollis in the 'neighborhood'. He was an orphaned street kid from Haiti who spoke little English. He had watched the tattered, sickly looking boy search garbage bins for aluminum cans. One day, Chance offered him something to eat and Hollis had looked up to Chance ever since. After Chance got out of

Juvenile Detention and ran away from his foster parents, he ran into Hollis again, by now nothing but skin and bones. Chance took care of Hollis as they both started sleeping in abandon buildings, until one day Hollis got so sick he was forced to get him help. Chance knew that if he took him to Harlem Hospital, the authorities would be notified. Worried for the little boy, Chance took him to an old man from the neighborhood who Chance had known since he was younger. The man's name was A.O., a local legend who specialized in everything when it came to the streets. A.O. had seen these symptoms before and called a house doctor to come look at him. After the doctor looked him over, it was determined that Hollis had a severe case of pneumonia, scarlet fever and malaria. The doctor said that Hollis was extremely lucky, because if the boy hadn't gotten medical attention when he had, he would have died in a matter of days. After Hollis was nursed back to health, A.O. let Chance and Hollis stay with him, since neither of them had any parents. They had been together ever since.

Though he and Hollis were raised together in the game and were considered brothers, Chance knew that, brothers or not, he would not tolerate him or anyone else jeopardizing his freedom. Chance had been locked down at the Bronx House of Juvenile Detention and Spofford for the murder five years earlier. Those sixteen months nearly drove him mad. Doing life in some prison became his mortal fear, which was why he was so careful and very cautious about every move he made. Being afraid in the street was an asset in his business because it kept you on point, kept your senses fresh. If any *real* drug-dealer tells you he isn't afraid, then that's a Nigger who isn't doing real things.

Chance cursed himself for putting himself in the mix, because he usually didn't involve himself in Hollis' side of the business. But when Hollis caught wire that a nigger that he had a contract on had emerged on the streets, Hollis begged Chance to back him up. Since it was on the spur of the moment, Chance agreed, but only because all he had to do was drive. Or so he thought. Chance began wiping down the trunk with a cloth as he stared angrily at Hollis. He then walked to the driver's side seat and wiped the dashboard, steering wheel and door handles and then threw him the keys. "You are a stupid motherfucker!"

"Damn nigger," Hollis yelled back. "I forgot, damn!" He fanned his nose from pungent odor emanating from the trunk.

Not since the Harlem epidemic of heroin in the sixties and seventies, when the Italians associated and formed an alliance with Black Murder Inc., run by Mister Untouchable himself, Nicky Barnes, had Harlem seen such a influx of drug money. But crack money made heroin money seem like chump change in comparison. However, even with all disadvantages, there were some advantages to capitalize on, and one was murder. It was one business in Harlem that never changed and could be very lucrative to the person who had the balls to handle it. One such was Hollis, and he had elephant nuts. Hollis was king in that domain, a cold-blooded murderer. He and his crew of teenagers – mere boys who called themselves 'Young Guns', committed some of the most heinous crimes in the underworld. Word on the streets – and only behind his back of course, was that he was called Heartless, as one could guess, because he was a cold-hearted bastard – and everyone feared him. Hollis had been murdering men and boys professionally since he was twelve years old. Only eighteen, Hollis no longer got a rush from a simple kill, not in the sense of what one is used to seeing in the movies or television. That 'Bang- bang – die shit!' No… he past that a long time ago. He got off by seeing them suffer – suffer hard and long! Hollis wouldn't blink to kill anybody – man, women or child, because he didn't care and that's what makes him so ruthless. Hollis had death in his eyes that nobody could deny, cold and icy.

The ages of his team of killers ranged from eight to eighteen, and male or female, not one of them would hesitate to kill. Hollis invented sick and demented ways to kill his victims and take them out scientifically. Since most of his victims were other drug dealers, as an extra incentive he would torture them until they told him where they kept their stash. Hollis became very effective at making them talk by slicing their stomachs open and unraveling their small and large intestines before their eyes. At times, if he really hated you, he would watch you die slowly, by pricking you with a hypodermic needle filled with the monster AIDS virus. He'd enjoy seeing you every day as your health declined. He once pricked a boy from the neighborhood, a seventeen-year-old High School basketball star, all because a girl

Hollis liked chose the dude over him. He would come up to the sick boy everyday and offer his twisted brand of compassion.

"Yo man, you don't look too good, you got a cold or sumptin? You need to get some of that Buckley's, its nasty as hell, but it might help!"

Heartless.

Chapter 18

Not In a Million Years

At Birdie's request, Silver stayed in the house all day, just in case. While things calmed down, Tommy took a special liking to Silver. Tommy, though he was fucking Birdie, was not a homosexual, just an opportunist, and a nigger had to survive somehow. Yeah, he fucked Birdie up the ass, but that was nothing. When Tommy was up north, this was the only way he got some commissary and money by giving niggers back shots and letting the stuff boys suck his dick. But he still loved a shot of young pussy every now and then. If it weren't for Birdie, and him having a big ass horse dick, he would be a typical homeless bum.

After two weeks or so, Tommy tried to make his pitch and feel Silver out by purposely leaving the bathroom door open when he took a piss, wanting her to see his girth. He would walk out of the shower wrapped only in a towel and would strut in front of her while she was watching television in the living room. Silver tried to pay it no mind, but he started growing bolder and bolder as the days went by. She thought of telling Birdie about it, but felt it would be awkward, and besides, she didn't want to cause trouble or friction between them, so she put up with it and stayed locked up in her room. In an odd way, she and Birdie had become rather distant lately. Birdie knew that Tommy has been acting differently ever since Silver had arrived, and had seen the way he ogled Silver's body – Birdie was getting jealous, not so much against her, but because Birdie hadn't been loved in so long that it was hard not to feel a little threatened. Even though Tommy was not a good-looking man by any means, he was all Birdie had, and that was hard too come by for him.

Silver reasoned that she just had to make it through the summer and she would be on her way. The scholarship couldn't come through quick enough for her. By now, she rarely left her room at all – even to eat. Birdie checked on her from time to time, but that was it. Silver normally waited till late at night to move about and maybe make a sandwich or some crackers.

On this particular night, Silver decided to take a quick shower and wash her hair while Tommy and Birdie lay up in bed watching a movie on VHS when they hear the shower come on. Tommy began to get a hard-on as he imagined Silver's naked and bare body inside the shower.

" I hope she doing O.K, cause this is the first time she came out of her room all day, she ain't even eat." said Birdie. Paying Birdie no mind, he rubbed his crotch and began scheming "Baby..." said Tommy with a false smile "I feel like some ice cream...some butter pecan. You think you can go to the store and get me some please?" Birdie looked at him with a smile and said, "We already got some butter pecan in the freezer, I'll go get you some." Birdie attempt leave but pulled him by the arm "No I meant that other kind?" snapping his fingers as he tries to remember he said " That green shit with nuts..."

"Pistachio?" said Birdie. Popping his finger bingo, he said, "That's it," and said like he was a big baby "You think you can go get you man some?" Looking at him pout, Birdie smiled and said "All right baby I get you some, let me just put on my shoes." Dressed, Birdie heads out the bedroom door and ask, "Do you want anything else while I'm out?"

"No" He said impatiently, than added, "I don't want that shit from the bodega, go to that Arab place... U.S Fried Chicken." Birdie turned around disappointed, and said, "That's all the way on 8th Tommy." Tommy grabbed his dick through his boxers and said, "Please" Birdie eyes lit up and said, "I'll be right back" Tommy quickly yelled, "And take your time!"

Just as Silver finished showering and drying herself off the bathroom door suddenly opened. She quickly covered herself with the towel. "I'm in here!" she gasped.

Tommy just stood there staring at her with his beady eyes. Silver tried to slide past him, but he blocked her by putting his arms across the doorway.

"Excuse me," Silver said.

"What did *you* do?" he asked sarcastically.

She attempted to duck under his arms, but he lowered them. Frustrated, Silver yelled. "Auntie Birdie!" He smiled. "Birdie's not here."

"What is it that you want, Tommy?" she asked warily.

"Oh, I think you know what I want."

Looking in his beady eyes, she yelled again. "Birdie!" She attempted to get past him once again, but he pushed her back.

"Scream all the hell you want, Birdie's not here to help your ass."

Tommy's large dick protruded from his boxers. Staring down at it, Silver grew scared. "Yeah lil' bitch, I'm gonna put all this shit in ya," he said, and began stroking his meat. Silver shook her head. "Tommy, don't do this," she said, trembling fearfully. You and Birdie is—"

"Fuck Birdie!" he snapped. "That ain't got nothing to do with shit!"

As he approached her, she threw up her hands. "Wait, Tommy, please I'm a virgin!" He smiled again. "Shit...you shouldn't have told me that...I ain't had no virgin pussy since pussy had me."

He snatched the towel off her body and his eyes nearly popped out of his head as he ogled her breast and neatly trimmed pussy hair. Cowering for cover as Tommy walked toward her, she cast a wild glance at the door. "Birdie!"

Tommy turned around. No one was there, but it was all the time Silver needed to run past him and out of the bathroom. She heard him curse and run after her, but it was too late. She slammed her bedroom door in his face as she locked it in the nick of time. He hit the door and cursed. "Bitch!" Scared to death, Silver quickly tried to put some clothes on as he pounded on the door, but only had time too put on a tee shirt before the door was kicked open. Tommy lunged for her like a maniac and slapped her, knocking her back across the bed.

"I was gonna put some Vaseline on my dick," Tommy said coldly. "But now..." He pulled out his huge dick "Now I'm gonna fuck ya lil' ass raw!"

He grabbed her by her hair and lay on top of her. Silver panicked. "Okay, Tommy, okay, okay...you got it baby, you got it!" She smiled tremulously and forced herself to relax. Slowly, he released his grip from her hair and searched her face unsure what to do next. He lifted himself off her slightly and she continued to assure him. "You were right...I do want some of that meat...I have since I first got here." He let her up but continued to eye her cautiously. She forced lust into her voice. "That day, when you were in the bathroom, you forgot to close the door..." She giggled. "Well... I saw it. Ever since that day I have fantasized you making love to me." He smiled. "That's why I started staying in my room," she lied. "Because I couldn't take seeing you if I couldn't have you." She stood. "Come on," she said, taking him by the hand. She stepped closer to give him a hug, and then viciously jabbed her knee in his nuts – he never saw it coming. Tommy keeled over and screamed in excruciating pain as she ran quickly to the front door. She flung open the front door and ran into Birdie, standing on the other side. She cried out in relief of his unexpected presence and threw herself into his arms.

"What the hell is going on here?" he yelled.

Tommy stumbled out of the room, rubbing his groin while Birdie stared at him.

"What the hell went on here?"

Silver sobbed. "He tried to rape me!"

Birdie placed a comforting arm around Silver and looked over at Tommy.

"The bitch is lying."

"You're a lying bastard! He came in the bathroom after me and pulled out his fucking dick." Birdie threw Tommy a distraught look. "Is that true Tommy?"

Tommy shook his head in dismissal. "She came on to me."

Not believing her ears, Silver frowned. "You lying son of a bitch!" She turned to Birdie. "Look at my bedroom door, he kicked it in." Birdie walked to the door to examine it. "What happened to the door, Tommy?"

"Bitch, what did I tell you? The bitch came on to me...now get ya ass in the room and let me talk to you!" Birdie put the bags down on the table and followed Tommy in their room.

Silver went back to her room to finish dressing, thought she heard the two arguing. Several minutes later, Birdie stepped into her room.

"Silver... this thing with you and Tommy is driving me crazy. Ever since you got here, things have been ...you know...first that thing with the shooting, now this thing with Tommy...well, it's just becoming too much for me to handle."

Silver was perplexed. "Auntie Birdie, what are you trying to say?"

Birdie spoke softly. "Well, me and Tommy thought that it might be best if...you know, you stay somewhere else until you go away to college."

Silver couldn't believe her ears. "You gonna put me out over that nigger who just tried to rape me?"

Birdie shook his head. "No, that's not it." He pulled out a roll of money. "No... we just think it would be best if you find a room or stay at a hotel for awhile...you know, until you go off to college."

Never in a million years would Silver have thought things would ever come to this. Anybody but Birdie, she thought, with a broken heart, she could only look at him and shake her head. She stood and went to her dresser while Birdie followed her.

"Silver, don't look at it like that baby."

She retrieved a picture frame, but left everything else where it was.

"Oh, Silver, you don't have to leave tonight baby..."

Silver continued toward the door. "At least take the money, Silver...please!"

Still silent, Silver opened the front door.

"Silver, wait!" Birdie implored.

Silver stopped when he placed a gentle hand on her shoulder.

"Silver, I'm sorry you feel this way... but at least take your clothes and your other important things."

She turned and looked Birdie straight in the eyes. "Auntie Birdie, I already took the most important thing to me." At Birdie's confused expression, Silver held up an old picture of her mother, Birdie and herself in happier times. Birdie stared at it, his eyes welling with tears. He attempted to hug her, but Silver quickly left, closing the front door softly behind her. Tears ran down Silver's cheeks as she walked hastily through the mean, dark streets of Harlem.

Chapter 19

The Reals

Silver had walked nearly an hour before it dawned on her that she was now homeless. A cold shiver raced through her entire body, as at each corner she heard the honking of horns from men seeking her attention. She did her best to ignore them as she made a beeline in the other direction, just to get away from them. In spite of this major dilemma, not once did she even consider going back to her grandmother and giving her the satisfaction of saying 'I told you so'. She thought of Missy, but ruled against it, knowing her living situation. She knew Missy would have held her down, but didn't want her catching beef with her Mom's over it.

She decided it would be best if Missy held her down in the daytime or gave her something to eat from time to time. She reasoned that everything would be okay by tomorrow, since she could always get a job at Burger King or McDonald's or something. That way, she'd have enough for a cheap room to lay her head for the summer until she got her scholarship in hand. She just had to make it through the night and get the fuck off these streets. She decided to walk to 125th Street and catch the D train, which she could ride all night since it went all the way to Coney Island in Brooklyn, then all the way back to 205th Street in the Bronx. Since it was the longest train route in the city, she wouldn't have to keep transferring as much. Besides, she reasoned, she might be able to get some sleep – with one eye open of course! She reached the train station, looked around for police and hopped the turnstile.

Surprisingly, she got through the night without any incident and woke when the conductor yelled, 'Last stop!' She was in Coney Island and opened her eyes to bright sun shining through the train windows. Rubbing her eyes, she saw the huge Ferris wheel and smiled. She had never been to an amusement park, but looking down at it, it was just as she imagined it would be.

She began to plan her day. The first orders of business would be a shower, clothes and a job. She could take a shower and borrow clothes from Missy, since they were the same size, and then she would

go to 34th Street and apply for a cashier's position at one of the
hundreds of fast food restaurants down there until she found one.

At Missy's house, Silver did not divulge to Missy what had
happened with her and Tommy at Birdie's house. She simply told her
that Birdie tried to keep her on lock- down and she wasn't having that
again, for if she had told Missy what really had happened, Missy would
have been waiting in the building for Tommy with a straight razor and
surely would have cut his throat. Missy asked her where was she
staying, but she lied and told her that she was staying with some
distant relatives in the Bronx. She confided in Missy that these
relatives were only giving her a place to sleep but that she had to feed
herself, and she would need to use Missy's telephone and address
when she went looking for a job. Missy replied without hesitation.

"Bitch, now you know you ain't got no problems. I'm just upset
that you ain't come here first, 'cause I would've held you down win –
lose or draw!"

Silver smiled but left it at that, knowingly explaining anything
further would have complicated matters. Missy made Silver some
bacon and eggs and then gave her twenty dollars. Silver headed out
and spent the entire day downtown, filling out application for any
position that she could get. Now, all she could do was wait.

After a week of spending her days at Missy's house and riding the
trains at night, Missy's mother began to notice her every day presence
and missing rations from the refrigerator. Missy simply told her to
mind her business, which created an argument. This was the last thing
Silver wanted, so she just started stopping by to check to see if she got
any job calls or maybe an occasional sandwich. While Silver was in her
apartment, Missy's mother purposely sat in the kitchen and monitored
the refrigerator activities. Seeing this, Silver often left without eating
anything at all. After a couple of days like this, she simply stopped
going back all together because of the strange and guarded look's
Missy's mother began giving her.

As the days passed, Silver grew so hungry at times that she began
getting headaches from hunger pangs. She past by Burger King's
garbage area and watched other homeless people ravage though the
bags and pull out discarded burgers or fries. She past them every
night, praying for the nerve to grab a couple of burgers also, but could

never bring herself to do it. But after several days on the street, pride was no longer an option and she found herself down on her knees with the best of them as she scavenged through the discarded trash at closing. She also became quite a good thief by stealing twenty-five cent Little Debbie's and Quarter Waters from the bodegas.

In a matter of thirty days, Silver acquired the survival skills of a seasoned transient, and after being on the street so long, she even stopped noticing the men honking and hawking at her. She would yell, 'Leave me alone!' at the top of her lungs and simply walk the other way. But for the real persistent ones, she would yell scornfully, 'Mister, I'm only thirteen years old! You like baby pussy or something?' That would be that. Little did she realize that her hygiene also fell off and her unshaven armpits started to reek B.O. to the tenth power. Her nails became caked with so much dirt that they looked like those of auto mechanics. She stopped wearing underwear after she had her period. Her red Reeboks, which she wore sockless, were torn and busting at the seams. Nothing mattered to her anymore, her primary focus now only food and shelter. She made friends with some runaways that hung out at Time's Square, and they told her about a place called 'The Covenant House', that sheltered and fed teen runaways. She kept putting it off because she'd heard rumors about the pimps who stood outside the complex to kidnap some of them and make them sex slaves.

One night, drop dead tired and beyond famished, she found herself walking all the way uptown to the train station on 145th Street. Police were stationed inside at both the 125th Street and 135th Street train stations, so she had to troop it to the 145th Street train station to hop the train. So tired she was virtually sleepwalking and ready to pass out from a mixture of lack of sleep and food, she barely heard a car honk at her. As usual, she paid it no mind, but this driver continued creeping behind her, and then the driver came to a complete halt. A middle-aged man with a soft face wearing a brown suit and tie jumped out. He stepped in front of her calmly.

"Young lady I would like to—"

"Get away from me!" Silver yelled.

The man, caught off guard, nervously threw up his hands to calm her down, but to no avail. Silver grew more agitated and yelled louder. "Get the fuck away from me, I'm not a fucking crackhead!"

Passersby watched the scene, but ultimately minded their own business, for acts like these were common at this time of night because female crack addicts regularly beat their tricks and ran off with their money. When their victims sometimes caught up with them, they wanted to crack their fucking skulls.

"Young lady, calm down...calm down...my name is Reverend R.C Davis. I am only here to see if you need any help."

Silver calmed down when she saw a Bible in his hand.

Voices from a loose circle of teens playing Cee-lo a short distance away seemed loud in the night.

"Come on, nigga, scared money don't make no money."

Another guffawed. "Please nigga, money don't make me, I make money, hoe!" He tossed dice and aced out. He stood up frustrated when his eyes caught the duo across the street. "Yo, peep this shit," Said Kevin and pointed.

"Yo, ain't that that old nigger Pookie running game on them crackhead bitches again?"

Adjusting his vision Vince said "Hell Yeah that's that bitch ass nigger..." He shook his head. "That stupid motherfucker don't do nothing but come out at night and trick with them dirty ass crack bitches!"

"Yo, I heard that nigger be beaten the shit out of them bitches ass and then take the pussy!" said Kevin. "Yo, that bitch musta just started smokin', 'cause she still look kinda good." He turned to another man who was hidden in the darkness. "Yo Chance, you see that shit poppin' off?"

Chance lowered the magazine and glanced toward where the couple stood.

"Yo, fuck watching some crackheads nigger and roll the fucking dice!" Hollis screamed.

Looking in Silver's frightened eyes, he reassured her again "Young lady, there is no reason to be alarmed, I'm just trying to help." He put his arms down and looked nervously across the street. "Like I said, my name is Reverend Davis with the Greater First Baptist Church. We have a convent on 106th Street and we provide assistance to people in need of temporary shelter and a soup kitchen to get something to eat." Not missing a beat, he continued. "Now, it's not much, but at least the food is hot and the beds are clean." He extended his hand towards his car.

Silver searched his face and then at the modest Ford sedan with a sticker that read 'Jesus Saves' on the bumper. "Thank you," she said softly. " I could use some help."

The Reverend proceeded to open the door for her and nearly broke his neck hurrying back to his own door. He smiled heartily, turned on the ignition and drove off. Silver looked around the interior and noticed another Bible on the dashboard and a little figurine of the Virgin Mary mounted to the dash. The warmth and soothing sound of Shirley Ceasar from the tape deck put her at ease.

Finally, Silver thought, someone was really trying to help her without wanting something in return. In an instant and beyond her control, she drifted off into a peaceful sleep.

* * *

A bump jostled Silver awake and she opened her eyes. She grew immediately alarmed when she opened her eyes to complete darkness. The good reverend had slowly pulled into a darkened area on 125th Street's West Side Highway. She heard a giggle from the drivers' seat and snapped her head in its direction. Silver turned to see the good reverend nude from the waist down smiling as he masturbated. Fear instantly jolted her to reality as she stared at his eyes glistening in the darkness. She turned and felt for the door latch, but it had been removed. His smile now turned into a deranged scowl, as he slapped her hard across the face. In a panic, she attempted to jump into the back seat to seek refuge and an exit, but was stopped cold when he grabbed her by the neck with his large hands and slammed her back in her seat. She looked back at him and froze when she saw him rubbing his genitals faster and faster while saliva ran down his purplish blubbery lips. Her mind raced as she tried to think of a plan when he punched her in the mouth. Bleeding and cringing in pain, Silver threw up her hands in submission.

"Okay, okay, mister, don't hit me no more... I'll give you some...please just don't hit me no more." She tried to calm him like she had Tommy – but this wasn't Tommy. Anger flashed across his face and he began to hit her with a barrage of punches.

"No...No...No...! That's not how it's done! That's not how it's done! You are supposed to be afraid of me...afraid of me...now I can't fuckin' cum!"

A deadly shiver raced down Silver's spine as she stared frightfully into the crying man's face – he was crazy! He breathed heavily and looked at her with disgust.

"I should kill you right now for ruining it!"

Silver quickly pleaded with him. "Mister, please, I can do it.... I can do it." She tried to placate him and give him what he wanted.

"Oh, please mister, help ...don't hurt me!" He eyed her suspiciously while arms folded, and smugly said "I don't believe you...you're nothing but a whore like the rest of them...and since you are a whore, I'm going to treat you like one and fuck you in the ass."

Fear deflated her as she once again tried the door. He yanked her back. With one hand wrapped tightly around her neck instantly cutting off her airway, the other ripped off her blouse and pants. He literally began chewing on her neck, breasts and nipples. Nauseous fear overwhelmed her as she felt his teeth gnaw painfully into her flesh. Unable to match his brute-like strength and no longer able to breathe, she grew light-headed. Just as she was about to pass out, she saw a flash of movement behind the reverend and then his head hitting the ceiling of the car while being snatched out like a rag doll. Relief instantly flooded through her as air once again filled her lungs.

Gasping for air, she leapt from the vehicle and saw her molester being brutally beaten by a single individual. Covering her exposed, bleeding breasts, Silver wasn't taking any chances to wait for the outcome. Off balance, Silver ran for dear life as she tripped and fell as she scampered away. It was then, when she froze when she heard the Reverend beg for mercy.

"Chance! Please Chance, don't kill me! Don't do it man!"

His words reverberated through her like a bombshell. She turned in time to witness the orange and white flash of gunfire that ended the violent struggle. Scared and confused, Silver walked like a sleepwalker toward the still standing man, unsure what to expect. She spoke nervously. "Chance?" He slowly turned around and looked toward her, and for the first time in over five years, she gazed into Chance's beautiful eyes again. Without a word, she slowly walked towards him and placed her head against his chest as they cradled each other tightly.

Chapter 20

The Reunion

Driving under a highway overpass in silence, Silver stared at Chance as he navigated his jeep into traffic. She spoke first. "It was you I saw that day in the car." Chance continued driving, not looking at nor answering her. "That was you, right?" He stopped for a light in front of the McDonald's on 125th and Old Broadway, and looked at her.

"Are you hungry?"

"A little, how did you know?"

He gave her a smile. "Either that or we have a growling lion in here with us."

He pulled into the drive through, where they ordered food, opting to eat in the parking lot and talk. Chance smiled as he watched her wolf down her Big Mac and super-sized fries and a soft drink. Catching his eyes, she realized just how she must've looked and apologized with a mouth full of food. Sarcastically, Chance put his hand to his ears.

"Excuse me, I don't understand you with a mouth full of food."

Silver smiled as she remembered that this was exactly how they had met in the cafeteria five years earlier, then looked down and laughed.

"Um Silver… I ask but one thing, and that is for you to look at me when I am talking to you."

The comment made them both laugh. After eating, Silver told Chance everything that happened over the years since they had last seen each other. Time flew by quickly, and they didn't notice the sun was starting to rise. They seemed to realize it at the same time and looked toward the radiant amber and orange hues of dawn that engulfed the horizon. She felt enthralled and turned to look into Chance's eyes, until she slowly edged closer toward him. A harsh knocking on the car window startled her. It came from the Manager of the McDonalds.

"Excuse me, we have a two hour parking limit," he said, pointing to his watch.

"Okay man," Chance said, and turned on the ignition. "Damn, we was talking for nearly five hours."

She smiled while an awkward, uncomfortable silence followed.

"Silver, I don't know how you feel about this, but you can stay with me if you want."

Silver looked at Chance. "I don't know, you look like you might get in trouble with your girlfriends if I stay with you."

Chance smiled at the comment but assured her that he had no girlfriend. "It's just one thing."

She smiled. "What, I have to put out?"

"No Silver," he said seriously. "I would never do nothing like that to you." He looked down. "I don't have much at my place, you know, it's just me."

"Is that all?"

He nodded. "That's it."

Chance lived a good distance away from where he set up shop in Harlem. He owned a one bedroom Co-op in the Fordham section of the Bronx. His mentor A.O., hip him to the game of not shittin' where you eat, only invested his money in real estate. So Chance paid a lady from the neighborhood $5,000 to purchase the place for him when he was sixteen years old. He slipped the doorman a hundred dollars a month to keep his mouth shut and to give him a head's up on any questioning outsiders. This would be the first time he had a guest in his apartment. Chance actually owned two brownstones in Harlem that were now worth almost fifty times the amount he paid A.O. for them. A.O. owned so much property in Harlem that he simply sold the two properties to Chance for the same amount that he paid for them thirty years earlier. Chance had listened to everything A.O. had told him over the years and it all proved to be invaluable.

Over his lifetime, A.O. had recruited and trained a number of great hustlers and killers into the underworld. Most of them were mere boys, usually in their early teens when he recruited them. Two of them had been Hollis and Chance. He had taken them under his wings and saved them from the streets or jail. He had taken a special interest in Chance because he had known his mother and father over good and bad years. He had seen how Chance, after his mother started spazzing on alcohol, had tried to hold it together for himself and his little sister. On the other hand, he had first seen Hollis when two local boys teased and harassed him because he was homeless, with dirt caked all over his skin. Hollis' hair had been so coarse and dirty that parasites lived in his hair, causing blistered patches in his head. The two boys relentlessly harassed Hollis until one day, one of the boys made the mistake of pulling a knife on him. Hollis pulled out a knife of his own, only bigger, and cut one of them with it. From then on, nobody bothered the homeless boy.

Both boys were loyal to A.O., until he died a natural death which was a major feat being who he was and the things he been through. A.O. was a throwback gangster who was part of Bumpy Johnson's Era. When he was ten years old, he and his older brother had been employed by Bumpy as 'spotter's' or 'point boys', that's someone who keeps an eye out for police or other gangsters plotting a hit or something, bootleg corn whiskey shit and number running for pennies. They had the bootleg whiskey game down to a science when prohibition was instituted. When alcohol became legal again, they just switched to the numbers racket, which he co-owned throughout Harlem with a powerful member of the Mafia. Though the brothers never mentioned it, they were also the silent and most powerful partners of Nicky Barnes. Toothless and all, A.O. would smile every time he heard someone mention that Nicky Barnes was the kingpin of Harlem.

While Nicky had met his demise in the game, A.O. remained untouched simply because he was untouchable, because he was smart. He stayed clean no matter what. Sure, the F.B.I. knew his name, but they didn't know his face. No one even knew what A.O. stood for, nor would he tell them. It was as if he didn't exist, because he didn't have a birth document or social security number. A.O. was less than 5' feet 3" tall and weighed about 125 pounds, but he was a person throughout Harlem that the gangsters mortally feared. They feared him not because of what he could do to them, but what he would do to others – and that's what gave him the advantage. A.O. was the type of man that had a prerequisite before you worked for him or did business with him – he demanded the names and addresses of your entire family, including any who lived down south and even the school your kids went to. See, if you fucked over A.O., he would murder your entire family and let you live, which was worse than a thousand deaths itself. He mastered the art of psychological warfare and used it to his advantage.

The reason A.O. remained on top all those years was because no one had the heart or will that it took to do what he was willing to do. He learned this art from an old associate of his from Sicily, who proved to be an invaluable tool to offset traitors and snitches. It was said that A.O. was the only Negro allowed to ever sit in with all of the Five Families of New York. A.O. did it all, saw it all and out-lived them all.

A.O. supplied the entire heroin trade in Black and Spanish Harlem, and distributed to major players in certain area of the Bronx and Brooklyn. The way the operation worked was that they had a designated pick-up and drop-off point for drugs and money. The drop-off for the money would always be the same, inside a rented apartment in a tenement building that only he had a key to. But the pick-up point would be a different place every time. At the drop-off apartment, he would leave the money and take the envelope with the location of the shipment sealed inside. That was it. Nice, safe and clean. Which is why A.O. survived that long in the business, because he never made contact with the other party.

He trusted Chance enough to make him the pick-up and drop-off man, trusting him with millions of dollars. When A.O. died, Chance thought that the life and operation that he had come to know so well would end, but it didn't and Chance assumed sole responsibility. Chance had money, but you would never know it by the way he lived so modestly. He never shined or propagandized his wealth. That was just one of the many pieces of advice A.O. passed down to Chance. It wasn't that A.O. didn't trust Hollis, it was that he didn't have that measure of intelligence that Chance had, which was imperative in his trade. However, A.O. was impressed with Hollis' primary skill — murder. He told Chance once that never in his sixty years in the business had he seen a person with Hollis' ruthless passion for death and carnage. He was a born killer, and that was why he allowed him to form a contract-killing ring that Hollis had run since the tender age of sixteen.

* * *

Inside Chance's building, he stood at his door with Silver, about to enter his apartment. He took a deep breath and opened the door. "Well, this is it."

Silver walked in, looked around the large, unfurnished apartment and smiled. "How long did you say you've been living here?"

He shrugged. "About three years."

The apartment was as empty as the day he moved in, with not so much a chair or table.

"Oh, I didn't have a chance to furnish the place yet." He smiled sheepishly. "I just ain't have a need to. The bedroom is hooked up though."

He showed her to the bedroom, which was nearly as big as the living room, only it contained a bed, a table with a lamp on it, and a dresser topped with a dusty, 19-inch color television set that looked like it hadn't been used in years. The room was also filled with books, stacks and stacks of them. Silver grew awestruck, as she looked on the walls and saw dozens of drawn images that looked like her. She turned to Chance. "Chance, is that…?"

He looked at the wall and nodded. "Yeah."

Silver was dumbfounded that Chance still felt the same way about her as she felt about him over the years.

"Silver, I never forgot about you. I thought about you every single day."

She looked up at him. "I thought about you every day too, Chance. I prayed that this day would come." They gazed into each other's eyes and kissed as if they would never see each other again.

Settled in Chance's apartment, Silver felt safe and secure for the first time in months. Chance was a real gentleman too, and had the entire apartment remodeled. In addition to a living room and bedroom set, he ordered cable, a VCR player and two 60-inch television sets to keep Silver from being bored. Silver said he shouldn't have done it, but he just said he had ordered them before she arrived. The once empty kitchen and refrigerator were now filled to the max. Chance took care of his business by day and came home by night. Silver would surprise him with a home cooked meal, and then they would spend the entire night talking. Chance, whose favorite pastime was reading famous American Writers like Yeats, Baldwin, Faulkner,

Orwell, Woolf, and Angelou, kept Silver up late at night while he read to her. Silver was mesmerized and enthralled by his powerful readings and vast knowledge of subjects. Though Silver was in the ninety percentile in the city, she knew that she was not even close to Chance's league. He had extensive knowledge in Astronomical Science, Philosophy, Literature, World History and Economics. She was baffled, but then, she always had been when it came to Chance.

Silver and Missy hooked back up and she updated her with the new developments. When Missy finally saw Chance face to face again, she couldn't believe her eyes. She joked with Silver that she had better give his fine ass some pussy before she let him get away, but as usual, Silver told her to mind her business. Silver had already thought this through in her mind, and didn't want to lose Chance ever again. With Missy's freak ass pushing her to do it every day, it became hard for her to resist.

In the meantime, Silver received word from Missy that the manager from 'Wendy's' had called and left a message for her to come in to work. Chance told Silver there was no need for her to work if she didn't want to because he would give her all the money she needed. Silver would have felt morally wrong to accept money from him knowing where it came from. He understood, so Silver began working the 3 to 11 shift in midtown Manhattan. Chance was there every night to drive her home so she didn't have to ride the train home late at night. With her first check of $113.18, she gave Chance $50.00 for rent. He declined, but she assured him that she would rather pay her own way, that she would feel much better for doing so. Reluctantly, and even though he surely didn't need it, he took it.

Friday night, on her day off, she made up her mind. Tonight was the night she was ready to seduce Chance. She even planned it out and went to Macys, where she purchased some inexpensive laced lingerie and some perfume. To top things off, she bought some candles for a romantic dinner. When Chance arrived home, the place smelled of delicious baked chicken, stuffing and with broccoli with cheese sauce. He was impressed, but after dinner she knew he would be even more so. Silver really went all out; she even filled the tub with apple-scented bubble bath, and had his slippers ready. When Chance finished taking a bath, he entered a candle lit bedroom with some Luther coming from the speakers.

Silver lay seductively across the king-sized bed wearing a red-lace sexy baby doll and thong. Chance stared at her until she felt the heat of a blush warm her face. He finally seemed to gather the nerve to approach. She reached for him and pulled him next to her, gazing into each other eyes, while the flickering candles maximized the romantic ambiance. Her heart was beating fast as they edged closer until their lips met. Silver's nipples hardened two folds as she felt Chance's butter soft lips, then his hot, lustrous tongue entered her mouth. A strong yearning overwhelmed Silver as his soft, magnificent hands explored her body, causing millions of tingly sensations to invade every inch of her body. Never before had someone touched her in such manner, so soft, so right, and as she lay back and closed her eyes, she felt helplessly caught in blissful heaven. Never in her life would she have imagined that such feelings were possible.

"Silver," Chance whispered. "I ...I've never made love before."

Eyes closed, Silver smiled and also confessed. "Me neither, Chance." She turned and urged him to lie on his back and began to sensuously kiss his chest and neck, causing him to breathe heavily. Unable to take it anymore, he flipped her on her back and returned the favor by softly nibbling on her ears, her lips and then down to her neck, all the while expertly moving his hands all over her body. Breathing rapidly and about to bursts, Silver cried out. "Put it in...put it in..." Moments later, she felt Chance's hot manhood slowly enter her, causing her to gasp. Seeking refuge from the pain, she squeezed his hands tighter and tighter as they found their rhythm. Chance slowly filled her with every inch of himself as a stream of her juices burst freely. As the pain ebbed, she gradually widened her legs with each thrust, inviting more and more of Chance inside of her. Tears begin to fall from her eyes as the erotic pain turned into euphoric pleasure. A new world opened for them both, as they became a perfect combination in an imperfect world. What a feeling, to love somebody who loved you back as much.

During the weeks that followed, Silver and Chance were inseparable, redefining the meaning of real love and affection that had eluded them both for so many years. So much so, that Silver made a silent commitment to never lose Chance again, because with him she never felt so complete and without him she would be so incomplete.

For a person to be totally alone in this big old world, by themselves with no family to lean on, makes you hold onto the one true person that you have. Silver and Chance spent many nights talking about their future, but a single problem ultimately caused a conflict within Silver, and that was Chance's lifestyle and business. Silver was morally opposed to anything that had to do with drugs and tried to convince Chance that there were other ways of making a living, because he was extremely intelligent. She even encouraged him to pursue his education. Reluctantly, Chance explained to her that it was not that simple to walk away from his business because he was in bed with the Italians, and to do so would be a sure death. Over the next few weeks, Silver nevertheless steadily tried to convince Chance to give up his lifestyle.

"Silver, why do we got to keep going over the same thing?"

"'Cause what you doing is wrong, baby. You better than anyone should know how it destroys families."

"I ain't ruining nobody's life. I ain't putting no gun to nobody's head, forcing them to shoot that shit in their veins!"

"You might as well, you push it and that's the same thing."

"I don't make them do shit they don't want to…shit, they grown!"

Silver shook her head in disappointment. "You know what, Chance…it is so easy for us to look at these addicts and not have compassion for them and write them off by saying they're grown, but what about the one's you don't see, Chance? Do you remember? The ones like you and me… your little sister – do you remember? If you can't relate to the grown ones, you can at least know what's it like for the children to suffer… is that what you want?"

Chance angrily shook his head. "No, that's not what I want, but that's just how fucked up this fucked up world is. The same fucking world that breaks up your family. The same world that puts you in the home of a rapist who does things to you that you still can't get out of your head and the same fucking world that throws you in jail where a pack of fuckin' bastards fuck you so bad that you have to get your fucking asshole stitched up! Then…just when you finally heal, you *once again* have to get stitched up 'cause they ripped you open again."

He stared at her as if he'd just lost his mind. Before she could speak, he continued. "Then, after awhile, you get smart and learn you got two options, either fight or you get fucked...well, guess what? I got tired of getting fucked, so I fought...no strike that...I fuckin' *killed* their asses! All of them, one by one!"

Silver watched mutely while Chance relived the horrors of juvenile hall.

"One night, I decided to get them before they got me. So I smuggled in a spoon, sharpened that bitch up nice and good, and went from bunk to bunk and stabbed each one of them motherfuckers in their throat – five of them – until they choked on their own blood! The courts wanted to put me away for life, but since they saw the pictures from the infirmary with my asshole hanging out, they figured I was the victim, that it was self-defense. I wasn't charged, but they don't just let a nigger off that easy, so they threw me in a psychiatric ward and filled me with so much fucking medicine that I didn't even know my fuckin' name or what fucking year it was, and then they wondered why I was crazy! Fuck that! Nobody gave a shit, so I don't give a shit either! It's sink or swim and I'm tired of drowning!"

Silver was taken back by his revelations but remained strong for his sake. "But Chance, don't you see? You had no control. You are not responsible for your past, but you're definitely responsible for your future...and you have choices."

"Choices? What choices?" Chance repeated exasperated.

"The choice to be who you were destined to become!" She took Chance by the hand. "And it's definitely not the purveyor of death and destruction to families!"

Chance looked up, speechless.

Chapter 21

The Dis

The summer seemed to go by swiftly and Silver forgot about her scholarship. She waited in front of Missy's building on 128th and 7th Avenues for her to drop off her bags so they could head up to the Bronx to meet Chance. Silver and Chance were actually going out that night on a formal date for the first time and she wanted to look nice for the occasion. Chance had offered to give Silver a thousand dollars to go shopping, but like always, she refused to accept 'that' money. She had no problem spending the money she received from Wendy's, even though it was barely over $150.00. Chance was going to take Silver to the best soul food restaurant in Harlem, Amy Ruth's on 116th Street, just off of Lenox.

Things were going perfect and began to get better when Missy came running through the basketball courts outside her building with a big kool-aid smile on her face.

"What's wrong with you?" Silver asked. "You look like you're about to go mad."

"I'm not going anywhere," Missy said with a sly smile, "But you are, bitch."

Silver frowned in confusion. "What are you talking about?"

Missy pulled a letter from behind her back. "I'm talking about this letter from Spelman College...you're in!"

Silver's mouth dropped open before she regained her composure. "Did you read it?"

Missy shook her head. "No, I just know that you're in," she said proudly. After staring at each other for a moment, Missy shoved the envelope toward Silver. "Well, open the shit already!"

Silver looked at the letter and slowly opened it. Looking at Missy once more, she pulled out the letter and began to slowly read. She looked up from the letter.

"Silver, what does it say?" Missy said.

"I got it...I got a full scholarship to Spelman."

Jumping for joy, Missy didn't notice Silver was not as elated as she was. Spelman College was in Atlanta, Georgia. Since she and

Chance had been together, she had forgotten about the scholarship, but suddenly the reality of having to leave him again became a hard reality. She knew that Chance would put her feelings before his, even if it meant that he would suffer a thousand days before he would let her suffer one.

While Chance was in the shower, Silver re-read the letter over and over. She pondered whether or not to tell Chance, and then decided against it. As she stared at the twilight, she didn't notice Chance walk up behind her, wrapped in a towel.

"What are you reading?"

Silver was startled by his presence and quickly hid the letter behind her back. "Oh, just some junk mail I got from Missy's house." She balled up the letter, threw it in the trashcan and then smiled. "I hope you didn't use up all the hot water as long as you were in there."

He gave her a hug and kissed her forehead. "I wasn't in there that long, now get you fine ass in there before we don't make it to dinner."

She hugged him again and looked in his eyes. "Do you love me?"

"Do Muslims hate pork?"

She hit him coyly on the chest. "No, Chance … I'm serious."

He frowned. "Silver, what's wrong?"

"Nothing," she said, and turned her back on him.

Perplexed, he turned her around. "Silver, I know you, and if something is wrong I want to know about it."

Searching his eyes Silver spoke. "I…I didn't get a scholarship." She put her head down in shame at the lie, but Chance gave her a huge hug and assured her everything would be all right. She felt rotten about lying to him, but justified her actions by reasoning that she could always go to City College and still get her degree, someday. For now, she wanted to remain by her man's side.

After dinner and a movie and visiting several game rooms downtown, Silver was exhausted and decided to take a quick shower, ending the night in Chance's arms once again. While Silver was in the shower, the telephone rang.

"Hello," Chance said.

"Hey, Chance…how was y'all's first date?" Missy asked.

"It was nice, we had fun."

"So where is Ms. Thang?"

"She taking a shower, want me to tell her to call you back?"

"Naw...it's too late, I'm just calling to be nosey and find out how you took the news?"

He glanced over his shoulders and whispered into the phone. "Yeah, she told me. I feel bad that she didn't get into that school."

"Didn't get in...what are you talking about...she got in, she got a full scholarship and everything."

Chance froze.

"Chance, you there?"

Chance forced himself to answer. "Yeah, yeah, I'm still here."

"Oh shit," Missy groaned. "She didn't tell you?" She cursed again. "Chance, I'm sorry...I didn't know...oh fuck me!"

"It's okay," Chance said. "I must have heard her wrong." Chance knew exactly what was going on.

"Chance?"

"Yeah, I'm here"

"Chance, do me a favor and don't tell Silver I ran my big fucking mouth...okay? 'Cause she will kill me!"

"Alright no problem...listen I'll talk to you later, okay?"

"Alright," Missy mumbled. "Chance...I'm sorry."

Chance slowly hung up the phone and thought for a moment. Suddenly his eyes fell upon the garbage pail and he walked over to it and bent down to remove the balled up letter. He looked toward the bathroom and began too unfurl the letter.

As the days passed, Chance started coming home later and later, and then one day he didn't come home at all. Silver beeped him all day and he still didn't call back. Worried, Silver decided to call out from work and wait for Chance to come home. When he still didn't come home, she began to fear the worst and decided to take matters into her own hands. She went to 144th Street, where he forbid her to come. As soon as she got out of the cab, she saw Chance in front of his spot with a group of young thugs, shooting some Cee-lo. Silver slammed the door, causing everyone to look up.

One of Hollis' boys named Butterfly Ty spoke first. "Oh shit…one of y'all niggers ain't got ya hoe's in check… rollin' up here like police!"

"Fuck that shit," Hollis said. "Honey is bad as a motherfucker, she could roll up on me anytime."

"Word to mother…who bitch is that anyway?" asked Squeaky.

Chance, sitting on the stoop in the cut, slowly rose to his feet and walked to the curb. The niggers were shocked when it became obvious that she was his girl. They turned their heads, more than likely hoping Chance hadn't heard their comments, but he had. To them, this was a major event because they never had known him to slip like this. He always schooled them about the game, to never shit where you ate and always kept his shit tight – strictly business. So naturally, they wanted to see how he handled his own shit.

"Chance!" Silver yelled. "Where have you been? I didn't know if you were dead or alive!"

As if it was no big deal, Chance shrugged. "I was taking care of some business, I was busy."

Silver frowned. "You so busy that you couldn't even pick up the phone to let me know if you were okay?"

All eyes were focused on Chance and he knew it. He knew that for business purposes, the outcome of this situation was imperative to his leadership position. He knew that something as little as not handling your bitch was a direct sign of weakness that street niggers took to heart. Bottom line was if they saw weakness, they would forever play on it, which could lead to your downfall. The next day, that shit would spread like wildfire, 'cause the streets are always watching and probing for a nigger's weakness. Niggers would say, *'Chance, that nigger from 144th Street, is pussy, he let a hoe chump him'*, or get the information twisted (which they always do in the ghetto). *"Yeah, I heard that Chance, that nigger from 144th Street, got his ass whup by three trick bitches who jump out of a cab on him the other night and then robbed the punk ass nigger'.* No matter how wrong it could be, the talk still jeopardized your rep, and this was all that was needed for a nigger to come and test you. But Chance wasn't that type of person. He offset all that shit by not giving them an opportunity to test him. One time and one time only, which is what A.O. had taught him and Hollis, and that was all that a nigger got.

Chance however, had other reasons to play the role that none of them would ever understand. "Look," Chance said. "I'm grown, I don't need nobody fucking clocking me."

Silver looked at him. "Chance, what has gotten into you? Why are you talking to me like that?"

"Because I can," Chance barked. "And don't be fucking rolling up on me out here with that other shit!"

"Chance, I'm just seeing if you are okay, 'cause I didn't hear from you in almost a week!"

"Now you see me," Chance snapped. "Now take your dumb ass home!"

Surprised, Silver looked around at everyone watching. "When will you be there?"

" I be there when I'm ready. As a matter of fact, what you need to do is start finding someplace else to live, 'cause I'm not feeling this shit no more, you know what I'm saying?"

Tears filled Silver's eyes. "Are you serious?"

He looked her straight in the eyes. "As motherfuckin' cancer!" Unable to look in her eyes any longer, Chance turned away. "I'm gonna stay at a hotel until you're gone."

Silver blinked back the tears and pleaded. "Chance, baby let's go somewhere and—"

"Bitch," Chance coldly interrupted. "I already told you I ain't feelin' you no more, so get your shit out my house and bounce!"

Silver stared at him in disbelief and then slowly backed away, clutching her body as if to hold it together. She fought to hold back the tears, but lost as she hailed a cab. As the cab arrived, she opened the door and looked back one final time.

Chapter 22

Four Years Later
Spellman College Campus Atlanta, Georgia

College life was everything Silver had hoped it would be. Over her entire four years in college, she again maintained impeccable grades, in spite of working two part-time jobs. She hardly ever went out or attended frat parties or dances, and during her four years away, she hadn't once come back to New York to visit.

Besides brief conversations with Missy over the telephone from time to time, New York ceased to have existed for her. Missy was now a big time dancer in some of the hottest Broadway plays. Silver always asked Missy to come down and visit, but she was always committed. Since the southern lifestyle was so good to Silver, she conceded that the easy going and friendly City of Atlanta was going to be her new home. But as fate had it, she was accepted to one of the best medical schools in the country, New York University Medical School. This was truly a dream come true, but with every dream there were a few glitches and one of them was that she was only receiving a partial scholarship. Even with government grants and stipends, she would still be short about $130,000 it would take to complete her training and education. That didn't worry her much though; just being accepted was the miracle. She would worry about the money later.

The graduation ceremony was beautiful. Looking out upon the sea of guests attending the ceremony, there wasn't one familiar face in the crowd, but when it was time to throw their caps in the air, Silver looked toward the sky. "We did it, Ma!" She threw her cap high in the air as hundreds of black graduation caps flew in the air like a flock of birds. Silver looked around at everybody kissing and hugging each other, smiled and took it all in. As quickly as the smile came, it was replaced by an overwhelming feeling of emptiness, a feeling that had followed her the last four years. She still missed Chance.

Silver arranged for Missy to pick her up at the bus station on 42nd Street. Missy now had her own apartment and her own car, so Silver didn't have to worry about not having a place to stay while she readjusted to life back in New York. Silver arrived first and was waiting on 8th Avenue between 40th and 41st Streets when she saw a black Honda Accord zoom to the curb and park. Immediately, an older white guy wearing a red cap approached the vehicle.

"Miss, this lane is for taxi cabs only."

Missy pulled her shades down, looked at the older man and sucked her teeth, dismissing him as if he wasn't even worth her comment. She glanced over the crowd, looking for Silver. The red cap approached her again.

"Ma'am, we have to keep it moving."

Missy tried to ignore him, but he was persistent.

"Ma'am, this is my final warning, we have to move!"

Angry, Missy turned on him. "Motherfucker, who the fuck is we? If you don't get your old funky ass out my face I'm going fuck you up!" Her voice dripped with venom as she stared the old man down until he backed away, not wanting any problems.

Silver watched the scene with a smile. "Same old Missy," she sighed. She picked up her bags and approached the car. When Missy spotted her, they both let out a big scream.

"What's up, bitch?" Missy squealed.

Silver dropped her bags and hugged her friend tightly. "What's up, Hoe!" They pulled apart and examined each other, admiring and hugging.

"Damn, I miss your yellow ass," Missy laughed.

"I miss your black ass too!" Silver smiled back.

They snapped out of their reunion when they saw the old skycap returning with a cop.

"Come on," Missy sighed, "Before these dumb motherfuckers want to tow my shit!" She popped her trunk and threw Silver's bags in and walked slowly to the front of the car. She took her time starting the engine.

"You got to go this minute," Red Skycap said.

Missy looked at him and the cop. "We gotta to go, huh? Why don't you try sittin' on his dick and pedal his balls, bitch?" She peeled rubber while giving both of them the finger.

Looking through the rear view mirror, Missy laughed.

"Yo, you still crazy as hell!" Silver shook her head.

"And you know it!" Missy admitted. She glanced at Silver. "Miss College Fucking Graduate...Go 'head girl, you did that shit!"

Smiling from ear to ear, Silver looked down and felt the heat of a blush warm her cheeks. Missy lit a cigarette and bragged like a proud parent.

"That's right; my girl has made something of herself...at least somebody made it out this motherfucker." Missy shrugged as she blew out the smoke.

"What are you talking about?" Silver came to her defense. "You're a Broadway dancer girl...you're doing real well."

Missy smirked. "Silver, I do work on Broadway, and I am a dancer, but not the kind you're thinking."

Confused, Silver didn't have a clue what she was talking about. Missy looked at her and smiled.

"Damn, bitch, you must've really been in the backwoods down south...I'm a stripper!" Silver didn't know what to say.

"Don't worry," Missy assured her. "It's only temporary until I find work, and besides, a bitch get paid for shaking her ass in front of them hard up niggers. I make sometimes five, six hundred dollars a night."

Silver's eyes widened. "Damn, in one night?

Missy smiled proudly. "Yep!" She glanced at Silver. "So what's next with you...you gonna move back here...you gonna get a job or what?"

"Oh, I guess I didn't tell you."

Missy threw her cigarette out the window. "Tell me what?"

"I got accepted into medical school here in New York."

The car suddenly screeched to a halt. Missy stared at her. "Silver...stop playin! For real?"

With a slight smile, Silver nodded. Unable to contain herself, Missy jumped out of the car in the middle of traffic and began jumping for joy at the good news. Smiling widely at Missy's jubilation, Silver couldn't be happier that her best friend was so happy for her. Jumping back into the car, Missy screamed.

"You fucking bitch! You really did that shit...I'm so fucking proud of you, Silver!"

"Thanks girl, I know you are." They embraced again.

Missy smiled. "Oh shit...me and my girl back together again...shit!"

Silver changed the subject. "So how's mom's duke's doing?"

"Talking the same old shit and still have them niggers laying up with her, she ain't change."

"What about your grandma?"

Missy chuckled and lit up another cigarette. "Grandma...shit, still fucking everybody's man in the project and still blazing more trees than me."

Silver laughed. "Still?"

"Hell yeah, still ghetto...man, if I can get one wish, I would move all of them out of them projects and break that 'perpetual ghetto cycle that my family is cursed with."

"Oh...what's up with Diego?"

Missy smiled. "Diego...shit, girl, I ran into that nigger a couple of years back and he lost all that baby fat and he was looking good as a motherfucker, yo."

Silver watched Missy smile lustfully. "Then what happen?"

"What you think?" Missy snapped, seemingly insulted by the question. "I fuck the shit out of that nigger!"

Silver giggled her ass off. "You fucking hoe—"

"You fuckin' right, bitch, ain't shit better than getting virgin dick and bid dick!"

"What the hell is bid dick?" Silver asked in curiosity.

"Oh, that's when a nigga just comes home from doing a bid in jail. Them nigga's be puttin' a hurtin' on the pussy yo, have a bitch waterfalling all night like Niagara fuckin' Falls."

Silver laughed again. This is what she missed most about her homegirl; she kept everything real and said what other girls' only thought. "Then what happened?"

"Well, me and him hooked up for a minute, but he was too fucking possessive, and I ain't living like that. I had to kill that shit quickly, fast and in a hurry! Besides, that nigger was still a mama's boy, he was too slow for me...but yo...guess what I found out."

"What?" Silver asked, almost afraid to ask.

"That nigger's uncle got the entire Washington Heights on lock!"

"What do you mean...on the drug tip?" Silver asked.

"Yep…and I ain't talking some street corner hustle shit, I'm talking pushing fucking elephant weight!"

"So you saying Diego is in the drug business now?"

"Hell no…his momma would kick his ass, that nigger work at the airport as a baggage handler."

They both laughed, and then Silver inquired about little Beasley.

"Beastly?" Missy said. "Oh, that nigger really changed. He's got his own locksmith company."

"So what's wrong with that?" Silver said.

"That's just a front… that nigger is a fucking cat burglar!"

Silver's mouth dropped open. "You're lying."

Missy shook her head. "Nope, I'm talking cracking safes and scaling buildings downtown with them whitey's and shit."

"*Little Beasley?*" Silver asked again, just to make sure.

Missy nodded. "Little Fucking Beasley!"

* * *

Missy lived in a nice, spacious two-bedroom apartment across the street from Central Park on 110th Street. Silver was impressed with her apartment. "Damn girl, how the fuck you afford to live like this?"

Missy smiled slyly. "I got a few friends." She opened a bedroom door. "This is your room, and you don't have to worry, I put all new blankets, sheets and pillows on them for you, 'cause my lil' sister used stay here with me for awhile until she started bringing them nappy head niggers up in here fucking and shit."

"Lil' Shay? She ain't nothing but thirteen!"

"Twelve," Missy snapped. "But that don't mean shit with these lil' bitches these days…spreading their lil' cooch open for anybody."

"That's fucked up!" Silver said sadly.

"Who you telling, but what can I do? Anyway, the towels are in that closet and the kitchen is over there if you get hungry, and here's my cell number in case you need me." Missy turned and headed out the door.

"Where you going?" Silver asked.

"Oh shit…I forgot to tell you, I got a date, but I'll be back in a few hours, so wait up for me, 'cause we got a lot of things to catch up on, okay?"

Silver smiled. "Okay."

Besides stripping, Missy supplemented her income by having sex with Big Willie niggers who weren't afraid to spend money for a good piece of ass. Most of her clientele were Dominican drug lords from all over Washington Heights. These Dominicans, over the years, now supplied 90% of the cocaine trade in New York City. They knocked them other nigger's out the box by offering a stronger and cheaper product, causing everyone else to retire. If any niggers in the city wanted to buy some weight, they now had to go through the Dominicans.

For Missy, this was a match made in heaven because once she threw her snapping turtle-like pussy on them; they become one step from wanting to marry her ass. But Missy made that shit known that she wasn't wifey material – only 'Strictly Rental' for the gushy pussy. As an added incentive, she had access to all the cocaine that she wanted. They threw that shit at her because the more Missy sniffed, the freakier she got, and she took full advantage of it. The disadvantage was that she had developed a huge coke habit in the process. In front of them, she sniffed all she wanted, but behind closed doors, she hit the glass pipe. Even though they sniffed coke also, they had a rule to never smoke it. Furthermore, they would not respect or fuck with a woman who smoked the shit, so she became an undercover crackhead.

Chapter 23

King Papone

King Papone was a rotund, thick-necked Puerto Rican in his forties, but looked closer to fifty because of bad eating habits. He had the goriest pair of eyes that you ever saw, that burned through you like a snake. At the moment, he sat in one of his many so-called offices, which were really in abandoned buildings in Spanish Harlem. He was the second largest distributor of heroin in New York, behind Chance's organization.

Hollis had completed dozens of killing contracts for Papone over the years, primarily low level dealers from the black side of Harlem or freelance dealers trying to set up shop without his approval. Hollis sat on an old plastic milk crate and listened to Papone ramble, as he always did. Standing next to King Papone was his ever-present, henchman slash bodyguard 'Lugo', a huge, grim-faced man. Hollis was unsure of his race, but he had a hawk's stare, and at the moment was eyeing Hollis carefully. A smiling Papone was speaking to Hollis with a thickly broken English accent.

"I goin' to give you a opportunity of a lifetime...I give you a shot, amigo...you crew show me loyalty...I like dat. " Never losing eye contact with Hollis, Papone shook his head, his facial expression changing every second. "You want to know how I made it to the top and stay de top, amigo?" Searching Hollis' face, he continued. "What ...you think 'cause day like me 'cause I hell of a guy?" Papone's friendly demeanor vanished. "Fuck, no!" he shouted. "Because I the most ruthless and dirtiest son-o-bitch in de world!" He shrugged. "Have to be...in dis bidness. They pull de knife, I pull de sword. They used de gun, I used de bomb, they try to fuck me, and I will fuck them and bury them and a year later I dig they ass up and fuck dem again! Really Chico, I stick my fucking dick through they fuck eyes and skull fuck dem!"

Hollis just stared at him as he continued.

"You see de difference, my friend? To me it's all de same." He spoke in Spanish. "Man, woman or child. They gotta go, they gotta go...Matenlos!"

Hollis felt the ominous presence of the Devil himself in the room, in Papone's image.

"I trust no one but me and my mother and I still cut the deck on that bitch!" He shrugged again. "So I guess I only trust myself." He chuckled.

Hollis remained quiet, admiring the man's coldness. In an instant, Papone turned on his charm, along with a wide smile.

"Enough about me amigo, dis is about you…your organization, huh?" Papone stood up and shrugged yet again. "Personally amigo, I like you." He nodded approval before he continued. "I like you and your brother, Chance…but I don't like your associates." He frowned. "To be blunt, I think you guys are being used. You do all the hard work and they reap all de treasures."

Papone paused and watched Hollis. He was a master of head games and deceit, and played on people's emotions and greed and used them to his advantage. He was simply planting a seed in Hollis's mind, and he would wait patiently until it grew.

"I don't know if you notice my friend, but there is no more Mafia as you once knew it, dat era was long ago, day no longer powerful. Hell…de Dominicans…El Flaco from Washington Heights, a mutual associate of mine, they are more powerful then them. What you got now is some ninety-year-old greaseball who uses you black boys like a Master uses his slaves…you a slave, amigo?"

Hollis glared at him.

"I didn't think so," Papone said. "You guys are boss…you hear me? Boss!" Nodding his head," he continued. "Now here's what I propose. Since you and your brother live in black Harlem, there's a lot of money to be made on coca, and if the right person can control all of it…ooh, amigo, sky de limit!"

He watched Hollis ponder this, and decided to drop the hook, line and sinker.

"All you guys got to do is cut dem Italians off, dat way I handle de heroin and you guys handle all de coke. We talkin' millions of dollars!"

Hollis stared at him. "So why are you so generous to me when you can make the money?"

"Conyo amigo," Papone said. "You forget you come to me. I just try mentor you. I got eye, I can see."

Hollis eyed him warily.

"Look amigo, you don't have to trust me and you shouldn't. I don't. Words lie, but math don't. It don't take rocket scientist to see dat you got what it take... you smart, you know de street, and most important, people fear and respect you."

* * *

A week past, but Silver hadn't once left the apartment. Missy was so busy with her life, she was hardly ever home, until one day, Missy walked into the house with a bright smile.

"Yo... get ready, we going out tonight!"

Silver was not in the mood for a party. "Naw...I don't feel like going out tonight."

Missy planted her hands on her hips. "Listen Silver, your ass ain't been out this house since you got here, so don't you think it's time for you to act you age instead of your temperature and have some fun?"

Silver thought about it for a moment than reluctantly spoke. "Naw...maybe I'll go with you next time."

Missy shrugged nonchalantly. "Okay, but Chance is gonna be there."

Silver froze and turned toward Missy, who now sat on the couch like she had the whole world in her hands.

"What did you say?" Missy remained silent and acted as if she was cleaning her nails. Knowing exactly what Missy was doing, Silver smiled. "Missy...what did you say about Chance?"

Missy sarcastically held her hand toward her ear. "Oh...did you say something?"

Silver rolled her eyes. "You heard me, Hoe!"

"Hoe? Look who's talking...as soon as I said that niggas' name, you came on yourself!"

Knowing Missy was right; Silver felt a flush of heat.

"Anyway...I was uptown taking care of some business and saw that motherfucker named Hollis, that dude you saw blast that nigger on 119th Street."

Silver shivered just thinking about it.

"...anyway, he was tryin' ta push up on me, and I'm ignoring his ass, so he started getting disrespectful. So I kept walking, 'cause that's one motherfucker that turns my skin, but then that nigga squeezed my ass like he's Mike Tyson or something. I was ready to cut that nigga on the other side of his face when Chance rolled up and checked him."

Silver instantly straightened at the mention of Chance's name as Missy continued.

"So we talking right, and I told him you was back in New York…and blah, blah, blah, he wants to see you!"

Not satisfied, Silver spoke anxiously. "What do you mean, blah, blah, blah?"

"Just like I said, I told him you were home and he wants to see you at the club tonight."

Silver rolled her eyes again and folded her arms across her chest. "That nigger got some nerve wanting to see me after he did that fucked up shit to me!"

"Silver, man…why don't you give the brotha the benefit of the doubt?"

"Benefit of the doubt" Silver said in surprise. "Benefit of the doubt? Missy, that nigger dissed me in front of all them nigga's and then put me the fuck out his house!"

Missy put her head down and spoke softly." How do you know he didn't have reason for doing it?"

Silver was ready to break on Missy but knew there was more than what she was telling her. Silver walked to her and put her hand on her shoulder. "What did you mean by that?" Missy couldn't look Silver in the eyes. "Missy, what are you not telling me?"

"Damn Silver…it was all my fault!"

"What are you talking about, Missy?" She lifted her friend's face.

"I was the one who told him that you got accepted at Spelman," Missy moaned, putting her head down again.

Shocked by the revelation, Silver stared at her.

"That night, when you and Chance went out, I called his house to ask you how your first date at Amy Ruth's was. He said you were in the shower, so I asked him how did he feel about you being accepted into the school…well, he said that you told him that you wasn't accepted." She looked up at Silver. "Silver, I didn't know you told him you wasn't accepted…how was I supposed to know?"

As Silver recalled the day, she thought about the letter she had thrown in the garbage can. He must have read it. All at once it began to make sense. Chance would have done anything in order for her to make it, even if that meant him losing her. A sudden epiphany overwhelmed Silver as she jumped up. "Yes!" she screamed. Missy looked at her as if she had gone crazy while she bent down and gave her a huge kiss on the cheek. "What time are we going?"

Missy looked momentarily confused. "About ten o'clock."

Silver looked at her watch. "Good...we got six hours to get ready." She hurried to Missy's room. "I'm gonna pick out an outfit out of your closet for tonight, alright?"

Missy frowned and shook her head. "Sure."

Silver picked out an expensive yet conservative Donna Karan outfit. This was no small task because it seemed like every outfit Missy had owned was tight – body huggers. While they got dressed they talked and laughed because it reminded them of their prom night, but this time Silver need not need to sneak around to do so. That moment was the first time Silver had thought about her grandmother since she had returned to New York. She promised herself that as soon as she got a chance, and the nerve, she would go and see her. But tonight, she had but one mission on her mind, and that was to fill the missing void in her life.

At the club, the girls took a table on the second level with a perfect view of the entrance. Silver sipped on a virgin Strawberry Daiquiri and sat impatiently, as it was close to midnight and Chance had yet to arrive. Silver, looking totally magnificent, had turned down dozens of guys who asked her to dance, unlike Missy, who started dancing as soon as she walked through the door. It was evident that Missy was a regular inside the club because the girls had yet to come out their pockets to even pay for a drink, nor had they paid to get in for that matter. Two full melting Daiquiris and a untouched bottle of Cristal on ice sat in front of Silver on her table, sent by admiring ballers. She glanced looked down at Missy, busy sexin' a nigger lovely as she shook her body, throwing the nigger her ass as if they were fuckin' right there on the dance floor.

Tired and frustrated from all the guys asking her for a dance, Silver decided to cut the night short and tell Missy she was ready to leave. As soon as she stood up she saw a familiar face walking through the door – it was Chance. Her heart nearly stopped when she saw him. He was dressed in black, sporting a baldy that seemed to glisten from the strobe lights. His mere presence and persona electrified the entire club as the crowd began to part as if he was Moses. They all knew who he was, a silent storm, the unofficial King of New York. Inside his arms he carried a large bouquet of red roses as he scanned the club. As if from a sixth sense, Chance looked up and saw her staring down at him. In an instant, he headed toward the staircase. Time suddenly slowed as she watched him stealthily walk up the stairs until he stood before her. It was as if Silver had met him for the very first time. What a difference four years has made since she last saw him, she thought. He was more refined and distinguished. It became quite obvious life was doing him well, and she felt his bulging muscles when they embraced. Neither had exchanged a word, as they could only stare and gaze into each other's eyes – they were both speechless. It wasn't until Missy, sweating profusely, came up to them that they broke eye contact.

"Ah sukey, sukey now...y'all two look perfect together!"

The ice was broken as they both looked toward the wide-eyed and smiling Missy, who ushered them into the booth.

"Now you two just sit down and do like Mary J. and reminisce and catch up on the old days while I get y'all something to drink." She looked down at the drinks already on the table. "Better yet, y'all deserve the best, compliments of all the suckers in the house!" She lifted a bottle of 'Bubb' and poured champagne into three glasses. She lifted her glass in the air. "I propose a toast."

Silver and Chance also lifted up their glasses, with embarrassed smiles. A guy rolled up on Missy and asked her for a dance, but she cast him an evil look.

"Can't you see we're in the middle of something?" She rolled her eyes and smoothly turned her attention back to Chance and Silver, shaking her head in disgust. "Niggers... anyway, as I was saying, I dedicate this night to two of my oldest and dearest friends, Silver and Chance, who if ever there were two people who belong together it is you two. I read something one day and it said *If you love someone and let them go and if they don't come back, it wasn't meant to be, but if you really love each other and let them go and they come back, they were truly, truly meant to be'.*"

The three lifted their glasses and sipped, except Silver who only smiled.

"And you two," Missy spoke softly. "You two really were meant to be."

Silver continued to stare at Chance while Missy continued.

"I ask only but one favor?"

Silver glanced curiously at Missy, who appeared to be near tears. "Anything, Missy," she promised.

"Promise me this will be the last time you two ever part?"

Silver again felt heat flush her face and then put her head down. After a moment, she looked up and nodded along with Chance.

Missy was not satisfied. "No! I want you both to say it out loud with a kiss on the lips."

Silver and Chance looked each other in the eyes, and electricity shot through her body. They both said yes and kissed each other while Missy looked on proudly.

"Okay, I'm gonna leave y'all two lovebirds alone to catch up, and hopefully y'all two can stay out tonight so I can get my groove on tonight, *'cause it's some cuties up in here that should be havin' my baby, baby!*"

Silver and Chance laughed at her brazen rendition of Biggie Smalls, but they both got the message.

"Now I'm going to the bathroom...hand me my purse, Silver."

Silver passed Missy her purse and watched her rush off to the ladies room. She then turned to Chance and smiled.

Inside one of the toilet stalls, Missy unraveled a small piece of aluminum foil filled with rocks of crack. She pulled out a glass stem, inserted a piece of crack inside it, and then fished around her purse. She pulled out her cigarettes and a lighter and lit one to mask the smell of the crack. Taking a quick, hard pull from the Newport, she placed it on the floor and nervously lifted the glass stem to her mouth and put the flame to it. She took a deep pull from the pipe and the stem crackled. Instantly, the euphoria of the drug invaded her body as her eyes widened and sweat oozed out her pores.

At their table, Chance and Silver made small talk. Silver seemed hesitant to talk about their parting four years earlier. He too, avoided the topic. "So how long you been back in town?" he asked.

Silver nearly had to yell over the loud music. "About a week."

Chance shook his head. "So how was Atlanta?"

"What?"

He edged closer. "How was Atlanta?"

She glanced at him. "It was nice, Atlanta is beautiful."

He nodded, and then looked down and saw Hollis at the bar talking to a girl. Chance never partied with his crew – ever. He tried to keep his business separate from pleasure and the only reason he was here tonight was because Missy told him Silver wanted to meet him here. Chance began to frown as he thought about how he and Hollis had seemed to be at odds lately over money.

Hollis wasn't getting many contracts these days, and because the way he tricked with different chicks every night, he was going broke. Hollis dogged Chance every day, telling him that these weak ass niggas' throughout Harlem were getting rich pumpin' crack while he starved. Hollis had a plan to extort or murder all other dealers and take over their spots. The way Hollis figured it, they should spread out and get a bigger piece of the lucrative crack business. Chance knew that it was fruitless to reason with him, so he stalled him by throwing him an extra two thousand a week, hoping to shut him up. Whenever Hollis saw him, he knew that it would be kickin' the same old shit.

After a few uncomfortable moments, he and Silver began to speak at the same time. They laughed over their timing.

"I'm sorry," Silver chuckled. "You go first."

"No, you first," Chance said.

"Missy said that you wanted to see me tonight."

"She told me the same thing about you." They both laughed when they realized Missy had set them up. He could tell something was on Silver's mind, something that needed to be said. She somberly looked at him.

"Chance, I need to know something before we go any further."

He said nothing, but waited for her to continue.

"Do you remember that night you dissed me in front of your friends and put me the hell out your house?"

Chance had known this was coming and sighed. "Yes," he said. "Let me explain." He frowned briefly.

"No, you don't have to explain a damn thing, Chance. I already know."

For a brief, painstaking moment, Chance wanted to beg for forgiveness, but Silver was speaking again.

"You did that because you loved the shit out of me, didn't you?"

Chance was at a loss for words. Silver grabbed his shirt and pulled him closer.

"Come here," she said and kissed him passionately. Her fingers caressed his face. "For four years, I tried to hate you." She looked deep into his eyes. "But I couldn't. So I did the next best thing and put you out of my mind. I never understood why you did what you did that night until tonight. You knew I had lied about the scholarship, didn't you?"

Chance nodded.

Silver shook her head. "You found out from Missy, and then read the letter I threw in the trash can." She paused, tears filling her eyes. "Chance, baby, you don't have to explain, I already know... you did what you did for me." She clasped his hands and placed them on her chest. "You put your feelings aside for me...for me, because you refused to allow me to lose focus on my life or dreams."

Chance broke in. "Silver, I love you more than I love myself, I always have. I knew that once you made up your mind to do something, that's it." He slowly shook his head. "What type of man would I be if I allowed you to do something like that? I wouldn't have been able to live with myself...I love you too, too much to be that selfish, so I did the only thing I knew to do...push you away."

Tears began to fall from Silver's eyes. The ambience could not have been better as the smooth and soothing voice of Sade filtered throughout the club. Chance caressed her face and kissed her tears away as she hugged him in return. "I'm sorry if I hurt you, Silver."

She laid her head in his chest and looked up at him "You know what?"

"What?"

She gestured toward the couples on the dance floor. "That's something that we never did before."

He glanced at the crowd below. "Dance?"

"Yeah, you want to?"

Chance shrugged. "Okay." As he stood, his cell phone slipped out of his coat pocket onto the floor, but he didn't notice as he took Silver by the hand and helped her scoot out of the booth. They walked down the stairs to the dance floor and then he cleared his throat. "Silver…I got something to tell you."

"What?"

"This is my first time."

"What, at this club?"

He grimaced. "No, this will be my first time ever dancing." She looked at him as if he were joking.

"Chance you never danced before?"

He shook his head.

"Don't worry, baby," Silver assured him. "I'm gonna hold you down no matter what."

She took him by the hand, led him to the middle of the floor, then took both his hands and wrapped them around her waist. She placed her arm around his neck. As if they were part of a finely tuned watch, everything fit perfectly – no instructions were needed. They danced through three slow jams by Sade, Luther and Teddy. Enough said. It was time to leave.

Chance whispered in her ear. "You ready?"

Silver nodded and said, "Let me go tell Missy we're leaving."

"Okay," Chance said. Silver handed him her purse and went upstairs to find Missy.

Silver disappeared upstairs, and then Chance felt a tap on the shoulder. He turned and saw Hollis smiling widely, a young girl behind him loudly smacking on chewing gum.

"Fuck you doing here, nigger?" Hollis asked, giving him a pound. "I thought yo ass don't get down like this and party with small timers?"

"Naw man," Chance grinned. "You know…nigger got to live sometime." Always suspicious, Hollis rubbed his chin.

"Nigger, you know goddamn well you on a pussy hunt! Where the bitch at?"

The girl Hollis was with stared seductively at Chance. Hollis made it sound as if he was a Willie ass nigga. Being the gold-digging hoe she probably was, she wasn't gonna let an opportunity like that slip by. Sticking out her bubbly chest, she continued to eye him as she spoke.

"Hollis, aren't you gonna introduce me to your friend?" She extended her hand out to Chance. "Hi, they call me Slim Goody."

Before Chance could shake her hand, Hollis slapped it away.

"Bitch," he looked at her as if she lost her mind, "If I wanted to introduce you to a nigga I would've. In the meantime, only speak when you spoken to and until then, shut the fuck up!"

Caught off guard, Slim Goody regained her composure and shook it off like a trooper. Still, Chance saw the malicious glint in her eyes.

"Bitches never know when to shut the fuck up," Hollis complained. "Anyway, nigga," he smiled. "So where is the bitch who got my brother nose wide the fuck open?"

"Come on, man," Chance said. "Stay out my business. You know I don't get down like that."

Hollis noticed Chance was holding a purse and jumped up and down. "Oh shit, this nigger is strung. She got you waitin' on the sidelines holding her purse like a straight bitch!"

"Fuck you, man, handle your business and stay the fuck out of mines!"

"Yo, come on man, you know I'm just fuckin' with you, but nigger, you better do like I do and treat all these broads like a prostitute, because that's all they are." He slapped the girl on her thick ass.

Chance grew bored. "Yo, I'm about to bounce." He gave Hollis a pound, but Hollis stopped him.

"Yo nigga, what's up with that thing I told you about? My man, Papone, wants to make us a sweet deal. We can put everything on lock."

Chance stared at Hollis while, like a fool, he continued bragging.

"Let's keep this shit gangsta, nigga, you know how I do. I already got these weak nigga's shook, all we got ta do is hook up with Papone. Give me the word and I'll air these fake Harlem bitches out, the Italians and whoever else, son! I don't give a fuck, I'm ready to touch sumtin' anyway."

Chance stared at him. "You know what nigger, you're a fucking idiot! You run your fucking mouth like shit is gravy." Chance looked at Slim Goody, then back at Hollis. "All it takes is one motherfucker to run their fucking mouths to the feds, and a nigga's is ass out. Nigger, I don't know what you're talking about, and even if I did, I wouldn't fuck with a stupid ass nigger who would get me trapped off!"

Hollis tapped his fingertips on the gun he had tucked in his waistband. Chance was the only person alive that could get away with talking to Hollis like that. Hollis wasn't afraid to die by any means, so it didn't matter to him. What mattered most to Hollis was maintaining the lifestyle that he led. He was a gangster and loved doing gangster shit, and he wouldn't give that up for anything.

Hollis merely smiled. "Aight nigger, you got it, I'll just handle my own shit. I was just giving a nigga an opportunity be independent from them Do-Wops. I guess some nigga's like being the fuckin' help."

Chance chucked him a sarcastic smile and walked away, though he glanced back once to see that Hollis' smile had evaporated. He heard Slim Goody speak to Hollis.

"Buy me a drink."

Hollis slapped her on the ass.

Walking toward the bathroom Silver saw Missy coming out quickly, walking as if she didn't notice her. "Yo Missy, you don't see me?" Silver yelled as she grabbed her by the arm. Panicky, Missy turned around and stared blankly in Silvers' face. Silver looked at her with shock and concern. "Missy what's the matter?" Sweating bricks and mouth twisted, Missy could barely speak. Silver backed up and looked her up and down. "What the fuck you been doing?" asked Silver "Umm…I sniffed a lil' bit of coke with my girlfriend inside the bathroom."

"Not for nothing, but that shit got you looking fucked up right now, let's go back in the bathroom to get you together." Silver took her by the arm and back into the ladies room.

In the bathroom, Missy came down from her high. Silver waited until she was presentable. She also knew from experience not to push or preach to Missy on the drug issue, because that would only make things worse. Addicts would slam the door on you in a minute, and so she promised herself she would wait until Missy was ready to talk. She gave Missy the once over. "Much better," she joked. "You think you can handle yourself now?"

"Girl, please," Missy said. "I just glad you gonna get some dick in your ass tonight, 'cause you starting to act like an old woman."

"Who said I was sleeping with him tonight?"

"Bitch, you ain't had no dick in four years. Don't even try it, 'cause you been creaming on yourself since I mentioned Chance's name."

Silver knew she was right. "Anyway hoe, I'm gonna go, you sure you're alright?"

"Girl, get ya ass on out of here before one of those scandalous ass bitches try to steal your man."

"Alright but, I'm gonna call you to make sure you got home okay."

"Sure, whatever you like."

Silver left, and then found Chance, who already had their coats in his arms. "You ready?"

Hollis sat at the bar, fingering the pantyless Slim Goody when he noticed Chance leaving with a good-looking woman. He stared at them and tried to remember where he had seen the light skinned girl before. He shrugged it off and got back to exploring the girl's insides.

As Silver and Chance left the club, a well-dressed and grim faced couple entered the club, a black male and a white female. It was obvious to everyone in the club that these were New York's Finest. Hollis spotted them immediately as they showed their badges to the bouncer. Hollis turned and smiled at Slim Goody. "Come on, luv, let's dance." He pulled her off the barstool.

"Okay," Slim Goody agreed.

Hollis pulled her closer into his arms while keeping his eyes on the detectives as they scanned the club. He looked down at her. "Yo ma, I want you to hold something for me."

She glanced up at him. "I hope its some cold cash."

Hollis watched the cops show a picture around. "Naw, baby...you close though. I want you to hold some cold steel." He discreetly showed her his nine-millimeter Desert Eagle. She looked at the weapon as if was a poisonous snake, shook her head and backed away.

"Naw, Hollis, I ain't fucking with you like that."

He grabbed her tightly by her waist and mashed the weapon into her ribs. "Bitch, if you don't slow your fuckin' roll, I'm gonna blow your fuckin' spleen out!" He watched the detectives get closer, looking from face to face. "Now police is right behind you, and I'm not getting caught dirty. If you fuck this up, I'm gonna have your crackhead momma and that baldheaded ass daughter of yours come the fuck up missing." Through gritted teeth, he continued. "Now spread your fuckin' legs – wide!"

Goodie stared wide-eyed up into Hollis' grim expression and had the good sense to realize his threat wasn't an idle one. She obeyed. Gun in hand, Hollis began working his hands up beneath the hem of her mini dress, searching for her vaginal cavity with his fingers. Suddenly, her eyes widened as he viciously shoved the weapon deep up inside her pussy, causing her to squirm in pain. He smiled as he pushed and probed. "You better stop moving, bitch, before this motherfucker pop off inside your ass and you won't be able to have no more them nappy headed lil' kids!" Just as he finished, the two detectives spotted Hollis and pushed Slim out of the way.

"Pierre Charles Joudan," the female detective said, flashing her badge. "You are under arrest!"

The black detective, already edgy, threw him up against the bar and handcuffed him. The female detective proceeded to check him for weapons and read him his rights. The black detective smiled.

"Pierre Charles Joudan, you are under arrested for the murders of Jorge and Marisol Jeminez." He turned Hollis around.

"I never heard of them," Hollis said in a bored tone."

The detective clutched his handcuffs tighter and looked Hollis square in the eyes. "Well, maybe you heard the name Awilda Jeminez? She was only three months old when she was shot... you sick bastard!" He pulled Hollis roughly off the bar. "Say goodnight to your friend."

Hollis glared at Slim Goody and then smiled. "Yo baby, keep that kitten tight, a'ight!"

"Let's go," the female detective said.

They escorted Hollis out of the club, leaving Slim Goody tight legged and sobbing silently.

Chapter 24

The Sin of All Sins

After driving about two-hours on the Pennsylvania Turnpike, Chance and Silver checked into the Hotel Gondolier in the Poconos for the weekend. The hotel included a heart shaped bed, blue waterfalls, and a Jacuzzi inside their room. Giggling as the cuddled, Silver searched for the bedside lamp, but Chance tickled her every time she reached for the light switch.

"Stop, Chance," she giggled. "I got to call and make sure Missy got home alright." She turned on the lamp and waited until her eyes adjusted, then picked up the phone and dialed Missy's number. While she waited for Missy to pick up, she affectionately rubbed Chance's chest. After the tenth ring, Silver glanced down at her watch. It was 8:34am. Missy should have been home by now. She dialed the number once again, no answer. She hung up the phone and turned to Chance. "I wonder where she could be this time of morning?"

After making love all night, Silver and Chance stayed up, talking and catching up on missed time. She told him about getting accepted at New York University Medical School, and how costly it would be, and how she planned to work three jobs if she had too. After she told him about everything going on in her life, she asked about his. Never inclined to speak about his business, Chance remained silent. Silver, still adamant about drugs, soon began questioning his dealing in drugs. She told him he was dealing in death and destruction, and how she honestly doubted if she could be with someone who pushed it.

"Silver, I don't sell it to no one, I'm just a messenger boy."

"Chance you cannot minimize what you do, nor can you sugarcoat it. No matter how you slice it, it's the same thing. It's death, baby. Why don't you just walk away from it while you still can? It's only a matter of time before something bad happens."

Chance turned away. "Silver, it's not that simple to just walk away, they don't get down like that."

"Who are they, Chance?" Looking at Chance for answers, she continued. "You told me before that you don't even know who it is that supplies you."

"Silver, it's just something's that you would never understand. We talking about the mob, a.k.a. the motherfuckin' Mafia!" Rising from the bed, Chance walked over to the window.

Sensing his pain, Silver walked over to him. "Then why don't we just pack up and leave New York?" She rubbed his bare shoulders and smiled. "Atlanta is beautiful all year round. And besides, I be damned if I let my man get away from me again!" Chance looked down at her, and she had to smile. She loved him to death.

"I fuckin' love you, girl!"

"I love you too boy, but …I just won't be able to take it if something happens to you, Chance."

* * *

At the Federal Court building in lower Manhattan, three large court officers led Hollis out the holding pen, to be arraigned. Twelve hours earlier, he had stood in a line up and was positively identified from behind a two-way mirror for the murder and execution of the Jeminez Family one year earlier. It appeared that the young kid who had been with Hollis at the time had spilled his guts to the police when he got arrested on his third felony drug charge, and was facing 25 years to life. He had made a deal.

Hollis fumed in the bullpen while he paced the floor, nervously waiting to appear before the judge for his arraignment. Hollis used his one phone call to call Chance on his cell phone, but he never answered. Hollis had been locked down for almost thirty hours now, and was pissed that he had to use a public defender to represent him. As he was escorted before the judge with his lawyer beside him, the copper double doors suddenly opened to display a well-dressed man in an expensive Armani pinstriped blue suit walk confidently toward Hollis' lawyer. After a brief discussion, Hollis' public defender handed his paperwork over to the newcomer.

The bailiff barked. "Court is now in session, The Honorable Patrice Roper is residing. Come to order." The Judge swaggered toward the bench and quickly reviewed the files in front of her while the bailiff continued. "Case on calendar, 427, docket number 3 in the case of Pierre Charles Joudan, charged in violation of US title 18 dash 848, three counts of capital murder."

The Judge stared down upon the court. "How does your client plead?"

"Not guilty your honor!" Hollis' new lawyers informed her.

Not impressed, the judge made a notation. "For the records, attorneys please state your names and addresses.

"Christina Richburg, Assistant District Attorney for the Southern District."

With a confident smile, Hollis's new lawyer spoke. "Good morning, Your Honor, Ms. Richburg and the Court. I am Allen Ginsberg of Ginsberg & Taft, 216 Park Ave.

Entering it in a document, the judge spoke again. "Any request for bail?"

The U.S District Attorney spoke up. "The government requests that because of the severity of the crime, that Mister Jourdan be held without bail."

Ginsberg quickly retorted. "Your honor, due to the fact that the people's case is based on a murder over a year ago, plus the fact that their information was given by a convicted felon, who happens to be incarcerated as we speak, we ask that Mister Jourdan be released on his own recognizance."

The D.A. was ready. "Your Honor, the fact that Mister Jourdan is not a naturalized citizen makes him a flight risk. Mister Jourdan has been arrested a number of times in connection with a notorious Harlem-based extortion, kidnapping and murder ring called The Young Guns."

Ginsberg was quick to respond. "Your Honor, I object and request that that statement be stricken from the record. My client has never been convicted of any crime, yet Ms. Richburg is attempting to prejudice my client in front of Your Honor."

The Judge stared sullenly at Ginsburg, and then turned to the D.A. "Ms. Richburg, this is an arraignment. We need only hear the government's position for bail, nothing more… strike Ms. Richburg's statement from the record."

Ginsburg smiled. "Thank you, Your Honor. Mister Jourdan has been gainfully employed at the same place for the last two years as a Youth Coordinator at San Clemente's Church in the Bronx." He turned and gestured toward an old priest who was at the moment being helped to his feet by Ginsburg's assistant. "Father Diaz is here to support Mister Jourdan morally and spiritually."

Hollis inwardly smiled as he watched the two men. The judge stared at the men, then at Hollis and his smiling lawyer.

"Bail is set at one hundred thousand dollars!"

'Thank you, Your Honor," Ginsburg said. He turned to shake Hollis' hand before Hollis was led away by three burly officers.

Silver and Chance had a wonderful weekend together. Chance told Silver that she would no longer stay with Missy; she was to stay with him. Silver was amazed with his assertiveness as well as flattered. He said he could no longer be apart from her, ever again, so he would help her pack her things. They found a parking space directly in front of Missy's apartment building and went upstairs. Inside, the apartment was silent. Silver called out for Missy, but there was no answer.

"Now where is this girl this time of morning? She never stays home." Silver and Chance walked into her bedroom to begin packing her clothes. When they finished, Silver wrote a note to let Missy know that she would be staying with Chance. "I guess I'll see her when I see her." She carried her bags to the front door. "Let me just put this note on her bed."

He nodded and Silver walked into Missy's room and over to her bed. Out of the corner of her eye, she saw something move. As she turned around, she saw the closet door move slightly. Frightened, she yelled for Chance. In an instant, he ran into the room with his gun in his right hand. He looked at Silver, who pointed to the closet. "I think somebody's in the closet," she said. He pulled her aside and edged slowly toward the door. She watched him cautiously place one hand on the doorknob and point the gun at the closet. Chance looked at her, and gestured for her to back away, then yanked the closet door open.

Breathing heavily, both hands tightly gripping the weapon, he scanned every inch of the closet, ready to blast whatever moves. Suddenly, he seemed to pause in disbelief as he lowered his gun. Silver looked at Chance, noticed his expression, and slowly began to approach him. "Chance what is it? As she looked in, she put her hand over her mouth and gasped. As if in intense pain, she fell to her knees as she watched Missy shaking and cowering like a scared animal in the rear corner of the closet. Her wild eyes darted nervously as she sat poised with a kitchen knife in her hand. Her eyes dilated as she scooted further back into the closet for protection.

After Hollis was bailed out, he stood in front of the courthouse, shaking hands with his lawyer. Hollis watched him walk off as he ripped open the plastic property bag that held his personal effects. He pulled out his money, put on his rings and watch, and then pulled out his cell phone, cursing when he found out the battery was dead. He was looking around for a payphone when a black Cadillac with dark tinted windows pulled up and honked its horn. Hollis cautiously eyed the vehicle as the rear window began to descend, then bent down and squinted to see inside. Through a thick cloud of cigar smoke, he recognized King Papone.

"Hola amigo, welcome home."

Hollis smiled and climbed inside the vehicle to shake Papone's hand. Papone's bodyguard drove off, the old priest sitting in the passenger side front seat.

"Yo, thanks for having my back dukes," Hollis grinned. "They acted like they wanted to hang my ass." Hollis looked at the priest and slapped him on the back. "Yo, nigger, thanks for fronting for a nigger by dressing up like a priest."

"He don't understand you," Papone said. "He don't speak no English, but he is a real priest."

"Damn, my bad nigga!" Hollis turned to Papone. "Yo, you did all this shit for a nigga?"

"Mira amigo," Papone shrugged. "I can't let my people go down de river like dat. Mira, but I can't say de same about…what he name? Chance…your so called brother?"

Hollis frowned, thinking long and hard about that. Papone eyed him.

"Why he not here right now? I sorry to say, but if I not get you a good lawyer, you be under Riker's Island somewhere right now. It looks to me like dey want to leave you high and dry, amigo."

Hollis's lips started to quiver. Why hadn't Chance been there to have his back? Why hadn't he answered his call? He had even left a message on his cell phone to come down and handle business.

"Look amigo, I don't try to tell you what to do, but if dat was me, I consider you should start thinking about what is best for Hollis and Hollis only."

Hollis looked at Papone.

"If your own people ain't with you, dat mean dey against you." Papone shrugged again. "What...are you afraid of him or something?"

"I ain't afraid of no motherfucker!" Hollis barked. "Especially that nigger!"

"Conyo, amigo calm down, I know you ain't afraid of him, and I know what you capable of doing. You remind me of myself in de old days, dat what I can't figure out for de life of me...why you ain't running you own operation?" Papone paused a moment. "Let me ask you a question...could you afford to pay the bail if a friend like me didn't put it up for you, amigo?"

Hollis remained silent.

"A person like you is supposed to be making millions, yet you don't have two nickels to rub together, but you know what?"

The car came to a halt as they parked in front of one of Papone's 'offices' in Spanish Harlem. A shiny black Suburban pulled up alongside the car with three beautiful Spanish women inside. Hollis sat up when he saw the women pouting their lips at him.

"You see dat car?" Papone asked.

Hollis, still looking at the girls, nodded.

"It's yours."

Hollis looked at him to see if he was serious. Papone nodded.

"And everything that's in the car is yours as well."

Hollis looked at the women, licking their lips and smiling. Papone continued as he inched closer to his ears.

"Inside the back of de car is a one hundred thousand dollars, all for you amigo!"

That did it, Hollis was sold.

Papone smiled. "Go 'head, go 'head."

Hollis smiled and exited the car, but halfway out, Papone grabbed his arm.

"*Now dat make us partner, and you know what you have to do?*"

Hollis stared at him.

"Dat mean *all of dem*, including Chance. Comprendey?"

Hollis put his head down for a moment and then nodded.

Papone smiled and released his arm. "Enjoy, amigo."

Hollis hopped into the jeep as a leggy girl moved over to the passenger side seat. Hollis was had already plotting the death of his next six victims; Shy from the Bronx, Old man from 116th Street, Spanish Tito from the Lower Eastside, Ally Mo from Uptown, and Supreme from Brooklyn. These were the 'associates' who had been supplying sixty percent of the heroin drug trade throughout the inner cities for the past twenty-eight years. Papone wanted to eliminate the entire group, but until now, their operation had been tight and untouchable. But Hollis was the missing link that Papone needed to infiltrate their network because of his knowledge of the operation and accessibility.

Hollis reasoned that Papone was right. Either a person was for you or they were against you, and eliminating Chance from his grip would definitely open the doors to control the crack trade. He would finally be the fucking man. After wiping out the associates, Hollis would wipe out all the freelancers in Harlem. He stood to make millions if he consolidated.

Silver and Chance admitted Missy into a private detox and drug treatment center named Visions. Chance paid the entire twenty-six thousand dollars in cash for a sixty-day treatment program. Missy fought for dear life not to be admitted, but fortunately for them the center was used to seeing patients like that come in, so they knew exactly what to do. Chance and Silver drove home in silence, devastated that something like that could have happened to Missy. Chance had seen many strung out addicts before, but nothing had ever affected him like Missy did. As they stopped at a light, he spoke. "That's it!"

Silver broke out of a fog. "What?"

"That's it, I'm not doing this shit anymore."

Not understanding him fully she asked again. "Doing what anymore?"

He pulled over to the curb and parked, looking at Silver. "I'm not selling that shit anymore."

Silver appeared stunned. "Chance, you getting out?"

He nodded and shrugged. "You were right, I'm no different from these other niggers. I was only fooling myself. I don't give a fuck what it takes, but I'm leaving all that shit alone."

Silver hugged him tightly. "I'm with you all the way baby, we'll do this together, okay?"

* * *

Hollis had waited for hours on Dumont Avenue in Brooklyn for Supreme to appear. It had not taken Hollis long to put his plan into action, and he had already killed four of the six men in one day. He killed each one old-fashioned style, with two bullets to the head. He was eager to make his mark in the game. Hollis had something special in store for Chance, and would use him for his fall guy. Since he was already hot, he needed someone to take the blame for the mass murders he had committed, and a trail had to be led somewhere for the cops to take the heat off.

At the moment, he waited across the street in his car for Supreme, a fifty-eight year-old man who fancied himself in still acting and dressing like a teenager. Finally, Hollis spotted Supreme emerge from his house on Miller Avenue, alone. Hollis quickly checked his weapons of the day, three hunting knives, and jumped out of his car. He pulled his baseball cap low over his eyes and crept closer and closer to his victim. Ten feet in front of Supreme, Hollis cuffed one of the knives in his hand and quickly stabbed him, two times in his midsection. Supreme never knew what hit him as he held his fat, bleeding stomach. Still on his feet, Hollis dropped another knife in his hands and expertly tossed it dead center in Supreme's back. The man staggered once and then fell on his face like a brick.

Nearly a week passed before Chance went back around the block. It was then that he discovered the drama going down. The first thing he found out about was Hollis' arrest, thorough Butterfly Ty.

"Yo, Chance we been looking for you Fam. Shit done hit the fan something lovely."

Chance tried to remain calm. "Aight nigger I'm here now… kick it!"

Without hesitation, Butter ran down the shit about Hollis being arrested, and other associates being murdered one by one. Tito, Shy, Supreme, Old Man and Ally Mo, all dead. As he broke shit down to Chance, luxurious cars of all types started screeching to a halt in front of their spot, Butterfly pulled out his GLOCK.

"Oh yeah, I forgot to tell you... these niggers was looking for you for two days," he informed him, keeping an eye on the newcomers. "Just say the word, nigga and I'll start layin' these niggas' down."

"Naa," Chance told him. "Not now, but keep yo shit on ready."

One by one, Ally Mo's people came. Then Shy's lieutenants, Gentry and Bosco came. In what seemed like a Puerto Rican invasion, everybody from Spanish Tito's side came looking for answers. So many people milled about that Chance had to open up the club and let them all in so the block didn't get hot. Bo- Bo, one of Ally Mo's people, spoke first.

"Yo, Chance man, this shit is smelling real funky. This shit wasn't no fucking accident, it was a fucking hit, plain and simple!"

This seemed to fuel everyone's anger, causing everyone to yell at once. Spanish Tito's younger brother, Tesio, glared at Chance.

"Yeah poppy...and the dirty motherfucker who did this shit shot my brother in broad fuckin' daylight while he was in the park with his five-year old granddaughter – his granddaughter, man! I only know one motherfucker heartless enough to do some shit like that."

Chance challenged him with measured anger. "So fuck you tryna to say, nigger?" It was obvious that Tesio had not meant to throw it out there like that, but he wanted some answers. He only said what everyone else was thinking.

"I'm saying, where the fuck is your brother at Chance? I heard nobody's seen him, or you for that matter, since they all started to get dropped."

Anger rose in Chance and his temper flared by his insinuation. "Yo, son, I know you're upset about your brother, but on everything that I love, and that ain't much, don't you ever... step to me with that bullshit, 'cause if I had something to do with it, you wouldn't even be here to inquire about it!" Tesio gritted his jaw but remained silent while Bo-Bo tried to relieve the sting of Chance's words.

"Bottom line is this... we all got a potential enemy, and for all we know, Hollis could be a victim too."

In the midst of their anger, no one had thought about this, which caused them to re-evaluate their conclusions and think. Bo-Bo continued. "Now, Chance," Bo-Bo said. "All we doing is process of elimination so we can look elsewhere. The more we know about the situation, the quicker we can handle all this fuck shit! So it would be to all our common interests if you tell us when you last heard from Hollis."

The entire place went dead silent. In Chance's heart, he knew Hollis had no reason to bump off these niggas' and bite the hand that helped feed him, but he couldn't get Papone's name from rattling in his brain. In spite of how guilty Hollis might be, he was part of his crew, so he had to represent him above all. Chance decided to give them only the minimum of information, and when he saw Hollis, he'd find out what's what.

"I last saw him Friday at the club. He was kicking it with this chick when I left at about one a.m. That's the last time I saw him." Chance really didn't give a fuck if they were satisfied or not, he had his own questions. He turned to Gentry. "Now tell me what y'all know?"

Later that night, Silver and Chance were both heavily burdened with thoughts. Silver was still concerned and worried about Missy, and didn't notice Chance's change in demeanor. Even if she had, he wouldn't have told her about his problems, because he kept them to himself. The entire situation left a bad taste in his mouth, as he tried to remember every conversation that he and Hollis had had over the past month. Nothing seemed to add up, even though he played the tape back at least a thousand times. It was then that Chance grew afraid, not from a fear of dying, but the fear of not being in the know. He knew that the answer would begin to reveal itself very soon, but little did he know that it would come sooner than he ever expected.

As dawn's early light began to creep though his curtains, he looked at his watch. It was 5:30 in the morning. He cursed and gently rose from the bed, not wanting to wake Silver. He stepped into the bathroom and took a long shower. By the time Silver woke, bacon and eggs were crackling in the frying pan.

"Chance, you cooking breakfast for me again?" she asked, hugging him around the waist.

"Of course, anything for my fiancée," he smiled.

"Now that's the second time you said that. You gonna get me open and I'm gonna hold you to it to marry me!"

Chance looked in her eyes and then reached inside his pocket. He pulled out a pink satin ring box. "In that case, will you marry me?" Silver's jaw dropped as she stared at the ring box, then his eyes. Extending his hand, he urged her to take it. She opened the box slowly, and gaped at the large diamond ring nestled inside.

"Chance," she whispered. "Are you for real?"

Chance got on his knees, looked up at her and took her hand. "Silver, will you marry me?"

Silver sank to the floor beside him. "Oh God, Chance, yes …yes!"

They kissed, and then rolled to the floor and made love right there on the kitchen floor.

After they showered, Silver told him she had something important to do that day. It was time to face her grandmother. After they dressed, Chance dropped her off on 138th and 7th Avenue with plans to meet up later in front of Missy's building. Chance kissed Silver and told her they would be making some big changes soon. In Chance's gut, he felt that too many things were happening too quickly. Years ago, A.O. had taught him to always go with his gut feelings, that if something didn't feel right, bounce and live to worry about it another day. Being that Chance wasn't anyone's fool, he would not hesitate to heed such advice. He went to his bank's safe deposit account that he kept for emergencies and took out five hundred thousand dollars in cash. Though he took every precautionary measure, he fell short of not noticing the black jeep following him since he and Silver had left their building.

Chapter 25

The Room of Love

With every step that Silver took, the muscles in her legs began to grow weaker and weaker until they felt as if they would give way at any second, but she kept forth. She finally saw her former residence, and questioned herself for the hundredth time since entering the block for a good reason to just turn around, but in her heart, she knew she had to get this over with. As she climbed the stairs of her grandmother's brownstone, she noticed it was cluttered with old supermarket circulars and Chinese take-out menus. When she reached the door, she noticed a thick chain wrapped around the gated doorway. Perplexed, she went down to the garden level, but it also had a thick chain wrapped around it. Silver then went back up the stairs and looked up toward the windows.

"They came and took her."

Silver turned to find a lady across the street sweeping the front of her building. She remembered Marie Riley. "What did you say?"

Putting her hands on her hips, Mrs. Riley repeated herself. "They came and got her long time ago, the ambulance people, and she ain't been back since."

Silver walked across the street. "What happened to her?"

She looked at Silver. "And who might you be?"

"I'm her granddaughter. I've been away at college for the past four years."

The woman looked at her more closely and then smiled. "Oh yeah, I remember you, you the one who got the name after your eyes. I haven't seen you in years, congratulations, child."

Silver tried to smile, but grew impatient. "Thank you, but can you tell me what happened?"

"'Bout a year ago, your grandma had a major stroke, almost died too, so they keep her in the hospital nearly six months before she came home in a wheelchair and everything. A month after that, they came and took her again, but this time they put her in a nursing home and she ain't been back since."

Silver looked at her a moment. "Do you know where she's at?"

The elderly woman slowly shook her head. "I'm sorry, dear, but I don't."

"Thank you," Silver said, and walked off in a daze.

Chance met Silver at exactly one o'clock. She told him everything that she had learned. He rubbed her hand. "I want to show you something that might make you feel better."

She sighed. "What is it, Chance?"

He smiled. "You'll see." He turned onto 122nd Street between Lenox and 7th Avenue and parked in front of a row of beautiful brownstone houses. He got out and opened her door, then went back to the driver's door to pop the trunk. He pulled out two bulky bags as Silver watched.

"Where are we going?"

"You'll see," he grinned.

The sky was beginning to cloud over. He took her by the hand and led her up the stairs. He reached inside his pocket, pulled out a ring of keys and opened the front door. Silver was obviously confused but remained silent. When they walked in, they immediately heard babies crying. Walking toward the back, Chance opened the door and was greeted by an older woman with a soft loving face, in the process of changing a diaper.

"May I help you?" she asked, turning around. She adjusted her glasses and gasped in pleasure. "Oh Chancellor, I hardly recognized you."

Chance dropped both bags and smiled. "How are you, Ms. Geneva?" He gave her a big hug and kiss.

She laughed. "Chancellor, I haven't seen you around here in months!" She placed the baby on her right shoulder, gently patting its back.

Silver looked at Chance with questioning eyes and he smiled again. "Ms. Geneva, I'd like you to meet my fiancée, Silver."

With a big, genuine smile, Ms. Geneva extended her hand toward Silver. "Oh!" she smiled. "Just like the room!"

Silver glanced up at him again, her brows lifted in question. Before he could explain, Ms. Geneva took off her glasses and began chiding him.

"Chancellor, why you never told me you had such a pretty girlfriend? You want to stay for dinner? We just 'bout to feed the families."

He looked at Silver and shrugged. "Yes, Ms. Geneva, that's a great idea, but I'd like to show her around first." The older woman beamed.

"You go right on ahead," she said. She grabbed Silver by the arm. "You sho' is one lucky girl to have the affection of a person like Chancellor, he's a fine young man. You make sho' you take good care of him, you hear me?"

Silver blushed and nodded. Before Ms. Geneva walked out the room Chance spoke to her. "Ms. Geneva, I need to talk to you for a moment." He gently pulled her aside and whispered to her as he pointed to both bags. Silver still looked confused when he turned to glance at her. He then picked up both bags and spoke to Silver. "I'll be right back." Silver nodded, and moments later, when he returned, she had not moved.

"Chance, what is this place?"

"I'm about to show you." He took her by the hand, led her to an adjacent office and guided her to a bulletin board on the wall. "Read that."

Frowning, Silver looked at bulletin board and noticed a golden plaque and read it out loud.

"This award is given to the Children's House for their dedicated and diligent service to their community by providing families affected by the addiction of drugs and alcohol. Let it be known that on this day, 8th day of May, nineteen hundred ninety-eight, the City of New York recognizes this as Jessica Jones and Ernestine Haze Day. Signed, the honorable Mayor, City of New York."

She appeared stunned beyond words, and Chance explained. "When you left the first time, I thought about the things you said, you know, about ruining families. For some reason, that shit stayed with me. Well, one day I ran into Ms. Geneva. I used to stay with her when I was in the system and she was the one foster parent that genuinely cared for me and never took advantage of me. She took in the kids that nobody wanted the mentally retarded and the problem ones – it didn't matter to her. When I brought this building a couple of years back, I decided to let her move in, since she still lived in the same cramped apartment with all those kids.

"Crack had hit the city with a vengeance, and all these unwanted crack babies started turning up in the system. Being the person she was, she didn't turn down one of them. Before long, she started helping their addicted mothers too, and now it's like a family shelter for addicted mothers who want to get their life together. After two years or so, it grew so much that I let them use my other house around the corner also." He smiled with the zeal of a little boy. "You want to see something really nice?" He took her by the hand and led her into the hallway. As they moved downstairs, they were met by a group of women with young kids and babies. They said hello to the group and let them go ahead of them. As they neared the bottom of the stairs, the delicious aroma of home cooking wafted through the air. As they entered the dining area, a sign read **'The Silver Room of Love.'**

After dinner, Chance and Silver were finally alone. He turned to her. "Silver, in some twisted way; I feel that I'm making some kind of difference, a sort of contribution. Or maybe it's just some way of me making redemption from all the foul things I've done." He paused. "Either way, what's done is done, and I can't change a thing, but... but you, Silver...you can really make a difference. It would be a travesty if you didn't utilize all resources to ensure that you succeed with your future plans without having to worry about how you are going to pay for it."

"Chance, I'm not sure if I'm following you."

Chance smiled. "Those bags I brought in...each contains two hundred fifty thousand dollars. One bag is for Ms. Geneva to continue running this program. The other is for you to continue your education to become a doctor." Before she could reply, he continued. "Now, I know how you feel about my money, but you got to understand that you can really make a difference and help so many people if you became a doctor."

Silver shook her head uneasy about the money.

"Silver, take a look over there." He pointed at a woman with three small children. " I remember when she got here over a year ago. She weighed about eighty pounds and was strung out on crack. She was homeless for two years after the city took her kids and found her system dirty with drugs when she gave birth to the last one. She was an incorrigible and habitual addict who would surely have died on the streets if she hadn't gotten busted for possession. The court mandated her into a program and sent her here." He looked over at the laughing woman. "Less than six months of being off drugs, the court allowed her visitation with her children again. Six months after that, she got full custody of all three, but only because of places like this! Ms. Geneva just told me that she would be moving into her own three bedroom apartment in two weeks." Silver looked around as he continued. "And that's about the same story of all the mothers here. Can you imagine what would happen to these kids if their mothers didn't get themselves some help? I do."

This was Chance's story; this was his plea for her to understand how bad he had it growing up in all those group homes. In that very instant she seemed to understand. He told she didn't have to say yes, but to think about it, but whatever she decided, the money would be there. All she had to do was come see Ms. Geneva, and she would give it to her, no questions asked.

Silver frowned and looked up at him. "Chance, is their something wrong? You sound like your going somewhere."

He tried to reassure her with a smile. "No, it's nothing like that. I just like you to be up on my every move, that's all, boo."

As they made their way to leave, Ms. Geneva saw them to the door. A small, wet and shrunken woman entered the front door from the outside. She was small, almost child- like, a seasoned addict. Her skin was ashen and wrinkled, and dark sullen eyes seemingly stared at unimaginable horrors. Ms. Geneva shook her head in empathy.

"Claresse," she said. "You can't keep doing this to yourself, baby, you killing yourself."

The woman simply broke down and cried like a baby as crept toward Ms. Geneva and tightly embraced her. "I know, Ms. Geneva," she muttered. "I know…but I just miss my babies."

"It's okay, it's okay, now you go down stairs and get yourself washed up and get somethin' ta eat."

Chance stared at her with compassion. He knew her from the old neighborhood, where they called her 'Tiny'.

The rain came down like cats and dogs, and Chance used his jacket to shield Silver. Hugging him around the waist, they laughed as they ran in a futile effort to escape the downpour. Unnoticed, a vehicle slowly crept toward them.

Chance opened the passenger side-door and whisked Silver inside. He covered himself with the jacket, and when he reached the car door, he noticed the slow moving jeep with tinted windows creeping towards him. Sensing danger, he put his hand on his gun and moved away from his car in case there was trouble. Suddenly, the vehicle came to a complete halt. Hand on the trigger, Chance stared cautiously at the vehicle as he watched a smoke-hued window begin to roll down. It was then that Chance realized that the driver was his brother, Hollis. He let out a huge sigh, reholstered his gun and smiled. It wasn't until he stepped closer to the jeep that he sensed something deathly wrong. Hollis had yet to look his way.

As if trapped in a bad dream, Silver watched in horror as the barrel of a shotgun extended out the rear window of the jeep that had pulled up alongside Chance's car—it was Butterfly Ty. Chance dropped his jacket and made a mad dash away from his car, but he had ran less then three feet when Silver heard the roar, followed by a flash from the weapon. The blast caused Chance to fly backward. He staggered to his feet and tried to continue, but more bullets tore through his body. Then another weapon was aimed at Chance, this time a 9mm fired off a volley of shots that caused his body to twist and contort as he fell to the ground. The vehicle slowly crept toward Chance's still body while rain caused the growing pool of blood beneath him to spew in the gutter like a river. The street was filled with the eerie sound of silence and raindrops as the two shooters watched Silver jump from the vehicle and heedless of the danger, run screaming toward her fallen man.

The headlights and horn from a sanitation truck behind them caused the attackers to drive off. Drenched from the rain, Silver collapsed at Chance's side. "It's okay, baby…they're gone, you can get up now, baby." She cradled his head in her arms. "Chance, baby, come on, we got to go home now. It's getting late. I've got to cook you your favorite dinner, baby." She smiled. "And then…and then we gonna watch some Jeopardy like we used to and see who wins." She did not register anything going on around her. Sirens were in the background. People were out on the sidewalk, looking, pointing. She begged Chance to get up. "Come on, Chance... don't leave me honey, don't leave me, not like this...please, don't leave me Chance, I need you."

A police officer arrived on the scene. "Ma'am, we got it from here, please give him some room."

He tried to bring Silver to her feet, but she wouldn't budge. The paramedics arrived and tore open their red medical bags as the officer again tried to pull her away. "Get off of me!" she snapped, holding Chance tighter.

Finally, two officers pried her loose and pulled her out of their way while the paramedics shoved plastic tubes down his throat and monitored him for a pulse. Silver put up a violent struggle. Suddenly, one of the paramedics yelled.

"We got a pulse!"

Chapter 26

Help Me Mother

Silver stayed at the hospital for two straight days, never leaving the hospital. The doctor told her, Chance was extremely lucky to be alive after taking seven shots from a high caliber weapon and one blast from a shotgun. It was nothing short of a miracle. They had him in I.C.U., under guarded and critical condition. Silver was relieved, but still extremely worried for her man. As she waited in the T.V. room to break the boredom, two detectives entered the room and flashed their badges. One was a large, black male, the other a petite white woman. Silver talked to about a hundred cops over the last two days since the shooting, but something was different about these two, she thought. The female cop spoke first. "Are you Ms. Jones, Silver Jones?"

Sensing something had gone wrong, Silver grew worried. "Is this about Chance?"

"I'm Detective Squassoni, and this is Detective McBeth from the homicide division."

Detective McBeth forced a smile. Hearing the word 'homicide' made Silver panic. "Why? What's happened to Chance? Is he okay?"

The woman detective reassured her. "He's still in intensive care."

Relieved, Silver sank back onto the couch while both detectives watched her every move. The man spoke impatiently.

"You are Silver Jones, correct?"

Silver looked up and nodded. "What is this about?"

"Chancellor Haze has been placed under arrest for murder and drug trafficking."

Exasperated, Silver rose to her feet. "What the fuck are you talking about? My fiancée is on his death bed after someone tried to murder him, and you're here to tell me he's placed under arrest for murder?"

"This is a murder that happened over a year ago," Detective Squassoni explained. "The drug charges are current."

Silver was speechless as the detectives continued their tag-team assault.

"How long have you known Mister Haze, ma'am?" Detective McBeth asked.

"That's none of your goddamn business!" Silver snapped.

"You better goddamn believe it's our business, since you're facing federal charges of aiding and abetting a criminal enterprise!"

He let that sink in while Detective Squassoni continued.

"Ma'am, what he is trying to say, is that we found enough drugs in his apartment alone to put him away for life without the possibility of parole. You, like the detective said, can be charged as an accessory that can put you away for fifteen years."

"And that would blow any chances of you going to medical school," Detective McBeth added sarcastically.

Silver stared at them, dumbfounded, wondering how they knew so much about her.

"Yes, we know all about you, and that is the only reason we don't bust you right now, but give us some time."

Not missing a beat, Squassoni jumped in smoothly. "Unless you do yourself a favor and help us out." She shrugged. "We might get you off with no jail time...if you cooperate right now."

Silver put her head down, feeling totally defeated. Moments later, she slowly lifted her head and spoke with the innocence of a five year-old. "Okay, if you head over the bridge into the Bronx, you gonna see this large white building." Both detectives pulled out notepads and began taking notes. "And right in front, there's a sign that reads 'Yankee Stadium'. Both detectives glanced up. "And when you get there, you can sell those wolf tickets to someone who don't know any better!"

Detective McBeth snapped his writing pad closed, stared at Silver and shook his head. "You know, it's the educated black girls like you who stand by these drug-dealing, murdering thug motherfuckers when good, decent hard-working brothers get noses turned up to them by women like you." He sneered and inched closer. "But you know what? I seen hundreds of girls just like you before and you gonna learn just like the rest of them, that loving these niggers only get you two things – a bullet or jail time!"

He walked off while the female detective stared at her. "Ain't this the part when you act like you're really concerned, give me your card and say, *If you should change your mind, give me a call?*"

The woman chuckled, reached inside her jacket and pulled out a business card. "If you should change your mind, give me a call." She extended the card.

Silver reluctantly took it and returned to the couch.

"Ms. Jones," Detective Squassoni said.

Silver turned around.

"All cops are not the enemy. We can actual help. If you should ever get into something over your head, give me a call." As the detective turned to leave, she spoke over her shoulder in a thick Brooklyn accent. "By the way, my daughter starts Med school this year also, congratulations!" She sent her a wink.

Chance was smart enough to have a lawyer on retainer that he paid two thousand dollars a month for, just in case of an event like this. Mister Morgenstern was from the old school, and had a reputation of doing anything to get his clients off. That included bribing the jury, the judge, or witnesses. Morgenstern was a no-nonsense kind of guy and knew the law like the average person knew their ABC's. He only had two requirements for his services, one, that associates refer you, and two, money – and lots of it. Chance had told Silver about him a couple of times, but she couldn't get his number from the house since the Feds had confiscated and sealed Chance's Co-op with everything in it. But as fate may have it, Chance had left his new cell phone in the car. Even though the authorities held his inquest and arraignment without him, Silver attended every one, along with his lawyer, while Chance recovered from his wounds. Morgenstern was quite frank with Silver about Chance's odds to beat the charges.

"Ms. Jones, the government has a strong case against Mr. Haze. They found one hundred forty-four grams of heroin, cash and guns in his residence. One of the guns, I might I add, was traced back through the F.B.I. system with several murders on it, including the massacre of an entire family over a year ago."

Silver refused to believe it. "No, that's not true. Chance never kept drugs in the house! He was set up!"

Morgenstern had heard it all before. "Maybe, maybe not, the point is trying to prove that to a jury. With all the evidence against him…" he closed his eyes and stopped walking. "And to be quite honest they will convict him, unless…"

Silver grabbed his arm. "Unless what?"

Morgenstern stared at her hands on his three thousand-dollar suit, pulled his arm away and wiped the wrinkles out. He looked her straight in the eyes. "Unless there's a miracle or these people that you say 'set him up' confess to these crimes." He chuckled. "You have a better chance of a miracle before someone takes responsibility for these charges. They carry a penalty of twenty-five years to life on each count, and he is being charged with a seventy-seven count indictment."

Silver somberly asked the ultimate question. "So what you're saying? He's looking at life in prison?"

"Doing life in prison is the good part. The government is seeking the death penalty." He allowed her a moment to process this, but then got down to business now. "Ms. Jones, you are Mr. Haze's fiancée, so I'll grant you the courtesy of handling the financial aspects of this case. I can almost guarantee that I can convince them to spare Mr. Haze's life, but it will take a ransom sum to do that."

Warily, she stared at him. "How much?"

"Well, I'll have to delay the trial for a few years until things die down, then talk to some judges, file motions, things like that, so I guess two hundred thousand might cover it. I'll need half of it up front."

Silver was taken aback, knowing it would be impossible for her to come up with that kind of money.

"You have my card. Give me a call when you get the money together."

Silver watched the man scamper off towards the elevator.

It was the loneliness and lowest point of Silver's life. Once again, she was alone with nobody in the world to turn to. She cried all the way home, dazed, confused and defeated. She knew she had to pull herself together, but how could she, when her life had been turned upside down? Just when she felt she could lay down and die, her mother's voice came to her. As if her mother was right there with her, she started asking her what to do, and at that moment, all the years of teachings – all the lessons that she ever taught her came back to her as clear as day – she had the answers. She looked toward the sky. "Thank you, mother!"

Chapter 27

Riker's Island

The bus ride across the bridge to Riker's Island was horrible. It doesn't get any more ghetto than this, Silver thought. The crowded bus was filled with chattering women, as though they were going on a field trip. Some of them sounded as though they had known each other for years. One particularly loud-mouthed girl from Brooklyn, nothing but ass and stomach, talked mad shit the entire ride to the island. She wore a one-piece spandex black outfit at least two sizes too small, and long, multi-colored extensions in her hair. She was with three of her six kids, all by different daddies, and yelled at them the entire ride like she was a drill sergeant.

"Tay-Tay, sit your fuckin' ass down before I fuck you up! Daquan, I'm gonna bust your ass if you do it again! Shauniqua, close you fucking legs and sit right before I slap you!"

If she wasn't yelling at the kids, she was talking to her friends about how every girl on the bus was there to take her man, and how they were all jealous of her. Silver didn't usually judge people, but this bitch really needed her ass kicked for wearing something like that. She wondered if the girl really thought she was sexy with her fat stomach hanging out the tight outfit.

Trying desperately to tune them out, she began to smile as she thought of seeing Chance for the first time in nearly two months. As the bus grew closer toward Riker's Island, the creepy sight of the compound came into view. Cold, murky water and the quarter-mile long bridge that separated it from the mainland, was the only way in and only way out. On the Island, stone-faced, armed Corrections Officers that aped as robots patrolled the perimeter of fence topped with stainless steel razor-spiked barbs that seemed to spiral for miles on end.

When they finally arrived at the visitors processing center, the women once again had to board yet another bus to take them to their loved one's 'house'. C-74, C-76, HDM, The Beacon, Rose M. Singer, Anna Kross, etc. The eeriest and strangest thing about Riker's Island was that even though they housed thousands of inmates in the facility, the silence was almost deafening. Silver realized that the bus ride was not the worst part after all, it was the cruel and degrading way the Correction Officers talked and treated them when they got there. They barked at them as if they were criminals themselves if they didn't follow their instructions to the letter. What followed next made Silver want to run. She had no idea that she would be subjected to a full strip search in order to see Chance, who was still placed in guarded condition in Riker's main infirmary.

The entire process was tiring, and it took over two hours before she was led into the core of the visiting room for Chance's arrival. They made the rules perfectly clear: 'No touching, No kissing, No passing any items.' To violate any of these rules would be cause for immediate removal off the Island and the visitors' list. After twenty minutes or so sitting at table number twelve, Silver heard a loud voice.

"Entering seven!"

A buzzing sound, followed by the clanking of a steel gate was heard throughout the room. Two c.o.'s, one in front and one in back of seven inmates entered the room. Each inmate wore an orange jumpsuit and flip-flops, and was shackled hand and foot with long chained cuffs. They all took short, choppy steps as they bobbed toward their assigned table. Despite such medieval conditions, each prisoner seemed jovial and alert as their eyes searched about, desperately anxious to sight their loved ones. Silver's heart began to race as she stood up to search each man's face, but her smile slowly disappeared as each man passed by to walk over to his assigned seat. Worried, Silver was about to walk over to the Sergeant's booth to inquire about Chancellor Haze when she heard another guard call out.

"Entering one!"

Hope resurfaced as she watched the gate open. As if a searing piece of hot steel slashed through her heart, her jaw dropped when she saw Chance enter the room with the aid of a C.O., who pushed him in a wheelchair.

In the five boroughs of New York, murder and mayhem was at an all time high. Over two thousand that year alone, but nothing close to the stacks of bodies showing up all over Harlem and the South Bronx. True to his word, Hollis caused such havoc and fear that other dealers completely shut down shop, retired or moved their entire operation further north to small upstate towns, or further south to ghettos like Baltimore, D.C, or Philly. In any event, niggas weren't fuckin' with Hollis now that he was even more powerful than before, since he had hooked up and allied himself with King Papone. Niggas was shook! With Chance and the Italians out of the way, Harlem became his own little candy store and the only people who were getting rich were Hollis and funeral parlors.

Silver desperately fought the urge to cry in front of Chance. She had to be strong for his sake and for herself because of what she would be attempting to do. With every ounce of strength she had, she fought the urge to hug him, remembering the rules. So she just sat and smiled widely. Chance's chin rested on his chest, unable to support his head by himself. As he sagged limply in the wheelchair, looking as though he had lost fifty pounds. But nothing was worse than the oxygen tube that protruded from his throat. In spite of seeing him so helpless, Silver blocked it from her mind. "Hey boo, how are you doing?"

He bobbed his head as he fought to raise it. He even managed a slight smile.

"I'm much better."

Silver was amazed he could speak through the tube. After they talked for about a half-hour or so, he almost sounded like his old self, with the exception of a few slurs and wheezes. After she had gained enough courage, Silver told Chance what his lawyer had told her at court, about his apartment and what he faced in the near future. After a long pause, Chance seemed unmoved by the news. He finally spoke, but in a low, measured tone.

"Silver, I know this is gonna be hard, what I'm about to say, but I just want you to listen." He paused to ensure she had his full attention, looked around the room to make sure no one was listening and continued between gasps for air. "I want you to get the money I gave Ms. Geneva for you and leave New York."

She watched Chance strain to find the words.

"Take the money for your education and forget about spending it on me, 'cause I'm already dead."

"Are you finished?" Silver asked. Chance didn't answer. Edging closer, Silver glanced down at her watch. "Baby, we don't have that much time left, so I suggest you just listen very carefully." Carefully searching his eyes, she continued. "As much as you're not going to like this, I'm going to get you out of here, and there is absolutely nothing you can do about it."

"Silver, please, don't be foolish. I won't be able to take it if something happens to you," he muttered.

"So now you know how I feel!" Silver quickly whispered. "All those years that we weren't together, I was nothing, you hear me? Nothing without you, baby. That's when I realized that I would surly go crazy without you. Chance, you are me and I am you, we are one and I'm never going to let you go, 'cause if I do I'll only be letting myself go. Do you understand that, Chance?" Chance turned away. "So it's either win or lose, and believe me," she grabbed Chance by the hand and looked him dead in the eyes. "I'm ready to die for my man!"

A tear fell from the corner of his eye as he turned to look out a distant window. Silver knew that she had to have the strength to carry both of them, so she continued as she turned his face toward her. "Chance, you have two choices. Either you help me and give me the information I need and I'll have a little chance of surviving, or I'll do it by myself and have no chance of surviving. But I do know one thing for sure…either I get you out of here or I'm gonna die trying!"

Chance stared at her for a moment then shook his head in frustration. He knew that when Silver had her mind made up, that was it. He was powerless, with nowhere to run this time, no way to bluff his way out of it for her best interest. He relented.

Chance listened intently to Silver's plan and they talked for another half an hour as he filled in the blanks by telling her the who's who and what's what. He told her if she had the remotest possibility of pulling this thing off she would need help, big help. She would need to recruit the right players she could trust who could play their roles and be willing to put their lives on the line in the process. Chance explained that she would need four or five people:

One – A front man, someone who was well connected in the drug game, someone who has big access to drugs – Diego, Silver thought. Two – A gorilla-type nigger who didn't give a fuck, who wasn't afraid to do stick-ups or lay niggas down – Chubbs! Three – a big bodyguard type nigger to play the henchman. Birdie! Four – a person who knew how to break into places, pick locks and safes.

Beasley! And Five – a person who could introduce one connect to another. This person had to be known to have past connections with drug lords. Missy!

Their time was almost up, but the last thing she and Chance discussed was Hollis. Chance explained everything about Hollis to her, how he was the most dangerous and ruthless man alive.

"Under no circumstances should you ever underestimate him!" he stressed.

Silver intently listened to everything. Just then, the men began to file out from their visit, and she knew their time was almost up, that they had only about five more minutes before his escort came for him. Silver smiled. "The doctors at the hospital were calling you Superman because they never saw anyone sustain so many bullets and live. That makes you invincible."

Chance chuckled. "Don't believe that. Every man, even Superman has his weaknesses. Superman has Kryptonite and I have Silver."

They both laughed. "So what are Hollis' weaknesses?" Silver asked as a joke. Chance thought about it for a moment, but was interrupted by the C.O. who came to escort him back to his cell. As he pushed Chance away from the table, Silver spoke to him. "Sir...I know you have rules, but do you think I can give him a kiss goodbye?"

The C.O. looked at her and then looked around. "Go ahead, but make it quick."

Silver thanked him and while he briefly turned his back, she bent down and gave Chance a passionate kiss on the lips, followed by a gentle hug. Before they pulled away, Chance whispered in her ear.

"Women and his mouth."

Silver looked at Chance, not understanding what he meant.

"Women and his mouth are Hollis' Kryptonite!"

Missy walked out of the rehab center after sixty days, looking totally fantastic. She had gained about twenty pounds in all the right places. When she stepped out the building, she was greeted by Silver, parked out front eagerly awaiting her arrival. They hugged like they hadn't seen each other in years. "Girl, look you," Silver squealed. "You look great!"

Missy did a 360, letting Silver see her new look.

"Damn girl, you finally grew an ass," Silver joked.

"Naw, I always had an ass, it's just that now I got ass on top of ass!"

They both laughed, then Silver loaded Missy's bags into the car and drove off. On the road, Silver told Missy everything that had gone down since she was away. Missy was brought to tears when she heard about Chance and what Hollis had done to him. And just as Silver thought, Missy was down to do what ever it took to get Chance out of the predicament he was in. Silver told her of her plan and how she needed to act quickly.

"Missy, I know you just got out of the clinic and I'll understand if you ain't up to it yet, just say the word."

Missy looked at her like she was silly. "Bitch, when did you ever know me not to be ready for no drama, I put the 'dra' in drama!" Laughing at her own silliness, Missy continued. "Besides, you don't know shit about the streets and I can't allow nothing to happen to my girl!" Missy shouted. "You know our motto 'I would die for you, bitch!'"

Silver looked back at her. "I would die for you too, hoe." They couldn't help but hug as the cars in back of them honked their horns for them to move.

The first person on their list to visit was Diego. They went to see him at his job at the airport. Silver drove slowly toward the baggage claim area when Missy spotted Diego tagging some luggage. "Oh, there he is."

Silver was amazed at how different he looked. He was now much taller and way more handsome, with no trace of baby fat.

"Damn! Milk must have done him some good," Silver said. Missy sent her an impish grin.

"Watch this."

She exited the vehicle. Diego's back was toward her, but she began to speak with a British accent.

"Oh boy, can you kindly get my bags from my car?"

Attending to other bags, he replied without looking over his shoulder. "Yes, ma'am, I'll be there in a second."

Stomping her feet Missy yelled. "Boy, look at me when I'm talking to you, now get my bags right now!"

Diego stiffened and spun around. "Listen lady, I told you I'll be with you in a second, and don't be calling me—"He recognized Missy, smiling from ear to ear. He smiled as well. "Missy, why you got to be fucking around like that?"

Missy laughed. "Ahh, I got your ass!"

Diego loved a good joke as much as the next person. "Okay, you got that one, but what you doing here?"

Missy smiled. "I brought somebody here to see you."

Apparently expecting another joke, he smirked. "Who?"

On cue, Silver exited the car. "What's up, Diego? Long time, no see."

He searched her face, looked at her eyes, and froze. "Oh shit! Silver, is that you?" He hugged her and swept her off her feet. He gave her a big kiss on the cheek, and then pulled away to looked at her. "Conyo... Mommy! Look at you! What have you been up to?"

Before Silver could answer, Diego's supervisor appeared.

"Diego, bags ain't gonna get tagged by themselves, come on now... chop chop!"

Silver broke up the brief reunion. "Listen, Diego, I need to see you about something really important." She handed him a card. "I'm staying at Missy's place and I need you to be there Saturday at 8 o'clock on the dot, okay?"

As if it was a no brainer, he looked at the address and shook his head. " I don't need no address, I know exactly where Missy lives." He smiled at a blushing Missy.

"Alright, but promise me you'll be there. It's real important, Diego."

He agreed, hugged them both and then watched them climb in their car and drive off.

In Harlem, they drove to a bar called Crystal's and decided to wait and order some virgin Piña Coladas, since both of them no longer drank alcohol. They asked several patrons at the bar if they had seen Chubbs, but everyone acted as if they didn't know him. After waiting nearly two hours with no sign of Chubbs, they decided to leave and try again tomorrow. Before they left, they decided to use the ladies room because those three drinks were working on their bladders. As they walked toward the bathroom, a large man appeared from out of nowhere and pushed them inside the men's room. The man pulled out two large guns and pointed them directly in their faces.

"You two lil' bitches better have a good goddamn reason to come up in here looking for me, 'cause if not?" Chubbs cocked both triggers. "Now who sent y'all lil' bitches? It was that Hollis motherfucker, right?"

Eyes closed and scared to death, Silver stammered. "Goddaddy, it's me, Silver." Chubbs used his gun to turn her cheek toward him.

"Open up your fuckin' eyes!"

Silver opened her eyes and Chubbs realized she was indeed his goddaughter, whom he hadn't seen in over eight years.

"Maafucker, ain't this about a bitch!"

His frown turned into a big smile as he hugged her like a big teddy bear. He hugged her so tightly she could hardly breathe.

"Well, I'll be goddamn," he said, proudly looking her up and down.

"Goddaddy, can you put those guns away?"

He glanced at the guns. "Yeah, yeah, come on, let's get out this maafucka."

Before they left the bathroom, he frowned and cocked a trigger again. "You still in college, right?"

"I just graduated."

"You going to medical school, right?"

Silver nodded.

Chubbs uncocked the weapons. "You would have made ya momma proud, baby girl!" Exiting the bathroom, he yelled to everyone in the bar. "This here is my Goddaughter, and she is a maafucken Doctor!"

A man standing by the bathroom door spoke to him. "So you not gonna be needing these, are you?"

He held up two large black plastic bags. Silver and Missy looked at each other, realizing just how close they had come to being killed. Chubbs hadn't changed a bit; he looked exactly the same, Tootsie roll pop and all.

He and the girls sat down, and after telling him everything that had gone down, he seemed to grow angrier each time Silver mentioned Hollis' name. Without hesitation, he said that he was in, but said that they should just let him clap the nigger and that would be that. Silver told him that it was more complicated than that. Chubbs said that he and Hollis were due to square off sooner or later, and besides, Harlem wasn't big enough for them both. He agreed to meet at the address she gave him on Saturday. He walked them outside, where he hugged her and told her how much he missed her mother. Silver agreed with him and said goodbye.

The next day, they were on their way to their old neighborhood to see Birdie. On the way, Silver finally confided to Missy the incident that occurred between her and Tommy. Missy was so furious that Silver hadn't told her about the attempted rape that it took Silver twenty minutes to calm her down.

They pulled up to the curb near her old building, and the first person they saw was Mitts the dope fiend. They were both surprised that he was still alive. They got out of the car, waved and said, 'Hey Mitts' and attempted to give him a few dollars, but he refused. Walking away, Silver turned around and saw that he was still staring at them. For some reason, he gave her the heebies-jeebies. As they walked towards Birdie's building, she saw him walking up the block with groceries in his arms. They stopped right behind him.

"Auntie Birdie," Silver said.

Birdie froze in his tracks. Either out of guilt or fear, Birdie slowly turned, his expression looking as if the Grim Reaper himself had come to get him. He dropped the groceries and clasped his hands over his mouth and started crying. Feeling his pain, Silver extended her arms toward him as he approached her like a sad puppy lost in a storm.

"I'm so, so sorry, Silver ... how can you ever forgive me? How can you ever forgive me?"

He kept saying it over and over again as they embraced. Silver found out later that Birdie had put Tommy out the very next day, and began walking the streets looking for her, but after several weeks, had been forced to give up. She assured him that she understood and had forgiven him long ago. The girls spent the night catching up on old times, and then Silver finally told him why they needed his help. Even though he was afraid, he agreed to go along with everything.

The last person on their list was Beasley. It wasn't too hard too find him, because all they had to do was look for his white van with thick smoke coming out of it. As they approached the van, they could barely see inside because of the thick cloud of reefer smoke. Cupping her hand against the window, Missy banged hard on it. Suddenly, the window began to roll down and a cloud of smoke rushed out, causing them both to choke.

Fanning her face, Missy coughed. "Yo Beasley, this is Missy, what's up, man?" He looked at her as if he hadn't a care in the world. "wen you a sa mi sistre?" Still coughing, Missy pointed to Silver. "Beasley, you remember Silver, right?" He lazily turned toward Silver. "Oh yah, I remember Silva, she use ta protect me in school."

"Yeah, that's right, it's time for you to return the favor. Are you down, nigger?"

He looked at both of them. "Anyting for you two, who save me punk ass when I came to de country, just ya tell me when ya need me!" Silver handed him the address while holding her breath. "Saturday at 8 o'clock. Be there, Beasley." Beasley nodded and rolled up his window.

One by one, they arrived at Missy's apartment. The first one to arrive was Diego, and the last one, of course, was Beasley. Missy had to go downstairs to get him from out of his van, as he puffed at a last minute blunt. With everyone there, Silver and Missy explained the situation and the risk involved. She gave them all time to think about. Chubbs was the first to speak. He had tears in his eyes. "Fuck that shit, man, ain't nothing to this shit but to do it." He pulled out both his guns and continued, "Let's take these bitches to war, man!" Birdie spoke next. "Silver, I did you wrong once, and I never forgave myself. Whatever you ask of me to do...I'm ready!" Silver smiled. "Thank you, Auntie." Chubbs and Beasley looked at Birdie strangely when Silver called him 'auntie', while Beasley nodded his head in agreement. They turned toward Diego. "So what do you say, Diego?" Missy asked. "Are you down or what?" All eyes fell on Diego, who sat still and silent, his head bowed. After several moments, he raised his head, his lips curved with a cunning smile. "This guy...Hollis, he didn't happen to have rob my Momma, did he?"

Silver and Missy smiled brightly, as they were the only ones who got the joke. The rest of the evening was spent going over the plan and their prospective roles in it.

El Flaco was the major drug overlord for Washington Heights. His cartel sold eighty percent of the cocaine on the eastern seaboard. He also happened to be Diego's uncle, his father's brother. His father had been killed sixteen years ago, when he was the overlord. He had been murdered by a rival drug cartel. After his death, his younger brother, Flaco, came to the country and picked up where he left off with a vengeance, killing everyone remotely affiliated with his brother's death, including their families.

Silver, Missy and Diego arrived on 165th and Broadway early Saturday morning. The only thing Diego knew about his uncle was that he owned most of the supermarkets throughout Washington Heights. As they exited the car, everyone stared at them as if they were strangers from another planet. As they began walking around, a peculiar thing happened. People began making the sign of the cross. The locals began to crowd them, and some even began falling to their knees and chanting in Spanish.

"Yo, Diego man," Missy said nervously. "What the fuck is going on? What are they saying?"

Diego replied, just as shaken. "I don't know, they saying something like, 'Oh mighty God, you brought him back to us,' something about being a resurrection?"

The crowd grew larger as they were soon surrounded, halting traffic. Suddenly, three men pushed the frenzied crowd to find out what the commotion was all about. Scared and unable to run, Missy, Silver and Diego grabbed each other tighter to prevent themselves from being separated. When the men finally reached them, their eyes widened and they, too, fell to their knees directly in front of Diego and began kissing his feet. Everyone else followed suit, falling to his or her knees.

Silver and Missy looked at Diego, not knowing what to say. The three men then rose to their feet and escorted them through the mass and into a nearby supermarket. Taken to an office in the rear, they sat silently and impatiently, unsure what would happen next. Suddenly, a door swung open and an older Spanish man entered. When he spotted Diego, he was visibly shaken. He slowly approached Diego and then spoke to him.

"What is your mother's name?"

Diego frowned. "What?" With a stern look, the man asked once again. "What is your mother's name?" Diego looked at Silver, who nodded for him to answer. "Maria…Maria Asencio."

Overwhelmed with tears, the man placed both hands on Diego's shoulders, kissed him on both cheeks and then affectionately hugged him. "I am your father's brother, and you are my nephew!"

El Flaco summoned his employee to get something out of the next room, and when they returned, they carried a large, framed picture. They turned it toward Diego. It was a picture of his father, a spitting image of him. El Flaco told them the entire story.

Diego's father had been a legend in Washington Heights before he died. He took care of the entire neighborhood and everybody loved him and called him 'El Mayimbe', which meant 'The King' or 'The Best'. He was like a modern day Robin Hood to the people in his neighborhood. This was why so many people had surrounded them outside, because they had thought it was some kind of miracle from God that El Mayimbe had came back to walk the earth.

Silver knew that for many years, Diego had believed that his father had abandoned him and his mother, but El Flaco explained to him that his father never abandoned him or his Mama.

"While giving birth to you," El Flaco explained, "Your mother almost died, she was in coma for three weeks. When she came to, she said that God came to her while she was in her coma and told her that if she cleansed herself from sin, He would let her enjoy her life with her only son. So she made God a vow that she would dedicate her life to Him from then on. The first thing she did was give your Papa a choice, either follow that same path with her or find another path without her, because she didn't want you to be mixed up in his business." He paused and lowered his head. "When your father didn't change quick enough for your Mama, true to her words she packed up and left and took you with her and vanished. Your Papa searched for years to find you and never did. We thought that she left New York, but your father never gave up hope of finding you, even 'till the day he died!"

He took some keys out of his pocket and opened a wall safe. He pulled out an envelope and handed it to Diego with a smile. "Those are the deeds and letters of ownership to a couple of homes and businesses in the Dominican Republic that he left to you before he died."

Diego appeared happy and relieved. After catching up on a few things, Diego explained to his uncle their dilemma. His uncle became apprehensive about the two Negra sucia women that he came with. Diego, seeing his uneasiness challenged him.

"Tio," Diego explained. "These two girls I knew my entire life. They were the only friends I had throughout school and never ask nothing of me until now. He lowered his head in shame. "Since I didn't have no one to teach me how to fight when I was little, I use to get the shit kicked out of me and robbed every day by the boys in my school!" Flaco's eyes began to water. "These two 'Negra sucia's' as you call them, and the guy in jail, was the only ones who came to my defense and fought them bullies for me when I didn't know how to fight for myself. They were the ones who had my back and gave me the courage when I had none. They were my big sisters, my big brothers, my father and yes…" Diego paused, "they were my uncles when I had none. Without them I don't think …no…I'm sure that I would not be here today."

Flaco turned away from Diego and then slowly rose to his feet. He walked over to Silver and Missy and hugged them both, expressing his deep and earnest appreciation by saying 'thank you' and telling them that they were now 'familia' and anything that they needed they could have.

With that, Silver, Missy and Diego put the wheels in motion. The first request they asked of El Flaco was to stop selling weight to his connections in Harlem, the Bronx, Brooklyn, and Staten Island and Queens. They assured him that this would not last too long, only long enough to cause frenzy on the streets. The other request was to sell them two hundred Kilo's for two hundred thousand dollars, with one kilo up front. El Flaco agreed without hesitation, and even though he didn't know their plans, he knew that it was more than about money, just as it had been with his brother.

The drug shortage in the city took effect almost immediately, and the small amount of product left on the street was garbage, full of speed, acetone and baking powder. Even the well-connected Papone had a hard time of obtaining quality coke, but even though he was a full partner with Hollis on the crack tip, his heroin business was unaffected. Silver and her crew waited patiently until the right moment, and when it came, Missy played her role beautifully.

* * *

'The Underground' was an after hours strip joint that was a haven for ballers and drug dealers to gamble or meet young tramps willing to perform unspeakable sexual acts. It held two full bars inside, one in the front and one in the back, and most importantly, two gambling tables – Cee-lo only. The elite thing about this spot was they let you ride in with weapons. They figured it wasn't necessary to sweat a nigger over his joint because that way everybody knew they could get got. It was a big balance of respect for each man to be cool.

Missy arrived at the club early that Friday night to ensure her plan would work without incident. Even though it was two a.m., it was still early for the spot. The real niggers usually fell up in there about four a.m. Missy cursed under her breath when she got to the bar and noticed that Butterfly Ty was already there talking to a girl she was very familiar with, none other than Slim Goody. Missy didn't want to seem too obvious, so she headed straight toward the back of the club in clear view of the bathroom and the couple at the bar. As she sat in a booth, she fished through her purse and pulled out some bills and started counting them. Satisfied, she sat back and waited.

Exactly thirty-five minutes later, the easy girl stood up from the bar, slung her purse over her shoulder and rubbed Butterfly Ty's cock before she left. Missy waited until Slim disappeared inside the bathroom before entering behind her. As she entered the bathroom, she noticed that Slim was already inside one of the stalls, so she pulled out her eyeliner and started doing her eyes in the mirror. Hearing the toilet flush, she watched Slim exit the stall through the mirror. Slim recognized her.

"Hey girl, what the hell you doing down here slumming with these broke ass niggers?" Slim asked, soaping and washing her hands.

"You know me girl, I take it how I can get it."

"I hear you, I'm sitting with this one buster and he ain't buy me but one drink and we been here about an hour."

"Yeah, I saw you two going at it at the bar when I walked in."
She watched Slim grab a paper towel and decided to work it.

"I heard about that fucked up shit Hollis did to you in the club
that night. I'm sorry it happened."

Slim wiped her hands harder. "Thanks, girl," she said with a
sneer. "But that's okay, 'cause I'm gonna make that black
motherfucker pay for that shit one day, that's for sure!"

Missy smiled. "Do you really mean that?" She flashed her two
hundred dollars and made her a proposition.

Missy left the bathroom and headed over to the bar where
Butterfly sat. Being the dog that he was, he totally forgot about Slim
Goody, who had slipped past him and out of the club without him
even noticing.

"Yo ma, what's poppin' with you tonight?" Butterfly said.

Missy ignored him as she ordered a 7-Up on ice. Licking his lips,
he looked her up and down in her tight fitting jeans. He pulled out a
knot from his pocket and peeled off a hundred-dollar bill, then spoke
with all the enthusiasm of a true player.

"Bartender, bring her four of those with cherries on top."

Missy gave him a slight smile and turned away, purposely giving
him a look at her perfectly shaped fat ass. He stared, just as she knew
he would.

"Yo, ma, forgive my rudeness, but damn, I just want to know
what time those jeans get off, 'cause that ass of yours is working!"

Missy laughed openly at the dude's game.

"Ain't your name Missy?"

Missy acted lightly surprised. "Where you know me from?"

Butterfly felt himself and grinned. "I'm from the streets, luv.
That's my job to know what's poppin!" He eyed her. "I didn't think
you fuck with black niggas because all those Spanish cat's I be seeing
you around with."

She turned it around on him. "Well, you know what they say? A
girl loves it when a man make love to them, but every now and then, a
girl don't want to be loved." She edged closer and spoke with the
nastiest voice she could conjure. "She wants to be fucked!" This blew
his fucking spot and she noticed his dick got harder than Chinese
arithmetic.

"Check!" he yelled to the bartender.

Missy knew he was only half-joking and asked him what he was pushing. Sipping on his Thug Passion, he reached inside his pocket and pulled out a set of keys.

"An all black Escalade, and my seat is just like my name...Butters baby, can you feel that shit?"

"Only thing I'm tryna feel tonight is something hard and thick!"

He smoothly stood up. "Let's bounce," he said, tossing the bartender a fifty-dollar tip.

* * *

At Missy's apartment, Butterfly couldn't believe his luck. Not only did he have a bad-ass freak, the bitch even had her own apartment. She made the nigger feel mad at ease, and offered to fix him any kind of drink he wanted.

"Yeah, fix me a Hennessy with some Alize if you got it."

Missy smiled at him. "You got it, baby!"

Butterfly felt like the motherfuckin' man, the fuckin' King! To top this shit off, he didn't even have to worry about hittin' this bitch off with some real ends. No, he reasoned, all she wanted was to get long dicked.

She brought him his drink. "I don't know if you fuck around, but if you want some blow, I got some."

He took a swallow of his drink. "Coke?"

"Yeah," she said. "But I don't fuck around; I just pull it out when I have company."

Wide eyed, Butterfly nodded. "Hell fuckin' yeah, I get down!"

Missy stepped into her bedroom and brought out a mirror topped with a large mound of cocaine. She set it down in front of him and Butterfly grinned when he saw the amount of coke in front of him. He stared at it for a moment. "Goddamn, all that shit is coke?"

Missy nodded. "That's what they say."

Butterfly had no reason to doubt her, because he knew Missy hung out with nothing but connected people, but he had to test it anyway. He wet his pinky finger with his mouth, put it into the coke and lifted it to his mouth to taste. In a matter of seconds, his mouth grew numb. He quickly tore off a matchbook cover, scooped up a hefty amount and sniffed it loudly and quickly, then took another hit in his other nostril. He then jumped to his feet and went straight to the windows, closing them. The drug made him paranoid. He went back to the coke and sniffed some more. He looked up at Missy and tried to speak, but his mouth was twisted, unable to get the words out – he was stuck.

"Slow down baby," Missy said. "That ain't none of that garbage that you're used too, that shit is pure." She bent down, removed the coke and took it back to her room, leaving him there stuck on stupid from the powerful drug. After relaxing him by sucking his dick, the powerful effect of the coke wore off and he came back down to normal. After he busted his nut, Missy handed him a washcloth. "Yo ma, check this out... where you say you got that shit from?"

She rose. "Now you know I don't mix business with pleasure, baby."

Butterfly grabbed her hand. "Fuck that other shit we did," he snarled. "I'm about business first and got the paper to back that shit up." Releasing her hand, he stood. "You ever heard of The Young Guns?"

Missy snickered. "Who haven't?"

"So you know how we get down. I'm a Lieutenant, and if you can get us your connect," he shrugged. "Shit...you can make yourself mad loot for simply playin' connect a dot!" Missy stared at him for a moment and sat back down to hear him out.

The meeting was set a week later in a midtown hotel, so the players had to be perfect if they were to convince Hollis they were real drug Kingpins. Being that Hollis didn't trust anyone but his own guns, he kept everyone at arms length at all times. If you slipped up or said one wrong thing, you were as good as dead. Diego, the mommy's boy, had to be convincing enough to play his role and they needed an expert to teach him how to be ruthless. Only one person was capable to teach him the thug life, and that person was Chubbs.

It took Diego nearly a week to lose his white boy accent and demeanor. Chubbs worked on Diego hard, teaching him how to walk, how to talk street shit and lingo, what to do if this happened, what not to do if that happened. He even made him spend time with some hoochie mammas to learn how to talk to them. And then finally, he taught him everything there was to know about cocaine; how to cut it, cook it, weigh it, bag it, everything.

The day had finally arrived. Diego was nervous but ready. They had needed to rent luxurious cars and buy fine, expensive clothing to play the role. Silver looked at her watch. They would be there in fifteen minutes. She cringed when she thought how she would act when she came face to face with the man who set her man up and nearly killed him. She knew she had to be cool for Chance's sake. Even though she had seen Hollis only in passing, she decided to wear expensive Gucci sunglasses in his presence so he would be less likely of recognizing her. She felt sorry for Birdie, who had been biting his nails till they bled. He wore an expensive all black designer suit with a Dobbs Fifty hat slanted gangster style over his eyes. Birdie looked the part as a no-nonsense bodyguard. Silver wondered why he was so nervous, because he didn't have to speak, only follow Diego closely and stare like an eagle at the enemy. Then again, she thought, he had every reason to worry, because they were about to come face to face with a notorious mass murderer. For some reason, Diego reminded her of an updated Tony Montana. Since Chubbs taught him how to be a drug-dealer, he had yet to talk or act like he used to. Chubbs thought it was best that he stay in character at all times.

So there they were; Silver, Diego, Birdie and Missy, sitting around in the hotel room, silent with their own thoughts while waiting for the chips to fall. Suddenly, the hotel room bell rang, causing all of them to snap out of their thoughts. It was now or never and no turning back. Missy and Diego scrambled into the bedroom as Birdie and Silver took their positions. Silver walked toward the door and took a deep breath before she opened it. As she opened the door, she found herself up and close and personal with the man himself - Hollis. She nodded and gestured to him and Butterfly Ty to come inside.

She escorted them to their seats and offered them a drink. Hollis declined, but Butter asked for some Hennessy. Silver nodded and went to the bar to fix the drink while Birdie stared at them without blinking. After handing Butter his drink, Silver spoke.

"Mr. Santos will be with you in a moment."

After nearly thirty minutes, it was obvious that Hollis and Butterfly were growing bored and restless. This was done on purpose, because Chubbs said this showed prospective buyers who were in charge, and that the visitors were there on their time. It couldn't have worked more perfectly, because as soon as the bedroom doorknob turned, the two jumped to their feet, just like Chubbs said they would do. Birdie did what he was told to do. He immediately pulled out his cannon and aimed it at both men while Diego walked out with a king's swagger, Missy hanging onto his arm.

"Oh poppy," Diego chided. "Put that away, you don't pull that thing out on our guests."

Both men watched Birdie put the gun away and breathed easier.

A charismatic Diego shook both men's hands and fell lazily onto the expensive sofa. Wrapped in a full silk robe, Missy reached inside her pocket, pulled out a cigarette and lit it for Diego. After taking a puff, she put it into his mouth. He took a pull and blew it out, looking at Missy. He kissed her on the cheek and she blushed and giggled. Silver stood poker faced, but thought they played their roles a little too perfect, knowing at that moment what they had really been doing behind that bedroom door.

"Missy here tells me some good things about you," Diego spoke to Butter. "Where you know her from?"

Butter began to stumble over his words, and glanced nervously at Hollis.

Picking up on it, Hollis jumped in. "She don't, all she know about us is that we know how to handle business."

Diego smiled. "Good answer." He motioned to Birdie, who reached into his pocket and pulled out an electronic instrument. He walked over to both men and motioned for them to stand up.

"What the fuck is this shit?" Hollis demanded.

"That amigo," Diego frowned, "is a debugger. It picks up on every kind of listening device or tape recorder."

"Man, I ain't come here for this bullshit!" Hollis snapped.

"Then leave," Diego shrugged. "I don't fuck with no narcs."

"Man, I ain't no fuckin' cop!"

Hollis watched angrily as Birdie checked him. Butter interjected, attempting to play the peacemaker. He turned to Hollis.

"Yo, Fam, it's for our safety too, and it ain't gonna take but a second."

Hollis glared as Birdie gestured him to lift his arms. After screening both men, Birdie nodded to Diego.

Diego smiled. "Now that we got that over with… it's time you told me who you work for."

In one swift move Silver, Missy and Birdie pulled out pistols and aimed at them. Diego kept his smile as Silver and Birdie collected their guns.

"What the fuck is this shit?" Hollis again demanded.

Diego stood up and grabbed the detecting instrument from Birdie, then showed Hollis the instrument. "When this red light comes on, it means okay." He whistled and gestured with his hands. "No problem." He walked over to Butter and scanned his pocket. The instrument light turned green. "But when it turns green, that means that we are receiving some type of frequency."

Hollis turned his glare on Butter as Birdie patted him down. He ripped open his jacket, reached inside his inside pocket and pulled out a Walkman with the dials glowing red. The radio was on. They lowered their weapons while Hollis continued to stare at Butter. Suddenly, Hollis punched him viciously in the mouth.

"Motherfucker, you almost got us killed over some stupid shit!"

Birdie returned their guns while Hollis apologized for his lieutenant's mistake, promising that it wouldn't happen again.

Diego smiled. "Good, I believe you." As an afterthought, Diego continued. "I like your heart." Hollis said nothing.

Diego sat back down, his eyes not leaving Hollis. "I'm going to be blunt with you. I don't like you!" He paused. "But … I going to do business with you because I had you checked out. You and King Papone are in bed together."

Still, Hollis said nothing.

"I don't like that fat fuck either, but I try to keep my personal feelings aside from business. Still, I'm not going to do long-term business with you."

Hollis frowned, obviously confused.

"What I will do is offer you a one time deal, in bulk." Diego snapped his finger. Missy stood and walked back into the bedroom, returning moments later with a fancy shopping bag. She handed it to Hollis. Diego urged him on. Hollis pulled out a wrapped bundle of cocaine in thick cellophane plastic. He examined it, and handed it to

Butterfly who then pulled out a knife and made a small incision in one end. He stuck his pinkie finger inside and then lifted his white-tipped finger to his mouth to taste the coke.

All eyes were on Butterfly as he works the powder around his mouth. His mouth twitched. Hollis then tapped Butter, who reached inside his pocket and pulled out a small testing kit. Butter poured a little solution inside a small bottle and handed it to Hollis. Hollis scooped out more powder and added it to the contents of the bottle, and in an instant the solution turned dark blue.

Hollis nodded in satisfaction. "How we gonna do this?"

Diego nodded in approval. "Amigo, you okay, you seem to have a twitch in your mouth."

Butter tried to control the twitch, but it was obvious to the others in the room that his mouth had grown numb.

"Here what I'll do, amigo. I'll sell you say...two hundred keys, at say..." Diego purposely lingered to build anticipation. "... say a two mil for the entire shipment."

It wouldn't take Hollis long to see the numbers, for he stood to make over ten million off this shipment alone. Hollis coughed.

"Cool."

"Good," Diego smiled. "Good!"

Hollis attempted to give him back the key, but Diego shook his head. "No amigo, that's my gift to you." For the first time since he entered the apartment, Hollis smiled.

"How will I be able to contact you?"

Diego snapped his finger again and Silver passed Hollis a cell phone.

"I'll get in contact with you. If you receive a call, you will automatically know who it is from." Hollis pocketed the phone as Diego continued. "Don't use it to call anyone and keep it on you at all times, even in the shower if you have to, 'cause I'm only gonna call you one time, comprenday?"

Hollis nodded, then moved to shake his hand. When he did, Birdie stepped between them and stared at him menacingly.

"Don't mind him," Diego shrugged. "He is just, how do they say, 'overprotective.'"

Hollis looked up at the towering Birdie and backed off. He tapped Butter to leave, but paused when Diego spoke again.

"Amigo."

Hollis and Butter turned around.

"Are you sure you can handle that much coke?"

Cocky and arrogant, Hollis smirked. "I wouldn't be here if I couldn't. I run Harlem, Bronx and Brooklyn!"

Diego nodded. "Not bad, not bad, but I hear you might be stepping on someone else's toes... a guy named Chance. I have heard he is the real Kingpin in Harlem and you are just his side kick."

Hollis looked at Butter and then turned back to Diego. "Chance ain't running shit, and he never did run shit. All he was was a fucking messenger, but you won't ever have to worry about that nigga, 'cause I already took care of his ass."

"Okay, amigo. You de boss now, just have the money ready at a moment's notice."

Hollis nodded, then walked out with Butterfly, closing the door softly behind him. As soon as he closed the door, they all collapsed into their seats in relief. Silver was the first one to her feet to check to see if everything was still being recorded.

Chapter 28

You're Forgiven

At Hollis' club uptown, about twenty patrons were inside partying when out of nowhere the entire place turned into the Wild Wild West as five men in ski masks barged in, pumping shotgun blasts into the roof.

"Get the fuck on the floor!" Chubbs yelled. He pumped a shot into the stacks of liquor on the bar, just missing the bartender.

One man, who apparently ran the place shouted back. "Motherfucker, do you know who I am? Do you know who I am? I'm John motherfuckin' Dough and y'all niggers are dead niggers!"

Chubbs and his brothers looked at the man and then sprayed his ass with a slew of bullets. Chubbs pumped his shotty again. "Now which maafucka in here wanna die next?"

Nobody made a move.

"Now I ain't gonna say this but one time! Strip! And I'm talkin' butt fuckin' ass naked!" The people in the crowd grumbled, unmoving. "The last one with their clothes off, I'm gonna turn their ass into change like John Dough here!"

With that, they quickly stripped. Chubbs nodded to one of his brothers, who exited the club and brought back a masked Beasley, carrying a briefcase. Beasley was led straight to the back office and started working on the safe while the others ushered everyone behind the bar so they could not see them hooking up the equipment.

Lloyd, one of Chubbs' brothers, reached into John Dough's pockets and pulled out a set of keys to the bar. He tossed them to Chubbs, then, seeing the discarded clothes and purses, and being the thief that he was, Lloyd decided to do the right thing and make it looked like a robbery. Chubbs gave the keys to Beasley, who expertly duplicated each and every key. After he finished, he set up bugging and video devices

With phase three completed, Silver went to retrieve the two hundred and fifty thousand from Ms Geneva to buy the kilos from Diego's uncle. Just as Chance said, she didn't have any problems. The older woman gave her the money with no questions asked. She was, however, still broken to pieces about Chance getting shot and cried the entire time Silver was there. Silver didn't tell her that he was locked up, only that he was doing fine and would be out of the hospital soon.

Ms. Geneva slowly shook her head. "We gon pray for that boy, okay? You just be strong."

Silver gave her a hug and a kiss, realizing why Chance trusted the woman so much. She had such a motherly personality that Silver didn't want to let go. She had to force herself away, wiping tears from her eyes as she quickly left. Outside, Diego waited in his car. Everything had been arranged. They were to drop off the money at his uncle's supermarket, where a moving truck would deliver furniture with the drugs stashed inside to Missy's apartment. After the furniture was dropped off, Silver would leave Missy and Diego at the house, telling them she had something very important to do and that she would return the following day.

* * *

Silver had found the nursing home where her grandmother was staying. Since it was all the way upstate and the visiting hours were only in the morning, she decided to check into a nearby motel and stay the night.

Diego had left Missy's apartment two hours ago, but Missy had trouble falling asleep. She had already taken a shower and a bath, but still couldn't sleep. Impatient, she walked to the refrigerator to find something to eat, but as she past through the living room, she stared at the new furniture. She glanced through the refrigerator but didn't find anything she liked. Irritated, she slammed the door shut. She cursed as she found herself staring at the furniture again, and with another oath, ran into her room and slammed the door shut. But the call of the drugs was too powerful for her to handle and ultimately, the urge finally took hold of her. She left her room and went straight to the kitchen, pulled out a cooking pot and filled it up with water. She opened the refrigerator and pulled out a box of baking powder, and then turned the flame all the way up until the water in the pot boiled. Missy then stepped to the new sofa and slit an opening in the back. With a defeated sigh, she reached in and pulled out a package.

The morning of the visit, Silver felt butterflies forming inside her stomach as she was led to her grandmother's room. As Silver stood at the door, she looked at the name on it. 'T. Jones'. Finding courage, she threw caution to the wind, opened the door and stepped slowly inside." Hello?" Not hearing a sound, she proceeded into the room, and the first thing she saw was a foot under some covers. She peered behind the curtain shielding the bed and saw her grandmother laying on it, headphones over her head.

The woman pulled them off and smiled. "Oh Jessica, you startled me."

Silver forced a smile. "Hi grandma, it's me, Silver. How have you been?"

Adjusting her glasses, the woman spoke in a sad, regretful tone. "Oh Silver, it's you."

It was several minutes of touch and go before they both felt more relaxed in each other's presence. Silver found out that her grandmother had been on her way home from the grocery store one day when she felt a slight pain in her hand and wrist. Then she had stiffened and passed out. The next thing she knew, she was in the hospital.

After about an hour, there was nothing left to discuss. Silver stared at the now shrunken and feeble woman. She had done her duty as a granddaughter, what was there left to do? But deep down, she knew there was plenty that needed to be said. They said their good-byes, but as she bent down to give her a hug, she thought 'Speak now or forever hold your peace'. So, without hesitation, Silver threw it out in the open.

"Why Grandma? Why?" Tears welled up in her eyes, partly due to built up anger and frustration over her current crisis, the other half due to seeing this wicked and deplorable woman in front of her. "Just tell me why you treated me like you did. I would like to know."

The old woman did not seem to be surprised. She was no longer in control, and was now the weak and vulnerable one without an ounce of fight in her. All she could do now was to cleanse herself from the sins that had been haunting her for years now. She gestured for Silver to sit down near her, sighed heavily and then proceeded to tell Silver everything.

"Years ago, before we, me and your grandfather, bought the brownstone in Harlem, we lived in Bushwick over in Brooklyn, in one of those old-fashioned railroad flat apartments. Well, it was me, my husband, Jessica and Jesse."

Silver frowned in confusion until her grandmother continued to explain.

"Jesse was your mother's older brother. Jessica was only six months old at the time, Jesse was four."

The old woman's eyes seemed to sparkle every time she mentioned her son's name.

"He was the absolute joy of my life. Anyway..." her face hardened. "Late one night we smelled something burning. We got up and opened the door and there was a big fire in the kitchen by the kid's room. Robert, your grandfather, raced through the fire to save the kids, suffering severe burns as he went through. I remember praying to God that he find them. As I waited, the fire grew larger and larger until suddenly, your grandfather came racing through the blaze covered in a thick blanket. When I got to him, the blanket had begun to melt from the intense heat. As he opened up the blanket, he handed me your mother and then attempted to go back and find Jesse, but by then," she sighed "the entire apartment was engulfed in flames."

Silver watched the woman's eyes grow cold and hard.

"I begged him to go back and save my son, and then the firemen kicked open the front door and pulled us out just as the ceiling began to collapse." She shook her head. "My son died that night in the fire...and since that day, I believe a piece of me died with him, because from that day on I just changed. I turned bitter and angry against the entire world." She looked at Silver. "There's a saying, '*A mother raises their daughters, but she loves her sons.*'"

Chills swirled down Silver's back, but she remained silent.

"I wondered to myself a million of times, 'What if Robert pulled Jesse out first?'" She lowered her head. "And to be totally honest with you..." She lifted her gaze and looked her granddaughter straight in the eyes. "I wish he had."

Silver said nothing, shocked.

"As the years passed, the older your mother got, the more she began to look more and more like her brother. Pretty soon my sadness turned into anger, and anger into resentment against your mother. I hated seeing her, because every time I looked at her, I was reminded of him, my dead son! When she got pregnant with you, that gave me an excuse to put her out, so I no longer had to look at her." She paused as she reflected. "But soon after, your grandfather died of what seemed a broken heart and left me with nobody, I blamed your mother once again for taking someone away from me." She stared out the window. "When your mother died and you came to live with me...I guess the same anger I had toward Jessica... I began to hold toward you." She shook her head. "I know I was wrong, but Lord knows I tried...I tried many times to love you, but I couldn't!" She grabbed Silver's hand. "That day when you left, and you told me you would love me until I learned to love myself... that really did something to me, to my heart."

Her grandmother eyes welled with tears, something that Silver had never seen before. Weeping loudly, the woman looked upward.

"I'm sorry...Jessica...I'm so-so sorry for what I did to you and Silver...Oh Lord, what did I do? What did I do? What did I doooo?"

She seemed inconsolable. Silver hugged her.

"How can Jessica ever forgive me for what I did to her? I treated her so badly."

Patting her back, Silver wondered if this was the first time she had cried since her son's death. Silver tried to console her. "Grandma, Mother forgave you a long time ago, and if she was here right now, she would tell you that." Wiping tears from her eyes, Silver continued. "Even though she is gone, she still lives inside of us. So does Uncle Jesse." Silver smiled. "Every time that I've ever needed mother most, she would appear and we would talk." Her grandmother slowly lifted her head.

"Do you think we can talk to them together?"

Silver nodded. "Of course." They clasped hands and began to pray.

Chapter 29

The Drop

After leaving the nursing home, Silver drove back to the city and arrived at Missy's apartment late that night. As soon as she entered the apartment, she knew something was direly wrong. She looked down and saw a trail of white powder on the floor. She locked the door and ran inside. The room was in disarray. She then went to the hall closet and opened it, nothing. She went to her bedroom, but everything was as she had left it. Silver checked everywhere but did not find Missy. She then stepped into the kitchen and saw baking powder, pots and bottles crusted with what appeared to be cocaine residue. On the counter by the sink, a half-filled kilo of cocaine was spewed all over the counter. Silver checked the rest of the shipment and was satisfied that only one package had been tampered with. Missy had cooked up enough crack to supply a small time dealer for a year.

She called Diego and the others to push the schedule date up because she didn't know what would happen if they ran into Missy. After she called everyone, Silver went to her room, retrieved a card out of her drawer and stepped to the phone. After the forth ring, a male voice answered.

"Fortieth Precinct, Sergeant Letizio speaking."

"Yes," Silver said. "I'd like to speak to Detective Squassoni, in Homicide."

* * *

Silver, Birdie and Diego waited in a silver Lexus parked on the corner of 163rd Street and Broadway. Silver had called Hollis five hours earlier to tell him where to meet them and to be on time. Hollis told Silver that King Papone would be with him. Chubbs told Silver that this would happen because he wanted to see for himself the people he would be doing business with, so without hesitation, she told Hollis that they would only be dealing with him. He agreed. Chubbs and Beasley had had Hollis under surveillance for over a week, watching his movements and habits. From what they gathered about Hollis, he was a major trick, and he fucked a different girl every night at the same place, an apartment above his club. He always met them inside the club and then took them home to sleep with them. He didn't drink or get high and was always on point. But they found out something else about Hollis that no one knew. Hollis went to church every Sunday up in the Bronx. Beasley followed him inside and sure enough, Hollis was inside on his knees, praying and praising God like the other folks.

Chubbs and Beasley trailed Hollis in Beasley's van and called him on their cell phone when they got within five blocks.

"Play ball!" Chubbs said, closing the phone. Beasley pulled up directly in front of them and the car came to a halt and parked. Hollis opened the door, got out and walked over to the parked Lexus.

Birdie eyed Hollis while Silver got out of the drivers' seat and walked to open the door for Diego. Diego shook Hollis' hand and glanced at Papone staring at him from the car. Frowning with disgust, Diego said to Hollis "Let's take a walk"

As they walked past the car, Papone stared intently at them. One by one, the locals walked up to Diego and started kissing his hand and making the sign of the cross. It was obvious that Hollis was shocked and realized that perhaps he had underestimated the man.

As they did a walk talk, Birdie was compelled to stop the people from crowding as Diego waved and smiled at them all.

"Why do you fuck with a cockroach like Papone?" he said. "I don't like that puta! What do you think of him, amigo?"

"Who, Papone?" Hollis asked. He sucked his teeth and chumped him off. "Fuck that fat fuckin' spic, I'm just using Papone's ass to get where I got to go. As soon as I get my shit right, I'm gonna take his ass out too!"

Diego smiled. "Good, good answer. Be ready to deal tomorrow. I'll call you to tell you where."

With that, Birdie stood in front of Hollis, blocking him from going any further.

Hollis look up at Birdie. "A'ight, man, I get the picture," he grumbled and walked off.

It was close to four in the morning as Beasley and Chubbs slowly exited the van. They walked up to the club's front door and stuck key after key inside the lock until they finally had a match. They got in so quickly that no one even noticed…well almost. Stickbroom Johnny, the neighborhood 'paperboy', watched them a moment and then went about his business.

With the last phase of the operation completed, Silver called Hollis and told him to bring the money and meet them at Pier Seventy-Nine on the Hudson at exactly six o'clock that evening. Papone, not trusting Hollis's crew, had told Hollis that he planned to use his own men to do the pick up and would be waiting nearby and watching his every move.

At exactly six, Hollis, Papone and four of his men pulled up and parked at an angle where they could see everyone who entered the pier. They waited about ten minutes before Beasley, who had arrived by boat, walked up to their car, startling them all. Hollis rolled down the window.

"Ya take de money to de boat," Beasley said.

Hollis popped the trunk and exited the vehicle, while Beasley hopped in the rear of the jeep. Hollis took a huge duffel bag full of cash out the trunk and nodded to Papone. Walking unsteadily, he approached the narrow pier. Silver noticed that he looked particularly gray. She smiled. They had done their research well. Chance said Hollis had come to this country from Haiti on a death boat. He had arrived in Miami harbor with the grizzly images of many people dying during his journey haunting him. Because the boat was undersized and carried a minimal amount of food, chaos and anarchy had mounted until the journey had become survival of the fittest. Old men and women that the younger men deemed unfit to take up the much-needed space were thrown overboard. Hollis had seen a swarm of frenzied sharks eat them alive. Since he was only nine years old, some had attempted to throw him overboard as well, but he cut the throat of the first man who put his hands on him. Seeing his tenacious spirit for life, the ruffian group of men let him be, but refused to give him food or water, so he survived on his own by eating maggots, seaweed and drinking ocean water.

Diego and Birdie waited on the boat. Diego told Hollis to place the money down in front of him. He did. Birdie, gun in hand, quickly hopped out of the speedboat and bent to retrieve it while Hollis cautiously eyed Birdie. Birdie picked up the bag, eyes not leaving him for a second, as he backed up and hopped in the boat.

"So what about the shit?" Hollis said.

Diego started up the motor and yelled over the roar of the engine. "The guy in your car will take you over to the next pier. There will be a truck full of furniture; inside is the product. My man will stay there with you until you count it up."

Diego sped off before he could ask another question.

Beasley waited for Hollis to get into the car. He knew that on top of a nearby bridge, Silver, Chubbs and his four brothers watched Hollis complete the transaction. When Hollis got into the car, he choked from the hydro that Beasley puffed. "Yo dred, can you put that out?" For an answer, Beasley took a slow drag of the blunt and blew smoke in his face. Hollis glared at him. "Where we going, man?" Beasley smiled. "Drive, Mon."

Beasley led them into another pier about a half mile down the highway and pointed to a white cargo truck parked at the end. Four Spanish guys stepped out of their car, and cautiously scanned the entire area. They nodded to Papone, who stepped out of his vehicle and also glanced around. Hollis climbed out of the jeep and walked to the rear of the truck and lifted the latch, but it was locked. He turned to look at Beasley, who smiled and swung a set of keys before tossing them to Hollis, who then opened the lock. Hollis examines the furniture for a moment and then pulled out his knife and began to cut the back of a chair open. He reached in, pulled out two bundles wrapped in gray tape and flashed a smile at Papone. Papone gestured for his men to get into the cargo truck, where the three of them slit open furniture and began counting the kilos. Others tested each and every bag. When they were finally finished, they nodded to a nonchalant Beasley. "Is ere ting irrie?" he asked them. They nodded and Beasley walked toward the highway with a Jamaican swagger. After Beasley was out of sight, Papone gave Hollis a pat on the back. "Amigo, everything you said was true. We should make millions off this shipment." Hollis smiled, not so much over the money at stake, but because he felt he had finally entered the ranks as a Drug Kingpin. Though Hollis was notoriously famous as a killer, he wasn't respected – he was feared. There was a difference. Only drug lords seemed to have it all – money, power and respect. Hollis had always wanted his name to be as renowned as ghetto legends such as Nicky, Fritz, Fat Cat, and Alpo.

Papone said that he would take it from there, that he would call him tomorrow to give him a million dollar advance. Hollis's dick hardened from the euphoria. It was time for him to celebrate his induction into the big time, so he headed uptown to his favorite spot. He smiled as he thought to himself that only the nastiest of nasty freaks would due tonight.

Chapter 30

Show Down

The sun was just beginning to set when the cargo truck pulled into traffic behind Papone's car. They had driven less than a mile before they ran into slow moving traffic pouring into an underpass. As they proceeded through the pitch-black underpass, traffic came to a complete stop. Behind the cargo truck, Chubbs and his two brothers patiently waited for the men in the truck to pass out from carbon dioxide poisoning. They had rigged a tube from the exhaust system to the underside of the instrument panel in the cab and removed the window cranks. After about ten minutes, the two men would not even know what hit them as the colorless, odorless gas filled their bloodstream as they drift off to a sleepy death.

The traffic jam had been prearranged and everything proceeded smoothly. After exactly fifteen minutes, Chubbs' crept to the cab of the truck, pulled the two limp bodies out and tossed them to the side of the tunnel, covering them with a blanket. That being done, Chubbs' brother, Lloyd, jumped into the driver's seat of the truck, smashed open the window and called ahead for the all clear. Lamont hopped in beside him. At the first exit, Lloyd swiftly turned off. Papone's car kept going, not noticing the unscheduled detour until, moments later, the car slammed its brakes and came to a sudden halt. Unmindful of oncoming traffic, the car peeled around and sped in pursuit of the cargo truck. Chubbs smiled.

Hollis was already at the Uptown Garage club throwing big money at the bartender telling him "Champagne for everybody." Girls from all over began surrounding Hollis as he pulled out fifties and hundreds and threw it around like money ain't a thang! Hollis had his choice of women tonight and was looking at all the desperate faces trying to get his attention. Suddenly, a thick booty girl bummed-rushed through the crowd of girls and whispered in his ear from behind and said "I want to put your big dick in my mouth, my pussy and in my ass! And when you're about to come... I want you to come all over my face!" Hollis's eyes lit up as he turned around and saw the familiar face and an even more familiar ass. It was Slim Goodie! Hollis said, "Oh, shit! If it ain't...?" Trying to remember her name she said, "Let me help you." She took his hand and put it under her tight dress with no panties, and pushed it deep inside her wet pussy. Staring him straight in the eyes, she pulled it out and licked his dripping fingers dry. The other girls watched in horror as they walked away from the freak show. Hollis knew that he found the right one tonight and all he could think was how he was gonna put a black eye on the pussy. He took her by the hand and led her out the door.

Papone circled the highway praying that the truck had broke down or something. But his question was soon answered when his driver noticed a foot sticking out of a cover at the side of the tunnel. Papone cursed vigorously in Spanish until they got out of the vehicle and lifted up the blanket and saw his two men lying dead underneath. He tossed his cigar to the ground and yelled "Hollis!"

Papone and his men arrived in front of Hollis' club, tires screeching. He jumped out of his car and headed straight for Butterfly, who was in the process of unlocking the front door of the club. Papone grabbed him, threw him up against the gate and then wrapped his fingers tightly around his throat. "Where is Hollis?" he demanded. Eyes bulging, Butterfly gasped for breath. "You're the one that introduced Hollis to that girl, weren't you?"

Butterfly nodded.

"Do you know where she live?"

"Yeah...I mean yes, Mister. Papone!"

Papone stepped closer. "You go there now and bring that black bitch back to me, you understand?" Butterfly nodded again. "And amigo, if you don't find her... you won't be coming back," Papone threatened, and then motioned to two of his men to go with Butterfly.

Missy watched Silver put her bags into the trunk of a cab, then look around one last time, perhaps hoping Missy would suddenly appear. She shook her head, and then hopped into the cab. Missy watched the cab drive east on 110th Street and round the corner, then hurried toward her building. After a three-day binge, she prayed that there was some cocaine left inside the apartment. Frantically, she put the key inside the door and rushed inside without closing the door. She quickly looked around for the furniture, but it was gone. She ran into the kitchen and opened up every cabinet and drawer in search of the opened kilo package she had left behind, but cursed when she didn't find any. She remembered she had left some coke on the mirror from Butterfly's visit and ran the closet, bingo! It was still there. She brought the mirror to the kitchen, opened the refrigerator, looking for the baking powder to cook it up with, but couldn't find it. She slammed the door shut and for the first time noticed the note attached to the refrigerator door. She snatched it off and read. *Missy, stay out of the apartment. I'm at LaGuardia Airport, leaving town, American Airlines Flight # 426 to Miami at 11:45pm.'* She put the paper inside her pocket and snorted the drugs, but still wasn't satisfied, so she lapped at the powder with her tongue, ingesting it orally. When she had licked the mirror clean, she sighed and looked up and saw three guns pointed in her face.

Inside the club, Papone's cell phone rang. He quickly opened it. "Yeah? Good, go there, pick her up and bring her back here, but don't kill her...but before you do, bring back the one you got now." Papone closed the phone and stared up at the ceiling.

Directly upstairs Hollis was fucking the shit out of Slim Goodie. She was yelling bloody murder, but told him not to stop "Ahh...oui...oui...yeah that's right, right there you black motherfuckaa!" Hollis had no problem filling the order "Oh, oh, now fuck me in my ass baby, fuck me!" Hollis said, "You freak fucking Bitch!" and pulled his dick out of her pussy and quickly shoved it up her ass. Slim Goodie's closed her eyes as he rammed her mercilessly. "Oui...Oww...Oui... that's rigggght da...daddy, right fuckin' there, right there...oh shit...fuck the shit out of me daddy...fuck me!" Hollis was pounding her so feverishly that dribbles of spit fell on her backside

Moments later, He busted off a 16 oz. sized nut deep inside of her as his sperm oozed out like a river! Hollis and Goodie were totally exhausted as they sprawled across the bed fighting to catch a breath. After ten minutes or so, Hollis finally found the strength to get up as he looked over at Slim Goodie who was sleeping. Hollis smiled wickedly because it was said that if you make a girl fall asleep right after you had sex, it meant that you fucked her well! Hollis frowned, as he smelled the pungent odor of shit in the air. He looked down and noticed that Slim's shit was on his dick and pubic hairs. He quickly got up and went to the bathroom to take a shower.

At LaGuardia airport, Silver breathed easier as she waited outside the terminal, desperately hoping Missy had found the note and would arrive before her flight boarded in an hour. She searched every face in each passing cab, and only idly noticed a black Lincoln that slowed to let out a passenger. It was only when the Lincoln stopped in front her that she noticed a grim-faced man inside staring intently at her. She knew immediately that she had fucked up. Her mind told her to run but it was too late. A man from behind quickly shoved her inside the vehicle, which speedily drove off without anyone even noticing that she had been kidnapped.

After Hollis closed the door to the bathroom, Slim Goodie jumped up from her faking slumber and look cautiously at the bathroom door. She grabbed her purse and pulled out a long pamphlet type paper and quickly stuffed it inside Hollis' jacket and lied back down. As an afterthought, she eyed his pants and reached inside and pulled out a roll of money and peeled off a few bills – all one- hundreds – and placed it back neatly. She smiled to herself and said "I told you I was gonna make you pay you black bastard!" and closed her eyes.

The car pulled up in front of the club like a bat out of hell, screeching to a halt. Silver was yanked out of the car and shoved through the front door.

Hollis had just gotten out of the shower, heard the tires screeching and looked out the window. He saw Papone's car and others parked in front and knew something was terribly wrong. His mouth dropped when he saw them pull Silver out of the car. Hollis ran over to the bed and dressed quickly. Putting on all of his clothes he grabbed his jacket off the chair and walked towards the door. Slim yelled, "Hey you forgot to pay me!" Hollis didn't even hear her as he flew down the stairs.

Papone circled Silver and said, "I don't know what is going on," Papone spoke to her. "But I know one thing. Either I'm gonna have my money, my drugs or your life."

Silver tried to bluff. "Mister, I don't know what your talking -"

Papone struck her viciously across her mouth. "I know everything about your little scheme, so don't lie to me!" he shouted. He turned toward one of his men, who stepped into the back room and emerged moments later with Missy, who looked strung out.

Silver's heart dropped while Papone smiled. The two men brought Missy toward Papone and Silver. Missy shook nervously, unable to look Silver in the eyes. Silver searched Missy's face, praying desperately that she hadn't done what she thought she did. "Missy," she said. Missy slowly raised her head. "Missy," Silver repeated. "Oh God, tell me you didn't?"

Missy said nothing, but lowered her head.

Papone smirked. "Yes, she did… she told us about your little plan, about Chance, everything. She sold you out for a twenty dollar bag of crack."

Silver looked at Missy, unable to believe what she heard. Anger overcame her emotions. "You fucking bitch!" she cried. "Do you know what you've done?" Missy started to cry and looked up at Silver. Her mouth moved, but no words came out. "Oh my God, Missy, you got us both killed!"

Missy quickly shook her head. "No Silver, they…they said that all we have to do is give them back the drugs and they'll let us both go!"

Silver looked at Missy and shook her head. "And you believed them?"

Papone smiled. "She is telling you the truth. Give me my drugs and I'll give you your lives."

Hollis burst through the front door, took one frantic look around and began yelling. "What the fuck is going on?" He walked toward Papone, eyeing Missy and Silver.

"Where you been?" Papone demanded.

Hollis gestured upstairs with his thumb. "Been partyin' with—" Looking in Silver's eyes he realized all at once, that the girl in front of him was Chance's girl – he's been played!

"Apparently, my friend," Papone said "we both have been set up by your friend, Chance."

Hollis glared angrily at Silver, and then pulled out his knife, ready to cut her throat. Papone stopped him. "No amigo, we got to get from her the location of our product first."

Hollis stared at Silver and spat in her face "I knew I saw your funky ass from somewhere." He snarled, and then turned to speak to Papone. "Let me take care of her. I'll make her tell me where the shits at!"

Papone smiled again. "No, amigo, you sit down, I'll handle this." Papone patted Hollis on the shoulder. He then looked at Silver, wrapped his huge hands around her throat and choked her until lights burst in her eyes. Papone gritted his teeth.

"If you don't tell me what I want to hear, I'm going to torture you so bad and for so long, you are going too beg me to kill you. Do you understand?"

Papone released his grip and Silver sagged to the ground, gasping for air. His men picked her up as she rubbed her neck, coughing. "I'll tell you," she spoke hoarsely, then coughed again. "I'll tell you everything you want to know, but you got to let my girl go first."

Missy looked up at Silver, eyes wide with surprise while Papone calculated.

"Okay, but if you don't tell me where my stuff at, I'm not going to give you no more chances."

Rubbing her throat, Silver nodded while Papone turned to Missy. "Get the fuck out of here!"

Missy's mouth said 'I'm sorry', but the words were unable to come out. Silver scowled at her. "Get out of here, Missy."

All attention turned toward Silver as she turned to Papone. "Before I tell you, I would like to know one thing before I die." She glanced at Hollis. "Why did you set my man up and try to kill him?"

Papone and Hollis looked at each other and chuckled

"Because he was a bitch ass nigger who didn't know how to get real money," Hollis said.

Silver stared at him. "But he was like a brother to you. He saved your life when y'all was younger."

"Bitch, please... you got that shit backwards. If it wasn't for me that stabbed that nigger in that alley years ago, Chance would have been dead a long time ago."

Silver frowned in confusion.

Hollis laughed. "What, he ain't never tell you? That big nigger was about to cut Chance's ass to pieces, but before he could, he didn't see my ass sneak up behind him. And when I shanked his ass in the back, Chance took the knife from me and told me to break out. He took the fall."

Suddenly, everything made sense to Silver. "And this is how you repay him? By planting drugs and guns in his house and almost killing him?"

Hollis smiled. "Shit! I would have set my momma up before I faced three counts of murder that was gonna put me away for triple life. But thanks to good old Chance, he's once again gonna take a murder rap for me."

"Enough questions," Papone interrupted. He turned to Silver. "Now tell me where my drugs are at."

Silver defiantly lifted her chin. "Why don't you ask my boss where the drugs at?"

Papone frowned. "What?"

"You heard me," Silver said. "I said why don't you ask my boss where the drugs at!"

"Who the hell is your boss?" he demanded.

Silver paused for a moment, looking from face to face. "Ask my boss...Hollis!"

Mouth dropping open in shock, Hollis looked at everyone now suspiciously eyeing him. He jumped to his feet. "Oh hell, naw!" he denied. "That bitch is lying!"

"Fuck that shit, motherfucker... you think I was just gonna stand by and let them kill me? Fuck that! Before I go out, I'm taking your black ass with me!"

Papone turned to glare at Hollis. Hollis broke out in sweat.

"Yo, Pap man, I know you ain't gonna believe this bitch?

Papone remained silent and Hollis looked at Silver. "You yellow fucking bitch, I'm gonna—"

Hollis reached for his gun to shoot her, but Papone's men quickly pulled out their guns, subdued him, and took it away from him.

"You see," Silver yelled "that's the second time he's tried to kill me so I couldn't tell the truth about his lying ass!"

Hollis nervously pleaded reason. "Papone, think man... think! What kind of proof does she have to base this shit on? She's just trying to save her own ass."

Silver glared at him. "You want proof, motherfucker? All right, here's proof. " She turned toward Papone and explained. "He made a deal to sell the drugs to some Dominican guy from Washington Heights named Flaco something, for one million dollars. After he sold the drugs, he was supposed to meet me in Miami in two days. I bought the tickets myself. If you don't believe me, check his pockets!"

Papone nodded to his men to check Hollis. One of the men reached inside his pocket and pulled out a plane ticket. Hollis stared at it, wide-eyed as if it was a snake. The man handed it to Papone, who slowly opened it.

"Flight 263 to Miami... one way."

"Oh hell, naw...hell naw!" Hollis cried. He glanced up. "Shit! That bitch, musta planted that shit on me!"

Silver didn't miss a beat. "I guess I planted some of the drugs in your office safe too, huh?" She turned to Papone. "And there's only one person who has keys to that, too!"

Hollis looked around fearfully, shaking his head in disbelief.

"Get his keys!" Papone ordered. A man reached inside Hollis' pants and pulled them out. He stepped inside Hollis' office, and the moment grew tense as Papone waited. When the man came out, Hollis's jaw dropped open and his knees buckled. The man carried an armload of bundled drugs, the same drugs they had gotten out of the cargo van earlier.

"He said the rest of it he was gonna hide under the dance floor," Silver offered.

The men immediately went to work on the dance floor and found the remaining kilos.

Hollis watched as they pulled out kilo after kilo. All he could do was shake his head in disbelief. "This don't make no sense! I don't even know nobody named Flaco! They are setting me the fuck up! Can't you see that?"

Papone stared at Hollis. "We'll see, amigo... we'll see."

Papone reached inside his jacket pocket, pulled out his cell phone and dialed a number. He looked at Silver, then at Hollis. "Me and El Flaco go back some years. We'll see who's lying in a moment."

Silver tensely watched Papone dial the number, hoping no one would answer.

"Hola," Papone said. "Let me speak to El Flaco. This is Papone from the East Side." He waited a few moments and then spoke. "Hola amigo, dis is Papone, yes...yes...very long time...listen I have my man here who said he got a big package for you. I just making sure I don't step on the wrong toes." He listened intently, looked at Hollis, and nodded. "Yes, a nigrito named Hollis...yes...yes...no, no, amigo, everything is okay. Thank you." He hung up.

On the other end of the phone Diego slowly hung up the phone and wiped his brow in relief.

"See," Silver said. "What did I tell you? And the motherfucker wasn't finished, either. He said after he sold the drugs, he was gonna kill you!" She quickly reached inside her pocket, pulled out a mini recorder and pressed play.

"Fuck that fat fuckin' spic, I'm just using Papone's ass to get me where I got to go. As soon as I get my shit right, I'm gonna take his ass out, too!"

Hollis listened to his voice on the tape and looked like he was going to be sick as he deftly cuffed a knife into his hand. Without warning, he took quick aim and tossed the deadly blade with expert precision straight at Silver.

Silver froze in horror as she watched the flash of the blade, but then from out of nowhere, she was knocked off her feet and out of harm's way. Stunned by the shove, she fell heavily to the floor as two of Papone's men shot Hollis dead. He dropped to the floor, with pools of blood spewing from his chest. Silver glanced over her should and saw Missy lying on the floor a short distance away, a knife deeply embedded in her chest.

The front and rear doors crashed open, startling everyone, as a score of FBI and DEA agents rushed inside, pointing high tech weapons.

Silver crawled to her friend and lifted her head in her lap. "Missy!" She began to cry, heart wrenching sobs. "Oh, God, Missy...what have you done? I told you to leave!" She frantically lifted her head and yelled. "I need some help!" She hunched over her friend. "Hold on, Missy, hold on, help is on the way real soon."

Missy looked up at Silver. "Silver, I'm sorry for what I did to you... will you forgive me?"

Blinking back her tears, Silver nodded. "I forgive you girl, but don't worry about that now." Blood began to drip from Missy's mouth and she began to gag. She looked at Silver and spoke, her voice whisper soft. "Silver, I don't think I'm gon make it...I feel cold." Silver hugged her tighter. "Don't talk, you gonna be fine, you be fine." Missy looked up at her and smiled. "We did that shit, didn't we?" Wiping tears away, Silver nodded. "Yeah, we did it, we did it."

"I didn't lie to you," Missy gasped. "Lie about what?" Silver asked past the growing lump in her throat. "I told you that I would die for you." Silver watched in despair as Missy's eyes became heavy and slowly began to close. Silver gently stroked her hair as Missy opened her eyes blankly. "Silver... Silver?" she screamed.

"I'm here, Missy." Gazing into Silver's eyes, Missy managed a tremulous smile. "Oh yeah...I love you, bitch..." Silver shook with grief and gently touched Missy's still lips with the tip of a trembling finger. "I love you too, hoe," she wept silently.

Squads of armed agents had Papone, and the rest of the men handcuffed. They confiscated the drugs and took pictures. As the coroner left with Missy's and Hollis's bodies, Detectives Squassoni and McBeth stood by her side, their expressions somber. Slowly, Silver removed the wire she had worn and handed it to Squassoni.

From the very beginning, Silver had figured out a way to save her man and manage to do it in way that didn't compromise her morals or the promise she had made to her mother years earlier to never deal the poison to anyone. Silver had not told anyone in her crew that she was cooperating with the police, not even Chance knew. But before she cooperated with the police, Silver had been smart enough, with Detective Squassoni's guidance, to get full immunity from city, state and federal levels, just in case. Everything that had been spoken from the hotel conversations and Hollis' club had been recorded and turned over to the Feds, who now had enough incriminating evidence to put Papone away for life. The authorities also had enough evidence to have the charges against Chance dropped. In addition to the confession Hollis had made on tape, he was also implicated in nearly three dozen other murders throughout Harlem and other boroughs, compliments of the cell phone that Diego had given him and told to carry around at all times. In addition to it being a cell phone, it was also a high tech bugging device that Silver requested from DEA. They had listened to hours of Hollis bragging about past and present murders and contract hits. Chance was right when he said that Hollis' Kryptonite was women and his mouth.

The DEA never recovered the two million in drug exchange money, and Papone wasn't about to make claims on it—that would have hit him with federal income charges. Instead, Silver divided the money with the friends who had risked their lives to help her. Silver gave Chubbs' four brothers a hundred thousand dollars apiece, but Chubbs declined his share of the money, saying everything he had done had been out of love. Silver tried to force him to take it, but he didn't budge. Seeing his reluctance, she asked him if he could then give it to his sister, Vonda. Jesse had always told Silver that if it weren't for Vonda, she wouldn't been here today. Chubbs smiled and said that he would. As they hugged and parted, Chubbs turned, grabbed his crotch and looked Silver up and down while licking his lips.

"It is one thing you can do for me?"

Silver looked suspiciously and said. "What is it Goddaddy?"

Chubbs grinned and asked. "Did Jesse ever teach you how to cook lima beans?"

Silver gave Beasley two hundred thousand dollars. The first thing he did was sell his business, pack up and move back to his native land of Jamaica. He bought a modest house in the hills and lived off the fat of the land, or shall I say, smoked it.

Diego also declined any money. He no longer needed it because the properties and businesses that his father had left him wound up being million dollar mansions and interests in a popular hotel and casino resort in the Dominican Republic.

Silver gave Missy the loveliest and most expensive funeral ever. Hundreds of former schoolmates and friends attended. Silver also moved Missy's family out of the projects and purchased them a four-family brownstone in a nice, tree lined section of Striver's Row in

Harlem. Missy had always said that, 'to break the perpetual ghettoness in her family they would have to move out of the projects first'.

They renamed the Children's House, 'Missy's House'. Missy's mother, grandmother and little sisters started working there full time as counselors for drug addicted teens and runaway girls, and set up a foundation in her name.

Silver donated the remaining portion of the money to various charities throughout the city, mostly to drug prevention agencies and battered women's shelters. Because of an assortment of rewards involved in many now-solved murders, Silver was given a total of two hundred twenty-three thousand dollars by local and federal agencies that she would use toward her medical school tuition.

Chance was released from prison and recovered from his injuries. When he got out, word on the street was that both King Papone and Mafia associates had a contract out on his head. He felt it was only right that he tell Silver before they got married, so they decided to pack up and move to Atlanta to start life anew. Birdie cried for nearly two days until Silver and Chance asked him if he wanted to come along, an offer that he tearfully accepted.

Chapter 31

Real Gangstas Move in Silence

Mitts loomed on the corner silently as he watched the moving men pack the last of Birdie's furniture. He looked up at the third floor window and saw Chance staring out the window as the moving men pulled down the truck door. Gritting his teeth, Mitts looked around nervously before deciding that it was time to make his move, and hobbled towards the building with his hands inside his coat pocket looking cautiously over his shoulders

After they finished packing the last of Birdie's stuff, Birdie looked around at the now empty apartment. Silver knew he felt sad and nostalgic. He had lived in that same apartment for over twenty years.

"I know how you feel, Auntie, I'm gonna miss this place too. But there's nothing left for us here."

Birdie swiped at his eyes. "You're right baby, but I was just thinking about all the good years I had here with you and your mother."

Silver hugged him. "You still got me, Auntie, and we're always gonna be together for now on." A knock on the door interrupted them.

"That must be the moving men with the bill," Birdie said.

He went to answer the door and Chance walked over to Silver and gave her a big hug and a kiss. Silver looked at him. "I can't believe we are actually leaving." He hugged her around the waist and planted a kiss on her forehead.

"Believe it Mrs. Haze, by this time tomorrow we'll be in sunny Atlanta!" As if in afterthought, he frowned. "I thought you said you paid the moving men already."

"I did," Silver said. Chance shrugged and then began gathering Birdie's remaining luggage. Just then, Birdie walked into the living room with a strange look on his face. Silver and Chance paused. "Auntie, what's wrong?" she asked.

Birdie tried to speak, but no words came out of his mouth. Suddenly, he collapsed to his knees and then to his stomach, and

Silver screamed when she saw the ice pick embedded in the back of his neck. From out of nowhere, a man appeared at the door, holding a pistol. Silver stared, not believing her eyes, but Chance chuckled softly and spoke.

"You've been supplying me heroin all these years." He sighed. "A.O. always told me that real gangsters moved in silence." Silver was confused. The real Kingpin of Harlem was none other than Stickbroom Johnny?

"Stickbroom, why don't you let her go? She has nothing to do with this."

Toothless Stickbroom Johnny frowned. "Nothing to do with it? Nothing to do with it?" he repeated. "This skank bitch is the reason why I no longer have a bidness! Before that shit with the Feds went down, everything went smooth, it was perfect... then this yellow cunt come along and threw ya ass some of her funky lil' coochie an' you got ya nose wide fuckin' opened and fucked everything up!" He shook his head and continued. "If you learnt one thing from A.O., boy, you should have learnt that every nigger that made big money in this bidness was brought to their knees by a fuckin' woman! And nigger... you ain't no fuckin' exception!"

"Come on man," Chance said. "I was loyal to you and the fucking Italians for years; I never even took one red cent man!"

Stickbroom only laughed. "For you to be so smart, you sho' is one stupid motherfukka! Ain't no fuckin' Italians been dealing dope in Harlem for over thirty year, dumb nigga!"

"But A.O. told me—"

"A.O. told you what?" Stickbroom coldly interrupted.

"He told me that he and his older brother was working directly with the Mafia and..." Chance paused. Silver looked from one to the other, heart racing with dread. Chance smiled. "You're A.O.'s older brother."

"And yo dumb black ass thought his older brother was long dead."

"All right man, I'll continue working for you as long as it takes," Chance offered.

Silver shook her head. "Chance, no!" Stickbroom laughed harshly. "You know goddamn well that you're hotter than a Park Avenue whore's pussy! You ain't no good too me anymore.

Chancellor Haze's name is in F.B.I. and the DEA files forever. You're damaged goods and you can't sell a loose joint without them knowing about it!" He reached inside his coat pocket, pulled out a silencer and screwed it to the gun. "Nigga...you know the game, no witnesses, no snitches!"

"Come on, Stickbroom," Chance said. "Just let her go and fuckin' kill me, motherfucker!"

"Stop showin' yo skirt nigga, y'all dead already." Chance looked at Silver while she stared back in numb fear. "If you're finished crying like... how dat Snoop doggie motherfucker say it...? Crying like a beeeiiitch... I got ta hurry up kill both you asses, I got some papers that has to be delivered!"

"How about I give you—" Stickbroom stopped him. "Nigga, don't try dat negotiation shit on me! I know everything you thinkin' before you think it. Who da fuck you think taught Adrian?" Chance was confused, He pointed the weapon at them. "Oh, that's A.O real name...Adrian Olsen." Stickbroom shrugged and aimed at them. "Silver couldn't breathe. Suddenly, Chance sprang for Stickbroom's gun, but he was no match for the bullet that ripped through his flesh, knocking him off his feet. Silver screamed and ran toward her fallen husband. Stickbroom smiled. "Ya know what, lil' girl? I always like ya mother...I wanted ta fuck her real bad." He smiled. "Damn...I getting a hard on thinking bout her ass... anyway, say goodbye!" He pointed the weapon at her head, when suddenly, Birdie's huge hands grasped Stickbroom by the ankles and yanked him off his feet, causing the gun to slip out of his hand. Birdie used his weight to hold him down.

"Silver run!" he yelled. "Run!" Silver leapt quickly to her feet and ran out the room, but when she reached the front door, she stopped and turned around, watching Birdie battle viciously with Johnny for the gun. Infuriated, she let out a banshee-like yell and ran over to join the brutal battle. She picked up the nearest weapon she could find – a thick glass ashtray – fell to her knees and began pounding Stickbroom repeatedly over the head until blood flew everywhere. Bloodied and still full of rage, Silver beat him until he showed no signs of movement. Exhausted and bloodied, she looked down at the unconscious man and then rolled Birdie over in her arms. Birdie opened his eyes and stared up at her. "Silver... you...you came back for me?"

"Yes Auntie, I came back for you. You just hold on, okay?" Tears began to fall from Birdie's eyes as he shook his head. "No baby, Auntie Birdie not gonna make it." Silver attempted to argue but he stopped her "No baby, it's okay. I'm ready." Silver remained silent as trickles of blood began to flow from his mouth. He gripped her hand tighter "Silver, you and your mama was the best thing that ever happened to me. Y'all was the only ones' who ever...ever... loved a big old faggot like me." Tears brimmed in her eyes. "No, Auntie, you can't leave me, we're all going to Atlanta and—"Birdie stopped her in mid sentence with a smile. "Silver, what's the worst word in the world?" Silver frowned. "Can't! But you—"

"What is 'But'? Silver smiled wanly. "But is a self-defeating word used by procrastinators. Birdie smiled back. "My baby!" And just like that...he was gone. Silver gently closed Birdie's eyes and kissed him on the forehead. "I love you, Auntie," she said softly and then slowly rose to her feet. She stepped toward Chance, writhing on the floor in pain. Blood streamed from his upper chest and back. She started to help him up when she noticed movement out of the corner of her eye, and turned to see a battered and bloodied Stickbroom Johnny standing and pointing his gun at them.

He sneered and without a word, calmly unloaded three shots into Birdie's dead body. Shocked, tired and bloodied, Silver couldn't move. She accepted her fate and stared down at Chance. Knowing it was truly over, Silver and Chance embraced and sealed their fate with a simple kiss.

Suddenly, a loud noise from behind Stickbroom startled them all. In growing disbelief, Silver watched a yelling Mitts charge into the room and tackle Stickbroom from behind. His forward momentum propelled them crashing through the window. She rushed toward the window and saw Mitts hanging tightly to the window sash. Stickbroom's lifeless body hung limply on the spiked gate below, where he had been impaled. Mitts desperately struggled to climb back in.

"Hold on Mitts!" she urged him. "Take my hand, I'll help you, just don't look down!" She reached for him. He lifted his head, and that's when Silver noticed that, for the first time, she was seeing him without his dark glasses on. A sudden and indescribable feeling overcame her as she stared into his bright, hazel eyes. She snapped out of her momentary trance and stuck her hands out. "Grab my hands!"

Mitts looked up at her and spoke gruffly. "Silver..." he said sadly "I'm sorry I was never there for you."

Silver gasped in disbelief as episodes of past encounters of Mitts flashed before her eyes, and it was then that she realized the man hanging from the window was none other than her father, Kenny.

"Daddy?" she said timidly. He nodded in shame. Grabbing one of his huge hands, Silver valiantly tried to pull him back in, but it was useless, he was much too heavy for her to pull him in by herself. Wide-eyed, she stared down at him and realized that he also knew it. His voice cracking he said,

"I think Jesse can finally forgive me for what I've done to you and her."

"Daddy," Silver cried. "Hold on, I'm gonna go get some help."

But Kenny shook his head. "No, I can't hold on much longer... just let me look at you one last time."

He stared up at her while Silver continued to shake her head. "Hang on!" she urged.

He smiled and rubbed her hand with one of his fingers and then let go, falling to the same grisly death as Stickbroom.

Chapter 32

Closure

Silver held Birdie's and her father's funeral on the same day. Both were buried beside her mother. After Chance recovered from the bullet wound, it was time for them to leave New York forever. But before they left, Silver told Chance that she had two important things to do before she could hope to have some closure in her life. Chance asked her if she wanted him to go with her for support but she declined, knowing it was something she had to do on her own.

* * *

Silver waited inside the dank and sullen visiting room at notorious Sing-Sing State Penitentiary. As she sat before the divided Plexiglas window that separated prisoners and guests, she patiently but awaited his arrival. At that moment, she was totally surprised by her sense of confidence, because she had thought about this day for many years and she often wondered how she would react when this day actually arrived.

Suddenly, the steel door clanged open, and a tall, lanky man with a thick mustache entered in front of a guard. He bobbled as he walked because of the chains connecting his ankles to his wrists. As the officer escorted him closer, Silver rose to her feet in nervous anticipation. The officer showed the prisoner his seat and he sat down. As the officer walked away, the man reached inside his pocket and lit an unfiltered cigarette. He stared at Silver and then spoke in a harsh voice.

"Who the hell are you?"

Silver eyes glistened with tears as she stared at the aging, leather-skinned man. He took a huge pull from the cigarette, eyes narrowed with suspicion.

"Did that fat bitch of a wife send you here for me to sign them dang divorce papers?"

Silver remained silent as she stared at the man who took her mother's life in a motel room almost twelve years earlier.

"Well, what the hell do you want?" he demanded.

Confidence built inside Silver as she simply stared and remained silent. The man waved her off.

"I ain't got to take this shit from no bitch." He turned his head and yelled "Guard!"

Silver remained unmoved and continued to look at him, but this time with a smile. He turned away from her as he waited for the guard and reached inside his pocket to pull out another cigarette. He lit it and then glanced up at her, eyes narrowed. He thought about the last black women he encountered. He continued to study her. She could sense his questions, his uncertainty. Surely he knew the date, not only was it her birthday, but the anniversary of her mother's brutal murder September 18th.

He fidgeted and grew impatient, calling for the guard once again. Sweat formed on his forehead. Unable to take the pressure, he snapped at her again.

"What is it that you want, lady?"

Silver remained calm and continued to stare. Staring deep into her eyes, the man dropped his shoulders and sighed. He lost his bluster and suddenly looked like an old man.

"I'm sorry I took your mother away from you," he said slowly. "I… I couldn't control myself, I was sick." He paused. "You got every right to hate me, but you don't have to worry, 'cause I'm already gonna burn in hell for the things I did."

The guard arrived and placed a hand on the prisoner' shoulder. He rose to his feet and walked somberly with the guard, then suddenly stopped and turned towards Silver again.

"I don't know if this means anything," he said timidly "but your momma bought you a Barbie doll and jump rope for your birthday." He lowered his head and disappeared through the doors with the guard.

* * *

Driving down south on the interstate and leaving New York behind, Silver and Chance stopped off in Bayonne, New Jersey to complete her final closure mission. After the morgue had released her father's body to her, they also gave her the contents that were on his person at the time of his death, including his wallet. After he was buried, Silver looked through his wallet and found a picture of him when he was younger and beardless. To Silver's surprise, she discovered she was the spitting image of him. She came across other small pictures and some telephone numbers. Curious and quite nervous, Silver decided to call them and inquire about Kenneth Duboise. To no avail, the people who answered said she had the wrong number. The very last number that she found had a New Jersey area code. She called it, and after the second ring a lady answered.

"Hello," Silver said nervously. "My name is Silver Jones, and I'm calling about Kenneth Duboise?" The lady on the other end was silent. Silver was unsure if she had just hung up. "Hello?"

"May I ask whose calling about Kenny?" the woman asked.

Chance pulled up in front of a large, Victorian-style home in a beautiful suburban neighborhood. He looked at her. "Well, this is it, you ready?"

Silver looked at the house, took a deep breath and nodded. They exited the vehicle, and Chance gently took her hand while they walked up the marble walkway. Silver looked at Chance one final time and then rang the front bell. Almost immediately, the door opened and a fair-skinned woman in her sixties appeared. She lifted her hands to her mouth as she stared at Silver, then extended her arms and walked toward her, tears slipping from her eyes. As they hugged, the door opened wider and a man about the same age with radiant white and wavy hair appeared. He took off his glasses, revealing bright hazel eyes. He looked as if he couldn't believe his eyes and gave her a tearful, loving hug as well. Silver looked exactly like their son, Kenny, who left home years ago after he became strung out on drugs.

Silver looked at Chance, unable to believe the loving welcome she received. These were her real grandparents!

"Welcome home," her grandmother said. She took Silver by the hand and led her inside the house while her grandfather hugged Chance. "Come on in, son."

Inside, about thirty family members had gathered to greet them. Her grandmother introduced them to everyone, and each member welcomed them into the family. Silver felt goose bumps course through her body, because as she stared at them, their bright hazel and silver eyes stared right back at hers – this was definitely family!

Silver was surprised to find out that in addition to having two grandparents, she also had three younger sisters, a younger brother, three aunts, two uncles, and a slew of cousins, nephews and nieces. Later that evening, Chance, who was having a conversation with his grandfather in-law, looked over at Silver, smiling and talking to her sisters. She winked at him. Chance knew one thing for sure – and that was she would never, ever have to be lost again!

The End

Epilogue

Silver enrolled in medical school that fall, and eventually went on to become a doctor. Chance also went back to school, where he received a doctorate degree in Psychology. He became a well-respected and prominent psychiatrist specializing in children. Years later, Silver and Chance moved back to New York and opened private practices right in Harlem, where they provided their services free of charge at Missy's House. They were also the proud parents of twins, a boy and a girl, whom they named, respectively, Jesse Kenneth Haze and Jessica Ernestine Haze, nicknamed 'Birdie.' They also moved Silver's grandmother out of the nursing home to live with them in the very brownstone that she had grown up in. The elderly woman loved them dearly because she believed she'd been given a second chance to have a son and a daughter. She was at peace with herself for the first time in her life and was extremely happy.

In time, Chance also found and was reunited with his sister, Karen, who was fortunate enough to have been raised by a loving family and was now happily married and working as a registered nurse in a Long Island hospital.

Silver and Chance dedicated their lives to helping other families devastated by drugs and alcohol. They often spoke at public schools throughout the inner cities and educated the children of the dangers of drugs and the importance of education.

Silver started every lecture the same way. "Hi, my name is Silver Haze, and I was born and raised right here in Harlem, poor and by a single mother. Today, I'm a doctor, and I owe it all to my mother for providing me with the secrets to life. Today, I'm going to share with you some of the secrets that she taught me, but first, in order for me to do that, I must tell you about a very bad word...it's a word that I haven't used in years. That word, children...is 'can't'.

For more information on our publications, contact us at:

Peaceful Storm Publishing
P. O. Box 126
Colonial Station
New York, N.Y. 10039

or visit our website:

www.peacefulstorm.com

Contact the Author at:

treasure@peacefulstorm.com

Give us your feedback for casting
Harlem Girl Lost - The Movie

Which entertainer should play Silver Jones?
Beyoncé
Jada Pinkett-Smith
Sanaa Lathan

Which entertainer should play Chance?
Usher
Mekhi Phifer
Tyrese
P. Diddy

For other characters in Harlem Girl Lost - The Movie

Write us and help with the casting!